CHINA WINTER

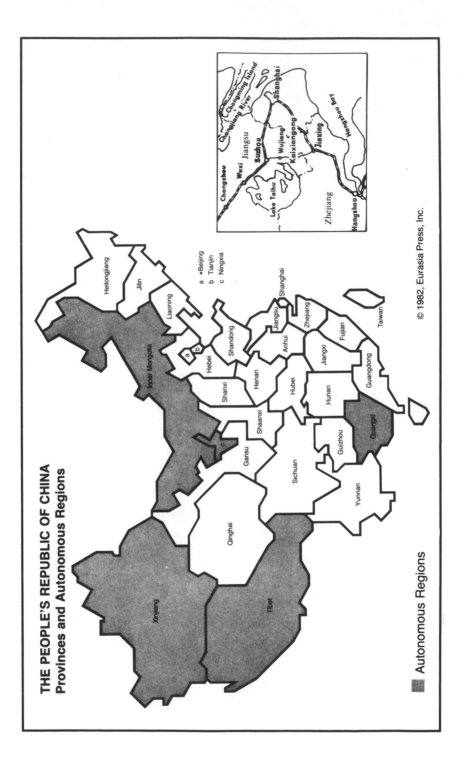

THE PEOPLE'S REPUBLIC OF CHINA
Provinces and Autonomous Regions

a •Beijing
b Tianjin
c Ningxia

Heilongjiang
Jilin
Liaoning
Inner Mongolia
Shandong
Hebei
Shanxi
Henan
Shaanxi
Gansu
Qinghai
Xinjiang
Tibet
Sichuan
Hubei
Jiangsu
Shanghai
Zhejiang
Anhui
Jiangxi
Fujian
Hunan
Guizhou
Guangxi
Guangdong
Yunnan
Taiwan

Changzhou
Changjiang River
Chongming Island
Shanghai
Jiangsu
Suzhou
Wuxi
Wujiang
Keixiangong
Jiaxing
Hangzhou Bay
Lake Taihu
Zhejiang
Hangzhou

■ Autonomous Regions

© 1982, Eurasia Press, Inc.

CHINA WINTER

Workers, Mandarins, and the Purge of the Gang of Four

Edoarda Masi

translated by Adrienne Foulke

E. P. DUTTON • New York

Published in the United States by E. P. Dutton, Inc.,
2 Park Avenue, New York, N.Y. 10016

Library of Congress Cataloging in Publication Data
Masi, Edoarda.
  China winter.

  Translation of: Per la Cina.
  Includes index.
  1. China—Description and travel—1976-2. Masi, Edoarda.   I. Title.
DS712.M3713   951   81-12502
                    AACR2

ISBN: 0-525-10764-9

Published simultaneously in Canada by
Clarke, Irwin & Company Limited,
Toronto and Vancouver

10 9 8 7 6 5 4 3 2 1

First Edition

This book is dedicated
to the Chinese people,
and directed at
those Westerners who love them.

CONTENTS

AUTHOR'S NOTE

This book will come to American readers more than three years after its publication in Italy, and more than five years after the events that it relates took place. Some things that were unknown to public opinion in the West in 1976 are now common knowledge; other things have been distorted by propagandistic manipulation and by an all too frequently superficial treatment in the mass media. So true is this that now it is very hard to offer readers an accurate perspective on those events, for in the interim their minds have been conditioned by interpretations that serve the purposes of one or another interested party. For these reasons, I believe it will be useful if I explain why I gave this book its particular form. In the introduction that follows I have attempted to clarify certain historical precedents of the events described in the book as well as to allude to recent developments. Readers already familiar with modern Chinese history may wish to skip over this section, which is of necessity rather long, or else refer to it occasionally while reading the main part of the text.

A more than twenty-year-long study of the language and culture of modern China has given me ever clearer evidence that a profound gap separates the sphere in which the specialist does his research from the area in which the ordinary citizen forms his opinions, even though he may be well educated and possibly a specialist in some other field. Also, my first long stay at Peking University from 1957 to 1958, my subsequent connections—which as often as possible were direct—with Chinese and with foreigners living in China, and, most recently, the months I spent in Peking and Shanghai in 1976–77, have all contributed to making me aware of still another divergence: the distance between what written words convey—whether they are propagandistic or ideological or scholarly (as in the historical and sociological interpretations that appear in both East and West)—and the reality of daily life, of relationships among individuals and diverse social levels, and of ways of communicating which, whether open and visible or concealed, course through the great corpus of Chinese society. The distance between these two dimensions does not imply that one or the other is authentic or false, but rather that both are somehow incomplete; in some way, they are mutilated. This hinders us in making full use of the theoretical material—distinguished and rich as some analyses are—and, on the other hand, in profiting as much as possible from direct contacts with Chinese while traveling in their country, or during cultural exchanges or other opportunities for meeting.

In addition to these considerations, chance determined one further circumstance. My most recent stay in China coincided with a crucial period in the country's history. At school, on the streets of Shanghai, from the windows of a mastodonic hotel, I and a small group of other foreign teachers witnessed the dramatic events that signaled the end of a great revolution. The echoes and repercussions of those developments extend well beyond even the vast Chinese theater; yet they are almost all voiceless, are almost all unrecorded for future historians, nor is there the sound-box alternative normally provided by newspapers and every other kind of printed matter from minutes of meetings, documents, and memoirs down to and including pamphlets and manifestos and handbills. Analogous events in the West have been well documented since at least the time of the French Revolution. The absence in China of any reference to public opinion, in the accepted sense of the term that Westerners inherited from bourgeois democracy, produces among us who are heirs of that tradition, but far-removed spectators of China today, the image of a deaf and blind history (or an absence of history). It is a false image, for in China paths of communication and ways of recording do exist but are different. They are subterranean, or if overt, they are ephemeral, like the immense number of handwritten statements that are posted on city walls, last for a few days, sometimes for only a few hours, and seem never to be photographed or filed for the record. They are, in large measure, fated to be lost, as throughout the centuries the sources for much of the history of this country of official historiographers have been lost—sources that relate to life, associations, political connections, insurrections, and the countless episodes of government opposition organized by the urban masses and the peasants.

So it seemed to me a duty to bear witness—a limited witness, to be sure, but worthy of some consideration because it is sustained by an earlier store of specific knowledge of China and by both theoretical and practical experience gained as a militant in the socialist movement. I felt this duty was owed not to specialists but to ordinary people, the general public, informed or not, for at issue are not academic questions but problems and conflicts dense with consequence for our shared present and future.

From diaries kept while I was in Shanghai I took material that in the book is cast in narrative form, with a defined time span and a conclusion and individuals as characters. But one character who is distinct from the author is, in some measure, the author speaking, and lives and reacts with her passions, idiosyncrasies, and prejudices. This character's voice I have rendered in italics, and in some of these passages the reader will discover my reactions to events as they occurred. Being contemporaneous to history, these reflections necessarily have a somewhat emotional content. I chose this form not as an expedient likely to make the book easier to read but because it best suited the explicit and implicit purposes of the work, in that it seemed the best way in which to integrate various orders of reality—science and subjective experience; universal, public reasons and individual, private motives; ideological abstraction and day-to-day concreteness; intellectuals/leaders and the people who are the governed.

For an observer in good faith and with some knowledge of the historical precedents who was in Shanghai in 1976, it was not hard to understand even then the direction events were taking. The worker presence is dominant in Shanghai, and at least since the Cultural Revolution years the people there have been involved in political struggle. As an observer I was drawn into a passionate empathy because there I saw the actual substance of the conflicts and not, as in Peking, merely the power plays at the top.

Also, the echoes of peasant resistance are more distinctly heard in Shanghai. And at a distance of years, the clear, courageous words of protest which Chen Yonggui addressed to the Central Committee in late 1978 confirm what one could understand at the time of Mao's death: a seemingly silent China, which matured during the long revolution, continues to grow. It is a real, an immense body in respect to which the factional shifts in government are irrelevant.

I have used the more accurate pinyin spelling for nearly all Chinese words in this book (i.e. Mao Zedong and Zhou Enlai instead of the Wade-Giles Mao Tse-tung and Chou En-lai. There are still a few exceptions, such as Kuomintang.). However, some pinyin words would only confuse most Western readers, so I have employed the more familiar Cantonese spellings of Sun Yat-sen, Chiang Kai-shek, and Hong Kong rather than the pinyin forms, which are Sun Wen, Jiang Jieshi, and Xianggang. Canton, the Yangtze River, and Peking are Western deformations; their pinyin equivalents are Guangzhou, Chang Jiang (the Long River), and Beijing.

—E. M.
Milan, 1980–81

1. Longhua Temple
2. Shanghai Municipal Children's Palace
3. Shanghai Industrial Exhibition
4. Jade Buddha Temple
5. Site of Founding of the Chinese Communist Party
6. People's Square
7. Workers' Cultural Palace
8. No. 1 Department Store
9. Shanghai Museum of Art and History
10. Garden of the Mandarin Yu
11. Friendship Store
12. Shanghai No. 1 Hospital
13. Shanghai Mansions (Shanghai Dasha)
14. Shanghai Foreign Languages Institute (Shanghai Waiyu Xueyuan)
15. Shanghai City Revolutionary Committee (Shanghai Shi Geming Weiyuanhui)
16. Culture Square (Wenhua Guangchang)

 Restaurants

Hotels

Consulates

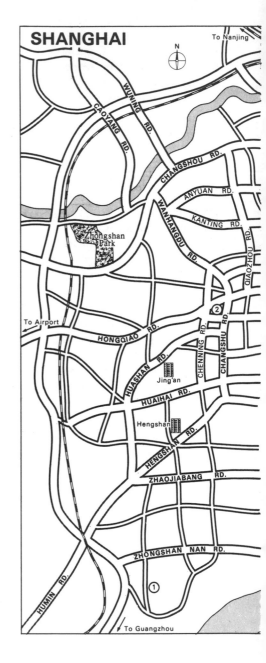

SHANGHAI

To Nanjing

N

WUNING RD.

CAOYANG RD.

CHANGSHOU RD.

ANYUAN RD.

WANHANGDU RD.

KANTING RD.

QIAOZHOU RD.

Zhongshan Park

To Airport

HONGQIAO RD.

CHENNING RD.

CHANGSHU RD.

HUASHAN RD.

Jing'an

HUAIHAI RD.

Hengshan

HENGSHAN RD.

ZHAOJIABANG RD.

ZHONGSHAN NAN RD.

HUMIN RD.

To Guangzhou

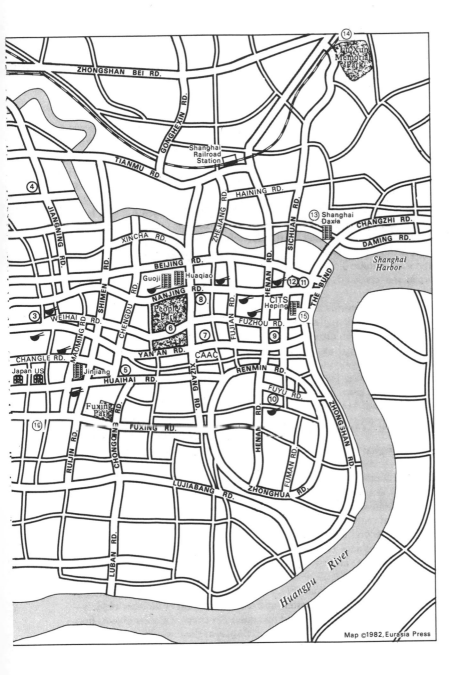

Map ©1982, Eurasia Press

INTRODUCTION

China in the Twentieth Century

The problems and conflicts of twentieth-century China are not only Chinese, but universal to our time. China exists in a world system that was founded on the supremacy of a colonizing Europe, and that has been progressively supplanted by the growth of two great imperial superpowers. It shares the growing crisis in the mode of production and of economic and social development inherited from this same European system. The methods of production and management offered by this model, as imposed today by the supremacy of the two imperial powers, are not those of decentralized, free competition with an emphasis on individual and national autonomy, but rather centralized power dominated by technology and based on a rigidly programmed domestic and international division of labor, and on a hierarchical ordering of individuals, social classes, and nations. As a consequence, centralizing, totalitarian managerial forms tend to prevail in the governmental and social direction of developing countries, whether they have been absorbed into the hierarchy of one or the other empire, or whether they lay claim to independence or assert a relative degree of sub-imperial power.

The process of totalitarian centralization has been furthered by the intervention in the class struggle of Communist parties guided by the monistic ideology of Leninism and the Leninist principle of "vanguards." When it became apparent in the early twenties that the Russian revolution was not part of a general European revolution, Lenin and the other Bolshevik leaders looked elsewhere for an internationalizing connection. They duly noted the overthrow of colonialism that was beginning to agitate the century. The struggles of African and Asian peoples to free themselves from their colonial status, including the struggle in China, were recognized by the Russians as one of the great

1

currents of our time, and redefined as part of a worldwide proletarian revolution. The movement for national independence was subsumed in the broader and more densely peopled sphere of the international class struggle. Where classical Marxism had rejected nationalism as a bourgeois ideology, the opponents of imperialism redeemed it.

The search on the part of an isolated and beleaguered Soviet Union for new alliances was pragmatic and reasonable; it also helps account for Soviet prestige and influence then and after the Second World War. But the totalizing ideology led to an attempt to unite under one emblem two things—nationalism and the revolt of the subordinate classes—that are not reducible to a single identity. The confusing of the two was reflected in the image of the Soviet Union: from the outset, no clear distinction was made between the national interests of the peoples of the U.S.S.R. and the country's character as the (international) "Socialist homeland." When the Soviet government intervened in support of liberation movements in order to prepare them and give them specific directions, allegedly it was motivated by their presumably being part of the worldwide proletarian movement; to this a postulate was appended decreeing that there should be a single direction of that movement. As time passed, the Soviet Union's national interests interfered in those of other peoples with ever more intolerable effects, while in various countries the class struggle was hampered within the parameters of totalitarian nationalisms, and instead of moving to abolish the state (which supervises capital), its growth as the exclusive possessor of power was nourished in opposition to individual interests and the group interests of workers.

Class conflict had been endemic in China's search for autonomy and national identity well before its encounter with the Comintern in the twenties. From the mid-nineteenth century, the world's most ancient and organic governmental system had been crumbling under the impact of gigantic popular revolts (one need recall only the 1850–64 Tai Ping Rebellion, which left 30 million dead) and of European aggression. The old governing class had sought unsuccessfully to rebuild its power by using the traditional methods of compromise and hybrid policies. In the past, these methods for reestablishing equilibrium had been predicated on the system's unity and universality—and on China's isolation. When a different civilization affirming the principles of pluralism and the equality of individuals and of nations erupted on the scene, the old Chinese system was shaken to its foundations. The nature of internal conflicts was conditioned and changed, for subaltern and ruling classes alike had to respond to the Western (or modern) challenge if they hoped to emerge from the pattern of cyclical revolts that led to no solution, to no liberation.

European attempts to colonize the country accelerated the empire's disintegration and political collapse, and spread extreme misery and degradation among masses of peasants and wage earners. At the same time, the colonizing effort helped to bring to the surface latent conflicts within the country and in its relations with the outside world. Contradictions that had accumulated over centuries seemed to explode and to fuse with new conflicts that China's encounter with the modern world created. Commencing with the first Opium War, in 1840, a process of change began that was to go on without interruption and at an ever faster pace—attempts at reform, cultural upheavals, revolts, and revolutions. This process cannot be said to have ended even today.

No new governing class emerged to replace the old declining mandarinate. The military revolt that brought about the fall of the last dynasty, in 1911, represented the aspirations of an agglomeration of groups that were only fuzzily defined. The urban middle class was growing in size and, thanks to its recent entrepreneurial activities, in wealth as well, but it was present in only a few large cities—Shanghai, primarily—and it was dependent on foreign capital and Western culture; in a word, it was unequal to the task of representing the cause of Chinese nationalism. At the same time, this urban middle class lacked a group identity vis-à-vis those exponents of the old order, the rural landlords, to whom it was bound by shared family, clan, and economic interests; accordingly, it was unfit to become the promoter and guide of revolution or of a reform of the landownership system.

In the absence of any socially defined principle that might have served as the carrier of reform, change initially appeared as a generational concern, and it took the form of a repudiation of traditional morality and of proposals for the renewal of education and culture. Young people became the champions of reform. Most of them came from the old governing class, from its impoverished or marginal branches, and from the immense reservoir of the provinces, as in the past. Also as in the past, the children of well-to-do peasants and of the urban middle class were to be found among them. But these young people could no longer look ahead to future careers in government as public officials. The mandarin system had survived into the first decade of the century but was now in its death throes, while the partially reorganized schools and private instruction were educating people for other things. New professional opportunities were almost nonexistent in a highly civilized society of very rich potentials, for foreign interests incapable of recognizing the country for what it was were moving over it as if over scorched earth, forcing it into abject dependency. With mounting enthusiasm, young people derived from their growing familiarity with Western culture principles that not only could liberate them from the shackles of the authority and moral code of the scholars, but that also collided head-on with the colonial status that same West was imposing on them and on their country.

Thus, China's entry into modern history (or, in the judgment of Mao Zedong, into the modern revolution) occurred with a great revolt of youth marked by the duality of nationalism and cultural revolution. The May Fourth Movement of 1919—a protest against clauses in the Versailles Treaty that sanctioned China's economic and political dependence on Japan—fused cultural revolt and insurgent nationalism in one vast current. So true is this that the term "May Fourth Movement" now denotes not only the combination of demonstrations and patriotic actions that in May and June of 1919 spread through the larger Chinese cities but also the entire process of cultural renewal that was initiated during the First World War and flourished during the twenties. The New Culture Movement was launched, in 1915, by Chen Duxiu (appointed two years later dean of the Department of Literature at Peking University and later first secretary of the Chinese Communist Party) and by Hu Shi (the most eminent philosopher of modern China, who in his youth had been a student of John Dewey). It differed radically from previous proposals for reform and modernization which had been directed toward safeguarding a Chinese "essence" or "singularity." This was a frontal attack on traditional authority, and on its intellectual and ethical foundations. All contemporary aspects of Western culture were taken up and promulgated—from science to philosophy and literature to democratic, socialist, and anarchist principles—as effective instruments for striking down Confucianism and the bases of the scholars' historical power. The revolt took off with an attack on the written literary language—which only the cultivated governing elite possessed and which served as a tool to perpetuate the illiteracy of the masses—and an attack on the traditional family and the morality that governed it; proceeding further, the Movement, with great courage, challenged Chinese civilization in toto. As Lu Xun wrote in 1918, Chinese civilization had been "four thousand years of cannibalism."

Extreme as their revolt was, substantially the May Fourth Movement was repeating a process already known in Chinese history. To orthodox doctrines they opposed a program based on heretical ideas to renew society and adopt new directions *within* the existing ruling class. However, the West had introduced a production mode that was incompatible with the continuance of the landowning class in a dominant position. Further, such disarray had been wrought in the collapsing power structure of the old scholars that no new generation of scholars could rebuild it or fashion a similar structure, nor could any purely cultural campaign resolve the crisis.

The May Fourth Movement had begun in Peking University, the cultural core of a city that was not only the political capital of the country but a lofty center of humanistic culture. While in all Chinese cities cultural and political life developed apace, the masses of the peasants were virtually excluded, although they constituted more than 80 percent of the population, and it was on their labor that urban civilization drew for material and spiritual sustenance. Although the Movement did demand that bureaucracies be abolished and illiteracy be wiped out, and called for a system of general public education, the preeminence of the cities increased in the decade between 1915 and 1925. It also acquired a new characteristic. While in traditional centers such as Peking humanistic culture was being renewed and enriched by Western ideas, literary currents, and educational contributions, other cities of a different origin which used to be looked down on by the mandarins were becoming of central importance; they were modern in the sense that they were growing or being transformed thanks to an industrial development engendered by foreigners. The most striking instance was Shanghai, the most densely populated of all Chinese cities and the most Western not only in its architecture and town planning but also in its citizens' style of living and thinking; only two hundred years earlier, Shanghai had been a small, relatively insignificant center, but it had been developed as a colony, with various quarters of the city apportioned among the various occupying powers. Industrial growth had partly transformed other ancient urban centers such as Wuhan, the big port on the Yangtze that actually comprises three cities, or Canton, a port with a long history in trade.

Inasmuch as the cities were modern, or relatively modern, industrial production sites, they became focal points during the twenties, as the reform movement was being politicized and taking on a class coloration. It is perhaps more than symbolically significant that the Chinese Communist party was founded in Shanghai, in 1921, just as, on the other hand, it was not merely an empty boast for Shanghaiese to claim that they were the "national bourgeoisie." The passage from cultural reform to politicization to involvement took place in the context of the West's economic penetration and capitalistic mode of production. In the vanguard were the city dwellers, belonging to, respectively, the bourgeoisie and the industrial proletariat, the former represented by the Nationalist party (Kuomintang), the latter by the Communist party. The two parties, although ideologically and politically polarized, did exist side by side in a several-years-long alliance and, indeed, at one point joined in a single bloc. The alliance seemed to develop from the cultural movement, which was unitarian in its global aspect and interclass aspect, even if divided among several political tendencies. Reformist and revolutionary intellectuals and students became the interpreters and cadres of this dual-faced context.

In the beginning, the Communists had very little political strength, and they were pushed into an alliance with the Kuomintang by the Soviet Union and the Third International. The Comintern's evolutional scheme called for the liquidation of the system founded on agrarian revenue to be carried out by a democratic-bourgeois revolution, in which the national bourgeoisie* would play the leading role under the direction of the Nationalist party. The cause of liberation from imperialism and from international capitalist interference would

---

*The term "national bourgeoisie" referred to the Chinese industrialists not financed directly or indirectly by foreign capital, and the class allied with them.

make this revolution part and parcel of the world proletarian movement, and assure the Kuomintang of the Comintern's support. The Comintern would be taking steps, meanwhile, to guide events in a direction that favored a subsequent evolution toward socialism. The Chinese Communist Party (CCP), allied with the Kuomintang and obedient to the Comintern's directives, was seen as an instrument of this design. The Nationalists agreed to the alliance. They, in turn, counted on using the support of the Chinese Communists and the Comintern for their own purposes. Actually, the decision that the Chinese nation's growth should follow the modern-urban route represented the view of both groups, but each thought of itself as being the leader and capable of incorporating the other in its own program as a subordinate ally. The Communists hypothesized that national independence would be combined with modernization and, for the moment would be spurred on by the workers and in the future controlled by them (or by a workers' party, which is why the CCP agreed, if with some reluctance, to form the bloc with the Kuomintang that Moscow's directives imposed). The Nationalists' program was the same except that it was to be under the hegemony of an enlightened national bourgeoisie.*

However, although for a while the alliance of Nationalists and Communists was compatible with the political scene in China, it did not correspond to social realities. In the mid-twenties, the two parties jointly launched a big military campaign from their secessionist capital of Canton, which was designed to liquidate the northern warlords, including those who had found niches for themselves in the Peking government;† the campaign turned into an attack on the landowning system, which the local militarists embodied, and a vigorous prodding to awaken the peasant masses. In the early twenties, the first peasant leagues had been formed under the leadership of Peng Pai in Guangdong Province; they were extremely combative and altogether capable of practicing a form of direct democracy. Now, as the Nationalist Army proceeded on its

*In foreign relations during the twenties and thirties, reformers and revolutionaries looked to the two large foreign countries unassociated with a colonializing past, the United States and the Soviet Union. For so long as the purpose was chiefly to redress the wrongs of old-style colonialism, these two countries represented to the Chinese the Western modernization that they, in the liberating vestments of socialism and democracy, should make their own. The special relationship that was established with both nations—especially through individuals, some of whom were official representatives—included impartially both Nationalist and Communist camps.

†Sun Yat-sen, the great Nationalist leader and president of the new Chinese Republic (1911), had founded a revolutionary base in Canton with the support of the Soviet Union, which sent him, in addition to financial assistance, advisers and technicians to help organize the Huangpu Military Academy; it had as its director Chiang Kai-shek (Nationalist) and as its political commissar Zhou Enlai (Communist). The majority of the new generation of military cadres were trained at the Huangpu Academy, and subsequently allied themselves with one or the other of the two camps, Nationalist and Communist. The Northern Expedition was in a planning stage for years; it was launched in 1926, under the command of Chiang, by which time Sun Yat-sen had died.

liberating march northward, similar agitation spread to other provinces in South and Central China.

The paradox was that the Comintern's program for the democratic-bourgeois revolution was pivoted on the emergence of an urban middle class—ergo of an industrial proletariat also—while the peasants were supposed in part to be phased out as a class via the proletarianizing process and in part to be designated lower-middle-class elements—ergo, to be represented by the Nationalist party. Never did the scheme envisage the peasants as a massive presence with an independent identity, with the result that they now became a disturbing element. It was impossible to face squarely the evidence that the peasants were not at all on their way to extinction, that the overwhelming majority of them had nothing whatever to do with the lower middle class, nor were they represented by the Kuomintang. Indeed, they appeared to be the only force capable of jolting the landowning power system to its roots. In fact, reality again turned theory topsy-turvy. The assumption that at that phase in history the emerging urban middle class and the landowners were the major antagonists proved to be unfounded. The urban middle class was so bound through personal relationships and shared interests to the agrarian propertied class that it could not see itself as being apart, much less in opposition. When the peasants began to rebel, not yet claiming ownership of the land but only calling for a reduction in the exorbitant agrarian tax, rental tax, and interest rates, not only did local landowners find the demands untenable but so also did the nationalist middle class that organized the revolutionary army. It showed itself not only powerless to carry out democratization in the countryside but also intrinsically to be allied with the social stratum it theoretically should have been opposing.

On the other hand, in the cities industrial workers were the objects of an exploitation and oppression typical of a colonized country, and the efforts of Communist activists accelerated their becoming organized. Increasingly strong unions were formed, and collective-bargaining struggles spread. They were directed against imperialistic capitalists and against Chinese owners as well, and the latter's earlier resentment at being overmatched by foreigners became secondary when both groups began to have a common interest in fighting the threat posed by the growing strength of the workers. In the end, class won out over nationalism, and instead of an alliance between Chinese capitalists and Chinese workers against the foreigners, it was foreign and Chinese capitalists who joined together against the workers. Hence the impotence of the urban middle class to make itself the protagonist of national liberation, and its close alliance with international capitalism, on which it was dependent.

All these combined factors led to an objective confluence of the interests of peasants and workers. (The workers had personal bonds with the peasants, because many of them were first-generation immigrants to the city, and their ties to their peasant relatives were still close.) The agricultural economy and the level of rural life had been so reduced that large masses of people, impoverished and without work, migrated or simply wandered from one place to the other, whether country or city. Such people were potential revolutionary allies for the employed workers and peasants, since they had, after all, a common origin, and the prevailing system was becoming intolerable in the extreme for them.

The situation steadily worsened, and the struggles of workers and of peasants especially were assuming a pre-insurrectional character. The Kuomintang responded by moving away from the Communists and organizing attacks on them. Finally, it broke up the common front and expelled CCP members from the government. However, in obedience to the Comintern's directives, the Communists remained faithful to the alliance, and after Shanghai had been liberated by 800,000 rebellious workers they handed the city back to the Nationalist Army in late March, 1927. On April 12, with the help of local gangsters, Chiang Kai-shek organized a massacre of union leaders and militants. Persecution and mass killings spread throughout the territory controlled by the Kuomintang, and Communists were ruthlessly hunted down also in areas occupied by the warlords.

The CCP leaders' policy had brought the labor movement to the point of catastrophe. The idea that the revolution was centered in the cities had also been blasted. This the Comintern was unwilling to admit, and although after great delay it did renounce the alliance between the Chinese Communist party and the Kuomintang, it pursued for some years a bankrupt program of urban uprisings; the case of the Canton Commune, in December, 1927, is the best-known of many; it was a generous and futile self-sacrifice on the part of thousands of workers and militants, who were massacred amid atrocious tortures.*

Since its organization in 1921, the Chinese Communist party had been led not by Social Democratic veterans but by democratic, progressive intellectuals who lacked political experience. The Party had been unable to fashion an image of its own, independent of the one the Comintern assigned it. However, during those early years and the period of disorientation that followed on the Party's defeat, the leadership was made up of people who had lived and been educated in a Chinese context, whereas the Comintern was quite distinct, its separateness being even physically apparent in the advisers, Russian or other, whom it sent to China. Then, in January, 1931, things changed. A group of militants who had been trained in the Soviet Union and who had returned to Shanghai, where the Central Committee was functioning underground, in a surprise move seized the Party leadership. These militants, ironically referred to as "the twenty-eight-and-a-half Bolsheviks," constituted the nucleus of a real "Bolshevik" or "inter-

---

*According to Jacques Guillermaz in *Histoire du parti communiste Chinois* (Paris: Payot, 1968), there were at least 5,000 deaths. This is the figure given by some Communist authors; others give the figure of 8,000, while one Nationalist author claimed there were 15,000 deaths.

nationalist"* faction at the service of the U.S.S.R. A murky period began in Shanghai then, in Communist circles and for others close to them, who included many writers and a majority of young intellectuals. A clandestine atmosphere is always unhealthy, and it was now made more oppressive by factional infighting, denunciations, accusations, uncertainty, and reciprocal suspicion. Orders arrived from abroad, and often were irrelevant to the Chinese situation; also, the authoritarianism implicit in this method of operating prevented clear thinking and open discussion. Because of the Kuomintang's severe, semi-Fascist police regime, labor's presence in the Party leadership was small and limited to vanguard groups from several factories. On the other hand, the fact that one or another of the foreign powers presided over zones free of fascism helped Party leaders maintain a dense network of contacts with the quite rich and articulate intellectual life in Shanghai, which was then the capital of a nascent cultural industry—large publishing houses, literary activity, Western theater, and cinema (unlike the situation in Peking, which was primarily an academic center). These years witnessed the birth of loyalties and enmities, hatreds and complicities, labyrinthine relationships among factions and subfactions—all of them politically and ideologically and personally motivated—that to this day constitute a concealed terrain of polemics, conflicts, and alliances that are not always understandable, and in which motivations are quite different from what they appear to be on the surface or are stated to be. They are the final outcome of the gradual degeneration of a Party conceived as an urban political species and centered in the unhealthy milieu of a big city. The remarkable figure of one writer emerges from this scene at a far higher level than that of his contemporaries: Lu Xun. More than forty years after his death, Lu Xun is still dragged into the polemics and exploitative maneuverings of opposed factions, as happens to great men whom all would wish but are unable to capture and claim as their own, and whom many who dare not confess it hate.

In those same years, the Communist party had still another face. After the 1927 catastrophe, a few leaders who had reluctantly submitted to taking their orders from abroad embarked on an independent line of action. It was not made overt; they maintained good formal relations with the U.S.S.R. and kept an organizational tie with those who were following the line of internationalist obedience, later called the "Bolshevik" line.

With some Nationalist Army units which, because they were commanded by Communist officers, had not followed Chiang Kai-shek, Mao Zedong and Zhu De led several insurrectional attempts that failed. They then established a territorial base in the Jing Gang Mountains, in Jiangxi Province, where others

*The term "internationalist" was coined by Western historians; it has never been used by the Chinese.

followed. They decided on this move partly to put themselves beyond the reach of Kuomintang persecution and to salvage what was salvageable of the armed forces at their disposal; however, the move also accorded with a strategic vision that was then in a formative stage and that was fully worked out in the years to come.

The assumptions are set forth in several essays of Mao Zedong published after 1925: "An Analysis of Chinese Rural Classes," "An Analysis of Classes in Chinese Society," and "Report on an Investigation of the Peasant Movement in Hunan." They are especially interesting in their original versions, in which ideas are not distorted by any concern to adapt them to orthodox doctrine. They make it quite evident that Mao had moved far away from the concept of an urban revolution carried out by the national bourgeoisie with the assistance of a Communist vanguard. The theoretical terminology is crude; what Mao was attempting was to describe Chinese society without using doctrinaire references. The terms "bourgeoisie" and "proletariat" are used empirically. For example, one finds a plethora of subdivisions: the bourgeoisie is upper, middle, small, agrarian, and urban; the proletariat is companioned by a subproletariat. Words are loaded with value content. Mao's "bourgeoisie" and "proletariat" are associated with unspecific ahistorical concepts like "the rich" and "the poor"— both terms being used with respect not only to money but also to culture and power. The reference to a front line beyond and above which each person and each category is situated splits society in two, but in terms almost diametrically opposed to those of Marx. Marx completes his interpretation of European history with a progressive, teleological concept which states that each historical phase overcomes and absorbs the preceding one. He assumes, accordingly, that the capitalist mode of production is a *necessary evolution,* and from this he deduces that all classes of society must be reduced to only two: owners of capital and wage earners. Such a necessity was not only alien but somehow incomprehensible to Mao, who was, after all, looking not at conditions in Europe during the period of bourgeois dominance but at conditions current in his own country, which were the result of a very different past. He looked on the rise of the bourgeoisie as an empirical fact that had occurred on another continent and could not cogently serve him as a model. On the basis not only of demonstrated facts but also of fundamental theories, the presumed centrality of the national bourgeoisie collapsed, as did the assumption that the revolutionaries must take the cities as their center of operation. Rather, they appeared as enemy citadels that must be besieged.

For Marx, the triumph of the proletariat and its leadership destiny are historical necessities, which intelligent revolutionary action interprets and so hastens the conclusion of an evolutionary process. For Mao, the struggle of the poor against the system of the mighty is necessary, and while victory is possible, it is immanent in social realities; the struggle is never concluded, the victory never conclusive. The positing of individuals on one or the other side of the front is determined not by knowledge of any scientific necessity but by utilitarian or ethical considerations. Revolutionary choice is a decision of the will, not a result arrived at scientifically.

Orthodox Marxists find this concept an instance of anarchistic primitivism, but it runs more or less subterraneanly through the entire theoretical and pragmatic work of Mao Zedong, from the early twenties almost until the eve of his death. He never arrived at an organic formulation of his ideas, and indeed it was not in his nature to do so. The same Mao who wanted to train himself as a Marxist oscillated continually between Marxism-Leninism and his own different concept, to which he was never able to give coherent, critically aware expression. His own ideas emerge more clearly in his early writings (when he knew very little about Marxism); intermittently they became more explicit at moments when he found himself in serious conflict with other Communists, foreign or Chinese, and only in his last years of renewed struggle and of defeat were they stated openly, albeit couched in discontinuous and epigrammatic terms.

The compromise with Marxism, which makes Mao's statements more contradictory and open to criticism, was motivated by a practical purpose, which was to link the struggles of the Chinese people to those of Western proletariats and to the world revolution. Without such a linkage, the possibility of success would have been ruled out, given the international character of the enemy present and holding power in China in the form of imperialistic capitalism.

The first result of Mao's thought was that the center of the revolution shifted from the city to the country. The peasants took the leading role both in the overturning of the landownership system and in the conquest of national independence since, in order to defend themselves, they were obliged to recognize and directly attack the capitalist forces in China.

Since the peasants, the people at war, were concrete entities, men and women of flesh and bone, they had a built-in sense of their identity; they were not objects behaving according to a logic that can be predetermined by some scientific analysis known only to political leaders or vanguards. All the more important, then, was the task of the leaders and vanguards to educate and persuade them; that task had to be well performed; the people's understanding had to become broader and more open, since their choices were to be free choices and the process of social and political liberation was to be one with the process of intellectual liberation: the possible but not the guaranteed result of "necessary behavior." Red power in the rural areas was founded not on the putschist action of a minority but on the active participation of the entire population. The Communists favored self-government of the people, educating them in democracy in forms and ways appropriate to their understanding and responsive to their needs. Economic policy, the confiscation and redistribution of land, the identification of the economic and social levels and categories on which to build and of those which were to be considered hostile—all these were the result of continual, minute study aiming to make them conform to social reality.

Complementing the choice of a rural rather than urban revolution was the strategy of armed struggle by the people. The objective was to turn to the people's advantage the disintegration of the central government whose weakness gave rise to the phenomenon of the warlords. On China's immense territory, it was possible to create territorial bases from which to wage guerrilla warfare aimed at destroying already disintegrating enemy forces one by one. It was a long-term process, in the course of which the holdings of the landowners were gradually expropriated, the people's education advanced, and their participation in the struggle grew.

This program was outlined during the early years at Red bases in Jiangxi and, later, in Hubei and Hunan Provinces. It was fully worked out during the period from 1935 through the war against the Japanese (1937–45) when the Reds were based in northeastern China and had Yanan as their capital.

However, Mao Zedong's freedom of movement, which had been favored by distance and the difficulty in communicating with Shanghai, was curtailed when the Central Committee moved from Shanghai to the Red bases—some members coming in 1931, and the rest in 1933. From then on, policy decisions about the conduct of the resistance to the Kuomintang's "campaigns of annihilation" (1930–34), agrarian reform measures, the Long March to the north (1934–35), a patriotic anti-Japanese front—decisions in all these areas of Communist party policy were arrived at after conflicts and compromises between the two divergent orientations—between the group adhering to the example and the directives of the U.S.S.R. and continuing the orthodox "urban" line, and Mao's heretical group favoring peasant nationalism. The meeting/colliding of the two Party components, which were incompatible culturally even more than politically, was fostered also by the arrival in Yanan of many intellectuals from the cities, Shanghai especially (among them Mao's future wife, Jiang Qing). Contradictions existed even within the same individual. For example, Zhou Enlai—to speak only of the most eminent figure—found himself close to the "Bolsheviks" because he shared Western culture with them, but also close to Mao in choosing independence from the U.S.S.R., and taking an antidogmatic, pragmatic position on questions of political action.

During the war of resistance against the Japanese (1937–45), the Communists functioned, in the main, independently—partly because they were forced to rely exclusively on their own strengths. Notwithstanding the fact that the CCP and the Kuomintang had re-formed a patriotic united front, their mutual distrust and hostility had abated so little as to permit the more or less disguised continuation of civil war. Several pressing considerations favored the Communists' opting for autonomy. It was important that they preserve their political power in their own territory, and that they maintain independent military units both to conduct guerrilla action behind enemy lines and to combine anti-Japanese resistance with the struggle for the land. Thus the internationalist faction's plan to reestablish an interparty bloc under Kuomintang leadership, as in the twenties, was frustrated, although it was supported by the Soviet Union, which not only did not furnish aid to the Communists but also maintained a position equidistant between the CCP and the Kuomintang, while explicitly recognizing the latter as the leading party and the government of the Chinese nation.

After 1945, both the United States and the Soviet Union favored a parliamentary regime for China, with the Kuomintang in power and the Communist party given legal status as either an opposition party or a member of the government but in a subordinate role. The program was unrealistic. There had been a massive growth in the strength of the Red Army, of the Communist party, and of people's power in the liberated zone, whereas the Kuomintang was sinking into corruption and impotence, and had lost the support even of a large part of the landowning class and of the urban bourgeoisie. Popular power had been strengthened because the Communists had gone their independent way, integrating leaders and people—in effect, transforming a war into a revolution of such dimensions that it could no longer be halted. The radicalized class conflict defeated attempts to arrive at an agreement between the Nationalist and Communist parties, the civil war openly resumed, and in little more than a year, the Red Army's advance, accompanied by agrarian revolution, became irresistible. "The materially inferior side conquered the materially superior side, the countryside conquered the city, the side denied foreign support triumphed over the side given foreign support"*—this slogan circulated widely at the time—and in short order the popular forces liberated the entire country.

The proclamation of the People's Republic on October 1, 1949, sanctioned the triumph of national vindication. After more than a century of dependency, China had regained full political, military, and economic sovereignty. The peasant revolution had also triumphed, and between the years 1950 and 1951 it was completed with the great popular movement in which the land was distributed among those who tilled it.

With the "entrance into the cities," however, knotty conflicts that had been accumulating over the years but had been held in abeyance by the armed struggle surfaced once more.

The split in the Chinese Communist party was concealed from foreign eyes, thanks to a show of unanimity that was energetically touted in inverse proportion to the fact. Indeed, after Liberation, the Party was in a state of permanent

---

*Jack Belden, *China Shakes the World* (New York, Monthly Review Press, 1970), Chapter XI.

conflict, deeper than the individual and factional fights for power. The basic dilemma lay in the disagreement over the "continuation of the revolution" (which is to say, growth of the class struggle, fissuring society to achieve equality and self-determination for the workers) versus the founding of a state through the establishment of a governing class above the masses to lead the cause of national unity. As the years passed, the opposed views were formulated and marshaled into two main currents: one assigning primary importance to the class struggle and a cultural revolution, the other supporting an elite-controlled, well-disciplined development and the restoration of order.

Not only peasants and workers had been set free by the revolution; the urban middle classes were now released from the control of a corrupt and conservative Kuomintang and from the deadly grip of foreign capital and of the financial interests and compradors dependent on it. The obstacles that had blocked the drive of the urban middle classes to assert themselves as the new governing class and as leaders of national construction were falling; potentially, they were the heirs and transformers of the government of the past and upholders of an honest and reformist political administration.

They constituted an emergent bourgeoisie in a country that had not known bourgeois development; they were the children of colonialism. They welcomed sympathetically the new government which was restoring national identity and dignity to China. At the same time, in seeking ways to legitimize their own role, they perceived a universal model in the history of Europe and were inclined to adopt European culture as their own—both its Western and Soviet versions. They accepted also the evolutionary concept of a unilinear development via gradually achieved economic and technical advances, and a scale of values that favored industry over agriculture, the urban over the country dweller, and a commitment to productivity and the accumulation of capital over the satisfaction of needs and a reevaluation of existing relations of production. In a word, from Europe there passed on to them the ethic of the bourgeoisie as the producing, capital-accumulating, and managerial class, both in the traditional Western version and in the Soviet version—i.e., socialism construed as economic growth directed by an elite for the good of the people.

In the first years of the People's Republic, the country suffered the impact that the Cold War had on international relations. Soviet pressures to absorb China into the "Socialist camp" under Russian hegemony mounted. The outcome of this was a direct Soviet presence which took the form of both economic and technical aid, the creation of joint enterprises, Soviet interposition in certain production sectors and in geographical areas of strategic importance, and propaganda, oral, written, and graphic. What's more, Chinese leaders and cadres, who lacked both theoretical and practical knowledge of how to set up the government and the economy "in the cities," adopted as their model ("copied" is how Mao Zedong put it) the cultural and economic structures and the administrative and managerial methods of the U.S.S.R. Although those Party leaders who had grown up in the school of the Third International and shared Soviet concepts of power, party, and centralism were a minority in the upper echelons of Party and administration, their ideas seemed to prevail. The "seizing of power" by the workers' party was thought to be the conclusive phase of the revolution; the next step was the Socialist phase of planned economic growth with rigid centralization, discipline, and respect for the hierarchs. Emphasis on the importance of production and a high regard for scientific, cultural, and managerial skills led to a confluence of the self-interest and tendencies of the cadres, who were making themselves into a political bureaucracy, and the concerns of the educated urban middle classes. From that fusion a new governing class emerged.

There was, however, no organic unity among the diverse components of the new governing class. The educated middle classes were distinguished from the cadres; and if some favored China's traveling the road the U.S.S.R. had taken, and accepted the system of centralized power, and were prepared to give up individual liberty for privilege, others were unwilling to tolerate chains on their freedom and continued to form their ideas after Western European and North American models. When, in 1956, the political leadership offered the outlet of the Hundred Flowers—an attempt at broad democracy in the cultural field, to do away with repressive methods like those that precipitated the revolts in Hungary and Poland—they let themselves be dragged into the antithesis the Cold War had induced between "socialism" (the Soviet camp and Soviet methods) and "freedom" (the Western camp and Western methods). What followed was inevitable. Empty aspirations to Westernize were suppressed, the attempt at democracy was defeated, and among the leaders and Party cadres the trend toward "Soviet style" management was reinforced. The Party secretary, Deng Xiaoping, led the repression with obtuse bureaucratic methods.

But Party cadres were not wholly replicas of Soviet bureaucrats. They did support the routine Soviet tradition; but also championed the innovative role that from their Yanan experience they had handed on to the entire country. Soviet-style development was, indeed, a contradiction of the judgment pronounced at the time of liberation by Mao Zedong according to which, now that "the center of the Party's work" had passed "from the country to the cities," the struggle against the urban bourgeoisie had commenced. So, far from conflicts having ended, they were transferred to the very fabric of the liberated country. Various difficulties arose in the attempt to translate Mao's statement into political action. First and foremost was the cultural immaturity of the workers, the urban stratum that should have embodied the alternative to bourgeois development (which was, furthermore, construed in a sense so broad as to include even the proposal to build in the Soviet style). Other problems included the unpreparedness of the cadres for so unusual a task—unusual not only for China—the spontaneous tendency to establish elites above the people's heads, and lastly, the indecisiveness and inconsistency of Mao Zedong and those elements in the Party closest to him.

In the years that followed, the Maoists' ambition was to be able to mediate between opposed exigencies: between patriotic collaboration and class struggle, between unity and criticism, obedience and rebellion, hierarchy and equality, building and revolution. On the strength of widespread discontent among the workers with the methods imported from the U.S.S.R., repeated attempts were made to find alternate forms of collective management that might increase the workers' influence in the factory, lessen inequality (not only in the distribution of income), and gradually attenuate the division of labor, in harmony with the Communist goal of eliminating the labor market. Attempts also were made at a dialectic between construction and struggle. The tactic of a "zigzag" procedure was adopted, whereby now the one and now the other prevailed in alternation. Planned growth was thus dislocated by mass movements that, having upset a preceding equilibrium, proposed a new one at a higher level (in line with a "spiral" development plan), and that were carriers of rebellion and mouthpieces for demands for equality and for power of the "poor" against the "rich": collectivization of the land (1955–56); the Great Leap Forward and the creation of the People's Communes (1958–59); "Socialist education" in the rural areas (1963–65)—to recall here only the bigger movements that affected the whole country. Despite serious imbalances, failures, and social trauma, the method, taken in toto, was efficacious, especially when the results are compared with the progressive decline of U.S.S.R. satellite countries and if one takes into account the aggression of the two superpowers with respect to China in the sixties.* The most fruitful results were obtained by adopting and spreading a policy of democracy at the base. Old customs and traditional ways of association were modified so as to function democratically, a new order of relationships among people was created which was ruled by a spirit of independence and collaboration, by simplicity, equality, and mutual aid. Obviously, this change did not always come about spontaneously; indeed, the authorities intervened continually, but on the people's part there was a basic faith in common values and a sense of ethical-political urgency that for societies today were exceptional.

These transformations affected a clearly delimited area of society which did not extend beyond the base communities. On a higher level was the sphere of national policy, to which the people as a whole were alien and indifferent, notwithstanding constant indoctrination. Furthermore, the hierarchic adminis-

*In the late fifties, China rejected further economic and military dependence on the U.S.S.R., whereupon the latter effected a kind of indirect aggression through the withdrawal of loans, technicians, and construction projects, and on the side it also mounted a military threat on China's northern frontier. The aggressive action of the United States, with whom China then had no diplomatic relations, was military, indirectly effected through the war in Southeast Asia in the 1960s.

trative system weighed even on the base communities and restricted their autonomy. And as the country moved further away from the revolutionary years and the power pyramid consolidated, the people's participation became less genuine and the tactic of periodically rousing the masses encountered a progressive decline in their sense of involvement.

It became increasingly clear that the Party lacked the suitable tools essential to achieve its goal. There were no adequate institutional means to permit any exposure of social conflicts or the development of democracy on all levels. Mao's own cultural limitations blocked any efficient search for such means. He never renounced the concept of a single party leading the nation's united front, with political direction assigned to the new class in power. Yet, to bear out the "continuation of the class struggle" slogan, the Party should have consisted of workers and poor peasants pitted against the "bourgeoisie," but this was an agglomeration of managers, cadres, and educated members of the middle class within the same party. The collaboration of the different classes under the guidance of a single party had worked effectively during the war when all their forces combined to fight the same enemy; but now, the common front embraced the "national bourgeoisie," which joined with the intellectuals, scientists, and cadres to constitute the new ruling class. The indigent peasants and workers were called up to take part in the struggle against the Party and state apparatus, with its managerial and intellectual components—the very apparatus designed to speak in their interests and give them political guidance. With the passing of time, by the 1960s the paradox became obvious. Compromise at the Party summit was no longer possible. Dissension broke out among the various currents, so serious that during the "movement for Socialist education" campaign, the different factional leaders were issuing contradictory directives, all of them in the name of the central committee.

Those Communists who were oriented toward class strife and a decentralized workers' regime denounced the Soviet system (nominally spurned by everyone) for opposing the population—as did the Chinese system, patterned on the Soviet model—and scorned their leaders as "bourgeois within the Party . . . on the road to capitalism." But they failed to propose an alternate route because no one, not even Mao himself, could explain what was meant by "bourgeois" or "the road to capitalism" in a Socialist society. While it was obvious that the workers held neither political nor economic power and that they were "merchandise" no less than their brethren in the capitalist countries, still no one troubled to question various Marxist postulates, first of all the contention that economic exploitation and political vassalage of workers have private property as their main motive.

This political current countered the oversight by inciting the people to rebel and by disseminating a dialectic of negation, inherited from the long record of cyclical revolts which have studded the history of China. This dialectic was unequal to the task of administering power or opposing others who already possessed power.

With greater mass education, an expanding working class, and the rise of autonomous government in the rural areas, the people became more and more restive with the straitjacket existence imposed on them by the Party's omnipresent authoritarianism, which denied the values of socialism inculcated in them. The ferment was especially heated among the young and the students. In May, 1966, Mao decided to "overturn the king of the Heavens and liberate the little devils," by allowing them to give free vent to their complaints. In China, an anti-academic and anti-authoritarian movement, not unlike the revolts that exploded in Europe and North America in the years immediately following, detonated a more general convulsion, which disrupted the urban population, particularly the workers. Mao Zedong and his closest henchmen attempted to challenge the widening gap between the population and its institutions by attacking the institutions (but only the Party bureaucracy and the schools seriously) and leaving ample space for spontaneity. This resulted in fearful disorder, with each social stratum venting its discontent and resentments on all other strata, everyone battling everyone else. If there were sharp divisions, there were also reconciliations in hitherto untried ways that discarded entrenched dogmas and schemes. It was a premature moment of anarchy that inflicted deep lacerations but at the same time focused the attention of millions on the basic problems of living together. The liberating thrust at the base could not long endure or reach out in all directions, primarily because of the clash of interests that separated the social strata, who shared nothing more than dissatisfaction. The workers, formulating their demands with varying degrees of articulation, asked for immediate egalitarianism, decentralized power, mass education, improved living conditions and work; eventually they wanted work divisions scrapped along with the labor market. The cultivated urban classes, however, when they reacted to bureaucratic control, sought opposite aims: anti-egalitarianism, centralized power granting broader freedoms for the cultured, high-level education for the elite, sacrifices imposed on the workers with rigid discipline in production as the primary goal, higher recompense for competence and greater scope for science and culture.

The outbreak of the Cultural Revolution in late 1965 had encountered tremendous obstacles in various Party organs; everything was done to transform it into simply one more of the many bureaucratic interventions among common people. At that moment, Mao Zedong was severely isolated, as he confessed to André Malraux on August 3, 1965. To make sure that the common people would have the possibility of attacking the Party apparatus, he was obliged to exploit group hostilities among the leadership factions, and ally himself with persons he distrusted. He had repeatedly, and cynically, resorted to this ploy in the past, and thanks to the solidarity of the common people it had worked for him, but he had become much more estranged from other leaders.*

Matters threatened to get out of hand in the summer of 1967 and the urgent need for a return to order became critical. Many rebels were gradually disposed of, at the summit through dismissals from office, at the base through the mass of young citizens sent to the countryside to work in the fields. The compromise between the moderate center and Mao was more conciliatory in 1970 and 1971 after the serious consequences that arose in the wake of the Lin Biao episode. The danger of a slide toward military dictatorship was averted, but only with a palace conspiracy and an assassination, two examples of expedient methods the Cultural Revolution had fought against. Moreover, the moderates' reaction led to an ulterior repression of the Left and the young.

The Cultural Revolution had served to prevent unresolved, unexpressed domestic tensions from being deviated against imaginary enemies beyond China's borders. It kept China from being dragged into a deadly war, toward which everything seemed to be prodding the country in 1965 and 1966—externally with the war in Vietnam, internally with the mood of exasperated "nationalism," the defensive structure of a ruling class unsure of its own base.

In 1971 and 1972, the Chinese reaped positive benefits from the Cultural Revolution in the area of foreign policy. Their indirect support of the North Vietnamese, their calculated abstention from the power games of the superpowers, their keeping equidistant from each (although the U.S.S.R. was considered "the principal enemy"), their noninterventionist solidarity with the struggles of

---

*Mao's well-known letter to Jiang Qing of July 8, 1966, bears on this: "The center is asking my permission to publish the speech given by my friend [Lin Biao], and I shall agree. . . . I have doubts about some of his views. I have never believed that my little red book contained so much spiritual power. When he praises it to heaven, the whole country will do the same. It is all exaggerated. . . . (I have been pushed by them onto Mount Liang [among the rebels]), and I cannot refuse my consent. To be forced to give it against my convictions is something that has never happened to me in all my life. . . . I feel sure of myself, yet I have doubts. . . . At the Hangzhou conference last April, I said that I did not approve of the formulas my friend uses, but my words had no effect. . . . They have used even worse expressions, they have exalted me to the heavens as the miracle of miracles. . . . I have become the Zhong Kui [a terrifying mythological character] of the XX century Communist party. . . . I'll break my bones in the fall. . . . If they have already demolished Marx and Lenin, why not us, too—and with more reason? You should think about this and not let victory go to your head. . . . Our task today is to knock out some of the rightist elements in the Party and in the country (to knock all of them out would be impossible); in seven or eight years we could launch a new campaign. . . . When can these lines be published? . . . Perhaps the moment will be after my death, when the Right will have appropriated the power. . . . The Right will exploit my words to raise the black banner, but without much luck. Since the Chinese empire was overt in 1911, the reaction has never been able to hold power for long. The Left, however, will use my words toward organizing itself, and the Right will be overthrown. . . ." (From an English translation of the letter in *Issues and Studies,* January, 1973, pp. 94–96, and in *Yearbook of Chinese Communism* 1973, pp. 2–3.)

the workers and youth in other countries (a reversal of Soviet practice)* won prestige for the Chinese government and its admission to the United Nations (October, 1971), and the possibility of dealing with American government leaders from a position of strength. These were the fruits of a convergence of Mao Zedong and Zhou Enlai's policies in foreign affairs.

In domestic affairs, the two statesmen were less in agreement—indeed, were mutually mistrustful—but both realized that their respective personalities functioned complementarily. Thus, so long as they were alive it was possible for the defeat of the Cultural Revolution not to turn into catastrophe and for many doors to remain open to a more thoughtfully prepared and a more measured resumption of its seminal ideas; their influence made it possible also for a return to public order and prevented the moderates' ascendancy from taking on the accents of a vendetta, a settling of accounts. A compromise among the political leadership was ratified by the Tenth Party Congress, in August, 1973, with a calculated balance among moderate and surviving leftist elements.

The presence of these two strong personalities could block dramatic developments, but the Cultural Revolution had brought out into the open conflicts among the different social strata and among the political factions which were not erased. Between 1973 and 1975, the struggle among political factions grew more and more severely aggravated; also, adherents of opposing groups coexisted at every level of the Party, which made for an ever more serious paralysis of society that a series of mass campaigns did not succeed in unloosing: "The revolution in education," "criticism of Lin Biao and of Confucius," "study of the theory of the dictatorship of the proletariat," "the four modernizations," "the three directives as pivot," "the limitation on bourgeois rights"—these campaigns were launched by one or another faction only to be instantly exploited by one or another faction for contrary purposes.

The semblance of equilibrium collapsed with the death of Zhou Enlai, in January, 1976. Mao himself was by now so gravely ill that if he made a public appearance it was like that of a ghost or an oracle. The enforced coexistence in the upper Party and government echelons of leaders who held opposing views and were animated by mutual hatred, like Deng Xiaoping and Zhang Chunqiao, had become untenable. In 1976, months went by while the people awaited the death of Mao; immediately after he died, in early September, the last match was played out by the rival groups. All odds favored the moderates. They controlled the major ganglia of power at the center and peripherally throughout the nation;

---

*The small Maoist parties and the pro-Chinese groups that sprang up in various Western countries had, for the most part, little understanding of Chinese policy, and made China into a myth to duplicate the shattered myth of the U.S.S.R., with Mao in place of Stalin. Such errors in judgment can be imputed only in part to the Chinese, whose culpability lay rather in their cynically making use of such groups and parties as errand boys and mouthpieces, to be discarded when no longer useful.

they were supported by the army and by the police; they had greater political ability and experience; and they had won the adherence of many older cadres who could not tolerate destructive innovations, and of almost all intellectuals, against whom the Left had conducted an obtuse and gratuitously repressive campaign. Only the reawakening of the great masses of the people could have checked the moderate faction's accession to power; it was actively supported by academic circles, by technologists and management personnel hostile to freedom for the workers, by aspiring technocrats, and by the educated urban middle class.

The fate of the Left lay in the hands of people from Shanghai's radical milieus, who were absolutely unequal to so difficult a responsibility. The Cultural Revolution from the outset had lacked leaders equal in stature to its aims, and those who had managed to survive the repeated violent shakeups were either mandarins in leftist garb or individuals of good faith but too mediocre to be capable of raising the morale of the weary people, who were frustrated and spent by ten years of contradictory exhortations. The current that had bound political spokesmen to the people was broken; what the people saw now in ideas and ideologies were the banners of battalions of the mandarinate competing for power. This was a return to the old days, and the spectacle of the powerful contending among themselves left the people indifferent or, at most, curious.

Ideas and ideologies were not, however, a gratuitous invention of political groups. Behind and above the factional contest something else was at stake and deep conflicts lay concealed. Substantial minorities of workers and cadres and large numbers of young people who had matured with the Cultural Revolution were aware of this, but they also took it for granted that the dreary top-level leftist leaders could not be the bearers of the revolutionary cause.

An attempted coup to eliminate the small group of leftists in the Party and government leadership (the Tienanmen incident) took place in early April, 1976, with unfortunate results. Mao Zedong intervened one last time, supporting the accession to power of Hua Guofeng, a well-balanced personality of the Left, who had kept to the middle ground in the factional disputes. Mao realized that after his death "the Right would prevail," and he was perhaps thinking in terms of avoiding a head-on collision, of leaving the way open for a nontraumatic contest for power. But in early October, it was Hua Guofeng himself, together with General Wang Dongxing and leaders from the old guard, who carried out a coup against the other four members of the Politburo—Zhang Chunqiao, Jiang Qing, Wang Hongwen, and Yao Wenyuan. The coup was initially presented as a move to reduce factionalism and completely restore public order, and perhaps some of its promoters intended it to be that, but eventually its true and inevitable meaning became clear: the elimination of various political leaders from the last vestiges of the Cultural Revolution, and the full reassumption of power by the apparatus and its allies who had been the target of that revolution.

Despite the passivity of the people, an immediate all-encompassing attack on the policy of Mao Zedong would have been inconceivable at that time, and was not even wanted, at least not by some leaders. The moderates played the winning card, directing the people's discontent and disappointment against the easy target of mediocre leftist leaders—the so-called Gang of Four. The term was taken from something Mao Zedong had said half-jokingly, and at first it denoted merely the four individuals who had been dismissed and arrested; subsequently, it came to be used in a figurative and gradually more comprehensive sense to refer to the entire period of the Cultural Revolution and to the policy "of the last twelve years."* The Gang of Four became a symbol, the scapegoat for all of China's past and present woes; at the same time, the public's condemnation of indefensible leaders was flexibly exploited by extending it to apply as widely as possible beyond the persons and policies of the Four.

In May, 1977, Deng Xiaoping "returned to work," taking up once more

---

*It should be noted that the Gang of Four—which is to say, the concerted actions of the four while in top leadership positions—cannot be carried back earlier than 1973. Yet political positions and choices were commonly attributed to them that go back to 1965. In the most recent propaganda, even the policy line subsequent to 1956 has been challenged.

In its parallel position to the Politburo, the "central group" of the Cultural Revolution constantly changed in its composition. In 1966, after the dissolution of the first "central group" presided over by Peng Zhen, its members included Liu Zhiqian, Guan Feng, Zhang Chunqiao, Yao Wenyuan, Mu Xin, Jiang Qing, Chen Boda, Kang Sheng, Wang Li, Qi Benyu, flanked by Nie Yuanzi and others of both the old and new guard. Between the summer of 1967 and early 1968, some of the "revolutionary rebels" were reprimanded, partially reinstated, then permanently expelled. Exponents of the Left were also relieved of their duties, among them Xie Fuzhi, Minister of Public Security, who nevertheless was still presiding over the Peking revolutionary committee in 1968, Nie Yuanzi, who wrote the first rebel *dazibao* (wall posters), and Yang Chengwu, chief of headquarters. Top leaders of the student revolt, some of them highly esteemed, like Kuai Dafu, were also liquidated after July, 1968, when the workers' propaganda squads moved into the universities and broke up the factional disputes.

Meanwhile, the central group assigned Zhang Chunqiao, member of the central committee, to take charge of Shanghai, where he supported the workers who had occupied the factories and set up management committees against the lockout of the cadres and technicians. He succeeded in quelling the heated infighting among the workers and helped to establish the Shanghai commune, becoming mayor of the city when the commune was disbanded by the center.

Yao Wenyuan, delegated by Mao to disseminate polemics against the Right, was a mediocre journalist who rose to power in the sphere of information over the years.

It was only during the Chinese Communist Party's IX Congress in April, 1969, that Jiang Qing, Zhang Chunqiao, Yao Wenyuan, and seventeen other persons took part in the Politburo (but not in the permanent committee, the real organ of direction). Following the defeat of Mao and the Left —and particularly in the wake of the Lin Biao episode—and the return to power of a good many leaders and cadres under attack during the Cultural Revolution (particularly Deng Xiaoping), the X Congress (August, 1973) reorganized the Politburo and permanent committee in such a way that Left and Right achieved a perfect balance. (Hua Guofeng appears in the politburo for the first time.) Only then did the alliance uniting Jiang Qing, Zhang Chunqiao, and Yao Wenyuan begin to take shape. They were joined by Wang Hongwen, promoted with others to the vice-presidency of the Party. Of the Four, only Wang Hongwen and Zhang Chunqiao sat on the permanent committee, along with seven other exponents of the various currents.

To represent the Four as close associates and, what is more, dominant leaders during the years of the Cultural Revolution is to perpetrate a pure fabrication.

the power that actually he had already rewon in April 1973, and lost again only in 1976. But this time he did not have to share power with a radical opposition. Over the next few years, all those who had been dismissed from their posts or hurt in some fashion during the Cultural Revolution were reinstated; the leaders closest to Deng were promoted to key posts; steps were taken to settle accounts with members of the Cultural Revolution, beginning with cadres nearest the base and the most fervent partisans, but going on to include the more lukewarm and reaching up into the upper ranks of the hierarchy, with the result that Chairman Hua Guofeng himself was maneuvered into greater and greater isolation. The action was carried out gradually and inexorably and most skillfully.

Now that, by degrees, the last positions of the heirs of the Maoist tradition had been dismantled, the time was ripe for an open attack on Mao Zedong. It began in February, 1980, when four men were removed from the Politburo—Wang Dongxing, Chen Xilian, Wu De, and Ji Dengkui—all of whom had either played prominent parts in eliminating the Gang of Four or at least endorsed their banishment. Secondly, the public celebrations that marked the postmortem rehabilitation of Liu Shaoqi were noteworthy, for Liu Shaoqi—more complex and nuanced historical realities apart—may be said to symbolize the opposition and the alternative to Mao.

The voice of the common Chinese people, particularly of the peasants, never reached us, and if we knew nothing of their reactions to the events of the past years, Chen Yonggui, former director of the Dazhai agricultural brigade, interpreted them for us at least partially. His antitechnocratic and ultrademocratic programs figure among the myths that have been demolished in the meantime. I believe it is necessary to quote a few of the phrases with which this man—certainly not to be suspected of sympathy for the Gang of Four—responded to his adversaries when he was virtually under accusation in 1978:

"I can read very few [ideographic] characters, and I've never studied Marxism-Leninism. . . . I don't really know what *Capital* and *The State and Revolution* are all about. . . . Some comrades quoted from the classics—history, Marx, the works of Mao Zedong—but I didn't catch many things. . . . If you ask me about the proper time to plant seeds, apply fertilizers, and weed, I can be at least 80 percent right, from my observations of the weather and my experience. . . . Seven or eight years ago, Chairman Mao wanted me to work in the Central Committee. I told him that I wouldn't feel at home in such a big office. . . . After the Lin Biao affair, the Gang of Four tried to enlist me on their side. The Chairman said to me, 'Old Devil, don't turn the Gang of Four into the Gang of Five.' After I heard this, I dared not even answer the phone calls from Jiang Qing, and I went back to Dazhai several times, feigning sickness. . . . I don't care to be a vice-premier or a Politburo member. . . . It means nothing to me. . . . Rolling up the bottom of my trousers to till the soil has always been my lot. . . . I already pointed out that since the 3rd Plenum of the CCP Central

Committee [July, 1977], the Party Central has been facing the danger of a capitalist restoration, has sent away Chairman Mao's holy tablet, and driven away workers, peasants, and soldiers. The phenomenon of campuses managed by bourgeois intellectuals has reemerged. At the same time, I also said more than once that the 3rd Plenum cut the Dazhai banner, abandoned self-reliance, forsook the Party's tradition, regressed into the past, stopped talking about the line and class struggle, wanted no more of the proletarian dictatorship, depended no longer on poor and lower-middle peasants, and practiced revisionism instead of Socialism. As I spoke these words, some people wanted me to disclose the identity of the behind-the-scenes instigator. . . . 'Comrade Chen Yonggui, these words are probably not from your heart. You were taken in and made a scapegoat by others. For the solidarity of the Party and the acceleration of the four modernizations, you must take a firm stand and divulge the identity of whoever wanted you to say these things. Then there will be no problem.' When I heard this, I felt strange. This is my viewpoint. Why should I implicate anyone either on the stage or behind the scenes? . . . I can either go back to Dazhai or go somewhere else. I am unfit to be a leader in the Party, but I can be an ordinary Party member; I am unfit to be a cadre, but I can be a peasant. . . .'"*

*English translation from *Issues and Studies,* May, 1980.

PEKING

Peking
June 28–July 20, 1976

This is not a flight from my own country. I have specified the exact duration of my stay here, which is to be a little more than one year. My purpose is to resume, after a long interval in academe, direct contact with this world, which has come gradually to occupy most of my thoughts and yet has grown increasingly abstract, become a locus of fantasy and ideology.

My prudence is great, my expectations are minimal. I should like to be useful in a modest way, and I know that I shall have to live in a kind of isolation. Companioning me is revulsion at what Europe and my own country are becoming, and the months ahead spread before me like a pause that will be filled with activity—for me, a descent into the concrete, an immeasurable remoteness from involvement. Because nowhere else in the world does the foreigner remain a foreigner as he does in China.

I shall be teaching Italian at the Foreign Languages Institute in Shanghai. Before that, I will spend two months in Peking as a guest of the Italian ambassador.

At the airport, I was nostalgically stirred by the well-concerted harmony of the buildings, by the people and how they move about. The Italians picked me up with affectionate dispatch, and drove me to the sheltering walls of the embassy. It is a building with enormous kitchens and soft-pile rugs; no rubbishy antiques, no chinoiserie; the lines and colors are right—the walls of the big drawing room are finished in a yellow lacquer, chairs are comfortable, floors black. Drinks were served by the elderly servant whom everyone calls Signor Chuang, of Shanghai, a polite, fragile-looking man (they say he used to be a tennis instructor). He is excellent in his present calling; convinced that he is the one sensible person in the house, he watches over us all. He worries about economizing and refuses to serve champagne when there are Chinese guests because, he says, they would not appreciate it. (When the time eventually came for me to take my leave, he obliged me to take along a box of tea I had in my room—otherwise it would be wasted.) His tone with me is that of an equal's reserved affection—a *laobaixing* (a "common man"), turning to a younger *laobaixing* in the home of wealthy people. Our conversations are carried on in a bastard tongue, a few words in an approximate English, a few in an approximate Shanghaiese. Having only read and translated Chinese without speaking it for so many years, my knowledge of the language had become bookish; in any case, I speak the national, or Peking, tongue, and the Shanghai dialect is almost incomprehensible to me.

When I got up the first morning, I felt dizzy and thought I must be sick. But then I learned that here this happens to many people in the summer. Apparently it has something to do with the low atmospheric pressure. It rained constantly, sometimes a drizzle, sometimes in torrents. The embassy itself is air-conditioned, but the instant you opened the French doors and stood on the threshold leading to the garden, a warm, moist canopy pressed down on you. Rare clear days came as a sudden, incredible delight.

Then it was lovely to get up a little early, step outside the new two-storied villa, cross the courtyard garden, and reach the street via a gate where a little soldier, bored but serious, always stands guard. On the opposite side of the small avenue is the Sudanese embassy, which is guarded by another little soldier; to the rear, our building is adjacent to the Norwegian embassy (during the earthquake in July there was an involved business having to do with feeding Italian and Norwegian cats). This sector is in the eastern part of Peking, and is known as Sanlidun—named after an old street—and many of the recently built embassies are located here. The villas are all low, all surrounded by gardens, all more or less of the same basic design but with variations or additions. The French embassy, for example, is much larger than ours; the Swiss looks like some sort of luxurious bunker and has both a swimming pool and an atomic-bomb shelter. An old suburban village, which has been largely rebuilt, surrounds Sanlidun, but otherwise this large quarter did not even exist at the time of my first visit here, some twenty years ago. Now there are not only embassies in Sanlidun but also street after street of private homes. The earliest built are simple, not to say amorphous; the later ones show more care. But taken as a whole, these avenues and streets are pleasant to walk along. Trees are beyond the counting, all planted in recent years; as many as four or five rows line both sides of the bigger boulevards. Acacias and poplars predominate, and when the sky is clear, they are a light, very luminous green. At many points, groups of buildings are surrounded by long, low walls, as is the custom here, and the houses are scarcely visible. Our little avenue, which is walled off on one side, is paved and well kept;

there are bins for refuse and fallen leaves. A short distance from the embassy, our avenue runs into the very long, wide boulevard where the Palace of Agriculture is located. I didn't visit it. Such exhibits, crammed with facts and figures, bore me, and, in general, so do even the panels of mounted photographs. I prefer books; one can consult a book sitting down and in one's own good time. Actually, the great exhibition buildings here are temples glorifying some nonreligion that does not speak to me. This particular building has pretensions to monumentality; I have a memory of white and green, not unpleasant.

If I turned left at the first little street after ours, I came to a big building housing a post office, a hairdressing parlor, a gas station (very few of these here), and assorted offices. Also a fruit store for foreigners. In the next small street, there is a grocery store for foreigners, very well stocked, where the diplomats' cooks and servants also shop. One finds items of better quality here than in the ordinary markets and stores, and also merchandise exclusively for us—cheese, yogurt, various kinds of salami, bread, brioches. All these foodstuffs are produced in China, however, and it is impossible to find imported brands of alcoholic drinks, even among those sold exclusively to foreigners in the Friendship Stores. To satisfy anticipated requests for whiskey, cognac, and so forth, imitations of whiskey, cognac, vodka—even of champagne—are sold. (Foreign residents of Peking who have contacts with the embassies arrange through them to get their supplies of imported brands of these and other items in Hong Kong, where you can buy everything, even Parmesan cheese.) To generalize, I would say that in no Chinese shop in 1976 was it possible to find one imported manufactured product, except for secondhand shops, where things that foreigners have sold through preestablished government channels eventually end up.

I often stopped at the grocery store for a yogurt (you ask for a straw if you want to eat it on the spot). A first-rate imitation of its Bulgarian original, Chinese yogurt is very good. It offers an instant freshness in this country of boiled water and cooked foods, where from one's very first days one runs about in search of fresh fruit, fresh salad greens, milk. Leaving the store, I would walk for a long time along low-walled avenues and streets, beneath a tree-filtered light that, amid the great silence and emptiness, so enfolded me that I had a sense of mild hallucination. Now and then, at a corner, a little green-clad soldier . . .

But I could push farther on, too, among the winding streets of the old Sanlidun, where I was one foreign body among the dense physical presence of the people—their laundry hung out to dry, their children playing at being grown-ups or, seated on tiny pillows in a circle on the ground, immersed in card games; girls were often playing that strange game of jump rope using yard-long elastic bands made of rubber.

When I would get back to the embassy, waiting for me on the table were the newspapers—the sole communication, plus radio and television, with the outside world if one does not count Signor Chuang, the cook, the *ayi* who cleans, the young butler, the chauffeur, and the interpreters. In Italy, I habitually read Chinese newspapers. But to read them here where they are actually published, and on the day they come out, is very different. An almost unbearable tension is exuded from these monotonous, rather formless-looking pages. It is the same tension one senses in the city itself if one goes to the center of town in the evening or late at night (in Peking, eleven o'clock is late at night). The streets are full of people, especially young people, who pour from the large buildings with lighted windows where their meetings are held. They are in high spirits, the way one is when one is young and is setting out for home in a group. They chase each other from one side of enormous Changan Avenue to the other; long, modulated whistles speak back and forth—like a call, a flow of allusions, a song the key to which is withheld from me and which I cannot interpret. But it is a signal with such a power of communication that it demands to be understood even by those who do not understand it. Like the pages of the newspapers. Like the few words I exchange with the few people with whom I have contact. Nothing is said *to* me; everything is stated, is spread before me.

I will transcribe the papers for the ambassador, and attempt to summarize the sense of what I read. The events were happening all around us, two steps away from us; indeed, we were—are—part of them, but we were separated by a veil. We were at once outside of and involved in an anxiety, in an expectation of something that could not happen, that did not exist yet that weighed down on us and made the days unbearable, like the gray canopy of sultry heat that weighed down on our heads.

There are many foreigners in Peking, and one wanders about, following along the articulations of the big body they form: embassy people, journalists, residents working for the Chinese, students at Peking University, students at the Foreign Languages Institute. For the Chinese authorities, each group constitutes a distinct entity that goes to make up a larger differentiated conglomerate. At the same time, the groups also form one aggregate category, with a few shared characteristics and general rules.

It is quite impossible not to see ourselves first and foremost as members of this big corpus, notwithstanding our different nationalities and situations and possible conflicts of opinion. There is an evident solidarity. We are all engaged in deciphering and interpreting the ambiguous messages transmitted to us. And we all tell each other what we learn, we exchange texts and translations. In this enclave separate opinions circulate.

The corpus does not cohere out of any inner necessity; its cohesiveness is determined by Chinese society, from which, inasmuch as it is not Chinese, it is excluded. As a consequence, this community is institutionally neurotic in na-

ture, and every connection within it is transformed into a neurotic relationship
—between friends, comrades, and even close intimates. Baseless divisions are
built up between those who belong to the pro-Chinese groups (*which* Chinese?)
of the European left, and opt to be their parrotlike spokesmen, heedless of the
contradictions among conflicting positions, and those who look speculatively
and with unshakable hostility on Chinese society en bloc.

You dine with embassy staff members who are housed in the brand-new,
many-storied villas that they fill with furniture and bric-a-brac from other Asian
countries, or you go to Peking restaurants, which are numerous and agreeable,
some built in the old style with courtyards and pavilions and tiny gardens, some
set amid the silence of the city's lakes. . . . You attend a cocktail party with
"sinologists" (the least traditionalist scholars of these last years had managed
to banish this term from the language, but it has been revived by the newspapers
in the twisted sense of "professionals who delve idly into behind-the-scenes
Chinese politics"). . . . To whom do these faces, these voices belong? I used to
ask myself. In what space do they move? It was China I had come to, and I was
unable to recognize myself in the unreality of the caressing, oppressive limbo
that enfolded me. It was as if we were on some Magic Mountain on the frontiers
of the real, infected by an illness known to all but of which, out of shame, no
one spoke.

I looked up other foreigners—students, residents. People who work for the
Chinese live at Friendship Hotel, on the western edge of the city, where most
of the institutions of higher learning and also the residences reserved for visiting
heads of state and other dignitaries are located. Walking westward, you come
to Beida (Peking University), Qinghua (Peking Polytechnic), the Summer Palace, and then the Fragrant Hills. On this side of town, too, they have laid out
new streets, planted trees, and put up so many buildings that I could not get
my bearings. If it had not been for a few points of reference—the Exhibition
Center, the Zoological Gardens—I could not have recognized the route that for
one whole winter, in 1957, I followed every day on my way from Beida to the
Peking Library. The transition from city to suburbs has been diminished, too.
Walls have been leveled, the great Xizhimen Gate no longer exists. Peking was
big before; now it spreads out of sight in horizontal space. Now enormously long
asphalt avenues are bordered by wide pavements of beaten earth, and behind
them the new poor houses—enveloped in green, invisible, unattainable even in
imagination—extend the old city, that labyrinth of courtyards concealed by long
stretches of low gray walls.

Friendship Hotel is an ensemble of numerous buildings, almost an enclosed
neighborhood. The Russians used to live there. They had made it a separate city
all their own, where one ate Russian food and watched Russian films; other
foreigners were hospitably admitted if a resident vouched for them. A few

specialists from Eastern European countries lived there, too, but the students always called it the Soviet Concession. Now I found it changed; there was still a check at the porter's, as there is wherever foreigners reside, but clearly the latter now were guests, not owners. Inside it seemed to me much less luxurious than I had remembered. It was now a complex of modest residences connected by little paths, like all the dormitory areas at the universities.

The residents included several scholars who were taking advantage of one of the few ways whereby a sojourn in China is permitted. But for the most part the residents were people who had accepted the ambiguous role of "friends of China"—and it would be hard to define the nature of the part. It is not that of the political militant or the internationalist partisan. The latter was definitively set at naught following the break between the U.S.S.R. and China, and political militancy requires at least an orientation and a set of opinions, whereas the function of the "friends of China" is to reproduce passively the opinions of the factions that come successively to power in this country. The people who work for the Chinese are not, as a whole, to be despised, however; something that could be termed a generous impulse pushed them initially to come here, even if the impulse was often accompanied by an avowal of failure in their own countries. Now their humiliation and frustration are patent. But since the struggle in the society around them is being played with virtually all cards on the table, some of the younger ones are taking sides, and in a few cases wanting to make up their own minds. The people who have been living here for a long time, who know, have little to say and are far less decisive in their judgments than tourists or journalists passing through, who fool themselves into thinking that in the space of a few days they can understand and judge this complex, unknown world.

I went to call at the Friendship Hotel a few times, and got along well with one or two of the people working for the Chinese. I didn't frequent them as a group, however, partly because of the great physical distances in Peking—the city's size shuts everyone up in his own quarter as if it were a village, and on holidays people organize hours-long trips to visit relatives—but also because the people who did know weren't talking, and their depressed conformism depressed me. (In 1957 things were much the same, if not worse. I remember my fear of being considered a counterrevolutionary because on a single occasion I had met with a Reuters correspondent on a purely friendly basis. People then were afraid of talking with strangers much more than after the Cultural Revolution. During that upheaval, foreign students were permitted to live in the same dormitories as the Chinese, whereas my friends and I were barred from them in 1957–58. Extreme repression had been clamped down on university and intellectual circles.)

The students, on the other hand, were loquacious in spite of being subdivided into opposing factions; newsmen considered them a primary source of news (the Italian students less so because they were more politicized, ergo more distrustful of the "bourgeois press"). I knew some of the students and we talked together like friends.

Taken individually, they expressed frustration and a sort of claustrophobia —those who had studied in Tianjin and Shenyang more so than those who'd been only in Peking. They bewailed the low level of instruction and complained of feeling like, indeed, of being, outsiders on the campuses. (Exceptions were those few who were cloaked in a lofty sectarianism, having managed to establish contact with the inscrutable Left.) From all they had to say, one deduced the distance that prevailed between propaganda and daily reality. Almost everything new in education that had begun with the Cultural Revolution had lost all meaning and had been transformed into bureaucratic administration; the workers' propaganda squads that in 1968 began to direct the schools had been largely forced out, and the worker teachers who remained had been co-opted among the other cadres to function in a still more parasitical way, if that were possible; the "May Seventh" schools had been made organizational appendages of various units *(danwei)*. (In the early years of the Cultural Revolution, these May Seventh schools—where cadres* went to learn how to support themselves through farm and manual labor—were burgeoning centers of great ethical tension, where the individual's commitment was often authentic, and not yet jelled into a hypocritical routine.) To save appearances, the cadres attended them in turn for a period of manual labor; many children of cadres managed to circumvent the rule that says one may enter the university only when proposed by one's unit and after years of work in the fields or factories.

As in Russia, here socialism is becoming identified with greater material well-being, and since in China there is not much material well-being, this is leading to mendacious propaganda about the horrible conditions of workers in capitalist countries. (Chinese students asked whether it was true that in Italy it was common for workers to be beaten by the boss.) The danger of a "return to capitalism" was interpreted consistently as an actual return to the semi-colonized China of pre-Liberation times. The instruction offered is obtuse, and the more so when it deals with political matters; for example, whereas the study of past history is fairly interesting, contemporary history is reduced to a series of trivial formulas that sometimes are contradictory, although nobody troubles to point this out. The overall picture is one of maximum bureaucratization. People are afraid to think, afraid of being criticized, afraid of worsening their material situation; mutual suspicion paralyzes everyone and increasingly mutes protest.

*The word "cadre" is my translation for the Chinese word *ganbu,* which has no real Western equivalent. The *ganbu* are both functionaries (members of the huge administrative apparatus) and party members, and they exist at all levels. It is the modern equivalent for the *guan,* the "official" of ancient China.

Foreign students share rooms with Chinese. Despite the latter's role as controls, often a friendship of sorts grows up between two young people; in that case, the Chinese lead their conversation away from politics and toward the private and personal realm—the only one within which one carves out a small margin of freedom.

The radical Italian students' discontent was the self-destructive attitude of the person who confronts an illusion—in their case, the China myth instead of a knowledge of China, the myth now threatening to become a mirrorlike error that compounds error.

To keep foreigners as much in the dark as possible about domestic events, the only admissible version of which is the one provided by official and public statements, is a constant aim in China, and it has remote historical origins. * The situation that has developed in the country in recent years has intensified this policy and has, as well, introduced some variations. On the verbal level, the seal has become even more hermetic. At the same time, there is an evident wish—and I would say pressure—on the part of the foreigner to grasp the controversial meaning of seemingly empty, homogeneous statements. He is invited to understand in the one way possible—not through a translation, which no one could supply since officially no dispute exists, but by learning to assign to words, and to the differences among them, the variations in meaning that those who are writing and speaking assign to them, as does the public to which the words are addressed. The more the first and official message proclaims an unseamed unity, the more the second and authentic message is summed up in the invitation to construe unity as division.

For about ten years, China has been torn by a very deep social conflict, which seems to manifest itself in a political form yet is unable to find political expression, much less find a political solution; this is true now, and will remain so presumably for a long time to come. The attempt to give the struggle political form resulted from the intervention of Mao Zedong at the start of the Cultural Revolution, in 1966. Unfortunately, this highest-placed authority was ahead of his times. Mao hoped that the Cultural Revolution would lead to a way of bringing the conflicts in Chinese society out into the open, thus preventing the bureaucrats' power from consolidating to the point where an attack against the state would become inevitable. But the new mandarins were already sufficiently solid to reject limitations to their power and the program for a gradual dissolution of any elite power. They are heirs to a two-thousand-year-old experience in governing; they also know well how to bolster their own strength by utilizing all the conflicts among the different

---

*Appearances to the contrary, this characteristic has not changed as of 1981. Freedom of communication in the private sphere, in opinions and tastes in literature and art is greater, but in politics the only voice that foreigners will hear is the official one.

components of society and within the working classes, aggravating the divisions among the people and introducing fresh ones, their ultimate purpose being to prevent the formation of a common front against themselves. The governing class possesses a solid organization, and has clear ideas about its own organizational and leadership tasks with regard to the peasants and workers. Further, it knows that the workers' fundamental interest—which is to free themselves from the conditions of a labor force that works for hire to which they are condemned by a market economy that goes on reinforcing itself in their "Socialist" country, against the rights and promises of the revolution—conflicts with their own development and production-oriented goals. The workers, for their part, do not possess a comparable political maturity; political awareness is still embryonic, and to the extent that it exists is found in a few workers and youth sectors—this in a country of peasants primarily, who in only a few places have cultural bonds with the big cities. Inevitably, then, the workers' opposition must be voiced to a great extent by elements from within the governing apparatus. The ripening clash of irreconcilable interests encounters a unilateral political maturity that is a monopoly of the cadre class.

The Cultural Revolution bared the conflicts and unleashed the forces of opposition, consisting of all those who, in different conditions and themselves in conflict, could no longer tolerate the impact of the authoritarian, bureaucratic system: students, some of the older teachers and intellectuals, factory workers subjected to rigid controls without a voice of their own, and even tertiary workers assigned to subordinate tasks. Although these forces were in no position to constitute a political alternative, they represented defiance of those who held power and challenged their actions in key sectors of production and culture, and wherever people had a more mature conscience—in the cities, in the schools and factories, for example. They may have been able to head off the building of economic and political structures on the Russian model, but the power of the bureaucracy they could not dismantle. For some ten years, and especially in the 1971–76 period, the result was a progressive paralysis, fostered by factors that only seemed to be unifying. The man who carried the greatest moral authority and who supported the Revolution was isolated and politically defeated, and too old and ill to return to the stage himself; the shared doctrine that imposes on one and all the programs for building socialism and for the class struggle became moot; members of the same mandarinate undertook to champion opposing interests, which inevitably transformed class conflicts into factional and personal struggles.

The Presidium and the Central Committee that emerged from the Party's X Congress (August, 1973) were the fruit of a compromise between the old leaders and the new forces that had emerged during the Cultural Revolution. (The latter had been reshuffled after meeting various defeats, and the already burned extreme intransigent wings had been eliminated.) In the following years, the factional struggle continued unremittingly, as now this, now that group launched an attack to better its position, with varying results. However, the apparatus as a whole did not seem to change, thanks partly to Zhou Enlai, who, in the interests of stabilization, favored consolidating the power of the bureaucracy and the old leaders, including those who had been the targets of frontal attacks during the Cultural Revolution. Today, some members of the Left share power with the old leaders in the top echelons of the Party and government, but power relations in the country at large—in the central and provincial administrative apparatus, the management corps of industrial and agricultural enterprises, the cultural and educational organizations, and the army—do not correspond to this situation at the top. Insofar as the ruling groups are concerned, the Left seems stronger in the unions and in some sectors of the entertainment world. What is commonly said today about the Left's controlling the information sector is not accurate. There is no question that the Left is represented in the direction of this sector, but it has no hegemony. In the entertainment field, its power is neither absolute nor unchallenged. The various film production organizations, for example, are dominated by one faction or the other. This accounts for the inconsistency of orientation and theme in the films now shown in movie houses and on television; on the one hand, some films vaunt the old glories and the old military figures, and they stupidly exploit traditional moral values; other films extol the struggle of the workers and of youth against Party bureaucracy, exalt the peasants and the barefoot doctors as opposed to the academic hierarchies.

The stasis has lasted too long; it is not tranquillity, not even stagnation, but a tension that is ever more strained. The people have been tried by very harsh living conditions, repeatedly they have been incited to rebel and forced to submit, and they will not hold out much longer; they will have to vent their protest no matter against whom. The precarious equilibrium among the competing factions is on the verge of collapse; whoever prevails at the top will have a good chance to direct the discontent of the masses against his adversaries.

Since the events of April, 1976, in Tienanmen Square, the Left has seemed to be on the ascendant, but its advance could be illusory. The leftists have been spurred to counterattack only because they were attacked first. The demonstrations held on the occasion of the Festival of the Dead in Tienanmen Square in early April and especially on April 5 were organized allegedly to honor the memory of Zhou Enlai; actually, they were designed to set up advance mass support for an eventual rightist coup against the compromise whereby power was to be shared among the various factions. There were a few incidents, none of them serious. Most of those in the crowds that flowed into the square chiefly out of curiosity remained indifferent when the Workers' Militia, supported by Peking's mayor, Wu De, intervened to restore order. Through which channels the demonstrations were organized never did become clear, but the Academy of Sciences, the majority of whose members favored Deng Xiaoping, certainly played a significant part.

That which took place publicly, witnessed by foreigners, was a confluence onto the square of many people—summoned, it must be, by someone, though not officially (when asked, those in the crowd would not answer). They came bearing flower wreaths accompanied by fliers carrying verses in memoriam to Zhou Enlai; these were placed beneath the monument to the people's heroes. Attaching themselves to this group were then many others who gathered to watch. These last might have belonged to any sector of the population, but those who carried the wreaths definitely belonged to the "cultivated" class.* Profiting from this homage to Zhou, which could not be challenged, the authors' verses slipped into their open attacks upon the leaders of the Left and barely veiled attacks upon Mao. The city leaders had these wreaths and handbills removed during the night, and the next day the Workers' Militia kept people away, though many continued trying to reunite on the square. †

Following the incidents, Deng was relieved of all his functions while Hua Guofeng was named Prime Minister and First Vice-Chairman of the Party. After this episode, the Left's campaign to continue the Cultural Revolution took on fresh vigor.

But the Left is blocked, in contacts with the outside as well as within the power structure. Those who support a resumption of the Cultural Revolution are in the minority among those in the central administration responsible for contacts with journalists and diplomats, as well as with important travelers or guests; it is rare that they disclose their ideological stance, and they do so only by extremely veiled, ambiguous allusions. Opponents of the policy "of the last twelve years" are more numerous and fairly sure of their own power; they vary in political orientation but are united in their dislike of this policy. In a private, confidential way, they allow a lot of information to be leaked about this or that prominent figure and about leaders' private lives. They drop clues about how a given article or literary work or film, or even a phrase or term, is to be construed. In a word, they supply some elements for understanding the ongoing struggle in its aspect as a struggle for power among factions and among individuals. Taken as a whole, the material they furnish is like a shapeless mass of gossip; as information it is analogous to the "news" about public figures and political events that in the West is published by the cheapest tabloids.

---

*To be certain of this, it is enough to read the poems, which were published in a volume in 1978.
†At the 3rd Plenum of the XI Central Committee meeting in December, 1978, the judgment of the event was officially reversed, and responsibility was laid at the feet of men of the Left. It was also stated, then, that there were deaths (although, according to foreigners present, the militia was not armed and there were no serious incidents, also thanks to the peaceful intervention of Mayor Wu De).
It is very difficult to judge the behind-the-scenes maneuvering that in fact went on, because of the lack of sufficient data and the total lack of public discussion of either of the two theses. In fact, when one of the two political directions has the floor, the other is forced to silence, and vice versa. This is true for very many of the episodes in Chinese history since 1949 (and even before), which are presented at first in one light and then in another, depending on whichever faction is predominant at the time.

This method of disseminating information, even if often it is on a par with the intellectual and moral impoverishment of the individuals charged with spreading it, is part of a precise plan of the moderates. The aim is to repress the free expression and explanation of the conflicts in Chinese society *and to substitute —first in the minds of the masses, then in the minds of foreign observers—the image of abstract power struggles among groups that are identifiable only through personal descriptions of the individual group members. A basic deep-seated solidarity unites the conceivers of this plan with almost all foreign observers (the professional China watchers, the diplomats, and the newsmen); the few among them who do not accept the ideological picture and its low level are ridiculed as oddballs. It is a solidarity established by common interests both within China and beyond her borders, and is the more effective for being tacit and unconfessed.*

Thus the Left presses on ineffectually. It's as if it wanted to demolish something but found no point of attack. Leftist polemics seem incapable of, or blocked in, concretely defining their objective, and too often their criticism, which is radical in the extreme, concludes blandly with the invitation to study Marxism-Leninism or the Thought of Mao Zedong, etc. The Left should be on the offensive, and instead is kept on the defensive. Most positions of effective power are in the hands of its opponents, and to reach the mass of the people the Left must pass through channels they control. Every directive and even every opinion expressed must beware the risk of heresy, the more so if it comes from someone highly placed. One of the few weapons the leftist opposition can make use of with relative tranquillity is the sayings of Mao Zedong; their adversaries are hostile to him but they do not challenge the Thought—to do that would be to challenge the very principle of authority, the pillar of bureaucratic power. *

In the attack on the bureaucratic managerial class, which is summed up in the heading "criticism of Deng Xiaoping and the revisionist wave of the Right to

---

*I use the terms "Left" and "Right" to label the different Chinese political currents, although I know that they are incorrect. The expressions derive from the European parliamentary system, where "Left" and "Right" refer respectively to the innovators and conservatives in bourgeois and democratic-bourgeois societies. Applied to Chinese Communists, the inference can be deviant (as it was for the early Bolsheviks) since what exactly is meant by the two words is unclear. Both sides have used them—and still do—in a deliberate ploy to create confusion. Thus, the same person (Lin Biao, for example) will be variously qualified as a man of the Left, of the Right, and of the "Left" (this reference in quotation marks manifests the void hidden behind these definitions).

Despite this explanation, I will continue to adopt these vague expressions simply because they are in current use; furthermore, it is not up to the foreign observer to change them or to invent more accurate definitions. One can say approximately that the Left includes those who seek a way out of bureaucratic dictatorship through greater public participation in economic management of the nation, in cultural affairs, and in political power. The Right includes those in favor of continuing or reinforcing the bureaucratic dictatorship and those who seek to attenuate it by borrowing the forms and substance of the Western political systems. (Leftists call their opponents "revisionists," a pejorative term commonly applied to the U.S.S.R.'s leaders, who impose a typical bureaucratic dictatorship.)

*overturn the verdicts [of the Cultural Revolution]," the dominant motifs empha-
size the class struggle, the development of "new Socialist things"—management
methods and social relationships introduced by the Cultural Revolution, the
advocacy of worker participation in management and opposition to individual
responsibility and the single manager (the Constitution of Anshan), advocacy of
the workers' direction of schools, the rejection of economic development that
follows capitalistic or Soviet models, the denial of scientific neutrality, the development of worker and peasant universities and of open-door instruction (the school
is transferred to the workplace), a public-health policy benefiting the peasants and
opposing the medical "barons." The basic theme in the papers of leftist leaders
and of the Beida and Qinghua study group is the attack against "the bourgeoisie
in the Party" and the exhortation that the working class "occupy the superstructure," the reference here being primarily to the areas of culture and education.
There is now open talk of "capitalistic" production relationships that must be
overturned, and reference is made to Mao's thesis maintaining that "except for
the property system" the present situation in China is just about what it was before
Liberation, since the same mode of production continues, together with the division of labor and class power. These subjects are argued sometimes with intellectual liveliness, sometimes in a dogmatic, routine spirit. Even in the best of cases,
however, they remain theoretical analyses that produce no concrete, operative
directives. The movement to renew the cadres seems to be more effective. Young
people are joining the Party in large numbers, and efforts are being made to
reinvigorate the youth and women movements, although what response there will
be from the base—the people at large—is not known. National congresses of the
League of Communist Youth and the Association of Chinese Women are scheduled to be held shortly. The planning group for the latter published an article in*
The People's Daily (Renmin Ribao) *on August 21 which signals a break from
the Association's conformist tradition and states a few truths with unusual candor.
"In the Socialist period, the principal target of the Revolution is the bourgeois
elements in the Party. . . . They are the most ferocious destroyers of the complete
liberation of the masses of women. . . . They brandish theories about "the back-
wardness of women" and "the uselessness of women" and affirm that "the destiny
of the husband decides the destiny of the wife" and that "there must be no talk
about freeing women from domestic work," etc. . . . If women are made to share
in productive industrial and agricultural work, it is in order to have a cheap labor
force. . . . As for culture . . . these aristocratic and bourgeois persons value it only
because it serves to "amuse" them, after their tea and wine. . . . We must wage
a long struggle against the bourgeoisie both in and outside the Party. . . . The more
violent the reversion to the past is, the stronger the will of the revolutionary masses
grows. . . . The big* guan *[mandarins] exert a heavy oppressive pressure . . . on
workers, on peasants, on women, and on revolutionary youth. Working women,
young women, feel great hatred for the bureaucratic class, and their resolve to*

struggle is firm. There is nothing strange in this, for it is in harmony with the development of things. . . . After Liberation, Confucian morality continued to spread its stench, to poison women. To free themselves completely, women must smash the yoke of Confucian morality. . . . They are destroying thousand-year-old customs, they are opening up a new era. . . . They are not "chattels" but masters. . . ."

I went back to Beida. Foreigners live in the first *lou* (a building of more than two stories) as you come in from the village of Haidian; Chinese and Russian students lived there when I was a student at Beida. Resembling dormitories for the Chinese, the accommodations are much more primitive than those converted for other foreign students at that time. Little wood is used, many walls are of old plaster, the lighting is dim, the showers have cement floors, and there seem to be piles of clothing and bathrobes everywhere. In all this there is both intimacy and apartness, the presence of bodies mingled with the abstinence of the poor literary man.

I ate in the old mess for foreigners, and on my way out ran into Zhao, a small-time functionary in the university's administration office. His hair is gray now, and I would gather that he has not made a career for himself. We were moved when we recognized each other; he invited me to come back to Beida, and said he would show me around. I have not gone back.

I have traveled about alone, on foot and by bus, and have rediscovered the city I used to know. It is the same and different. People have changed. Their smiling delicate reserve has dissolved into hard expressions; they are well fed, quite well dressed, and they look as if their feet were firmly planted on the ground. Stores are well supplied, little greengrocer shops are frequent, and there are no queues. Bei Hai Park is closed to the public, and you catch only a brief glimpse of it as you cross a bridge. The Dong An Shichang Market has disappeared; with its arcades and open areas, restaurants and cafés that you used to reach via tiny hidden stairways, the market was an adventure in itself, a city within a city, the preferred place for our excursions as students. Now on its old site are the large, formless sheds of a modern market that is full of produce yet seems poor.

The air is no longer so clean, for lots of factories have gone up, and the city's onetime quiet is only a memory. Peking has been proletarianized, but in a measured way. Its rational, peaceful order survives; the immense crowds move about within its vast area in a given rhythm, at one pace in almost uniform movements, as if each person were an element in a single rational or musical pattern, with no false notes, no disparities, or any visible individual autonomy. I have retraced the streets north of the Imperial palace, walls of dust, the vegetation, the grand canal as broad as a river, and the long red wall of the Forbidden City. Almost nothing noteworthy here; even the half-collapsed little buildings one does glimpse bespeak poverty, and yet it is one of the places on this earth which possess a most perfect, unending beauty. One does not notice it immediately, and often it escapes the hurried traveler. But once you are penetrated by that beauty you will never be free of it; and it will extend to include the little perpendicular streets, the low walls, the dusty courtyards, even the stones and the lumber piled up in the *hutong,* where life spills out into the street as it does in villages, but modestly and within well-defined limits.

Xidan Avenue, joyous confusion. . . . The thoroughfare is lined with shops and markets and places that resemble big popular mess halls where you can drink an orangeade or a glass of milk.

Endless, colorful Qianmen Dajie was transformed from boulevard into river by one of the frequent summer thunderstorms the evening after my arrival, when my hosts and I drove along it on our way to the Tian Qiao Theater. People took it all in good part; with no trace of self-consciousness, they removed their shoes and rolled up their trousers—even the soldiers—and everywhere bare legs protruded from beneath light plastic rain gear. Bicycles kept on the move, having literally to ford the street. Some people took shelter beneath overhanging roofs, standing on the windowsills, pressed against the glass panes, quite aware of what a spectacle they offered. It was almost dark. Then our car stalled, and we also began to roll up our pants legs. But the Chinese driver got out, and balancing an umbrella with one hand, he fiddled around a bit and managed to start the engine up again.

The main part of the program at the Tian Qiao that evening was a modern Peking opera. In what has become a famous passage, a woman gives suck to a wounded soldier who has not a drop of water in his canteen and is half-unconscious. She then hides him in a cave and brings him food. There follow scenes in the woman's house, with her nursing infant, and a brief appearance of her warrior husband. Enemy soldiers arrive and threaten to kill the baby if the woman does not tell where the soldier is; the women dance against the enemy; the soldier arrives; still very wobbly, he tries to carry the baby off, but is overpowered. In the end, the peasant militia arrives, together with the woman's husband, and saves everyone after a scene of acrobatic struggle, which is a Peking opera's usual finale.

Mediocre music, half Chinese, half Western. But the dancing sequences are exceptional, especially the solos of the wounded soldier, who was played by a first-rate male dancer. None of the Grand Guignol that the plot might suggest, but an underplay of complex emotions and even an erotic identity in the woman's part. These are signs that the society is in a process of transformation; one dares introduce motifs and allusions from the old repertory into the austerity of the present.

The theater as theater is flawed, approximate, searching for a form, as are all the other performing arts, and literature as well. This is not so very important, I believe, and it's silly to try, out of goodwill, to find qualities the works do not possess. What for the moment we do not find in them may exist elsewhere.

Zhu De, the famous Red Army commander during the civil war, was very old, almost a government pensioner. His death had been expected, so when it occurred it created no great commotion—also, the people interested in public life are taken up with very different matters. I went to his funeral, which is to say I went to pay my respects during the hours reserved for foreigners. In the red wall of the Forbidden City, to the right as you look toward Tienanmen, a gate leads to the People's Cultural Palace, where his ashes were on view. In the square outside, girls and boys were lined up at some distance from each other, all wearing white shirts and black armbands. To enter the palace, we took our places in a seemingly endless line in which people were standing two by two; far to the other side was the line of those who were leaving. Once through the first gate, we heard the cadenced music of the "Varshavyanka." It was repeated uninterruptedly; the sound paced our steps, neither too slow nor too fast, and multiplied our collective presence. The succession of courtyard after courtyard, of gate after gate, the people and the music defined time and space forever in one circumscribed moment. Presently we reached a larger courtyard and stood before a building similar to the central hall of a temple. Its façade, like the earlier ones we had passed by, was draped from on high with great black banners tied in bows; beneath the banners, a horizontal script in black on white, to glory everlasting. . . . And rising up from ground level, wreaths upon wreaths upon wreaths of the many-hued bright paper flowers of Chinese funerals; under the blinding white light, they covered the entire wall in perfectly ordered rows.

Inside, high-ranking officials were standing side by side (they spelled each other), and shaking hands with each person in the kind of gentle, intimate way that I would say someone who has lost a friend would shake one's hand. To the rear, at the top of a few steps, on either side of the urn and two huge wreaths (Mao Zedong's on the right), stood the dead man's closest relatives, his daughter and grandsons, who were almost in tears as they also shook hands with the people passing by; the younger boys were in uniform, army or navy.

Then the return, again paced by the music, between red walls and greenery. Before entering the second courtyard we had signed an open ledger and taken a white fabric flower to pin on our chests, which we now returned on our way out.

Everything that is written, read, fashioned, or done in China is at the antipodes of the "spontaneity" many Westerners assume to be synonymous with "creativity." No other people has so absolute a need as do the Chinese to define its own form in order to recognize that it truly exists. That funeral ceremony was linked to a tremendous tradition, and it was also new—and how unlike the immense proletarian crowds you see in films of Lenin's funeral.

The opera, films, sports events; organized visits to factories, communes, and residential neighborhoods; admission permits for museums, free access to the Friendship Store and the International Club (restaurant, swimming pool, projection room)—like everyone else, the staffs of the embassies are prescribed their dose of "after-work activities," which for them are not only more numerous than those assigned the Chinese but also better, since they include some entertainment. Although the geographical areas in which foreigners are permitted to travel are limited, they do include one section of the Great Wall and the roads leading to it, as well as the nearby thirteen tombs of the Ming emperors. Long-term resident aliens pooh-pooh this excursion, and it is indeed always the same. But it is very pleasant, of a Sunday, to pause by a little-frequented tomb, where grass grows among the stones and the scent of the pines is quickened by rain. Hundreds of cicadas chorus constantly, as they do throughout the city, too. One is reminded of the romantic travelers' ruins in ancient Rome, but here there is an inhabited countryside as well. Houses and fields are only steps away; grain is strewn to dry on the floor of the upper, open part of the tomb, as if it were a threshing floor. Stretched out in one corner, a young peasant lad is peacefully reading. On the newly asphalted roads, wheat and hay from the adjacent fields are also spread out to dry; trucks and jeeps maneuver around.

Travel
July 21–29

A return visit to walled Xi'an, central city of the Han and Tang empires, set amid the yellow burning drought of the loess. The heat is unbearable. The stone statues, the Buddhist treasures are marvelous. . . . But again what commands respect and amazement is the dogged will to make a thankless earth fertile, to bring the desert to flower; almost invisible threads of green sprout the moment one has managed to carve out a small level space on the sandy high grounds that are bare of vegetation. The villages are built of rough blocks of earth—mud on mud—yet they are noble in form and are adorned like castles. The hills of Hua Qing Park, now called "thermal springs," are green; this is where the beautiful Yang Guifei used to bathe, and where Chiang Kai-shek lost his dentures in his haste to escape.* Every time people come here they retell these

*The famous "Xi'an incident" occurred on December 11, 1936. Chiang, who was sleeping in one of the buildings in the park, tried to make a hasty escape when officers of Marshals Zhang Xueliang and Yang Hucheng came to arrest him.

stories, and the smiling, intensely green countryside that lies amid encircling dust and mud is a luxuriant oasis, reflecting the past onto the present. Girls and boys bathe by the dozens in a recently built swimming pool fed by natural hot springs.

In the Middle Ages, Xi'an was the arrival point of caravans from all over Asia. During the war against the Japanese, it was a border city. Here the troops of the Kuomintang and of Yanan met—mutually suspicious allies who nominally were part of the same army. Anyone going to Yanan had to pass through Xi'an; who held power there was not clear. The erstwhile quarters of the military commands are now a museum; low buildings, partaking of both barracks and old-style dwellings, they are a complex agglomeration of pavilions and courtyards in clean, linear style, Chinese and military, in which already the Nationalist Kuomintang is indistinguishable from the austere poverty of Yanan.

Yanan, up in the mountains, is reached only by truck or by plane, and to go by air sometimes one must wait days for favorable weather, since the plane must land in a very narrow space between windswept valleys. They say that in winter the landscape looks like the desert, as much of the Chinese countryside does, but in summer one descends to a small city that sits fresh and green among the yellow-red earth of terraced hillsides, which are tunneled by grottoes.

It is a town of poor, dignified people. They have all the essentials—fresh vegetable shops, one large general store, small tailor shops where women sit behind sewing machines. You see many people pulling heavy loads, but also many animals—which is one sign of a degree of well-being. The town is, however, primarily a pilgrimage goal, "the sacred seat of the revolution," as all Chinese call it. The summer green of the vegetation is fused with the red of the flags. Commemorative writings, sayings of Mao, the fine Museum of the Revolution, where one reads the story of the revolution in photographs. . . . The Yanan Pagoda on the hill, and the Yan River below, bordered by caves and by new buildings that imitate the caves, look too much like the color reproductions of them which are sold all over China. Things are transformed into holy picture cards—just as in Assisi; actually, the man assigned to accompany us does resemble a thick-witted priest, and the girl custodians recite the same set speech from memory.

But no matter; such places make too deep an impression to be lastingly spoiled. We visit the headquarters of the Central Committee and of the General Staff and the private houses of the leaders. They stand at various points on the outskirts of town, well apart from each other. The caves are sparsely furnished in extreme simplicity and with only what is needed for decent daily living. One wall is taken up by a wide-arched window topped by wooden Greek fretwork; an opaque light filters down onto a rough table. Behind the table, a wood-slatted bed, little mattresses neatly rolled, mosquito netting. . . . A photograph of the young Mao seated and writing. Outside, wild apple trees are growing; we gather the fruits that have fallen on the grass and eat them. We hear the sound of a fanfare in the distance. Young people and groups of soldiers are walking silently between the courtyards and through the houses; sometimes they stop to listen while the guides explain. The remoteness of the place, the seclusion of the monk absorbed in meditation as he writes his work—a supreme detachment from the world. . . . This was the functioning center of a revolution that only a few decades ago shook one quarter of the earth.

These grottoes bear witness both to the Yanan rebels' alienation from the world during the Civil War and to their historic significance to the world.

The fourth and last residence is the most complex; in addition to the grottoes, there are buildings of wood and brick—offices, workrooms, and a sort of shed, its wooden trusses exposed, for meetings. It is a poor yet noble architecture, which repeats traditional lines but is modern because it is reduced to essentials. The same is true of the famous Red House *(Hong Lou)* in Nanniwan, with its interiors of brick, varnish, and lacquer, where at one time the offices of the General Staff were located, and where fabric panels inscribed with poems by Zhu De hang on the walls.

Today, building is not being done in this style, perhaps because of the intervening influence of the Soviets.

We arrived in Nanniwan in a drizzling rain, after a long trip by car through deep-green hills and low mountains, where the people live among fields and also rocks on the hillsides. It seemed a kind of happy *via crucis,* for our route was marked here and there by little signs—these, of course, bearing quotations of Mao.

In the village, we ate a meal at the cadres' school, which they themselves prepared, after which we rested on their beds. (A function of Buddhist monasteries even more than of Christian ones was to offer hospitality to travelers.) We saw the famous spring.

Here one comes to something that symbolizes a high point well documented in the Yanan museum: the years in the early forties when the Kuomintang imposed an economic blockade on the impoverished border regions then occupied by the Communists. Lacking means of subsistence and deprived of all outside help, the Communists decided to build agriculture and industry from nothing: print shops, chemical plants, presses for printing paper money, mechanics' workshops, cotton mills. . . . There are photographs of Communist cadres spinning, of soldiers in rags working the stony ground—in Nanniwan, where now there are fields, the ground had until then been judged totally infertile. Schools and universities were founded. The Communists managed not only to survive but to fight and to extend their territory. It was considered by the whole world to be a miracle. When *there is nothing* it is possible *to build everything.* The same logic led, later, to their abandoning heroic building and

Yanan and to their relinquishing the conquered territory, and in less than two years they had occupied the whole of China.

That period holds the key to all the successes in the years that followed, which are not to be construed as miracles. Those successes were not utopian nor based on a warlike heroism, which by definition is destructive and temporary; they were the result of constructive actions.

One must ask oneself, If this state of affairs has indeed vanished, then why? Last January, two poems of Mao were republished. One ends with the lines: "Nothing in the world is difficult—provided one dares climb high." But poetry alone is not enough.

The red earth and smiling countryside of Henan. Cheerful peasants by the hundreds were carrying foodstuffs to market; hundreds of carts were loaded with fresh vegetables and suckling pigs. People paused at improvised stands along the roadside to drink tea and stretched out in the shade for a midday nap. It was a hot, sunny, green land we drove through to revisit the Long Men caves, with their enormous statues and tiny bas-reliefs—grandmothers coming here used to place their little grandsons in the Buddha's lap (it brings good luck), and "educated" girls would warn them that they must not do this.

In Luoyang, however, there was great tension, and we were able to walk about a bit—escorted—only after much insisting. The walls were covered with big slogans attacking provincial leaders and some Party documents. I don't know any details, for I glimpsed them from our moving car, but there were so many that they could not escape notice.

For that matter, our stay proved to be very short. The ambassador was notified by phone that he should return immediately to Peking because there had been a serious earthquake in the Tangshan area.

Peking
July 30–August 25

For almost the whole month, we have been on an alert, for the big earthquake was followed by hundreds of small ones. In and around Tangshan the damage is frightful. Train service has been interrupted, and hundreds of casualties have been transported by plane to Shenyang. In Peking, they have relaxed the residence controls, and people are permitted to take in relatives from Tianjin—who have been left homeless. There is talk of fatalities running into the hundreds of thousands. The area around Tangshan is a major coal mining area; one can imagine what a blow the disaster must be also for the economy (coal is still heavily used, not only in the steel industry).

In Peking, many old houses have been damaged so severely that it is not practical to repair them but preferable to tear them down and rebuild. Even a few concrete structures show slight cracks. One was not aware of this at first; it seemed that there was no damage here at all, such is the order, the busy composure, that has reigned in the city from the outset. Four million people have been camping out in the streets, in plastic and old canvas tents held up by lengths of wood found who knows where, but built according to the rules, not hit or miss. First-aid stations were set up at all street crossings. Within a matter of days, provisional water pipes replaced the emergency tank trucks; temporary electric cables were strung up, and gas was supplied in cylinders. In a word, everyone got himself organized as if living in the middle of the street was the most natural thing in the world. Work was not interrupted for a moment. Even offices were moved out onto the sidewalks, complete with telephones, abacuses, tea glasses, notebooks, and thermoses.

Adjustments are being made continually. People have moved on from the shelters of the first few days to rather sophisticated arrangements.* The Chinese exhibit a prodigious capacity for adjusting to the provisional—in actuality, they do not discriminate between the provisional and the permanent. Among the camping-out tactics: Very small children have set up little tables and benches, so they can sit down to do their lessons. Nursery school teachers hold their classes and play periods in the street, as if they and their small charges were in a classroom or garden (but then this is an old practice, even without any earthquake). Everyone goes about his business, however intimate or improbable it may be, not bothering about other people yet with a kind of humorous, unexpressed awareness of their presence. One man lies on a long bamboo armchair, smoking and reading, with his feet propped on a second chair, as tranquil as if he were alone in a meadow.

Not one instance have I seen of the contemplative passivity of the Indian or Neapolitan. People work slowly and inexorably, and not for one moment do they stop adjusting, modifying, building, in search of.a final form, of perfection in the provisional. Precariousness is redeemed by the performance of great theater.

The naturalness is not natural; often it costs unbelievable sacrifices. Among the less serious is the trekking from one end of this immense city to the other; to go from their place of work to home people travel for hours on public transportation or by bicycle.

In normal times, many people stay in the dormitories of the factories or offices where they work, and return home only on their free day.

For the duration of the alert, the government has prohibited occupancy of living quarters above the second floor. Accordingly, embassy staff members and

---

*A year later, the alert having long since been lifted, I still found along the sidewalks of the big avenues long rows of real brick structures, little chalets of the poor (but with some aesthetic pretensions), which people who lived in adjacent houses had built with their own hands as permanent refuges, perhaps from the crowding if not from the earthquakes.

their families have set themselves up in the garden, in army tents hastily supplied by the Chinese. A few are bivouacked in the large salon and in the hallways. People who felt the initial strong tremors are terrified; indeed, a diffused hysteria reigns, and few of us are up to maintaining much order. The pointless activities that serve foreigners as surrogates for a normal life have been interrupted; what with tents spread the length of every street, the intimate life of the city is still impenetrable, and our claustrophobia mounts dangerously. The ambassador provides meals for everybody in one of the three large kitchens, which has been converted into a mess hall. People watch television and still read the papers. Something has become blocked, and not only here among us. The earthquake is being used to jam political discussion; everything is a call to dedication and to sacrifice—who can possibly object to that? You hear even wild exhortations, like one demanding that human life be evaluated hierarchically. Cadres would be the first to be saved, with the right of precedence over one's family and friends.

From the living quarters in the residence to the offices to the garden to the mess hall, we keep perpetually running into each other. We speculate endlessly, even into the small hours of the night, about what is going on; this is especially so ever since most dependents were sent back home and relatively few of us are left; an exaggerated calm has taken the place of the earlier agitation. The uneasiness that weighs on us from the outside is reflected among us in an artificial arguments, in which each person takes one or the other side in turn.

The sultriness is oppressive, too, but thunderstorms bring momentary relief. The garden is thick with cicadas, and they sing constantly. In the evening, old films are shown in the small salon attached to the commercial offices, but sometimes out in the open, in the garden, which leads to speculation about what "they will think"—"they" being the soldiers on guard duty, who can take advantage of their assignment to steal a glance at the screen. Sometimes the Swiss come over, or we go to them. We have interminable, absurd, but peaceful discussions with semi-Fascist officials.

In the last few days, it seems that the Left may be trying to break the suffocating blockage that grips the country by reviving the political discussion, apart from the monotonous subject of the earthquake.

During the day, I circulate as little as possible, out of some kind of shame to be breaking into the privacy of people who must live exposed in the streets. When it grows dark, A.B.R. and I take bicycles and ride through the sleeping city. A few soldiers are on patrol, boys sit in a circle on the ground playing cards, voices and coughs are heard from the tents, there are a few lights; a man seated on a little bench beneath a street lamp almost squarely in the middle of the street is reading a book. Now and then the sky becomes very clear and fills with stars.

The alert has ended almost imperceptibly, even if not entirely. The summer sultriness is relaxing, and the pure light of autumn is at hand. One sunny afternoon, I went through the streets of midtown again. Most of the shanties had been taken down; in a flash, everything is clear and orderly once more. Heaps of red bricks were everywhere, and soldiers and young people were busy demolishing or already rebuilding. I noted the poverty and the dignity of Peking, people's quiet pride, their irony when confronting their own misery. Tacked to the walls were little slips of paper with inscriptions: "Man conquers nature." . . . "Unite to struggle against the earthquake," etc. These slogans emanate from the Right; but on the walls their significance is close to that of the little shrines on the street corners at home in Italy.

The authorities are also checking cracks in multistoried buildings before declaring them usable. The big shop on Wangfujing is displaying its merchandise on temporary counters out in the street. Other shops are doing the same; each displays a red banner with its name. People are cheerful; the shops are filled with fruit, and everyone is buying watermelons.

The Ministry of Education informed me some time ago that I may go to Shanghai when I wish. The ambassador and his wife are in Xinjiang on a diplomatic visit. I take my meals alone in empty rooms. Tomorrow I will leave. It seems to me that now, having said good-bye to the Italians, I am really about to enter China.

3.

SHANGHAI

Arrival
August 26, 1976

I took the plane from Peking at six-thirty in the evening. I should have left in the morning, but the interpreters at the embassy neglected to have me obtain the travel permit every foreigner must have who leaves the place for which he has a residence permit. I was accompanied to the airport by M—— and an official from the Ministry of Education. Some poetry by Mao, which M—— read aloud, was quoted in a huge red poster on the departure-lounge wall. It amazed the official that he was able to translate it. M—— knows Japanese. We talked about ideograms. Presently, the official said to me, ironically, "In Shanghai, you'll be able to share in all the experiments in the revolution in education."

The flight lasted about an hour and twenty minutes. It took us fifteen minutes just to fly over Shanghai, from outskirts to airport, a seemingly endless dark surface that was sprinkled with lights, like a starry sky. When I stepped from the plane, a wave of humid heat rose from the ground and enfolded me — the "autumn tiger." A number of people were waiting for me; they had been there in the morning because even the phone call about my delayed arrival had not been made in time. The mistake was not of my doing, and it had ruined my day, too, but they, while seeming to be tolerant, managed to make me feel at fault. I will learn to play this game. The point of it is to maneuver always to be in an irreproachable position; without ever seeming to try, and indeed with every show of modesty and disinterest, you chalk up an advantage of half a point or a tenth of a point over the person you are dealing with.

The people who came to meet me are on the staff of the Waiyu Xueyuan, the Institute of Foreign Languages, where I shall be working. They introduced themselves, but there were quite a few of them, and for the moment I had only

48

a confused idea of who was who. I could identify one older man, who was the most important cadre present, and a few associates—Zhang Shihua, an instructor of Italian, whom I know from the time he studied at the Oriental Institute in Naples, and Chen Shilan.

Chen is short, quite thin, and she moves rather awkwardly; beneath her pleated skirt her skinny legs seem to be propelled this way and that because she is slightly pigeon-toed. She wears glasses, looks intelligent and thoughtful, and is a bit of a show-off about how well educated she is; she speaks a passable Italian. She is an instructor at the Institute, and now has the accessory function of being my interpreter, so she instantly took me in charge. I could get along without an interpreter, actually, but, as I know, everybody must have one, even people who are perfect masters of the language. For every person who works for Chinese there is a Chinese, called an interpreter, who is responsible for the guest's safety, his physical and psychic well-being, his words and his thoughts, his morality, his felicity—in a word, his life. Because Chinese society did not anticipate the existence of any such foreign body in its midst, the outsider is offered the chance to live through an intermediary and to let himself be led about by the hand. During the foreigner's sojourn here, for the purposes of his connections with the world, ergo of his own existence, the personality of the interpreter who falls to his lot is decisive. Reality begins where the Chinese language begins. The foreigner is *barbaros;* that is, by definition he is a nonspeaker, he can approach reality only through a mediator. Everything in Chinese that he understands directly is considered unreal or at least uncertain. His institutional status is that of the person who does not understand. The foreigner who does comprehend Chinese is an anomaly, and insofar as possible is to be adroitly guided. It is permissible at any moment to quibble about what the foreigner claims he has understood, and even repeatedly to turn his account of it topsy-turvy with the impunity of the person who is master of the game. This is true of more than language; it can be carried to a point where one doubts the evidence of one's own senses.

There is one escape hatch in this setup: relationships among non-Chinese. Normally the interpreter abstains from interfering in this area; such intervention is not one of his duties. These relationships develop within the barbarian world, in the sphere of nonspeech over which the interpreter has no control, because usually he understands only one variant of the universal barbarian tongue. Therefore, the connections foreigners have among themselves are among the things that are permitted, but they are considered not to exist.

We climbed aboard the Institute bus, which was waiting outside the airport. The Chinese chattered and laughed among themselves; it was a bit rude of them, for they were speaking the Shanghai dialect; it was as if they were on vacation or an excursion. When we reached the Shanghai Dasha, everyone got out of the bus, and we went, in a body, up to the fourteenth floor, to the room where I shall have to live. The fourteenth floor is occupied entirely by foreign instructors. For families there are double bedrooms and apartments; since I am alone, I will have a bedroom with bath.

Chen gave me an advance on my salary, which is payable on the fifth of every month, and a little ration card that allows me to buy food in a specified store (I don't understand the reason for this, since one can buy food anywhere; maybe the card is for rationed items) and coupons for cotton. Tomorrow she will go with me on a turn around the city and to do some shopping. Classes begin officially on September 1, but Chen said one can go to school a day or so in advance. It was by then nine o'clock and rather late. She told me to speak to the *fuwuyuan* (service employees) on the floor if I needed something, and with that, the group took a joyous leave.

I am trying now to take possession of my lodgings. Shanghai Dasha is a hotel seventeen stories high, built by the British on the bank of the Suzhou River, where it flows into the broad Huangpu River. It is a mastodon among the low buildings that surround it; walls, plumbing, closets are all solid and functional, without the colonial geegaws you find in many hotels here. The furniture is nineteenth-century eclectic, generally in less good taste and quality than the building itself. My room is quite large, with very commodious wall closets and pegs. The wall opposite the entrance is almost entirely taken up by a big window of small, square, leaded panes. The view is panoramic: below, the two rivers, separated by the bridge; to the right, the city; then the Bund, with its many trees, ships at anchor, and tall buildings—the monument the colonizers built to themselves—then Huangpu Park; and finally, the big Huangpu River. Here is none of the nighttime silence and desolation that is so frequent in China. The city is full of light, and beneath my window there is a lively river traffic— large boats, and tugs hauling immensely long lines of barges; an illuminated clock tower sounds the hours (and twice daily, a carillon plays the first few notes of the *"Dongfang Hong"*—a popular song the people have substituted for the national anthem). The din on the street below is hideous. Buses, jeeps, trucks honk incessantly, gratuitously sometimes, and other times to clear a way through the dense throng of heedless cyclists and pedestrians; louder still are the boat sirens and, directly below my window, a loudspeaker, used by the people directing the river traffic in their incomprehensible Shanghai dialect.

The tap water, I discovered, has a disgusting smell. If ten million people put up with it, I told myself, I shall have to get used to it. I decided to change the arrangement of the furniture, for the two beds side by side, with the head-boards to the wall, did not work—too much bedroom. And too much chinoiserie to have the two armchairs with their backs to the window and the small table lengthwise between. Also, I decided to replace the pink terry-cloth coverlets on the beds.

I wondered who lived in the other rooms around me, and realized I was hungry. On the plane, no food had been served, and by now it was too late for supper. I would have to wait for breakfast in the morning.

I emptied my suitcase, took a shower, holding my nose, and went to bed. I was tired and fell asleep at once. But the noises outside kept waking me. I couldn't even reduce them by closing the window because then it was too hot.

In the morning, I got up feeling groggy. On the main floor, the restaurant was deserted; a plump, unwelcoming fellow told me to sit in a small inner dining room. They brought me a Chinese-style breakfast. I didn't know yet whether I had the right to order something else. I like the Chinese cuisine, but not for breakfast; I can't manage that cold food.

Chen arrived in a taxi paid for by the Institute. Two students came with her, who have had a first year of Italian with Zhang. They said a few words with difficulty, but then, they were intimidated. In the taxi, we went along Nanjing Road, Yanan and Huai Hai Roads, stopping now and then to go into a store. The crowds were immense—*thick*. You say "crowds" but the word conveys no idea of the fact. After a while, you are overwhelmed, your head swims, and you want nothing so much as to find some place to hide. Our first stop was the No. 1 big department store, a tall building with towers, like all the others which were built in the colonial era and dominate the center of Shanghai. The city has numerous large stores, but this is a major one. Someone coming here from Peking, which has decently supplied shops, feels as if he has arrived in the land of consumerism. People stand rows deep in front of all the counters on all floors. Not only the abundance but the great variety of the merchandise is striking. And it is attractively displayed, as if to say, "Do look at all these nice things," but any explicit device inviting one to buy is ruled out. The floors are tiled, a great luxury, and tiny children somehow manage to find room to run a few steps and then slide. The counters and display windows are made of dark materials, as in village stores thirty years ago—they reminded me of photographs of an older England in a children's encyclopedia I once had. Things have that same look of being born of the machine, crude in appearance but precise and functional. Chinese workers, like artisans, are all proud of their trade. Things must be well made.

People in Peking have an impassive serenity (or self-control), and even in dress present a uniform, unchanging appearance. Here there is restlessness; the young girls are pretty and less inhibited; they try to give a touch of elegance to their pleated skirts, and look for variety in materials and choices of colors. (However, just now some *dazibao,* or wall posters, are appearing against the wearing of skirts and against "beauty." "What is all this 'beauty' about?") The streets throughout China become a sea of white shirts in the summertime; here in Shanghai you see young men in short brownish jackets of some man-made fabric, trousers longer than the usual style, cut less full over the backside and leaving the ankles exposed. People here have the wherewithal to be dissatisfied, they are tensed for change, and oblige you almost violently to be aware of it.

Chen is intelligent and has experience in dealing with Italians; for two years, she acted as interpreter for the Italian couple who taught at the Institute before me. One of her duties is to meet my wishes insofar as possible, accepting them as matters of fact that are not to be judged, especially when the requests seem to be connected with the uses and customs of my country. The more happy and satisfied the foreigner is, the fewer headaches to be taken care of, the better. Most Italians who come here present their Chinese hosts with several shared ethnic and political characteristics. They like elegance; they enjoy eating well; they are ultrafraternal, ultrademocratic, and sometimes ultraleftist; they want to move about by themselves; they prefer buses to taxis—and this, according to the norms of good behavior, is becoming in the foreigner; they wish to be treated as companions; they love to be independent (hence are often saying or thinking, "Don't keep bothering me"); they appreciate beauty; they are anti-Fascist; they have nothing good to say about priests or the Italian Communist party.

So today Chen took me to shops that in her opinion are more sophisticated, the ones "Sandra liked" (Sandra was my predecessor), where gourmet specialties are sold, and to dress shops that she judges have a certain elegance. (Chen is somewhere between thirty and forty—still of an age to have a notion of elegance. She does what she can to translate it into fact, while recognizing the limits imposed on her by poverty and today's ritual sobriety. She knows that our ultrademocratic attitudes about clothes—our bundling up in semi-Chinese attire—is a mask that, even if we put it on with good intentions, not wishing to "give ourselves a foreigner's airs," we will remove the moment we have left the country.) My habitual request for a map of any city I am in was answered with alacrity: "I'll try to find you one." She ran from one bookstore to another, knowing quite well that the maps for tourists are worthless.

Chen and the students who were accompanying us are proud of this big industrial city of theirs. The smile I suppressed when I heard that they think of Milan as being a sort of Shanghai was pretty idiotic; after all, Shanghai *is* a big industrial city, even if in appearance it is a big market of impoverished customers. Yet the moment you say, "I'm glad to be in Shanghai," or "I'd rather be in Shanghai than in Peking," or, heaven forbid, "Shanghai is the most advanced city in China," they instantly stiffen, refrain from making any reply, and change the subject. At first I attributed this attitude—and I was mistaken —to a programmed, generic abstention from passing any judgment whatever. Only later did I learn that Shanghai is itself a political symbol, and therefore to express any opinion on it is tantamount to professing a political stance, which could be risky.

When we got back to the hotel, I was so done in by the heat that I hadn't the strength to go down to the restaurant. I drank some tea, ate some apples, and threw myself on the bed until two, when Chen came back to pick me up and take me to a basketball game. The rule is, Never an idle moment: work, amusement, food, sleep. There must be no empty hours, no uncontrollable lacunae.

On the bus, I met several Chinese and, for the first time, several foreign instructors at the Institute. A Peruvian under thirty, likable; his wife, full-bodied, with a dusky half-Spanish half-Indian complexion, large limpid dark eyes, and magnificent hair; their most beautiful little daughter, three years old. A young, rather melancholy Englishman. A blond, clear-skinned German girl, smooth-haired, sweet, pedantic. All are in their first year of teaching, but some have been here since before vacation started in June or July. (So it was possible to come earlier. Why did the people in Rome keep raising objections in my case?) The stadium was far from the Dasha, in the southwestern part of the city; we passed along Huai Hai and the nearby streets in what used to be the French Concession. Here the streets are quieter and the buildings more attractive, residential for the most part—large and small villas behind long walls—and there is a feeling of freshness beneath the endless galleries of trees. Then we came to an area of new construction, the usual shapeless houses, but the more recent ones are better—multistoried towers such as one finds on the outskirts of some Italian cities. Chen said she would not like to live so high up, and then there's an extra charge for the elevator. In building, they use small prefabricated panels, made of some cheap scrap materials, with decent results.

The stadium is a vast, roofed, circular building, more or less on the same model as the one in Peking. It can hold twenty thousand people. There is air conditioning; the lighting and the equipment are modern.

In the periods between games, Chen asked me the Italian words for mechanical equipment in the stadium, much of which I was unfamiliar with; she jotted down what I could tell her in one of her little notebooks. She never stops working, and she knows that I am a tool to be put to use wherever and however possible. I don't find being used in this way disagreeable; my usefulness was one of my reasons for coming here, and so I don't avoid it but cooperate. Tomorrow morning, we will be going to visit the industrial exhibition, one of the glories of the city, and Chen will be able to enter more words in her notebook.

We left the stadium in an ocean of people and had some difficulty making our way toward our bus and singling it out, since hundreds of similar buses were also parked. There were also many bigger buses, and a few automobiles.

The buses, large and small, belong to individual units, or *danwei*. People can buy tickets to the theater or to sports events, which cost very little, by queuing up, but that way you lose a lot of time, and risk losing it to no purpose, for few tickets are placed on sale. Most are distributed through the *danwei,* which are the basis of organization throughout the country. The clans of old have been overturned and replaced by the *danwei.* (In the countryside, often the substitution is in part nominal.) Every individual belongs to a *danwei;* generally it is his work or study unit or, failing that, his residence unit. Whatever business it is he must attend to—even paying for his bicycle license or eating in a railway dining car—the forms are prepared for the *danwei,* not by the person. One has recourse to an individual only if he does not belong to any *danwei.* But in general, someone who did not belong to a *danwei* socially would be a marginal case, he would be living on the fringes of illegality—where, for that matter, many people in the big cities do live.

Even foreigners must be part of a *danwei,* whether Chinese (as in the case of people working for the Chinese or studying in their universities) or autonomous (as, for example, in the case of foreign embassy personnel). The *danwei* disposes of certain specified goods that it administers, as it does itself, according to preestablished models that allow a measure of autonomy. Your *danwei* controls you within its sphere of responsibility and protects you against the outside. If someone in today's typically small family—a child, say—suffers from another member's offense or tyrannical behavior, the *danwei,* in principal, can protect him. However, if an agreement is arrived at between the elders in the family and the directors of the *danwei,* there is no escape. (S—— told me later about a girl friend of hers who was in despair because her mother and the school where she was employed as a worker were in agreement that she should marry a fellow she didn't want; to that point, she was resisting, but she knew that sooner or later she'd have to give in. Marriage before the age of twenty-five is discouraged, but it is considered a disgrace if one does not marry after that. Parents and *danwei* cooperate in helping one not to become a disgrace.)

It is through the *danwei* that information, newspapers, and directives reach you. It is through the *danwei* that it is legitimate for you to voice your ideas and criticisms.

This explains the Chinese society's organizational efficiency, otherwise incomprehensible, which is attributable to the *danwei* network, and the speed with which it acts, as well as the elasticity and independence of its action—of groups of people, not of individuals. So long as a cadre has the unanimous support of his unit he is secure; it is very rare—in practice, it never happens—that a punitive measure is taken against him until his standing has been undermined among those at the base who have been supporting him. This is one indication that the *danwei* are independent but not impervious. What the established channels are by which one can get through to them, and to what extent conditioning from above or outside affects them, I don't at this point know.

When membership in one *danwei* is superimposed upon membership in another, or if their spheres of jurisdiction overlap, the mechanism jams, especially if such a development has not been foreseen and pertinent rules have not already been laid down. Further complications arise when the irrational behavior of the foreigner is injected into the procedures. (Foreigners tend to ignore the *danwei.*) Suppose someone says, I'm teaching or I'm studying in such and such a place, or I'm working in such and such an embassy or press agency, but at the same time I want, on my own and for personal reasons, to do this and this research in such and such museum; or I am not a student but I'd like to attend classes at such and such a university. . . . Such things turn out to be virtually impossible. At best, an ad hoc arrangement must be made, which requires laborious negotiations, preferably with the support of a high-placed cadre. No provisions have been made whereby individuals singly and on their own initiative may combine or superimpose activities and functions. This gives rise to, among other things, a continual sense of frustration in every foreigner here.

Back at the hotel, after a short rest, I went up to the eighteenth floor. Banquets are held here, and I had been invited to one by the Institute cadres. A welcoming banquet when you arrive and a farewell banquet when you leave are ritual imperatives.

A banquet is a very different thing from a meal. A meal includes one or more bowls of rice, vegetables, and soup; for someone who eats well, also meat or fish, or *baozi* or *jiaozi* (buns and dumplings that have been filled and steamed), or *miandiao* (spaghetti); for the person who can allow himself tea, a glass at the beginning or end of the meal. A banquet is de rigueur when invitations are issued, but even if you simply go out to a restaurant and order for more than a certain number, a meal automatically becomes a banquet and must be served as a banquet, which is to say, at a round table and according to established rules for the quantity, quality, and succession of dishes. A banquet always begins with cold starters, followed by different dishes that are served one after another and gradually fill the table. The effect to be achieved is that of an endless series, an effect of superabundance and of excess. With each "course" you must believe that you have come to the end and instead discover that you have not. At big banquets, there is a cyclical return, which may even be repeated. After you have come to ever more delicate dishes, the soup, and the almond-milk pudding, and after they have brought you the boiling-hot sponges to clean your hands and face, lo, the thin-leaved steamed stuffed buns appear on the table again, and you're off to a fresh start. The incautious guest who does not confine himself from the outset to small samplings is undone at a certain point and can only wonder when the end will ever come. In reality, such a moment does not exist; the banquet simply dwindles imperceptibly when the participants' sensibilities are deadened. Then the purpose has been attained—not to nourish the guest but in some way to overcome him with an excess of giving that is also a demonstration of power.

In China, people often eat standing up and with bowls in hand, as if incidentally and while on the run, in canteens where the bowls are carelessly rinsed; often they forgo chopsticks and use a spoon, in order to eat faster (and that is a big sacrifice of a primary token of civilization). In the country, you see adults and children standing, or crouching, each holding his bowl and eating by himself, and as if apart and withdrawn. Today, no one lacks for food, but the majority eat chiefly rice. A dish of *miandiao* is a great treat. Eating is, and manifests itself as, an elementary need that excludes the slightest degree of ritualization, almost like going to the toilet.

The banquet is the opposite of this. Eating as a physiological imperative is canceled out, and only pleasure remains; the abundance, indeed the waste, are signs of one's liberation from need, proof that one belongs to the world of the master and not to that of the servant. Each dish should be only tasted. Alcoholic drinks are served at banquets—usually at official dinners, tiny glasses are filled with *maotai* (distilled from rice) and a lighter, sweet distilled rice drink. An alcoholic drink is not taken to quench thirst, as wine is in Italy and France, or beer elsewhere, but exclusively for pleasure or in celebration. At banquets, these drinks are downed accompanied by toasts, and the rite exorcises the indulgence, which, in any case, is confined to festive occasions. A concession to the West is made in the growing consumption of beer as a thirst quencher with meals, and beer is now permitted even during a period of mourning. In practice, however, it is mainly foreigners who take advantage of this concession, and the virtuous and well-educated—especially women and effeminate men—when confronted by a glass of wine or beer defend themselves by professing to be teetotalers.

Chen was a case in point this evening; she was as grave as can be and full of her official responsibilities. There were no other instructors and no students present. The older cadres were receiving me: Lao Bai, Lao Zhang, Lao Ji, and Xing from my section. *Lao* ("old") is customarily placed before the last name in addressing or referring to persons who are older or in a somewhat higher position than the speaker; it is frequently applied to the "old cadres." (*Xiao*— "little," which is to say "young"—is used in the inverse sense. Both terms are also part of friendly/affectionate speech.) Lao Bai directs the Institute's office for foreigners; he is nearly sixty, and speaks with not too clear an accent, which doesn't matter since he talks only in conventional language, in that special politico-bureaucratic singsong in which monosyllables are grouped together in rhythmic little strophes separated by pauses. (One of the games foreigners play is learning to imitate this way of speaking.) Lao Bai has one eye with a drooping lid—a suspicious, malicious eye—while the other is youthfully lively and laughing; although he is thin, there is something soft about him, something very elusive. A young man with a well-bred air, broad face, wearing glasses, accompanied him. Lao Zhang and Lao Ji are also Institute cadres, whereas Xing is assigned to my section. Unlike Chen, they all ate and drank with manly cheerfulness; we were far removed from the correct rigidities of Peking—but perhaps that was also because here the connection with me is different, more direct. We do, after all, have to work together. They made me drink and chatter on, and seemed much amused by what I said. The relaxed and affable atmosphere was too overdone to be genuine—or perhaps it was genuine, for these people seem quite well versed in the art of steering a course among opposing factions; they can permit themselves the ambiguous joke, which is inexplicable, in any case, to the foreigner. We drank quite a lot, and ideas grew a bit muddled. We got around to speaking of *The Dream of the Red Chamber,* which I have translated. I asked whether young people today still read it. "They read it" was the prompt, complacent reply.

At the end, Lao Bai delivered a brief speech for my benefit: Now you are no longer a tourist, he said. You are here to work. We all hope that we shall be able to collaborate in the best of ways, etc., etc. I responded in modest, exemplary style. We took leave of each other in high good humor.

August 27

Second day in Shanghai. I went with Chen to the industrial exhibition on West Nanjing Road, which is wider and greener than its very crowded eastern end. The exhibition is housed in one of those structures with a central pinnacled core which the Soviets have scattered all over Asia. (Someone dubbed them "Stalin's spit.") The Shanghaiese are proud of this exhibit, which testifies to some of the results of their labor. They want to prove that they are capable of doing what others do. Since I understand nothing about machinery, I can form no opinion, but experts say that their pride is justified. I helped Chen translate some incomprehensible technical terms—I managed to cope only because, luckily, explanations were given also in French and English.

I lunched in the restaurant at the Dasha with colleagues, and learned several things from them. The small dining room where they sent me yesterday morning is reserved for us residents; they give us special discounts, and one may order either a la carte or prix fixe: one yuan twenty (1.7 yuan = $1.00) if you order Chinese food (with a choice among three menus), or one yuan fifty ($0.90) if you choose Western cooking. Drinks can be ordered and are extra; beer is the favorite and it's excellent. The Chinese meal is a bit too much for one person, a bit meager for two. Breakfast, Chinese or Western, can also be had in the dining room, they told me, but you waste a lot of time. In the evening, almost everyone takes bread, butter, and milk or yogurt to his room; this is packed for you in a little box. On the fourteenth floor, we have four kitchens for our use, with two stoves in each. The kitchens are at the far ends of the two corridors, near the apartments where families live. (These apartments, two on each side of the hallway corners, have windows all around and a magnificent view.) Arrangements are worked out for sharing use of the kitchens. In addition, there's a small room that has thermoses already filled with boiling water, and a tank containing boiled cold water. My room is the first at the end of one side of the corridor, conveniently close to the water supply and kitchen.

There was no time for a rest after lunch, for the bus came to pick us up and took us to the Institute for a meeting of the foreign teaching staff.

The Institute is in the Hong Kou district, in the northeastern part of the city, where the Dasha is also located. You reach Hong Kou Park—the Lu Xun Museum and also his tomb are in this park—by Sichuan Road (or on the first stretch, by Wusong Road), and continue a bit to the north. Fudan University is in this direction, too, but lies farther ahead. The Institute stands behind the park; to get there by car from the Dasha takes ten to twenty minutes, depending on how crowded the roads are. Sichuan Road is one of the important north-south arteries; all such streets are named after provinces, while the big roads or avenues running from east to west generally are named after cities. Since the main arteries are so very long, they are divided into three parts—north/central/south, or east/central/west—a system that makes it easy to find your way about. Our bus follows North Sichuan, passing the site of the old International Concession and, farther north, the Japanese Concession. It's a wide street, but not wide enough to accommodate present-day traffic and crowds, very lively, and full of simpler shops than those on Nanjing Road. A few tall buildings and other colonial hybrids, but also many two-story houses; the first-floor outer wall is plastered white, the second is of wood, with or without a balcony. Trees line both sides of the street but especially in the first stretch of Sichuan they are not very tall. Much dust, many colors. But if you follow Wusong Road, to get to the park you must drive along a curving stretch of road that runs between low walls and is bathed in light filtering through the transparent foliage of trees; here are the houses and small villas of natural brick of the erstwhile Japanese Concession, some of which are now the residences of cadres while others have lost any architectural character because of overcrowding. Behind still other walls, there are schools and institutes. This is a deliciously restful and fresh drive; you divine the strong southern light from the shade itself, and from the exuberant colors glowing beyond the grayness and the dust.

The main and oldest part of the Foreign Languages Institute has an entrance on the peripheral artery that you enter after the park and that leads out of the city; the trains pass by here, also. The Institute is a conglomeration of buildings set among tree-lined paths and green lawns, and surrounded by a long wall. The buildings house lecture halls, reading and work rooms, administrative offices, a medical consulting room, libraries, the language laboratory, other laboratories for various kinds of reproduction (photographic, phonic, typographical), the mess hall, the large room for meetings and theatrical and film performances, and residences for students and a part of the staff. There is even an athletic field and a swimming pool.

The paths have a shambling, dusty look, like something abandoned in midconstruction; there is no dirt, no litter—surely the pathways are regularly swept—yet they look neglected. Still, everything is pretty much in order. The buildings are all two-storied, the floors on the ground floor are unpainted cement, on the second, wood. There is a vague smell of food and toilets, of old plaster and dust; windows are not washed and in some places the glass is broken —and yet people are forever going about washing and cleaning in an unceasing, ineffectual busyness. Passing through the entrance gate, you enter a shady walk lined on either side by wood and bamboo billboards on which *dazibao* are posted. Behind them, on the right, is a patch of garden, then the athletic field; on the left, the row of billboards is broken by several entrances to various classroom and administrative buildings. At the far end, the walk is closed off by a flower bed and a large billboard; it is painted red and carries a quotation from Mao. At that point, you can turn either right or left into a smaller walk where the billboards are covered not with real *dazibao* but with official notices. They are written with care, the characters are neat—they look almost printed —and are embellished with colored decorations, a detail as indispensable as it is meaningless. However, they do instantly identify the notices for what they are, and no one reads them.

Our meeting was held in a large room on the upper floor of the building that adjoins the Mao quotation. Windows on all sides, a huge table in the middle, a vacant conventlike atmosphere. Present: Lao Bai and his young colleague, two women from administration, and three or four other cadres, each of whom is responsible for something. "Responsibilities" are so numerous and so intertwined that I will never manage to understand what it is each actually does. Also present were some worker-teachers—that is, leftovers from the Propaganda Teams of workers which in July of '68, during the Cultural Revolution, went into the schools to run them. Today, at least on Chen's part, there was some hesitation and confusion in identifying them as such and in defining their functions. A thin, disagreeable type is the person responsible for "the Revolution in Education" at the Institute. We took places around the table. My colleagues—the Peruvians, the German girl, the Englishman, and two Japanese men—had their respective interpreters at their side, as did I. Purpose of the meeting: to inform us how the Institute functions, about our own work, and about the struggle in progress. Lao Bai opened (and closed) the meeting. The man responsible for the Revolution in Education did the talking.

A résumé of his remarks, taken from my notes:

"The semester is about to begin. We will speak about the work of teaching in this Institute at the present moment. The situation in China is excellent. The criticism movement against Deng Xiaoping is developing; there is in progress a furious struggle against his line. In the field of education, the situation is good, but here also there is a furious struggle. The revolution in education began after the first phase of the Cultural Revolution; it is not a new problem today. Deng wishes to upset the verdict of the Revolution. Cadres and teachers throughout the country come, in large number, from the old prerevolutionary schools, therefore bourgeois ideas are widely disseminated, especially in the universities. But today do the universities not belong to the proletariat? No, not yet, not even if the directors are proletarians and the students are of proletarian origin. The road still to be traveled is long. In the curricula there have not been fundamental changes.

"This Institute was founded after Liberation [1949], but because the revisionist line was strong prior to the Cultural Revolution, in character it was old —old in its teaching methods and materials and in ideology. The chief problem that confronts the Revolution in Education is, What position should be taken with regard to the seventeen years that preceded the Cultural Revolution? We maintain that after seventeen years the Mao line had not yet been realized in education; the bourgeoisie had exercised dictatorship over the proletariat. According to Marxism-Leninism, the university is a tool of class dictatorship; at the university, Lenin said, the sons of the proletariat receive a bourgeois education. Naturally, there had been some changes here, but no radical changes. Leadership continued to be in the hands of *zouzipai* [leaders who are capitalist-roaders]. The students who wished to become one with workers/peasants/soldiers were few. Also, in their first year here the children of workers and peasants remembered their origins; in their second year, they became estranged from their families; in their third year, they did not recognize either father or mother. In a country under the dictatorship of the proletariat, it was, in actuality, the bourgeoisie that exercised dictatorship over the proletariat. The masses were displeased with this.

"In 1966, Chairman Mao issued the May Seventh directive ordering the period of study to be shortened, a Revolution in Education, and proclaiming the need for the Cultural Revolution. The school was the stronghold of the bourgeois class, since a large contingent of educated proletarians did not exist. Even in our Institute, bourgeois thinking was preached in class. The only foreign language taught was Russian, and the teachers were White Russians. Then, a revisionist Russian [i.e., a Russian from the Soviet Union] became head of the Institute. Soviet teaching methods were adopted. The period of study lasted for five years. Graduates did not go into the factories or into the fields to work, or into the army, but instead sought fame and success.

"Teaching was entirely theoretical; some graduates were not even competent to be interpreters. The followers of Deng say that in the first seventeen years of the Popular Republic, things were going well, but now the university level is low, lower than that of a middle school. Before the Cultural Revolution, the period of study from elementary school through university was eighteen years. There were many books; one memorized everything for the examinations. Once an examination was passed, the subject matter was forgotten, but bourgeois ideas remained alive. And bourgeois arrogance. Chairman Mao teaches that students must also raise their political consciousness in order to become cultivated proletarians.

"Problems related to the two lines in the field of education: the recruiting and enrollment of students; the program of study; how to develop individual abilities. Should one or should one not follow the May Seventh directive about integrating workers and peasants? Should one have open-door or closed-door schools? The experience of the last years shows that open lessons, open doors, are the right way. . . . Even the foreign professors have now taken part occasionally in open-door lessons, they have discussed and decided together with the students about how to teach the lesson, they have given examinations in factories or out in the fields. The followers of Deng say that everything today [1976] is practical activity, while theoretical study is neglected. In actuality, they are against the Cultural Revolution and against open-door lessons. The Chaoyang Agricultural Institute has been a positive experiment. It is ridiculous for agricultural sciences to be studied in the city. One does not grow rice or wheat in concrete. According to Deng, graduates cannot be ordinary peasants because they are in a higher position than peasants. This is a wrong way of thinking, but not easily uprooted. It comes from Confucian thought. Let those who succeed best in study become high officials. We must learn from what has happened in the Soviet Union. The majority of the leaders who have come from the university are revisionists ("satellites in the sky, the Red Flag on the ground"). For us, this is a difficult task, with a thousand and more years of feudal thinking behind us. We must commit ourselves to it from generation to generation. The revolution has barely begun. The new things started by the Cultural Revolution are showing how vital they are. But it takes a long time to develop and improve them. The quality of instruction is being raised. The revolution in the school is still in an experimental phase. We hope that the foreign professors will give us the benefit of their opinions about the work in this Institute. You come from faraway countries to take part in the revolution in education. We welcome you warmly.

"The foreign professors are asked to share actively in the educational revolution, in collaboration with Chinese professors: to contribute toward improving the level of the Chinese professors' knowledge of foreign languages, if possible forming study groups with them, and if there is no time for that, then studying with them after the lessons with the students; to carry this program out in a planned way; to give lectures on various topics, for both professors and students; to make voice recordings for slides and films; to draw up lists of study materials in collaboration with the Chinese professors and with the students and, when going out to the communes, also with the peasants. The task of the foreign professors is, above all, to improve the command of foreign languages, to maintain a close collaboration and exchange of experiences with the Chinese professors. If they so wish, and health permitting, the foreign professors are invited to share in open-door lessons in the factories and countryside. For foreigners, the weekly schedule is six mornings and three afternoons (one devoted to political study). Periodic meetings will be arranged at which the students can comment upon the professors' work. . . ."

At the conclusion of these remarks, Lao Ji, representative of the Foreign Office, spoke on political education. Before the Cultural Revolution, he said, emphasis was on education only for a profession. Foreigners were excluded from political study. During the Cultural Revolution, some foreign professors criticized this system, and even wrote *dazibao*. After 1967, many foreigners who had been working in China returned to their own countries. They were invited again starting in 1973. Initially, experience was lacking, but toward mid-1973 a plan was worked out for them to have political study. That foreign professors should share in political study is a new thing in the Cultural Revolution, and was initiated early in 1974. The experiment is now two years old; it seems a good method to encourage an understanding of China and communication with the Chinese people. In political studies, like the Chinese, the foreign professors have followed the development of the various movements: the criticism of Lin Biao and Confucius, criticism of the famous novel *Shuihu,* and of Deng. Plans for the next semester include a more profound criticism of Deng based on an examination of the "three poisonous grasses," which is to say three essays [attributed to him]: "On General Principles of Work for the Entire Party and the Entire Country," "On Several Problems of Scientific and Technical Work," and "On Several Questions Relative to the Accelerated Development of Industry (Regulations)." Deng's revisionist line emerges clearly from these articles; they are three poisonous plants that are against the Party, against Chairman Mao, against the Chinese people. They will be studied as negative examples.

The method of study: reading of articles and discussion, also with students, and eventually with workers and peasants. Before National Day, on October 1, we are to finish reading the first article. Every foreigner can participate in this study if he wishes. It will be an opportunity for you to come closer to us. Even if Deng is finished and done for, his revisionist influence persists; therefore, it is essential to deepen the criticism. . . .

When it is our turn to speak, John, the Englishman, says that in order to carry out this study, it is indispensable that we have the three Deng texts. We all second this request. The reply is vague: We will do everything possible to supply you with the texts; if this is impossible, oral reports on them will be made; then you will be able to go outside the Institute to discuss them with theory groups in factories and communes.

From what I heard in Peking, the Left is exerting pressure to have the texts published, while the Right is resisting. *Neibu** is already being widely circulated. I have got some idea of the essays from reading substantial quotes and comments in the leftist periodical *Study and Criticism (Xuexi yu Pipan)*. In part, the "Deng line" seems similar to Italian Communist party policies, putting great value on technocrats, productivity, and discipline, stressing centralization and national unity, and stifling critical, libertarian ferments on the Left in regard to domestic policy. As for foreign policy, it favors opening the door to Western technology and capital, too, perhaps.

Impossible—at least for the moment—to grasp what the people who make speeches like these to us really think themselves. Maybe nothing. I am a transmitter, not a creator, Confucius said. Russian influence in the early years after Liberation must have been very profound, more so than we assume.

Streets and Spectacles
August 28

This morning I had nothing I had to do, and I went out alone. I walked along the iron bridge over the Suzhou River—to the left is the wide expanse of the Huangpu River, the innermost area of the harbor with warships at anchor, and beyond the great river in the distance, the southeastern part of the city. On the far side of Huangpu Park, I crossed the street and walked by the Friendship Store, the Seamen's Club, where foreign sailors may stay while they are in port, the Office of Foreign Trade, and the headquarters of the textile workers' and longshoremen's trade unions. I turned right into Nanjing Road, which is wide here and has not one tree, then walked on as far as the Xin Hua Bookshop.

Just before you reach the bookshop, on the left, there is a big wall, painted red, with two poems by Mao that were published early in the year for the relaunching of the Cultural Revolution. The shops on Nanjing Road are the best-stocked stores in all China, and they are of every kind, from those that sell machinery or silks or tea to little doorway stalls selling clothing and booths offering fruit and drinks. Noise accompanies you everywhere; it is as dense as the crowds. The Shanghaiese consider Nanjing Road a splendid street because it is lined with tall buildings, like cities in the West. Only refined types like Chen prefer the less central and more aristocratic streets of the French Concession, Shanxi Road, and the residential areas bordering Huai Hai Avenue.

Crowds on Nanjing Road have a surface uniformity, but if you look carefully, it is possible to differentiate. Many workers, with serious, severe faces; young boys who, to all appearances, are idle, and who range from the rather elegant to the tough; young daughters of cadres who, with their handbags, look

---

Neibu is restricted informational printed material circulated exclusively among the party's thirty million members. Hence it reaches a wide readership (and is inevitably passed on secretly to nonmembers). Other *neibu* material is reserved for the cadres of the various ranks.

rather fad-conscious; elderly women in rags, dragging carts behind them; bewildered soldier boys (the soldiers are volunteers, recruited mainly in the country-side from families of proved probity and political unimpeachability); minor cadres; young families; tiny elderly women, their hair tightly drawn back, who are beautiful and very dignified. This diverse crowd is nonetheless unitarian in its chaotic disorderliness, which is so unlike the rhythmic movement of Peking crowds, whether on foot or on bicycles, among whom you move about peacefully because everything seems preordained and lasting. Here *and* there you are not, as a stranger, looked on with favor; people regard you with diffidence and unfriendly curiosity, perhaps with suppressed envy.

On the ground floor of Xin Hua, books are not sold; a kind of circulating library has more books on display than are on sale upstairs. A foreigner does not have the right to take advantage of this or any other of the public libraries. An area is set aside, with benches, where children may read, and there are wall cases with notices and propaganda. You climb a sort of wide staircase; at the top of the first ramp, an illuminated case, where the works of Mao are displayed on red velvet; you turn right or left to climb the second ramp. The bookshop on the second floor is divided into sections: many books by and about the Legalist philosophers and related to the *Pi Lin pi Kong* campaign; collections put together by worker study groups; material on the revolution in education; works of fiction, drama; Lu Xun. . . . Many, many posters and collections of reproductions of paintings by peasants and workers. (Some good things, some less good, some dreadful. But varied in style and origin.) I didn't linger in the science or technology sections, out of pure and simple incompetence. Xin Hua seems to me less well stocked than the shop on Wangfujing Street in Peking; however, you find books here that you don't find in Peking, and vice versa.

A certain number of books and magazines are sold everywhere, but in all Chinese cities you also find materials that are published locally. This regionalized publishing activity is good particularly for university publications. If a person doesn't have friends here and there who will alert him, he can miss new works even in his own field of interest, because they are not systematically or even frequently reviewed in magazines. In actuality, the person who wants to be informed about such things does manage, but through what channels I don't know, because professional societies have not been re-formed since the Cultural Revolution. The channels for disseminating political information are obvious; *neibu* pamphlets addressed to various readership levels circulate in quantity. But I so far don't see that similar booklets exist for nonpolitical subjects. No doubt the people make up for the lack of public informational media by intense, endless exchanges of news among themselves. But is this enough? How these channels of information function escapes me.

It became too hot, and I couldn't go on any farther. I turned back, via Sichuan Road, for I wanted to pass the food shop for which I have a ration card.

I couldn't locate it at first; at the number written on my card I found a large doorway leading to a courtyard. I spoke to a man standing by the door, and he told me to walk on in; there, almost hidden before the courtyard entrance, was a little door. The shop is tiny, carelessly arranged but stocked with all kinds of supplies, even items one does not find elsewhere, from meat to fruit to canned goods. There is much more merchandise than one at first sees and, as I was to discover later, a back room filled with treasures. Is this store for foreigners only, or also for some special categories of Chinese? (I never did find out.) It is certain that ordinary people do not have access to it—not even the instructors at our Institute, for example. The fact that you see Chinese shopping there doesn't mean anything, since they may be servants in foreign households or hotel cooks. And for that matter, it isn't enough to be a foreigner in order to be able to buy there; you must show your card, and the dates of its validity are checked. Everyone is interested in each new customer, and curious. Today, the person who checks my card: "Ah, Italian. . . . Where are you working? What language do they speak in Italy?" Here even rationed items for which we have no coupons can be readily bought—olive oil, flour, sugar. The fact of having to come into this half-hidden place gives you the sensation that you also have something to hide, that you are an accomplice in a slightly shameful operation.

I continued along Sichuan Road and crossed a bridge, one of several over the Suzhou River, coinciding with the principal north-south streets. People were leaning against the railing, open-mouthed, watching the boats come and go, and the barges that are permanently moored along the banks; others had spread their little wares out on the ground; halfway across the bridge, some others were selling cabbages from a small cart. This is a hog-backed bridge; cyclists dismount for the ascent, leap onto their bikes, and take the downgrade at top speed. I continued along Sichuan Road for a bit, then turned right into Tiantong Road and, after passing one intersection, returned to the Dasha, turning right again at Wusong. Like much of Shanghai, these streets are a hodgepodge of buildings put up in the colonial period which are in poor shape but still decent, and of two-storied Chinese houses that have tiny shops, restaurants, and apartments on the ground floor, and more apartments on the second; through the open windows you see row after row of clothing hung up to dry on lines strung across the rooms. These houses are not in good condition; the walls are peeling, and the wood of the doors and second-floor exterior walls has not been painted in years. From the few that have been recently repaired, one visualizes what they all could be if they were better cared for, especially those that are not in the hybrid colonial style.

Outside the street-level apartments and tiny shops, women do their laundry in small washtubs, and take pains in cleaning the small wooden refuse barrels. Old men, their trousers rolled up above the knee because of the heat, sit on small bamboo benches in the middle of the street, beside little children who read, write, and do their sums; an occasional chicken, tied to a door, pecks at the ground. Pavements are narrow and uneven and crowded; there is always some-one busy at some kind of work with whitewash, paint, tools, but, especially, people are forever moving things; often the street is obstructed by serried piles —boxes or scrap metal or reams of paper. This is not room enough for people or things. But objects are arranged according to some criteria of appropriate-ness; the disorder is necessary and, to some degree, apparent rather than real, the way it is in a blacksmith's shop or on the desk of someone who is studying. To our way of seeing things, which is distorted by our passion that everything should sparkle and gleam, all this presents an image of something vaguely not clean, and yet there is no filth. Nor does one detect the smell of filth.

The humid heat is unbearable, and one must do things a little at a time. Toward midday, an agreeable, middle-aged Frenchwoman came to see me—Paule Garçon, who teaches at Shida, the upper normal school. She doesn't live at the Dasha, because the Chinese have built lodgings for Shida instructors on the university campus, but she has lived here, and now, at her own expense, she reserves a room for weekends so as not to remain too isolated from the city and from people—which is to say, from other foreigners. She is a veteran in the profession of teaching abroad. She has been in Shanghai for two years, is now waiting to leave for Argentina, and before coming to China had taught French in Sweden. One sees straight off that she is a master of her calling. You must struggle, she told me, to convince Chinese professors that a foreign language is not Chinese translated into that language. For years, foreigners have been battling against an obtuse resistance to the reading of texts written by native speakers; instead they are required to use the strange jargon of the various foreign-language editions of the *Peking Review* (or worse still, the foreign-language broadcasts of the Peking Radio) as if it were really the language in question. The most that has been conceded so far is that foreign teachers may make some corrections in these and other translations from Chinese. But to use an original foreign-language text is still ruled out. The Chinese professors find this arrangement very convenient, and most have no intention of exerting them-selves to change it. They want to continue with the present routine; the question of whether or not the students learn something useful is not pressed by them. Luckily, the students don't see it this way. At Shida, for some months they have been demanding to read newspapers from the country whose language they are studying. This has led to consternation among the profs, who have subscriptions to such papers—to *Le Monde,* say—but don't read them because they don't understand them. The student requests at both Shida and Fudan echo the battles of the young people in Peking, where some time ago students at Beida and Qinghua Universities won permission to read and study foreign publications. (This is one of the factors that account for the Peking universities being cur-rently in the educational vanguard.)

Paule says that the Chinese bureaucrats deliberately place a barrier between us and the people not only in order to isolate us but also to put us in a bad light, to show us as privileged bourgeois. She fought for one year against being provided with a curtained taxi for her use exclusively; when, finally, she got authorization to travel by bus, she heard her official escort say in the presence of the other passengers, "You see, at last we have reeducated her." Perhaps things are a bit more complex than Paule presents them as being. There is the notion that we *should* be given privileges because we come from countries with higher standards of living, and China must not lose face by making us endure inconveniences; and somehow or other, this has got to be made clear to the common people. The upshot is that people either conclude that we are all privileged bourgeois in our own countries, too, or they think that in our countries everybody is a privileged bourgeois. The latter is perhaps the prevailing attitude, at least in Shanghai. There's also the fact that flesh-and-blood foreigners, whether residents or transients, do more or less resemble each other to a Chinese eye, and relatively speaking we do look rich.

What with this sultry heat, the only thing to do in the early afternoon would have been to lie down for a bit. Instead, at two o'clock, a member of the Institute staff arrived to explain the political situation to me. Chen was (pretended to be?) ill; she does suffer from sinusitis, and occasionally the condition is worse than usual. So Zhang acted as interpreter. The man spoke at length, and I barely followed him, for my eyes kept closing with weariness.

He said that the current struggle in the field of education began at Qinghua University, against the revisionist wind from the Right which had arisen last summer. "The Right attacked via the schools because it knows that education is a key problem. It is arguing for the primacy of a technical and scientific education over education in politics and in class struggle because it asserts that the latter would hinder high-level scientific training. The rector of Qinghua was only a front for Deng, and Chairman Mao personally launched the struggle against him. The wind from the Right reveals the existence of a sharp class struggle," said the man. "The Cultural Revolution and Chairman Mao are under attack. The danger of a capitalist restoration in China is real and present, as we have clearly seen in recent months. The restoration of capitalism relies on the hypothesis of the extinction of the class struggle; in reality, the aim is to extinguish the struggle of the proletariat, not the dictatorship of the bourgeoisie over the proletariat. Chairman Mao has said that bourgeoisie are in the Communist party, that they are the leaders of the capitalist-road line, which is still alive. The theory of productive forces pits economic development against management by the proletariat, and against the class struggle.

"According to us, however," said the man, "the class struggle is the basis of economic development; we must set a great economic growth into motion, but take the class struggle as its pivot and thus eliminate the influence of revisionism. Deng and the other rightists deck themselves out in the prestige of Chairman Mao, they unfurl the Red Flag, they exploit the enthusiasm of the Chinese people for growth in production. Not only do they distort Chairman Mao's directives but they put lies into circulation. From last summer until the Tienanmen events they have sought in this way to disorient people, to create confusion; they have circulated false directives, false documents that allegedly came from the Central Committee, false speeches by outstanding public figures in the campaign around the name of Zhou Enlai. It is necessary to counterattack with revolutionary truth. After the Tienanmen incidents, things have become a little clearer, they now stand exposed before the eyes of the people. . . ."

Why did this speech—which, actually, in large part I am inclined to agree with—manage only to make me sleepy and bored? It's not only that the delivery was so muddied and repetitive—actually, it was a montage of newspaper clips —or that I doubted the conviction of the man making it. (Not to mention Zhang, who in translating it either watered it down to meaningless pap or simply omitted other parts, particularly those having to do with class struggle.) The real reason is that this speech, like all the others, remains in the stratosphere of abstract concepts. Even when it is plots or lies that are at issue, what those plots and lies might consist of is never made explicit and clear; when speech is not abstract, it is allusive. If you happen to be already informed about the facts, you are given an interpretation of them—or rather, you are told what position to take. Words themselves are divested of meaning. What percentage of the Chinese masses, I wonder, suffers from this separation between words and things. And to what extent do they have access to the facts so that they are better able to understand the words?

When the man went on this afternoon to talk about the struggle in the Institute, he did not become more concrete but took off into the realm of purest generalities. He spoke of attack, counterattack, study, criticism, "open-door classes" (classes held in places of work, in the cities, and in rural areas), thousands of *dazibao,* mobilizing the masses, training activists, raising consciousness . . . he talked on and on and said nothing. If he were a pro-Deng man, he could have said almost the identical things, with only a few word changes, in order to exalt the struggle in the contrary direction. The one single fact he brought out—it was in connection with a lessening of the "three great differences" (city/countryside; intellectual work/manual work; workers/peasants)—was that this year five graduates of the Institute went to Tibet, several others to Heilongjiang, and the rest to remote country areas to fulfill the manual-labor requirement. This bit of news, supplied as it was without other related information—what used to happen? where did the others go? etc.—meant nothing.

Before saying good-bye, Zhang left two articles from *The People's Daily* for me to translate into Italian "for the students"—that is, as language texts. We're off to a good start: One is an editorial against the "deviationist wind from the Right"; the other is an article about the earthquake, a topic the Right exploits as a diversion. Obviously Zhang knows how to play both sides of the fence.

In the evening, we went to a *zaji*—the so-called circus—performance. When there's nothing better to do, they take you to these spectacles. I've seen so many that I'm a little tired of them. Especially since the acts are always the same, no matter where you happen to be, in Peking or Xi'an or Shanghai. I took the line of least resistance and went. But the evening turned out to be a delightful surprise. The acts were nearly identical to those in Peking, predictably. But the audience was interesting, first of all—with its peasant China character, its youthful warmth and vivacity, as in a workers' quarter on the periphery of Milan after the "reawakening" in the 1960s, and very much "with" the exceptionally gifted performers.

Acrobatic skills are taken for granted here; the real test is the grace and lightness with which the actors recite their lines. One of the stupidest numbers, in which the actors imitated sounds, was transformed into a cabaret number and sparkled with satire. There were the usual birds, chickens, trains, motorcycles, and so forth, but two actors, using only sounds, acted out a big public gathering, which actually was *the* gathering par excellence—when Red Guards marched by the tens of thousands into Tienanmen Square in August 1966, at the beginning of the Cultural Revolution. In the theater, a "hallowed" episode was deconsecrated, celebrated instead with affection and smiles, like an event that belongs to the people and therefore can be freely transformed for the occasion into an entertainment. You could positively hear the crowd movements, the shouts, the singing, the *wansui*— "May you live ten thousand years!" The Communist party was not left out, nor was the name of Mao Zedong. People tonight laughed, applauded, and called for an encore. (And this from a public that normally does not applaud at the theater, to the consternation of foreigners, including me. "The actors know all the same that they are appreciated," Zhang explained.) A current joins together actors and public in divertissements that allude to ambiguous political episodes of a highly dubious nature. But they end with everyone taking delight in the game of mirrors, during which ideology is abandoned and only sublime artistry remains.

Right? Left? Is it true, after all, that Shanghai is the city of the Left? Or is it merely a place that is running precipitously ahead in comparison with much of the rest of China? No doubt, economically and culturally it is a privileged area. Yet, all the same, the battle against the bureaucracy to win actual rather than nominal worker management and the effort on the part of proletarians to acquire culture comes from places like this, not from the more backward zones, and not from the peasants, who are the bastion of conservatism and the alibi adduced by the promoters of construction, production, order, and morality.

August 30

Yesterday, Sunday, I went for another little walk through the city. Then I translated one of the articles for Zhang. I do ask myself what sense it makes to have students read these things in Italian. Translated, the content is too difficult for them at this point, and many of the words and terms are useless to beginners. Then—a pleasant task—I went over the translations of some of Mao's poems which have been sent on from Peking so that the Institute people can comment on them; they've been passed along to me because no one at the Institute knows enough Italian to suggest variants. I don't care for the translations; they're overemphatic and pedestrian. The originals should be looked at and other solutions suggested. I'll do one or two in the evening, when I have time.

This morning, my colleagues went to the Institute. I went to the hospital for my medical examination and to get my medical card. The hospital is way out in the west, in an agreeable, tree-lined district. It had the customary cleanliness and the extreme simplicity and efficiency of Chinese hospitals. Doctors and nurses were the kind you dream of, or so they seemed to me: attentive and unassuming. Chen (restored to health) accompanied me, and we got everything taken care of very quickly.

In the afternoon, I translated the earthquake article, and prepared a little speech that—so Chen tells me—I will have to make to the students tomorrow. I tried to use simple words and explain why they must study the real Italian language and not Chinese rendered with Italian vocables, and why it is essential for them to get to know the non-Chinese world as it really is.

School
August 31

This morning, on the bus that leaves the hotel at seven, there were the two Peruvians, Marcial and Olga (she teaches not only at the Institute, like her husband, but also at the middle school affiliated with the Institute); John, the young English teacher, together with his slender Thai wife, who also teaches English; the two Japanese, Mr. Ohara, who is pushing sixty, and Makita, who is around forty. (I don't know why among all of us only Ohara and Shinto, who teaches at Fudan, are addressed by the title "Mister.") There is a kind of distance between the Japanese and the others, which is owed to more than a language problem, although contacts are courteous enough. Yet they say Makita is a "comrade." But then, Japanese are very reserved. There was Dagmar, the young German; a little girl; and two babies. The babies—Aymin, Peruvian, daughter of Olga and Marcial, and tiny Maya, English daughter of John and Alissa—were dropped off at the nursery school near the Institute. The little girl, Felicitas, is Dagmar's daughter, and she will have to attend the school attached to the Institute; she looked displeased and sad to be alone. In the beginning, her mother has told me, she rejected everything Chinese; things are going a little better now. John and the Peruvians got off with me; the others continued on. Two sections of the Institute have their quarters here, in the main and oldest part of the building—the English section and another which is linguistically rather mixed, being primarily Spanish and Russian, to which are added the classes in Italian, Albanian, and modern Greek. The other language sections are in buildings enclosed within another wall; they are not far away, just one street and beyond the railway tracks. (Everybody crosses them as if they were tram tracks, and it seems that accidents happen occasionally.)

In the middle school attached to the Institute one studies a foreign language —English, Spanish, French—as one's major; it is a special school that prepares the student for entrance into the Institute. (Unlike Shanghai's other middle schools, this one is organized to take boarders; students eat and sleep here, and go home only on Sundays.) Privately, I wonder how this fits in with the regulation that says after middle school everybody goes to work for several years, and after that, those who are chosen by their respective units may then enter the university. I have the impression that many things that were to have disappeared during the Cultural Revolution haven't disappeared at all, that, on the other hand, things introduced by the Cultural Revolution and which one would expect the subsequent reaction to have eliminated may continue to exist even now. There is a juxtaposition of both. Reforms are made in contrary directions, but each thing is added to the preceding thing rather than made to replace it; one moves ahead by accumulation and, depending on the circumstances, chooses this or that from the heap. Thus what is modified is the arrangement of the diverse elements. Or sometimes even only the name of a thing is altered. The individual is continually adapting and, at the same time, resisting. Much of what appears to be uncertain and confused is, in reality, the intermeshing of complex, defensive structures.

I came to the end of the little entrance path, and after wandering around in the courtyards of those barrackslike buildings and asking several times for directions, I found my classroom in the first building to the right of the Mao quotation. It has the same squalid look as all the others. Each student has a set of headphones for his own use, which is connected to the receiving and recording equipment; when headphones are not in use, the sections of wood into which the jacks are plugged are slung at the back of the room. Fourteen young people were seated at desks; two absentees will come tomorrow, when lessons begin officially. This is a second-year class, nine boys and seven girls, adolescents, in appearance. They looked at me somewhat anxiously. Presently, we were to go upstairs to the large hall for official introductions, so we had only time to exchange a few words. I made the acquaintance of Tang, a graduate last year and now an apprentice professor. He has bristly hair and, behind glasses, a very intelligent, unusually candid glance. He is not at all like Zhang, who never looks you in the face and seems to come from another world. Tang is rather close to Chen, but I would say that he does not belong to her professorial mandarin category.

They called us for the meeting. We went upstairs together, and took places around the table. A few section cadres were present. The meeting opened with a series of vapid little speeches: The new instructor and the students must meet each other, make each other's acquaintance, say a few words to each other. The meeting was formalized to the point where it became a ceremony instead.

And there was I yesterday afternoon, preparing things we might talk about! I held my few notes in one hand. I would have felt frustrated, had I not had an overwhelming sense that I was not part of what was going on. However, I said a few words about what it means to learn a foreign language, although actually I could have talked about anything under the sun—wildflowers or the leaning tower of Pisa. Everything would have been fine, nothing would have mattered. I was not perceived as someone who talks, who expresses ideas. I am an object to be treated well so that I may be put to use. Everyone was kind and, to please me, smiled.

After the meeting, the students took off, and the three profs escorted me to my office; it's a large room with two desks, one for me and one for Chen, two armchairs with a small table between, a shelf with thermoses, and a closet. The furniture is old and had been mended, but on the whole the room is comfortable. One could make it less dreary with a few posters and such. Other people would do this; I cannot. These surroundings are what they are; they say something definite, and I would not be able to introduce heterogeneous variations. I can do no more than settle in as best I can, and what that really means is being in this room with a provisional identity, pigeonholing myself and my reservations in these drawers that are full of crumbs and old dust, seating myself at this desk as if it belonged to someone else.

I have asked to take my meals at the Chinese mess so as to be with the students as much as possible. At eleven, Chen and I went to lunch. (Tang has his meals in the building where he has his room, on the French section side, and Zhang is in another office on the ground floor, with other Chinese.) The mess hall is huge and barrackslike. Students and professors were standing in line before little windows; one side for rice, the other side for various dishes among which one chooses. There were soldiers in the queue, too, and pupils from the middle school, elderly women, and even a few little boys who are children of staff teachers. Everybody had his little enameled ironware bowl (the students leave theirs on shelves installed for the purpose). Chen darted about to read menus, greet this and that acquaintance, and get me chopsticks. This first day was, as I learned, typical. Steamed rice arrives on two broad superimposed containers, and is divided with a wooden paddle into box-shaped servings of two, three, or five *liang*. The various dishes are quite good and cost very little (you pay with coupons that you buy to last a month or longer). When the students have been served, they move on into an adjacent room, also huge, which is rather dark and has a damp concrete floor. (These floors are always wet because people are constantly pouring water over them; the idea is to keep them washed down, but it makes for a slimy surface.) They sit on long benches in front of tables that are rough wooden planks supported by trestles.

Today Chen said to me, "There's not enough room here for us," and so back we went to my office with our bowls. Even my project of eating together with the students, as I often used to do in Italy, is dissolving into nothing. They are doing this to isolate me and to protect me, and it is intolerable. But I'm not sure I would have had the strength to eat among people who are so crowded together, who belch and spit almost onto their neighbor's plate, and at the end of the meal leave uneaten food on the table as if they were in a pigsty. Well . . . Chen and I ate our lunch in my office, and went downstairs to rinse out our bowls in cold water in the washbasins; vague bits of food were sliding along the bottom, and nearby someone was gargling vigorously. Then, to sterilize the bowls, we poured a little boiling water from the thermoses over them. "I never saw it done this way in Italy, how is that possible?" Zhang asked. I looked at him, startled. Chen was clearly annoyed by his stupidity. Zhang had come to get something, and he and Chen went off to their rooms for the midday nap. Some people have a folding bed, others stretch out on two tables that they have cleared and brought close together. I dozed in an armchair in my office.

On our return to the Dasha and before dinner, which must be ordered no later than seven, I went out again for a little walk. Many shops were already closing; people passed by with bowls like ours, on their way to buy their food somewhere. I think I will have to buy a bicycle, otherwise I'll never get beyond the environs of the hotel.

The streets of Shanghai rarely give you a feeling of pleasure, but they are eloquent. A gigantic London East End is superimposed on the China of the lower Yangtze, with plane trees and low houses such as one finds in a village, except that here they line interminable streets; then suddenly tall buildings and dismantled churches of the colonial period stand like the remains of a shapeless past.

September 1

This morning I was face to face with my class. Chen, Zhang, and Tang were present, too; they sat in the back of the room. I gave a short account of my trip to the northwest and of what Peking was like after the earthquake. The students had trouble understanding my Italian. I simplified as much as possible, but they are not advanced enough to take in a story. Zhang must have known this, and he should have prevented our losing time in this way. I'm beginning to suspect that it matters more to him to look well in the eyes of his superiors than to achieve positive results in the teaching.

I tried to get the students to talk a bit, asked how old they are, where they come from. Most are from Shanghai, either the city proper or the suburban communes; a few come from the nearby provinces of Jiangsu and Zhejiang; one comes from Jiangxi, and one from Sichuan. Among the Shanghaiese, only a few actually said, "I come from Shanghai." In order to find that out, I had to put the question differently: "Where does your family live?" Almost all said that they were "settled in the country" in one or another area of China. They are unable to express even very simple concepts in Italian, but they know by heart the standard translation of many phrases such as that one. I'd have liked to counter and say: If you are here—here in Shanghai— you can say "I have worked in the country at such and such a time," but not that you are "settled" in the country. But I let it pass, because I understood that it was not a linguistic lapse but rather their way of using the word to exorcise the fact that they are *not* settled in the country, whereas every virtuous young person should be, and virtue is the precondition for entrance to the university.

Some of this group have done several years of manual work, however. For others, such work (after middle school) has been virtually nominal—a year or even less spent in a suburban commune; these are children of cadres, or the brightest children in an agricultural brigade in some suburb. It's easy to pick them out because they're the youngest. The students themselves jokingly point them out to me, and implicit in the joke is the traditional superiority of the older child over his "little" brother or younger sister, together with a kind of resigned envy, a recognition of the elder's inferiority because the younger one is, the more quickly one learns. Their pride in the years spent in the countryside is very great, on a par with the bitterness they feel for time irredeemably lost.

The class prefect, Liu Fenghua, is the youngest member of the class: twenty. He already has the round face, the slow reflexes, the comfortably well-off air of the minor cadre. The vice-prefect, Zhou Shiliang, twenty-four years old, has served in the army; he has a broad, intelligent face, as pimply as an adolescent's—or maybe it's lightly pockmarked. Assignment of the function of prefect is not a casual matter. It is made according to a precise political dosage, as is the case with the Revolutionary Committees: No. 1 is someone moderately rightist, No. 2 someone moderately leftist. Theoretically, the students should elect the prefect and his deputy, but, unless there is an actual rebellion, they simply endorse the choices of the directors, which are presented as suggestions. Probably the whole business, like much else, is discussed beforehand by the Party cell, to which some students belong; and perhaps at headquarters these students do express their own opinions.

The girls in the class are of two kinds: the very well-mannered Shanghai girls—some of them seem to have stepped from the pages of an old-fashioned novel—who are no doubt from cadre families; and the peasant girls, timid, audacious, who know what they want and go straight to the heart of the matter. One of them, Wang Jianhua, twenty years old, comes from the model suburban commune of Hongqiao; she is very popular with everyone; when she speaks, she smiles and her plump cheeks redden. Her companions call her, laughingly, "the baby." In fact, she is the most mature of them all and, making nothing of it, often cheerfully helps the others. Wang Min, older, has headed an agricultural brigade in Jiangsu Province; she is very shy, not brilliant, her handwriting is sloppy, and she makes a lot of spelling mistakes; I'll need a little time to understand how capable she is. She sits next to Ye Shengwang, also a peasant from Jiangsu; he is so restless that it is almost a sickness with him.

I asked what cities they are familiar with. Very few. Among all of us, I am the person who has visited the most Chinese cities. For more than one student, traveling to work in some faraway rural area has been a unique opportunity to stop for a day or two in towns along the way. The Chinese need no travel permits; everyone is free to move about. But they have no vacations to speak of; the two to three consecutive days of vacation that they have twice a year don't permit them to go very far. Students are fortunate in that they have a month-long vacation in summer, and two weeks in winter. However, for them, as for everyone else, there is the problem of money. A few have been to Peking, a few to Peking and Nanjing. "Which do you like better, Peking or Shanghai? Peking or Nanjing?" I asked, just to get them to talk. The reply: "All the cities are beautiful." There's nothing for it; even given a choice among three or four cities, they will say that all are equally beautiful. I insisted, tried a little irony to get a response. Finally, someone went so far as to say that he prefers the country to the city; no one chose the reverse. With some effort, Ye Shengwang confessed that he likes Nanjing better than Shanghai. Is it fear of shattering the equality among cities? . . . But perhaps the point lies elsewhere. Perhaps one must avoid bringing out into the open something that is a great responsibility and a great affliction—the fact that as a city Shanghai is *different.* It is a symbol of political difference; the local students' pride in belonging to China's greatest industrial city, and a relatively rich one, transpires through their every word and act. But its singularity is something else, perhaps dangerous to mention, something they want to conceal.

Uncertainty about what it is permissible to think or say, or to say to the foreigner, lessens as you move up through the ranks. For the profs, there are no taboos when it comes to comparing the beauty of Chinese cities. As we were talking later, we were as one in praising Suzhou. Chen comes from Suzhou, and Tang from a village nearby. The people of Suzhou have the reputation of being cultivated and agreeable, and their dialect is thought to be very pleasant-sounding.

In the afternoon, I held a conversation-lesson with the three teachers about the state of affairs in Italy. My exposition was a bit fuzzy, for I despaired of making myself understood.

I am very tired. Too little sleep, because we have to get up so early, yet the idea of going to bed at nine in the evening is hard to adjust to. There's an advantage to growing extremely weary—it makes it possible to sleep despite the rumble of the boat engines on the river and the stink that comes in through the window. But I move about in a perennial daze.

September 7

Seven days of school already. I teach six hours a week, which is to say, two hours on three days. Zhang teaches six more. My students attend four classes per day: two given over to Italian, two to other subjects (Chinese language and literature, politics, and background material on Italy). No one expects me to meet the teachers of these other courses, or to have the vaguest notion of what they are teaching. I am trying to work together at least with those who are concerned with Italy and Italian. I attended Zhang's classes twice, to get some idea of the level of the students and to coordinate my teaching with his. But I've gathered that it would be better to stop so as not to upset him; he's not at all sure of himself, doesn't want to let the students see that, and is afraid of what I will think of how he teaches. "Help each other" indeed! We are at the antipodes of that; in fact, we get nowhere near the minimal spirit of cooperation that exists even among Italians, who are notorious for their individualism and their inability to work as a group. The prevailing attitudes among my colleagues here seem to be diffidence and rivalry toward each other, and toward the students a more or less authoritarian paternalism. Zhang actually has his students read aloud in unison, and he's not the only one; when you walk along the corridors, you hear choruses of voices. Then he checks on whether they have memorized little set phrases. When someone makes a mistake, he corrects it rapidly and without explanation, and moves on. Now I realize that I was being a little heavy-handed with my first class when I straightway ruled out reading in unison, argued against learning by rote, and emphasized that the first thing one must do is learn to think.

Probably Zhang felt humiliated. But there's nothing I can do about that. If I were in a position to choose—or at least to have a voice in choosing—a working relationship with my colleagues, things would be different. But since that's not so, there's nothing left but for me to use as I see fit at least that margin of freedom which cannot be taken from me.

When I don't have classes, I work in my office. At my request, Chen has shown me where the Institute bookshop is located. Sometimes in bookstores affiliated with an educational institution you can buy books that are not always to be found outside, and sometimes they may give you some periodical from among those usually forbidden to foreigners—from among those, of course, that are not *neibu.* The Institute's bookshop is a small, modest room at the entrance to one of the buildings in the English section, next to a tiny cake and cookie shop.

I have asked Chen also to ask for permission for me to use the library— my Italian predecessors had told me that there you can read virtually all the periodicals allowed the Chinese masses. The matter proved immediately to be complicated. There are two libraries in our section: one for teachers, which contains material in foreign languages, and one for students. In addition, the Institute has a general library, which houses material that is specifically related to this or that country, this or that language, but that is in Chinese for the most part. Chen did not even mention this one to me; I learned of it from foreign colleagues. As for the other two, I don't know where the one for students is located, but I have ascertained that it is a small library for press and periodicals, with Chinese magazines that are to be found on sale elsewhere, and a few Italian Marxist-Leninist, or "Maoist," publications. Whether there are also books in Chinese I don't know; I am sure there are none in Italian. Chen accompanied me to the library for the teachers in our section; it's on the ground floor of my building. It is kept locked, and evidently no one uses it. If you needed to consult something there, better think of it a day or so ahead and alert the person who has the key and who, it seems, is not always to be found. The division I had access to was the Spanish, which is joined with the small Italian section: two rooms with wall shelves; quite a few books, but old; one would say a library that has not been kept up to date for years. Maybe that's why nobody uses it. Half of one shelf is given over to Italy: two or three short rows of books—fiction, history, publications about China, the Sansoni encyclopedia in four volumes, current papers and periodicals—*Il Corriere della Sera, Panorama, Epoca,* and the usual Marxist-Leninist papers. The Italian material is meager, which is natural since instruction in Italian was begun only a few years ago, but at least it's recent. The collection is hit-or-miss, because it is based on the advice or gifts of Italians. My visit was useful for purposes of information, and also to find out what material I can make use of for my work here.* But there is no place here where one finds Chinese reading materials of any kind.

In conversations with Chen and others about local libraries, no one suggested where I could go for material about China in Chinese. So I talked about this, among other things, with John, who came to see me last evening in my

*I plan to write and ask some Italian publishers to donate books; other materials, like dictionaries and catalogs, will be arriving, I know, also as a gift, from our Ministry of Foreign Affairs. And I'll have as many language-instruction books as possible sent to me.

room at the Dasha. He knows classical Chinese well and speaks many languages, but his real passion is music. He plays the flute quite well and knows how to tune pianos. I don't doubt that he has been "apolitical" in the highly politicized sense in which the English usually are, but he is a restless man who has most likely come to China expecting that things which elsewhere were beginning to elude him he would find materialized here. And instead, here he is, confined within a rarefied sphere, in a limbo enclosed by walls of cotton wadding. "I've experienced many frustrations," he confessed sadly. But he stubbornly persists in adhering to concrete daily realities and in reacting to the ambience here as if he were in England. He knows nothing about Marxism, he told me, and asked me to suggest some books he might read. For my part, I ask him about Shanghai, for he has been bicycling about the city for months and knows it like his own turf—the vegetable shops, the tailor shops, the tobacco shops serving Chinese where he buys things and exchanges a few words with people. I admire and envy his analytical approach; it's the only way to make a dent in the screen of ideological blah-blah. As for the libraries, he insists that we have the right to use the Institute's big library. However, even his interpreter, who seems a little more open than Chen, didn't go there with him; he found out about it on his own and simply walked in. Nobody stopped him. He urged me to do the same. I asked what the library is like. It's quite rich, he said, but, as in the libraries of the various sections, the material is old, and the catalogs are so dusty that clearly no one has touched them for years. Once you have located a book in the catalog, you must obtain a permit from your superiors to read it. The rule applies to the Chinese students, too. This news discouraged me. I could foresee how much time, effort, and wave-making that would involve me in, how askance Chen and Zhang would look, and in the end my Mediterranean indolence dissuades me. But even more, the sense of profound alienation I am beginning to feel is making me weak, already prepared to give in, and utterly incapable of sharing John's quiet assumptions about his human and civil rights. In point of fact, John relies on a solid constitutional sense which I, as an Italian, do not possess, and I am already imprisoned within a mechanism into which I will eventually integrate myself without having actually decided to do so. The first visible link in the chain is my being led around by the hand by Chen. The only way I know how to resist is through mental reservations.

But to some extent what appears to be passivity pure and simple is more; it is also a way of holding my own—as I see it, the only way that will let me preserve my independence. I will ask for something just once, clearly and precisely. If what is asked for is reasonable and they don't respond, then they'll be the ones to "lose face." But I'm not going to put myself in the position of asking over and over again, to let requesting become begging. A few days after I arrived, I presented in writing a list of what I should like to acquaint myself with in Shanghai; it included the Central Public Library, and scholars concerned with the work of Lu Xun. I specified that I should like to speak with a specialist about certain aspects of his writing which particularly interest me. This second request has already been brushed aside. Notebook in hand, Chen has asked me exactly what these aspects are, because, she said, a woman teacher of Chinese at the Institute could have a chat with me about them. Obviously, I've no wish to listen to this lady rehash secondhand opinions. Nonetheless, I specified that I am interested, first of all, in the polemics between Lu Xun and the *Chuangzao She*—the Creation Society, which was one of China's most famous literary groups in the twenties. Secondly, I was interested in the question of the united front of the Communists and Kuomintang in the thirties. I know what positions were taken in the period of the Cultural Revolution with regard to the united front—they are amply stated in the press—but am less clear about how the debate between Lu Xun and the Creation Society is now assessed. What I know from foreign students of Chinese literature suggests that there is great confusion, an unwillingness to put Lu Xun in the wrong, but ditto for members of the *Chuangzao She* who are important public figures today. Actually, what need is there to take part in passing critical judgment on a dispute that is fifty years old? But people here keep going over and over it, dividing the world into black and white, not only for the present but also for the past and future. As to the library permission, we'll see, but I am skeptical. My other requests I do anticipate will be granted, since they fall within the range of things usually shown to foreigners.

In addition to John, in these last days I've come to know Uta, the young German woman who teaches at Fudan. Vigorous build, chestnut hair, vivacious eyes: Uta exhibits the passionate nonviolence of the post-'68 generation, a thoughtful attention to the person talking with her, and the nondogmatic attitude that in the best Germans reverses and redeems what in so many of them is an angelic or bestial defiance of reason.

Also, Susan, who is an English instructor together with John, is back from vacation. I was sitting alone in the restaurant, at one of the small tables, and I noticed that from the large round table where she was seated, although alone, she kept looking up from the books and papers she had with her and glancing at me curiously. Susan is small—tiny even, like a little girl—and looks more Indian than English (her father is Indian); her body and expressions betray a basic insecurity masked by the knowing little airs of the star pupil. At the end of the meal, she came over to introduce herself and brought greetings from a mutual friend she'd met in Paris. She speaks excellent French and is connected with French leftist groups. She kept watching me uncertainly, as if she were sizing me up, and allowed herself no easy cordiality.

That evening, we met again in Uta's room, which is furnished with individuality and hospitable; young Dagmar was there, too, and the four of us drank sweet Chinese wine and talked a long time. All Susan's reserve melted away. (Perhaps she was afraid of finding in me the older overbearing professor.

Instead, after a full year's stay, it is she who knows much more, in addition to speaking the language fluently.) Europe manages still to produce admirable people, especially among women of the younger generations, who have succeeded among themselves in overturning that disagreeable relationship of competitiveness or of silly complicity in the dominating shadow of the male master always looming behind them—a clearing away and a rationality that make for trust, even if so far only a minority of women is involved. Among the young men and women living here there is an implicit, a reciprocal trust that we all realize is essential if we are not to be divided and lost, whatever the circumstances. They all evidence a remarkable involvement in work, almost as if they were staking their best against obstacles that the bureaucrats and petty academics seem to be putting in the way of mass education—which is, after all, a part of official programs. "That's not all there is in Shanghai," Susan said. "There are many positive things, too." She seemed not to want to say more.

"Extracurricular Activities"

On Friday afternoon—September 3, before Susan had come back—we met for our first political-study session, again in the second-floor room with the big table and with all the foreign teachers present. The same cadre who had come to see me at the Dasha made a two-hour *baogao* ("report") on criticism of the three articles by Deng, repeating what has been published over and over in the newspapers for months. Anyone who had not read the papers—and more particularly not read *Study and Criticism* or the polemics over the schools and the Academy of Science and the management of production units—would not, I think, have got very much out of the man's rehash. Repetitions and tautologies so emptied of meaning the theme of discussion, which in the press reports was detailed and explicit, that it seemed stupid and gratuitous. For example, the argument against reintroducing work rules in the factory, which insists they are really intended to establish a rigid control of the workers from above, was restated in these terms: "The introduction of management norms into industrial enterprise signifies the restoration of capitalism."

One asks oneself, Is this distortion intentional? In any case, cadres and little professors like these are brought to a standstill when they are confronted by the ideas of Deng's critics, the young critics especially, because they perceive them as an attack on their own roles, even more than on their own opinions. They are in an ultradefensive position and are afraid of free discussion. They make a long, long *baogao,* and allow only a few minutes for questions or objections, which are reduced to nothing. On this particular occasion, Chen, who in other matters is even too diligent, translated some things but not others, which suited me, for I prefer to understand on my own, but that was certainly not her intention. Dagmar, who doesn't read Chinese, asked to know the content of the articles; otherwise, she said, the gist of the criticism escaped her. John asked for clarification of the historical background and evolution of the debate. No response. I pointed out that they were discussing the struggle, but then everything seemed to boil down to an exercise in theoretics, whereas we wanted to know how they moved on from theoretical study of the problems and of Marxism to the real political struggle. (The Beida-Qinghua group has written that if one judges the Left and Right by their words, they seem identical; everybody is saying the same things; whereas the whole point lies in confronting words and the actual politics being carried out.) The response to my question: You have been here too short a time; you will see for yourselves, or you will see when "you talk with the workers."

Monday, the sixth, in the early afternoon, we went to visit a factory that produces candies and canned foods, the Yimin Shipin Yichang.

A big bus came to pick us up, together with the young man and two women associates of Lao Bai and our interpreters. Everyone, including Aymin, Felicitas, and Maya, embarked on a drive that took us through unfamiliar areas of the city. Long crowded streets, small houses, factories, big buildings, walls, signs, a network of activities and connections spread over a space that one couldn't quite master—Shanghai suddenly seemed like London. When a city exceeds certain dimensions, it becomes a world; neighborhoods, units, and blocks of buildings become adjoining villages.

Like most Chinese factories, this one was a functioning disorder. There is always something in the process of being built or altered; collapsing old sheds stand side by side with new structures. The workers passing by looked at us curiously as we walked to a neat, well-kept small reception room. Here we were met by a representative of the factory's Revolutionary Committee and someone from the union, plus a dense crowd of workers, both men and women. The first shift was about to end, so they took us without delay on a tour of the plant. It has grown by accretion. What must have started out as a small semi-artisan enterprise has had new sections added little by little. Mechanization has now largely replaced manual labor; they showed us machinery invented and built by the factory's own personnel. One got the impression that the work is quite hard, and that it is performed not under compulsion but rather in good spirit and with much freedom of movement.

Back in the reception room, the woman union representative told us the history of the factory. The workers, male and female, seated around her kept close tabs on what she was saying. It turned out that, in fact, this is an old factory, previously owned by Japanese, then by Chinese ("compradors of the Kuomintang," the union woman said, in an obviously critical reference to the national bourgeoisie, which is the pride of many people in Shanghai). In 1949, the old owners partially dismantled it, but production was quickly resumed.

With the workers' enthusiasm no longer exploited by foreigners or Chinese, particularly not during the Cultural Revolution, there was an enormous increase in production and an expansion of the types of products manufactured; from an initial output of cakes, the factory has moved on to produce chocolates, ice cream, caramels, and all sorts of canned foods. The work force now numbers 2,500. According to the woman, diligent efforts have been made to invent new machinery and increase mechanization through the plant's "three-in-one" technical group—consisting of workers, technicians, and cadres—established during the Cultural Revolution.

They listened and responded to our questions, which had to do with sanitary controls for the production of canned food in Shanghai, the quality and quantity of the production, criticism of the three articles by Deng, the workers' participation in management, wages, women's organizations, the union, admission of workers to the university, and recreational and cultural activities.

Tea was set out on a table, together with a quantity of sweets of every kind, and the women workers sitting with us urged us to try them. Aymin stuffed herself with excellent little chocolates. Everybody was in high good humor. One sensed their feeling of security and their trade-unionist strength. There seemed to be no barriers between supervisors and workers, and it was as if they wanted to show us that, all together, they were mounting a defense against something hostile on the outside. They were not sure whether we ourselves were people with whom to be solid or whom they should treat with a certain reticence in self-defense, but we felt that they rather gambled in favor of trust.

I do hope to visit other factories often, and I'd like to be able to work in one. The factory is a powerful antidote to the obtuseness of those in the scholastic milieu.

This afternoon I went to a film screening at the Institute. The projection room, also used for mass meetings, musical performances, and entertainment of other kinds, is a separate building next to the one where my office is. I liked the interior—it resembles an unembellished hangar. A handsome wooden girder supports the roof; the whole is reminiscent of the revolutionary style of the twenties and thirties. The auditorium is large, seats (on benches) are numbered, and tickets (free) must be requested in advance. People not connected with the Institute are admitted, too (many schoolchildren), who obtain tickets through their respective units.

Today they were showing *Chun Miao* (literally *Buds of Springtime,* but it's the name of the heroine). By everyone's account, it is the best in a series of recent films about the barefoot doctors, and, together with *Juelie;* or *The Breakdown,* one of the good productions coming out of the resumption of the Cultural Revolution. It was made when Deng Xiaoping had returned to power, ergo it is a "countercurrent" film. The story is about the people's struggle in a village against the imperious doctor-barons. The doctor-baron chief opposing the bare-foot paramedic heroine is also the local political authority; he declares that she is rebellious, unworthy of obtaining her membership card, and he bans her from the Party. The film shows the abandoned state of the peasants, whose children die without anyone wanting to care for them (the doctors think only of their studies and careers)—the dilemma of the disinherited throughout time. The actors' delivery is forced, the doctor-barons are ridiculously villainous villains, but their chief, who is also the political power, is the personification of the familiar Russian-style minor bureaucrat. When a little boy stricken with pneumonia is ignored by the doctors, the girl throws herself into a desperate, anguished effort to save him with herbal medicines. Her breathless search for the herbs, by night on the mountainside, is replete with hyper-romantic symbolism but does not exalt "traditional folk medicine" over "bourgeois science" so much as it represents ordinary people's unwillingness to be crushed and trusting to their own means in order to survive. Yanan all over again.

The dialogue is very strong. Exhortations to obey the authority of the Party are answered resoundingly: "What authority?"

Yet here in China every day is geared to the rhythm of a conventlike iron discipline that would seem to exclude the possibility not only of a challenge to authority but even of the most modest objection. Is it a matter of the conflict's being too extreme to allow for mediation? Or, on the contrary, are they searching for a nontraumatic road to change?

At Fudan, the students are calling for an overhaul of teaching methods. Some are said to be refusing to read *Pékin Information* because "it's not written in real French."

When I have no work to do after dinner, I can walk over the bridge for an ice cream at the Friendship Store, which stays open until ten. The street is quieter then but not deserted. The bridge is guarded by members of the Workers' Militia—often girls, who are quite aware of how charming they look in their blue overalls, belted close around the waist, and their sun helmets and rifles. They lean against the parapet and chat with passersby, or walk back and forth, patrolling the bridge.

By late afternoon old men and women, alone or in groups, are intently going through the slow motions of traditional Chinese gymnastics in Huangpu Park. All around are the sounds of a port, of boats, engines. People go to bed early and get up early. But in the evening and late at night, too, you can glimpse some elderly person intent on shadow boxing, or *taiji,* as the Chinese call their traditional gymnastics.

One must be careful not to mistake Shanghai for China. Here, rebellion and repression, in both intensity and form, are abnormally strong—although they are indeed common to many industrial areas. Even in seemingly small things there are differences. For example, in Peking there are no restrictions comparable to the ones in effect here on access to libraries; there, reticence and reciprocal suspicion do not lead to such paradoxes as here; the surveillance and isolation of foreigners is milder, so much so that if one perseveres, it is not impossible to establish direct, friendly contact with accessible individuals on the Right or the Left. Also, Peking's cadres and minor intellectuals are less vulgar.

In looking at China from Europe—or, more generally, from the West—too often we fail to take into consideration what Chinese society was and is. The Chinese were a people living in the most extreme poverty, whose patterns of reference had been either destroyed or debased. The plan has been to take off from the blank page of poverty, from the very lowest level, and to permit no one to rise higher alone. The result: an enormous night school and an enormous convent. . . . But the night school is reductive; it is a place where adults repeat what they are taught like children, trusting or feigning trust. But someone is doing the teaching, someone who is already "above." He is, or at any moment he can become, the enemy. The person who teaches, or who manages, *must be obeyed, and at every moment he must prove his loyalty to the people, his humility; he must never "claim bourgeois rights," and must do manual work, must live in poverty.*

This is a tremendous Confucianist game. And it is continually passing from a liberating to a tyrannical function. "The bourgeoisie is in the Party." "Bourgeoisie" here means the separate power of a class or a caste, and is not embodied in this or that faction, in this or that individual. The split is cultural, ergo it is everywhere, and the Cultural Revolution was intended to be a response to that split. A dominant class or caste is not incompatible with lively social mobility, as has been true in the Chinese tradition.

As individuals, A, B, and C—and even E, F, and G—can be banished or neutralized. But this will not settle the question. Whoever *may be banished, the* zouzipai *(capitalist roaders) "will continue to be on the move."*

The revolution born of the old China was a revolt that, unlike those of Europe, had not destroyed the principle of authority and overturned institutions. The revolution did not create new institutions or formulate a system of institutional guarantees. Masked as a "democratic-bourgeois revolution," it did, yes, provide itself with a constitution, which it plumped out with words more or less copied from existing bourgeois-democratic constitutions—but no Chinese ever believed they were other than empty words. What counts is the danwei *(base unit) instead of the clan, the production brigade instead of the village, Chairman Mao instead of the emperor, the* ganbu *(cadre) bound to the people instead of the* guan *(mandarins), the friends of the landlords.*

But little by little this mirror image of the old society began to reveal itself as the same old society in a process of progressive rebuilding, solid now, having arisen from the rottenness into which it had sunk and strengthened by infusions of peasant blood. It seemed as if the perennial cycle of history was repeating itself once again.

The revival was thrown into confusion by the Cultural Revolution, which shot ahead toward the only goal possible in the circumstances: an attack on the entire power structure. "The revolution . . . fell upon their own heads."

The Cultural Revolution sought to overthrow the Confucianist game, to be the other side of the medal.

But the two sides, the two faces of the medal are inseparable. In Peking, often you cannot tell the new from the old, or freedom from tyranny.

In Shanghai, anyone who presents himself as a mandarin sickens the people because he is a false mandarin and a false priest. The Western bourgeoisie that came here created nothing if not ghosts, but it did overturn the culture of the mandarins. Inhabited by workers, Shanghai became one of the remotest peripheries of the capitalist world. The proletarian revolution in this distant outpost was attempted but crushed in the twenties. In 1927, insurgent workers were massacred while an educated Chinese middle class—half intellectual, half petty bourgeois, torn between westernization and nationalism—emerged in poverty, amid rancorous sectarian controversies and in a treacherous climate of clandestinity, yet enjoying the pitiable privileges of civilized elites that live on the fringes of the colonial world. Shanghai knows nothing of Yanan; in those years it was the city of the Kuomintang, of the national bourgeoisie, of underground Communists, and subsequently of Japanese invaders who occupied it.

After 1949, generations of young workers joined with their elders, and their class entered a new era of enlightenment. A modern proletariat with modern exigencies arose in the industrial centers, in the ports, and on the railroads; opposed to the technocrats, they rejected the production-oriented logic and demanded that their needs be met immediately. To fend them off, the technocrats are prepared to grasp any weapon in their determination to dominate the producers and, in defense of production, to force them to renounce their own aims. They are ever ready to reward them financially within the limits of what is possible and reasonable.

For all workers, the Cultural Revolution was the "January storm," the Shanghai commune of 1967. There and similarly in other cities, they strove to assume the role of modernizers, like the bourgeoisie in the West, and at the same time to liberate themselves from their age-old dependence on the technocrats and bureaucrats. But their struggle was (and still is) confounded and complicated by an immense population of indigent peasants beyond the industrial zones—poor materially and culturally, naturally in thrall to the mandarins. Thus, the two factions are at once antagonistic and complementary.

The Chinese workers are too weak culturally to take on the burden of such a demanding mission—not only to fight for their own interests but also to guide

*the peasants in their efforts to emancipate themselves from their backward mate-
rial and cultural circumstances and, at the same time, to overrule the power of
the bourgeoisie acquired over the centuries of their ascent. This mission cannot
be delegated; mediators are essential—but do such mediators exist?*

*In the China of Yanan, students and educated young people became guer-
rilla and Party cadres, writers became schoolteachers, women became soldiers.
They were a heroic minority in a small heroic republic amid the vast sea that was,
and is, China. After Liberation, the great class of the educated and the half-
educated—government officials and academicians, teachers, writers, artists,
professors, students, later scholars and scientists—willingly accepted new tasks out
of nationalistic pride and in obedience to an ancient discipline; they reacquired
the legitimacy lost to them during a century of national shame, and took upon
themselves once again the responsibility for teaching and guiding the people. The
language of the Socialist revolution did not disturb them, even though it was
peppered with anarchistic parlance. Given the old dialectic in which Chinese
historical cycles develop, the overthrow of authority was anticipated and taken for
granted. The mandate had to be taken away from the* guan *and from the emperor
who did not govern* in the service of the people. *To govern well means to serve
the interests of the people; service to the people makes for a power more deeply
rooted and invincible than that held by masters of wealth or leaders of armies.
The educated and semi-educated classes responded positively to the call of duty
to their country, and setting themselves to their task, rebuilt the pyramid of sound
government, and they trained millions of new* ganbu *(cadres) big and small.*

*The leaders, the cadres, the educated, and the semi-educated are old and
young, men and women, varying widely in their social origins and life experience.
If not homogeneous as a class, they are even less so in ideas and behavior; they
range from revolutionaries to conservatives, and among Party members there are
interwoven political persuasions and loyalties that derive from the involved history
of the twenties and thirties and relationships with the Comintern and the Soviet
Union, from the mixture of ideologies—democratic, anarchist, and Soviet-
Marxist—and from a succession of generations, some having lived under the
Kuomintang, others untried in a struggle against the overlords.*

*If one examines the vanguard and base sectors, among those calling for a
resumption of the Cultural Revolution, they appear immature and incapable of
providing a theoretical and pragmatic political form for the confused, embryonic
demands of workers, young people, and women, who oppose authoritarianism and
press for self-management. The middle- to high-ranking cadres and the leaders
of what has been dubbed the "leftist" tendency would be more culturally adequate. Even among them confusion is great in matters of theory, since different
orientations converge in the so-called Left that are analogous to what in the West
we would classify as liberal, Radical Socialist, Leninist, Stalinist. Actually, their
greatest inadequacy lies elsewhere: as leftists, they do not differentiate themselves*

from the cadres and leaders of other political currents, but together with them form what is, to all intents and purposes, one homogeneous social class. This explains, among other things, why the criticisms and accusations that ricochet back and forth between the factional battle lines are identical. All factions profess the same doctrine (the Chinese version of Marxism-Leninism), and to possess the doctrine and be authorized to transmit it is now, as in the past, what basically legitimizes a caste—or a ruling class.

The workers in industrial zones and students in the vanguard schools do not know how to express their rebelliousness except in the doctrinal language, which they take from the by now rich repertory of the several-centuries-old bourgeois revolution and the more than one-century-old worker movement, up to and including the most recent subversive appeals issued by the country's highest authority, Mao Zedong. But the search goes on in ways however contradictory because there is one thing that all those words fail to express satisfactorily: to win freedom from an increasingly centralized and hierarchical politico-economic system, with managers and political directors oppressing the people who work, and the so-called common good relating less and less to the individual's real life, is a difficult new task, for which democratic-bourgeois and Marxist theories are altogether inadequate.

Western democracy and Eastern socialism have both evolved toward greater centralization in the supervision of production, in science, and in the exercise of power, toward a new despotism (whereas the bourgeoisie cherished the illusion that it was forever defeated). In the war on tyranny, in the East as in the West, reviving the old formulas of socialism or democracy, which ring more and more hollow, is not enough.

Of all the Communist leaders—and not only Chinese—Mao Zedong came closest to understanding the new reality, but his thinking was contradictory because he persisted in expressing himself to a great extent in terms of the old formulas. He warned that the dividing line between socialism and fascism was uncharted, therefore it was easily crossed, but he never explicitly denounced the despotic character of socialism; this would have undone a good part of his own work. Instead, he sidestepped the issue by resorting more and more to generalized discourses; human destiny, he said, repeats itself within immutable limits: equilibrium and imbalance, order and disorder, unity and division, authority and rebellion: like a return to the cyclical vision of history in great Chinese thought.

4.

MOURNING

The Death of Mao Zedong
September 9, 1976

The mildest of September days. . . . I came back from school a short while ago. The sky is such a limpid blue that it lends an azure tinge even to the great yellowish river. The city is still half-lighted by the sun—below my window it is dark—but all of it is swathed in red flags. Loudspeakers everywhere talk back and forth. The communiqué is repeated over and over, well phrased, no rhetoric. Walls are already covered with white paper streamers on which young people armed with cans of glossy paint and thick brushes are inscribing "Our great leader, Chairman Mao Zedong, will never perish." The local militia has been mobilized. The city is awake.

Today I was at the Institute and should have come home after four-thirty. I was working with the Chinese professors when, shortly after two, an announcement came over the radio that at four there would be an important communiqué from Peking. A little before four, the three Chinese left, saying that I should probably expect the bus to come a bit ahead of schedule. I walked along the street that leads to the exit; the golden light was filtering through the plane trees that arch overhead—it was a heavenly afternoon. Then the radio began to intone "The Central Committee of the Chinese Communist Party, the Standing Committee of the National People's Congress. . . ." I gathered what it was about before the sentence was finished. Teachers, students, elderly workers scattered here and there. . . . A clutch of little girls piled on a tricycle. . . . Many people seated side by side along the low pavements on either side of the street, but each bent over, head in hands, alone. Some were sobbing.

I walked on slowly toward the gate. The communiqué was speaking of a great Communist. At its conclusion, the Russian folk melody, the "Varshavyanka," was played, then the "Internationale." The way they instantly busy themselves with paper and paste and brushes, the bewilderment, the feeling of confusion and weeping and stupefaction as when a close and dearly loved relative dies. (A few days ago, with my two-bit Machiavellianism, I had criticized the way people speak of "ardent love" for the leader. I realized that I had offended them on a point where sensibility is shared, untouched by factionalism.)

The "Internationale" is for us foreigners, too; it brings everyone in. The sound of it is reaching me now through the open window. (Yesterday I went to a mass political meeting in the film auditorium, and came away full of irritation, telling myself it was like Kafka's *The Castle;* you turn and turn and never get anywhere. . . . Damn intellectual generalizations. Why do they continually show us up as arrogant adults who end up always missing the real point?)

Today I was assailed by a sudden memory of small empty streets in Venice in September, like another world without connection to this one where I now am. China cannot *not* be this passion, this splitting off from the land that has nourished you and fracturing of yourself, the imposing of different structures. But the truly great, like Mao Zedong, do not belong only to their own land but break across borders. And then the figure of Mao reminds me of other images, all mixed together confusedly, Bakunin and Lenin, the Paris Commune, the Chinese peasants, the howl of the *miserables,* and the proletarian vanguard—the sublime years between '27 and '42. Surely he was the greatest liberator of men in our century. . . .

Among the white strips of soft paper that the girls had piled up to await inscriptions, a woman who was seated on a low curbstone suddenly keeled over. The girls stopped their pasting and hurried to lift her up. She couldn't stand alone, and they accompanied her slowly on her way. Throughout the city there were dismayed faces, reddened eyes.

I listened to the radio, which is broadcasting details of the funeral ceremonies. The mourning period will last until the eighteenth of the month. I went to Uta's room, where there was a meeting of the foreign instructors—English, Peruvian, Japanese, German. Paule Garçon was there, too. And the Fudan people: Bob, our well-born French Marxist-Leninist. Shinto, Uta. Also Marjorie, a gentle-mannered half-sinicized Australian who has lived here for years; she keeps very much to herself, and until now I did not know she even existed. Dagmar is at the factory in connection with the open-door program, but Felicitas was with us. We decided to offer a wreath and write a letter. We had a few editing problems about the letter, which Susan and Makita had prepared. Our discussion was a model of democracy in action, everyone making his point peacefully. The letter was revised several times before it was approved. It's not easy for people to write a brief joint message in circumstances like ours. We speak different languages, we have different attitudes, and we find ourselves in the strange situation of being only partly integrated as a group yet having to make ourselves understood in the correct way by the people we are addressing.

September 11

Yesterday and today no classes have been held at the Institute. (There's been no general ruling; each unit decided on its own.) We foreign instructors asked our Chinese colleagues for guidance, and now have decided to offer two wreaths. One will be presented jointly with the Fudan and Shida people, and will be taken to the People's Square, where the city's public observances will be held. The other will be offered at a ceremony to be held at the Institute. In every inhabited locality throughout the country one place will be designated, in conformity with the precedent set in Peking, where everyone can go to pay his respects. Smaller ceremonies, like ours at the Institute, will be held in individual neighborhoods —here, in Shanghai's many public gardens—and in individual units. As for the letter, our Chinese colleagues have told us we can send it either to Peking or to the local city government, but we've finally gathered that the proper addressee is the Shanghai Revolutionary Committee, which is the local authority directly over our *danwei,* the superfamily to which we belong.

One does not buy wreaths, one makes them. (On this exceptional occasion, there are wreaths for sale, too, but as a kind of ad hoc public service available to foreigners and those who, for pressing personal reasons, are unable to make their own.) For this, we all met in my office, which is bigger than the others, and the Spanish-language students came along to help us out—indeed, they did most of the work. Everywhere in the school, in offices and classrooms, everybody was taken up with the same task. Rolls upon rolls of the lightweight crinkly paper Chinese stationery shops are always full of, lengths of wire, scissors. . . . In the corridors and courtyards, people are fashioning bamboo frames, which they wrap first in straw and then in paper. Making the flowers is fairly easy, and the effect is splendid. The paper is reinforced by a wire attached to a pointed stick which acts like a needle in threading the wire through the straw frame.

The preparation of these wreaths is a highly civilized ritual. The labor is light, less effort and pleasanter than knitting, but all the same you have to work with your hands and pay some attention. While you work you talk sometimes, and sometimes are silent. As you become emotionally more relaxed, you become reflective. You are in company, and at the same time alone. You cannot help but think of the person who has died, but it is the opposite of cries of lamentation. Equilibrium is restored, and in the midst of grief you meditate. This is the chorus in which you are free only through becoming one with an organic whole.

I interrupted the gentle task of helping to fashion the wreath in order to help Zhang in translating the communiqué on Mao's death into Italian. We didn't use the Chinese text but transcribed Peking Radio's "Italian"-language broadcast. I do hope this version is not broadcast in Italy; it is full of those strange terms like "Mao Zedong Thought" and "renegade gang" and "unity and unification" and "correct party" and "deviationist wind from the Right," etc.

The people most out of place these days are the Peruvians, Marcial and Olga. And yet they are among those of us politically closest to the Chinese. But they are the bearers of formal Latin-American traditions where the Indian and Spanish heritage produces exuberant explosions such as the Rio Carnival, and artistic constructions of enormous dimension and violent color, from baroque colonial architecture, up to and including the films of Guerra or Rocha. Marcial wanted the wreath to be not round but heart-shaped, and in the center to have a bunch of flowers—red, *"como el sangre proletario."* There was a horrified reaction from English John (who had not been warned) when he saw the result. . . . Our affectionate, well-mannered young Chinese were doing what we asked them to do. But their corrective touches—almost imperceptible and I would say unconscious—were in exactly the opposite direction from what Marcial wanted. Olga kept asking for "strong" colors. On the contrary, the Chinese were envisaging the dazzling, sorrowful white-yellow-sky-blue of their funerals. Then, this morning someone—perhaps an older person—recalled that red is the color of joy; it is not funereal, one cannot put it in a wreath. So we remade the wreath, removing the red and crimson flowers and replacing them with white, sky-blue, and lilac flowers. Order has been reestablished, to the sorrow and frustration of the two Peruvians and to the satisfaction of the English.

What enables us to communicate with the Chinese is our old culture, even our Hellenism, our Goethe, our Brecht. But not its popular elements. During the funeral ceremony today, I was noticing in the long lines of people how easily most of the Europeans adapted to Chinese forms in behavior and clothing, and how less integrated the "uncouth" Americans and Australians were, with their gaudy plaids and their overbearing physiques. However, the foreigners, the "barbarians," who are beyond hope are the Africans, and the more African they are the more that is so. The colors of their clothes, their manners, and language are so much at variance with the context, and thus they find themselves beyond any possible rapport.

And yet a black is not a "barbarian" in Paris or London, not even in Rome or Milan. Late capitalism—that iconoclastic destroyer of forms—has nonetheless arrived at the premise of universal equality; it has torn up all streets, and produced building materials made up of fragments so unrecognizable that any aspiration to reconstruct the past is foolish and futile. In comparison, China is too organically structured, too perfect.

We—all the foreign instructors—left at one o'clock this afternoon in two buses for the funeral ceremony. Unlike the arrangements made in other cities, here in Shanghai foreigners were invited to the ceremony on the first day. The lovely September skies are still with us. The plane trees are so numerous and so luminous that one is reminded of Suzhou, the beautiful town not far from Shanghai. We got out of our buses a short distance from the great People's Square. Lines upon lines of people were already waiting, all very orderly. Everything was organized to the nth degree, and well. Every group was assigned a precise moment when it was to enter the big hall in the People's Park. Every foreigner had by his side a Chinese; this time it was not for the usual protection-control but a grateful hospitality offered to those who "come from far away" and were sharing in the mourning. "We are very grateful to you because you have been close to us in these days" is something we would hear repeated many times.

Inside was an enormous space, hangarlike in proportions, an example of beautiful modern architecture. By the entrance, rows of militia, men and women, with rifles, were carefully drawn up; groups of them, seated or standing, were at the far side of the square, all wearing belted bright-blue overalls and helmets. They were very handsome, the women especially—perhaps they had been handpicked. Inside the hall, other militiamen were stationed; these were unarmed.

To the right of the door as we entered, the vast hall was literally filled with wreaths placed on benches that usually are meant for the public. To the left, on one of the short walls of the hall, a large portrait of Mao, surrounded by flowers. On either side of the portrait, eight people—top city officials, who, I understand, spell each other—were standing on a platform or stage. Beneath the platform, large wreaths from the city's more important units and public figures. We filed by, stopping for a moment to face toward the stage as two of our people carried our wreath over to it. And then we took our leave. In the glare of the floodlights installed for the film and TV cameras and in the white-yellow of the wreaths, there was a severity—a hardness, almost—a precise language that was an attempt to be modern and unlike the ritualism of Peking. We passed between more rows of militia, and were out on the street once more.

Everyone was weeping. We wept too. The collision of different emotions was too great. A thought occurred to me: Workers and peasants carry arms in civil life. (The constitution, by placing the People's Militia—defined as "the workers' and peasants' own armed force"*—on an equal footing beside the army, continues for a time the traditions of Yanan and the Paris Commune.) The "stirring strains of the 'Internationale'" accompanied us, followed us, and then the "Varshavyanka." This was both historical event and family mourning.

*In the new constitution of 1978 the militia is mentioned, but as a force subordinate to the army.

Two messages came through with powerful urgency: the pressing invitation that you participate and a simultaneous rejection of you—the unknowing you, the foreigner tolerated because you are sharing in the host's grief. Both messages were authentic, they were not subjective projections; an accumulation of contradictions becomes concentrated in certain given moments.

The present pattern in China for communications regarding political and social matters and for economic management is the tiaotiao zhuanzheng *(dictatorship from branch to branch): from the individual to his base group, either a factory team or agricultural production squad, to the base leader; from this leader to the base unit (production, administrative, educational, residential, etc.); from here, via its leader, to intermediate groups of various kinds and at various levels of the ladder (provincial organisms, for example) on up to the topmost central authority. An individual or a base group wishing to communicate with another individual or base group must address the message upward along the ladder to one or another higher level, depending on the circumstances and the importance of the question at issue; the message then descends the ladder toward the other group; the two are put into communication under the control of the higher authorities (or they will never be in contact), and messages are screened and transmitted by these controllers.*

"Dictatorship from branch to branch" is what Franz Schurmann has termed "vertical rule," and it corresponds to centralization. In this way, "an agency has full policy and operational control over all units of organization within its jurisdiction." In the period prior to the Cultural Revolution, as analyzed by Schurmann, alternating with and superimposed upon this system was "the dual rule," according to which a "lower-echelon agency receives commands from two or more higher-echelon agencies . . . in practice . . . an agency is partly under the jurisdiction of another body at the same administrative level."

This system was shaken up by the Cultural Revolution, and in localities where people are politically more alert and more independent in spirit it is continually violated, as it is where leaders encourage autonomy at the base instead of thwarting it. However, the system has never been done away with, and at least in theory it prevails. The Left accuses Deng Xiaoping of wanting to establish it, but it is rather a question of his proposing to reinforce it and make it generally operative, thereby eliminating whatever latitude of independence the base has won for itself and would like to expand.

The Left advocates the "dual initiative." This is no longer a matter of "dual rule" in the old accepted meaning of the term, nor is it an instance of a generic decentralization but a combination of original proposals based on some positive experiences, especially in Shanghai. If the relationship of the central government to the units assumes the form of "dictatorship from branch to branch," the mechanisms of the old society are likely to be reproduced and the base community (family, clan, village, etc.) will tend to function as the elementary cell in a despotic organism—even, and all the more so, when the center assigns to it relative autonomy in management and decision-making exclusively within itself. *The intermediate levels serve as authoritative transmitters, and their share of effective power increases in proportion to their nearness to the top. "Modern" economic power is perfectly grafted to this structure, and takes it over, extending the network of units that are subject to central production plans and to rigid control to include the industrial and scientific sectors. The "dual initiative" does not exclude the vertical rule but companions it with a functionally opposed series of "horizontal" communication channels whereby units belonging to different production sectors, and the local population in its various organizational centers can be in communication. Communication means collaboration, taking the problems of others into account in solving one's own—therefore, the possibility of modifying orders vertically received even in the area of selecting products, determining the quantity and quality of production, the organization of work, research programs, and so forth. For both productive and nonproductive units, it is a question of subordinating their own programs to the general interest—not as that interest is defined by some abstract version passed along by the center but that sense of the general interest which is received and acquired through direct communication and collaboration. This method is incompatible with a system of rigid planning, but it does not frontally attack the center's plan, since it would offer no alternative general program to oppose that plan—unless it is a "return" to free enterprise, which is incompatible even with a capitalist structure. Horizontal communication implies the gradual wearing down of the power system through initiative at the base, which in socialism is presumed to be capable of building while at the same time it destroys; it implies also the leveling of the walls that separate units from each other and blind them to everything that happens outside their respective boundaries.*

Mao Zedong occupied the position of greatest prestige (if not of greatest power) in the seat of central authority. He shattered the "vertical rule" more than once, in both its downward and upward flow. He aimed at a gradual extension of the self-administered sphere, to the point where personal, family, group, and community interests become integrated with the general public interest.

Hypotheses of this sort are realistic only if there is a modicum of goodwill on the part of those who currently control the vertical structures, and a willingness gradually to be deprived of their authority in the name of communism (and, what's more, a willingness to assume responsibility for a large share of the serious technical and economic difficulties that would inevitably arise in the course of the process). Without such willingness, the hypothesis of a "peaceful" transformation becomes unreal.

The terms in which the political struggle is posited today (on one hand, the Soviet-type production-oriented centralizing programs of Deng Xiaoping, and, on the other hand, the attack on the bureaucracy as the class enemy), the paralysis to which the country has been reduced by the years-long challenge put to "people in power" by certain sectors in some classes and some political circles that tended to undermine their authority and were therefore considered hostile—all these factors seem to indicate that a peaceful transformation is precluded. Not only this, for by now it seems to be a fact that in the government apparatus and among those who "possess culture" there is no willingness to cooperate in the "extinction" of their own roles. In the short run, the more likely hypothesis is a recourse to repression on the part of the strongest, for so long as the power balance favors them. Mao was concerned with furnishing guarantees to the people. He proclaimed it was their duty to "go against the tide," their right to pass over intermediate groups and approach leaders directly (a duty and right sanctioned by Party statute);* their duty to post dazibao and their right to strike (guaranteed by the Constitution of the Republic); he maintained that workers should share in the direction of schools, that the schools should be open to all, that the workers should have the right to be armed. . . .

These guarantees are inadequate and can prove to be utterly illusory once the authority that has made them operative disappears. The Chairman was a living guarantee of liberty and of liberation. This is why today the Chinese people feel decapitated.

Evening, September 11

At dinner, I talked for a moment with Dagmar, the German teacher at the Institute, who had come back from the factory for today's ceremony. She's lost some weight, and in her pale face her pale-blue eyes look larger. I asked what the factory stint had been like, and she answered in an admirably simple, forthright way. She does not sleep in the quarters for workers, which are already overcrowded with students, but in a nearby hotel for Chinese; the small room is for four (herself and three Chinese from the school). She eats in the canteen with the workers, and spends the whole day working side by side with them. It isn't tiring, she said. "The atmosphere is amazing. Great freedom, high spirits, and lots of discussion. People work calmly, there's no pressure. . . . For me it's been an extraordinarily positive experience. Even the reaction to word of Mao's death was genuine emotion. In comparison, everything that happens at school seems artificial, even false."

She added that she'd found the hours when she wasn't actually working

*This duty/right was practically suppressed in the new (1977) statute of the Chinese Communist Party, and replaced by the duty to oppose anyone who contravenes the three principles: to practice Marxism and not revisionism; to unite and not divide; to be open and frank and not to conspire. Also, the "four great freedoms," including the right of every citizen to promote public debate and to post dazibao, have been deleted from the constitution by the National People's Congress, September–October 1980.

—during meals and in her free time—upsetting. The problem was living in such close quarters, never having a moment to herself. "Even before I opened my eyes in the morning, I'd hear someone asking how I was. . . . In the evening, if I started to read a book I wouldn't get beyond two lines before I was interrupted. *Never* to be alone for a second, to be interrupted the moment you start to do something. . . .

"I couldn't eat. Not because the food was bad. Actually, it's more plentiful and better than at the Institute. But everybody around me was continually spitting, and their noses were always running. It made me feel as if my throat had closed up. What little I ate was not from my wanting to; they made me."

If I go to work in a factory, I'll take a supply of chocolate with me. That's always worked for me when my stomach has refused other food.

Will the less exclusivist Chinese be able, I wonder, to understand that for one of us to work in a factory and to live with workers presents no problem and is a welcome, positive experience—contrary to what it means to their educated people, who for thousands of years have been conditioned to despise manual labor? Will they come to understand that what is hard for us, on the other hand, are the cultural habits that unite all of them, educated and uneducated alike— the non-Western aspects of their life? This is a problem in relations with the Third World, which intellectuals cope with somewhat better, because they are able to think abstractly, than does a European worker or, worse still, a peasant. (I remember a case in which young Italian peasant girls in a camp went for a week without going to the toilet because the toilets had no doors.)

Ceremonies
September 16

When I walked into the classroom on Monday, I found that the desks had been pulled to the middle of the room, arranged so as to form a large table, and the benches set around them. Attached to a sort of placard were "statements of commitment" which the students had written individually—pledges of their political fidelity to the legacy of Chairman Mao. Such declarations are all over the school and even outside, posted like *dazibao.* Each student in my group spoke in turn, commenting on the Party and government communiqués. As always in these "discussions," it's hard to say whether there is something behind the ceremonial and, if so, what. Each speaker gave more or less a résumé of the communiqué; any difference among them lay in nuances of tone and in an emphasis on this or on that detail. Gradually the girls began to sob, and the young men wept, too. The class vice-prefect, Zhou Shiliang, carefully read the communiqué that lists the many leaders who are conducting the funeral ceremonies. Behind the general stupefaction, a furious struggle is going on which is concealed from us. They are all on the qui vive.

The Chinese need to express themselves in visible symbols. They are also unremitting perfectionists—excessive, maniacal. Mourning banners are becoming more and more numerous, more and more beautiful. Walls and doors once red and black or red and white are now carefully covered with inscriptions in white on black or black on white, as if for an extraordinary celebration. And as if for a celebration, white and yellow paper flowers have sprouted everywhere: on gates, walls, trucks, jeeps, the handlebars of bicycles, the fronts of buses. Red flags fill the streets; they look most splendid in long streets lined with two-storied houses; one flag after another juts out on a pole into the sun rays filtering through the plane trees and willows. The city has a different light.

Virtually nothing is left undecorated. Paper flowers are artfully arranged around portraits of the Chairman to alternate with black mourning bands. Two girls came to help us put up flowers in my office. The portrait hangs high, and to reach it they had to drag over a table and even put a chair on that. They climbed up on the table in one jump—no steadying of themselves with their hands. (It is a pleasure to watch young Chinese move. Between gym and military training, they acquire marvelous body control.) On the long blackboard, some of the boys have written "Our great leader, Chairman Mao, will never perish." To make sure the calligraphy would be beautiful, they first traced the characters with a wet rag, then applied chalk. That inscription will always remain my strongest memory of the room. It stayed on the board for months.

On Tuesday, in the early afternoon, the ceremony at the Institute was held. I had eaten lunch at school and, feeling very tired, had dozed off in an armchair in my office, while the Chinese went off for their siesta. At one-thirty, we all went out to the athletic field, where a big portrait of Mao had been framed with paper flowers. Quantities of wreaths were arranged around it, made by the students, professors, and cadres. In a long line, two by two, we walked by the portrait. For a moment, one paused, turned to face it, and bowed three times. (A ritual; on TV I've seen them doing the same in Peking. In the municipal ceremony here, however, there were no bows.) Young guards, with rifles, were on duty here, too —school militia, I was told. Seeing the students all together like this, one recognized the high percentage of the working class—from the work-worn hands, from the faces, which have the ugliness that comes from generations of poverty, although human intelligence lights the eyes. Many wore military uniforms.

The service at the Institute smacked of a mere formality; it was almost false and quite out of tune with the feeling that prevails these days. We all noticed it. The students and, generally, the foreigners who have been working in factories during this period have spoken to us about how completely different the atmosphere there has been in comparison to the schools.

Every evening, on TV, they show again and again heartrending scenes of people crowding to see the body. The despair is almost hysterical, especially among young girls. What does it mean, and why is such a show being made of it? Mao's body is wrapped in a red flag with the hammer and sickle, and lies under a shield of glass. The funeral march (the "Varshavyanka") and the "Internationale" are played continually. No one understands why Mao was not cremated. There is an evident effort to emphasize his internationalist and Communist aspects. This is the counterweight to something *very* heavy in an altogether different direction. A rumor is circulating that the leaders of the Shanghai Revolutionary Committee have been summoned to Peking (but by whom precisely?) because people in Shanghai seem less moved than people in Peking. And, in fact, here people do weep less and make fewer scenes. Which accounts for the repetition and the beefing up of ceremonies, and the invitations—not public, needless to say—to cry harder.

September 19

Things repeated over and over, where variations provide nothing but unneeded emphasis. These days of mourning, in addition to being a rite which in Shanghai is assuming spectral tones, are the visible manifestation of apprehension, almost a sense of desperation, about things to come. Paule Garçon says, *"Quand le père meurt. . . ."* I don't believe it's that simple. But the same acts, the same words, the same filmed reports four and five times, ten and twenty times, and were it possible, it would be a hundred and a thousand times—for a Westerner, this becomes impossible; you can't take it. After the fifth identical repetition, even if it were of the most sublime truth, you collapse. Everything becomes opaque, indistinguishable. This is not ritual for the sake of catharsis or redemption. The perfection that is dreamed of—if not, however, attained—is the annulment of the slightest diversity of whatever kind, the annihilation of the persona. Even for them, all this cannot have a positive significance. Blessed be Shanghai, where it strikes a decidedly false note.

Yesterday, the final ceremony in Peking was shown live on TV throughout the country. It was watched by virtually everyone in China—except for people who were taking part in similar local ceremonies in the major city squares and public parks and neighborhoods. We watched it with the Chinese professors in a hall at the Institute across from my office. At one point, everyone was weeping and sniffling. One half hour later, they had scattered to shop and were chatting lightheartedly as they chose blouses and lengths of cloth.

The Shanghai TV station first showed the Peking ceremony, then telecast the proceedings in the local People's Square. In Peking, the Vice-Secretary of the Party, Wang Hongwen, presided. The immense square and the wide adjacent streets were filled by a dense crowd assembled in orderly ranks. Soldiers and civilians, unit by unit, were lined up in a preestablished, rigid order. The aerial shots made the scene look like an enormous geometrical pattern of closely packed human bodies—squares and rectangles, some lighter, some darker, depending on the colors of jackets and shirts, which were alike in each group. Again they played the "Varshavyanka" and the "Internationale," and at the end, also "The East Is Red." At the center of the platform, in addition to Hua Guofeng and Wang Hongwen, were Ye Jianying and Zhang Chunqiao. Also present: Jiang Qing, Song Qingling, and other top leaders. The funeral address was read by Hua Guofeng. It followed the same general lines as did the joint editorial of *People's Daily, Red Flag,* and *The Liberation Army Daily* except that, on the whole, the tone was more moderate and there was no mention of the quotation from Mao, which figured prominently in the editorial and in other newspaper articles: "Keep to established policy." However, the funeral oration did affirm that "the bourgeoisie is in the Party," and the criticism of Deng Xiaoping will continue, as will the struggle against the "wind from the Right." There is a strong emphasis on proletarian internationalism.

The speech would seem to be the fruit of a compromise. Radio Popolare telephoned me from Milan, and I said that the Chinese are very strong and united, and that all the speculation about internal conflicts is exaggerated. I believe it is fair to say this, but it amounts, I know, to taking a position in favor of the Left. For in fact they are by no means united, unless, perhaps, in their shared anguish over being divided. The expression of grave preoccupation on the face of Wang Hongwen during the ceremony was so eloquent that it seemed deliberately put on—a wordless message. During Hua Guofeng's address, Wang leaned over to scrutinize the sheet of paper in Hua's hand, almost as if he were verifying that the words being read aloud were the words that had been agreed upon, and he did this with a diffident air that looked very much like a hint to the public. Beside him, fat Ye Jianying looked his habitual uncommunicative self—whether it is due to age or to an inveterate habit of hiding his intentions you never know. The faces of Jiang Qing and Zhang Chunqiao were rigid. . . .

The Chinese have the capacity to transmute the most terrible events into theater, annulling the contingency of the moment in which they are experienced. This ceremony had nothing "real" about it; it was an abstract, livid performance of a funeral in which everyone played a prearranged role—a moment that exists outside time and becomes forever fixed in images. In this fashion, a system that seems enclosed in a rigid informational structure reveals itself to the eyes of the world with a shameless openness that has an analogy only in a work of art. Also, it has the potential for shifting abruptly from tragedy to carnival, as in the theater of Shakespeare. There is no one here, from the first to last in the crowd, who does not have his role to play.

City and School
September 21

It's eleven o'clock. The city is quiet, if not entirely asleep. (Of course, we're near the port, which never sleeps.) A veil of dampness and rain. Seen at a distance, from above or in the perspective of its streets, rivers, and canals, Shanghai can be most beautiful. From near at hand, the squalor, the peeling walls, the spittle, the dirt suffocate its beauty. (The skill of the people who run the city lies in their being able to contain this within bounds; things never get to the point of being indecently filthy, to the loss of self-respect that one encounters in so many parts of Asia.)

I've been walking a lot these last days, on Sunday morning and on my free afternoons. I have wandered by the bookstores on Nanjing Road, Fuzhou Road, Sichuan Road, or in the direction of the old city: along the Bund, the broad avenue that parallels the river, with its flower beds and monumental buildings, which is now called Zhongshan (Sun Yat-Sen) Road, then the People's Road, then Jing Ling Road; then northward to Fujian as far as Nanjing. It's like walking around Naples. Life is all in the street. Long rows of two-storied brick and frame houses are set among trees, flags, and colors that the black and white mourning cannot quench. Countless tiny shops sell incomprehensible things, but everything is small, fragmented into tiny packages and packets. The appetizing smells of biscuits and sweet fritters are prevailing odors in this city, together with the aroma of smoked fish. And occupying every vestige of space, the protoproletarian crowd of all ages.

Yesterday, after two days of rain, the sky cleared a bit. It was already dark as I walked north, without crossing the Suzhou River, along Bei Sichuan lu. How lovely it would be if I could be relaxed. The shops, the lights at the ground-floor level filtering through shutters in the patterns of their handsome disintegrating frames, the curtained second floors—an intimacy that is a little dirty and full of bodies. Peking was like this when I lived there. . . . If I could only give myself to enjoying all this. Instead, I am always tense. I receive and reflect back the tension and hardness around me.

In secondhand bookshops I've found old issues of magazines, but none of the *neibu* publications some Italian students have asked for.

The crowds are very human. The Chinese are the most likable people in the world, it's been said, and that is true. But you are kept at arm's length, you are an outsider. You are, fundamentally, an enemy until you establish firsthand contact with someone and maintain it with at least a minimum of continuity; then affection reigns, and the same warmth enfolds you as when you step into the homes of peasants. But in the generic garb of the foreigner you are tolerated only because for the good of China repugnant creatures like you have to be tolerated. It is pointless to pretend that things are otherwise. Toward us taken as a whole there is the subterranean hatred of the poor, of the Third World, for the rich. In point of fact, they see nothing about us except our enviable wealth. The moment of solidarity is the moment when you as an individual appear in a position of weakness—weak because personally you don't seem rich, or you're sick, or you're carrying a heavy burden or are working hard. Or you are an unmarried woman or you've been separated from your family for a long time. This is an unconfessed, urgent seeking for equality.

At school, the professors would rather we talk about our ruling class, they prefer to read a "right thinking" newspaper such as the *Corriere della Sera;* they don't want to hear about our workers as they really are, about either their relative prosperity or their profound wretchedness. For reasons of principle, they cannot say they are enemies of workers, yet they feel ours are remote because it is only their economic situation that they compare with their own.

September 22

Chen came to see me, which was an occasion for maintaining distance and delicacy. True discourse with every Chinese who is close to you proceeds only via allusions. Chen has sensed a lack of ease in my working with Zhang— aggressiveness on my part with regard to his inadequacy as a teacher. She also knows that I have become aware that she has become aware of this. A mirror game. Not one word was said about it. We spoke to each other about it while talking of altogether different things. She gave me to understand that my intervening to correct certain matters of instruction is very acceptable.

I must be careful. They find our violence unbearable. Their gentle, mild eyes are capable of endless, refined maliciousness, but a head-on encounter is out of the question; it would be tantamount to self-annihilation. They are unendurable persuasive enchanters.

September 23

Peaceful mornings and afternoons in my office at school, with Chen, who works at the table opposite. The students have already gone or are leaving for their open-door classes. The program is quite poorly organized. Until the last moment they did not know when they would be leaving, nor to do what. The Institute's directors, especially those in my section, take a negative view of the open-door classes, and to get around that obstacle it was decided to send my class for one month "into society," which is to say, send some of them to help out the clerks in the Friendship Store, and the others to snoop around the handful of Italians who are here to set up an exhibit of sanitation equipment and packaging machinery at Shanghai's Palace of Industrial Exhibitions. Contrary to what we had been given to understand at the beginning of the school year, I was not asked to take part in the meetings held to prepare for this exodus from the Institute, nor was I even told what the students' activities would be. They have not managed to prevent my stating that all this perverts the purpose of the open-door classes, which is to bring higher-level instruction into the workplace. Seven or eight young people will waste their time in the limbo of the Friendship Store; another seven or eight will get in the way of a few Italian technicians, who are terribly busy with preparations for the exhibit and with whom they will exchange a few little conventional remarks, maybe picking up a proverb or two.

They meet them only during work hours and cannot lend a hand in that work since they do not know Italian well enough. What has happened to the close relationship, the reciprocal give-and-take between workers and students that this experiment should be activating? If at least we had programmed these days together so that, the political purpose having been sidestepped, they might be useful for learning the language, if nothing more. But not even this. It seems to me that among the unstated purposes of the Institute's directors there may be the aim to demonstrate that the open-door classes are a waste of time.

Who knows, do the young people submit passively, or do they make some attempt to question or object during the preparatory meetings? The fact that I have been excluded would lead one to suppose that things are not going entirely smoothly. But then, what do I know of their daily life?

I see them seated in order at their desks, each one always at the same desk; there are shifts now and then, but they are organized shifts that involve everybody; one row that was on the left moves over to the right, one row in the middle moves to the side. Most often, a girl sits beside a girl, a boy beside a boy, and there are a few exceptions to this.

They seem asexual, yet dominated by a sexuality that is more than diffused; it is omnipresent. They are not adolescents but children in adult bodies. They blush like Victorian maidens at the slightest reference not even to the erotic, but merely to pregnancy or childbirth. Their relationship to their own bodies one would call infantile, and this is more obviously true of the young men. (But perhaps I am not seeing the same things in the women only because, according to European prejudice, in them such things are more acceptable.) They are continually touching themselves and others—people of the same sex, that is, because it is taboo to touch the opposite sex. In public, they touch face, head, hands. They jostle each other, the way our boys in secondary school do. Or perhaps like seminarians. During class, two boys—among the most intellectually mature—are oblivious of the world around them; they giggle together, elbow each other, whisper with no sign of embarrassment. The one boy gently scratches the other's neck. Girls walk along a path or a street holding hands.

In the hotel restaurant, at dinner, girl students from the Fudan French section come over to my table; their open-door classes consist of working in the Dasha kitchen and serving at table. As an example of open-door schooling it's a compromise, albeit better than the one arranged for my class. They are hesitant but curious as they stand close by the table, determined to make conversation. *"Mon professeur"* is how they address you. They tell you something about themselves, about where they come from and about their families, and they ask endlessly for explanations, having mostly to do with language. They gently keep within safe, circumscribed limits, where the ground is solid beneath their feet. You don't know, nor do they, what there may be beyond those limits. They come from the country or small cities; they are far removed from the working-class vulgarity flaunted by Shanghai waitresses.

Still other men. Visibly excited, his eyes flashing, Tang brought an ex-fellow-student to my office, Wang Li-chun, who had also graduated in 1975. Passing through Shanghai, I had met Wang years before, in the classroom of an Italian teacher. He was the best student in the class (so Chen told me later). Now he is working in an import-export office in Wuhan, and is afraid that he's forgetting his Italian; however, he is still able to express himself pretty well. He told me what Wuhan is like, about his three-day trip on the Yangtze, about his work and what he is reading; he asked me urgently for Italian books, which I promised to get and send to him through Tang. He asked me whether Italians like my translation of *The Dream of the Red Chamber.* It was not the usual polite question; clearly, he recognizes the book's stature and its primary impor-tance as a medium of knowledge of China. When I told him that I was far from satisfied with my translation, he said to me serenely but firmly, "When you go back to Italy, you must do it over." He is also perfectly aware of the worldwide significance of Lu Xun's work.

In both Wang and Tang, as they were together in my office, I felt I was seeing the incarnation of an image familiar to me in literature and in the written pages of history: those who have taken up again and multiplied the revolt of the twenties and rediscovered the idea of freedom. I thought of Mao Zedong's poem *"Changsha."*

When he is alone, Tang has little to say. Unlike the older two, Zhang and Chen, he never chatters about nothing; also, in connection with language he asks sensible questions and not before he has first given the problem some thought; he's quick to grasp answers and explanations. His reserve comes not so much from his being timid as from his having a very strong sense of respect for others and for himself. Never will one hear from his lips any of the hypocritical or foolish talk that is Zhang's current stock-in-trade and seems to be the standard here at the Institute.

Tang now has an outside assignment as interpreter for the Italian techni-cians who are mounting the exhibit. He sleeps at the Dasha. He greets me in the morning as I am getting into my bus and he with the Italians into his, which will take them to the Palace of Industrial Exhibitions. Yesterday I met him in the elevator, and he told me the number of his room. He defies the separatist system.

A Very Great Generation Gap

Usually, when you meet a middle-aged person, either he is reluctant to speak or he utters a few prefabricated banalities, whereupon both parties feel embarrassed; you make an effort to fill in—and to fill up the silence—with some dreadful bromides of your own; it is all very false. On a small scale, this repeats a scene that is so often photographed and is always identical: the Chinese political figure seated in an armchair flanking another armchair in which sits the distinguished foreign guest. A small tea table stands between the two armchairs, and behind the two dignitaries, vigilant in the shadows, stand two interpreters who are taking notes—most often patently conscientious women. The two people who should be conferring wear identical inexpressive smiles. In these circumstances the foreigners, whoever they may be and of whatever race or station, always look alike. Unwittingly, they conform to a conventional model desired by the Chinese—they are no longer ambassadors of barbarian and tributary states but messengers of something preestablished by the rulers of the Middle Kingdom. The imposition is so total that in most cases the victim doesn't become fully aware of it, and he has no means at his disposal to react, much less object. Everything moves forward, controlled by the formal machinery of a most courteous hospitality, and in conformity with the customs of the person who is host. No more, no less. One loses face, literally and totally, without even knowing it—except that a vague sense of unease may gradually penetrate. (If so many political figures, even powerful ones, submit to this, it is because the code in terms of which the rite is carried forward is peculiar to the Middle Kingdom, and without practical consequences beyond its borders. Paradoxically, it entitles, where appropriate, the foreigner to maintain his colonialist stance, to abstain from any genuine communication, and to exploit his adaption to the native—read "barbarian"—rites.)

Today's students, young people under twenty-five, are less manifestly hypocritical than middle-aged people, and seem more trusting. But they seem also very fragile, as if they felt on none too firm ground. City-born youth and the children of cadres are already inclined to cynicism and conformism; the peasants are more naive, without having lost the slightly diffident cunning characteristic of the peasant, which in today's conditions is rather innocuous. One and all are extremely uncultivated. If only this were just a matter of their having few ideas; but their lack of culture is the lack of the means with which to express something universal or general even if only approximately or in a distorted way. The sole generalizing language they know is that of a doctrinaire, formula-ridden ideology, which everyone accepts as a public ritual and which no one recognizes as having any relation whatever to reality. To express what is real there remain slang and dialect, which is limited to and also delimits the specific, the particular, the analysis that is not supported by the possibility of generalizing; that lies beyond them, that is entrusted to others, and is unreal because it belongs to the public ritual sphere.

A similar situation holds true also for sexual morality. Repression is severe. Young men and women live so mixed up together that you ask yourself how they can endure such a rigid pattern of chastity. But if you look closely, what the priests once upon a time would have called "promiscuity" is only a matter of appearance; in fact, the taboos have been internalized. If you ask a girl to translate the sentence

"Yesterday I went out with a boy I know," quite without realizing it she amends it: "Yesterday I went out with a girl I know." Also, homosexual practices and masturbation are very prevalent; even illicit heterosexual relations are rather more numerous than they might seem—bearing in mind the physical obstacles that are created by overcrowding and by collective residences, where inevitably everyone knows everything about everybody, which amounts to a reciprocal control. The network of propaganda against this or that form of behavior—spread group for group, person for person—in itself indicates that such behavior is widespread. However, one learns of it also from stories the foreign students tell and from firsthand confidences. Despite the leaflets warning against masturbation (they adduce arguments and lies worthy of the most contemptible of priests) and the general acceptance of a repressive morality (which corresponds to old customs and is therefore less alien to the political-ideological discourse), it is evident that, as a whole, the people adopt tacit rules of a lower order, so to speak, according to which certain kinds of behavior that are not officially allowed can or cannot be tolerated, or are considered a current practice that one does not wish to judge. These roles conflict with the general centralized precepts; accordingly, they vary from place to place, from city to country, from city to city, and from community to community. Therefore, the foreign observer who ventures to generalize on the basis of a few specific instances does so at his peril.

One must not draw too hasty conclusions. Cases vary enormously. You have only to talk with the students at Fudan, also here in Shanghai, to discover that they have a higher cultural awareness than those at my Institute, and above all a greater political maturity, which here can mean a great deal. And then, the generation between twenty-five and thirty-five, to which Wang and Tang belong, is a different breed, with a scale of values that has no connection with the values of their elders. Things that appear to be insurmountable mountains of difficulties to the older people for them become natural and simple. The young seem alien both to the old rites and to the petty bourgeois dream of the Shanghai of days gone by. This is no longer May 4th, but the Cultural Revolution.

Questions of language. They all have a passion for literature, especially for fiction. Even when students ask me for things to read in Italian, they ask for fiction. Perhaps they are searching for a language apart—one that is neither the official doctrine of politics, ideology, newspapers, nor the particularistic local dialect. The language of fiction is as concrete as the vernacular, but it is also universal. It opens onto the outside world, and is perhaps the one channel where a margin of real communication exists.

September 24

Discussions, visits, meetings. . . . In class last Monday, the twentieth, the students "discussed" for three hours Hua Guofeng's funeral address. As usual, each of them made a résumé of the speech. Even this extremely tedious repetition would not be utterly meaningless, perhaps, if the verbal signs of the dispute now in progress were better known (the substance is already pretty much public knowledge). It's true that the résumés were not identical. Some emphasized these words, others those words, some stressed the struggle, others unity, and so on.

I went with Marcial and Olga, the Peruvians, and a young French couple who have just arrived, to the headquarters of the First Party Congress. It's one of the ritual visits, and I'd made it years ago. The cadre who welcomed us delivered an account of the history of the Party, at the end of which he recalled how, in 1949, Mao had said that to seize power was only a first step, and that the road ahead would be long and harder; the man observed that some leaders (like Liu, Lin, Deng) want to repeat the unfortunate historical phase that had occurred in the Soviet Union, but Mao had weighed the Soviet experience, and the Cultural Revolution was a movement from below to unmask leaders traveling the capitalist road. He even uttered the slogan "act according to established policy," which at this moment is a kind of badge of the Left.

At least in Shanghai, it's likely that among people with at least a little political involvement the terms of the current fight are clear and that they are participating in that fight to one degree or another while all the while what they say to us is empty talk, meaningless except for a thinly veiled allusion.

Steelworks No. 5

This afternoon, in the period scheduled for political study, four workers—three men and one woman—from the Steelworks No. 5 plant came to the Institute. They introduced themselves, giving last and first names. They're members of a group of workers who follow a program of study while continuing to work in the plant. The four of them resembled, almost physically even, our young Italian workers; the girl, especially, was very like some of our militant women workers —rather short, high shoulders, wide, large, very intelligent eyes. When she spoke, she smiled that intense smile of the person who is pursuing an idea. This was in no way silly, as the smiles of Chinese women often are, nor vulgar like those that aren't silly.

The eldest member of the group spoke first. He was a rather tall man, lean, with strong features. The other two were shorter, wore glasses, and might well be student workers.

Their topic was criticism of the "General Program" of Deng Xiaoping in relation to the internal struggle at the factory. From my notes, here is a résumé of the first statement:

"Steelworks No. 5 was founded in 1958. In the last ten years, the political consciousness of the workers has risen steadily. Since the beginning of the

Cultural Revolution, production has doubled and the range of products has multiplied tenfold. At present, workers engaged in the study of Marxism-Leninism number eighteen hundred, about one-tenth of the work force. The plant is producing not only steel but men and ideas [a slogan these workers launched which I've read somewhere]. It trains cadres, it compiles texts. The workers have published ten books, totaling two million words.

"In these days the workers, as heirs of the last wishes of Chairman Mao, are carrying forward the criticism of Deng Xiaoping. Ever since he returned to the government, this man has conducted a methodical attack against Mao's line. The 'General Program for All Work of the [Whole] Party and the [Whole] Country' is now his flag. Last year [1975], in March, Deng had already presented—in the name of the Party—a proposal for the 'four modernizations' [in agriculture, industry, defense, science-and-technology] as a preliminary to the struggle to limit bourgeois rights. The 'four modernizations' were to be achieved in two phases, the first by 1980, the second by 2000. In May, 1975, at a meeting on the development of steel production, as guidelines Deng proposed the 'three directives' [study of the theory of the dictatorship of the proletariat, stability and unity, development of the national economy]. In the following August and September, the 'Some Problems in Speeding Up Industrial Development' directive was formulated. The 'three directives' were proposed as the Party's 'General Program,' and were a reversal of Mao's line. By the late summer, there were many rumors [about the elimination of the Left]; the restoration move peaked in October. Then Deng's collaborators formulated the 'General Program' on the basis of some ten articles Deng himself had written.

"In the General Program, there is no mention of the dictatorship of the proletariat, of 'politics takes command' (the emphasis is all on productive forces), or the results of the Cultural Revolution; the contribution of the masses is undervalued. Deng said that the publication of the General Program was a 'coup.' We say it is a coup against the working class. Later, in reply to criticisms, Deng defended himself, arguing that the General Program contained some inaccuracies. In actuality, it had been carefully pondered and much revised. It was a program of restoration. In many offices, moves were underway to launch an organizational reform even before the Program was circulated."

The woman worker spoke next, describing how Deng's program had been criticized in the factory. Discussions began in April of this year, she said. At first, not everyone understood; some people did not realize why the Program was not all right. So, the general feeling was that they needed to go deeper, to make a detailed analysis of it. The Program is divided into five parts (one of which is introductory), and fifty-six paragraphs; it contains fifty-four quotations from the classics and from Mao. Because of references to socialist theory, it was decided to combine the study of theory with the analysis of the program. Opportunist trends from the past were studied, as was criticism by Marx,

Engels, Lenin, Mao. From the texts thus studied, an anthology was compiled, consisting of forty-one points, and this was distributed to all the workers. As for the quotations Deng had used, the workers had gone back to the texts from which he had taken them, had studied those texts in their entirety, and related them to their historical context in order to reconstruct their original meaning. The works studied, sixteen in all, were by Marx, Engels, Lenin, and Mao.

The criticism, the young woman continued, was developed analytically. In analyzing the Program, eight deformations of Marxism-Leninism were identified: (1) no account is taken of the fact that in Socialist societies the market system, salaried work, and the division of labor continue [that is, no account is taken of the fact that a class society persists]; (2) the quotations Deng cites are removed from their historical context, and their meaning is thus distorted; for example, a quote of Lenin from the NEP (New Economic Policy, 1921) period, which deals with education in general, is used as if Lenin were talking about political education; (3) quotations are incomplete, which amounts to another distortion; (4) arguments from the classics are utilized arbitrarily, for only one aspect is taken into consideration while others that complete the sense of the discourse are omitted; (5) quotations are used as a protective device to mask the substance of the text itself; (6) opponents' terminology is used in order to clothe the text's very different content (that is, the terminology of the left is used, but emptied of meaning); (7) the thinking of the classics is deformed and used for different ends than was intended; (8) ideas from the classics are used only when convenient (for example, one is allowed to understand that Engels dealt only with the struggle between man and nature, without revealing the connection between man and man that lies behind the connection between man and things).

Through this analysis, the young woman continued, it is possible to unmask for the workers the real content of the Program. The function of study groups is to point the way, but the basic force is the mass of workers (that is, the *immediate* function of the groups' study is to raise the consciousness of the mass of workers). It has now been decided that they will study Marxist theory more seriously, and then go back to the criticism of the Program point by point. This criticism must and will be closely linked with the class struggle in the factory, in society at large, and in the international field.

At the end of their statements, the workers answered our questions. They did not monopolize the entire time with *baogao*. Their style was poles apart from that of the school cadres and the routine followed in our political study periods, where they cast about for little dodges whereby they can avoid questions—in a word, not communicate, not respond to anything. This afternoon, we were persistent and even pedantic in asking for clarification. (Chen was acting as interpreter. She had given a rather approximate translation of their opening remarks; now, whenever questions of mine struck her as being traps, she seemed to persist in giving them a polemical tone in translating them.) The workers never replied evasively; they were passionately involved. They believed what they were saying, and they wanted us to understand.

I asked whether they had the text of the Program, and if so, when and how they had obtained it. They answered that the Program was to have been the lead article in a projected new periodical, *The Ideological Front,* that never reached publication. Early in the year, extracts from the essay were already in circulation; then—as *neibu*—the entire text became available. (They spoke frankly about *neibu* material, though they knew that normally one did not even admit the existence of such to foreigners; these were seasoned people and quite accustomed to meeting foreigners. Neither this year, nor during earlier stay and trips in China, had I heard the term used in an official exchange with foreigners. Today, Chen did not translate it.)

Roland, the Frenchman, asked for clarification of foreign policy. In response, they criticized a policy of capitulation vis-à-vis foreigners which, in the economic sphere, was evident in programs to export raw materials and import industrial structures, sometimes including foreign technicians. In order to promote oil exports, Deng was obstructing the modernization of domestic facilities; specifically, he had issued orders to block the conversion to oil of furnaces fueled by other combustibles, such as coal. Revisionism, they went on to say, is an international phenomenon, and the publication of the Program is part of this phenomenon. Also, Deng's economic policy imitates the economic policy of the Soviet Union (material incentives, the theory of productive forces, economism, emphasis on individual management and opposition to collective management, technocracy, management through vertical channels from above to below): a linkup with the interests of capitalism is an objective reality. In the end, the development method the Program proposes would necessarily lead to dependence on foreign capitalism. On the ideological level, this orientation is accompanied by scorn for the workers.

One example: last year, Deng came to visit the Shanghai petrochemical plant where a new chimney had been built in record time—seventy days against a hundred, which is the international standard. Deng asked what they had done to speed up construction; the answer was that they had tripled the eight-hour work shift, so that construction continued uninterruptedly twenty-four hours a day. Whereupon he commented: But that means you spent not seventy working days to do the job but seventy times three, or two hundred and ten instead of a hundred. (That is, Deng's reasoning had reduced success or failure to a mere matter of hours of work, denigrating the workers' sacrifice.)

Pascale, the French comrade, asked how their criticism of the Program is related to daily realities in the factory, to society at large, and to foreign relations. They replied that the criticism is directed against the "integral rectifi-

cation" Deng has proposed. Today, some "new things" exist which were introduced by the Cultural Revolution: worker participation in factory management,
study groups, etc. In industry, the political position of the workers is steadily
growing stronger. According to the revisionists, worker criticism violates "objective" laws. (That is, it does violence to the "objective" laws of a profit-
oriented production system that is presented as being the only one possible, the
only one conforming to the findings and postulates of science. In this system,
workers exist only as producers in the work force. Their "criticism" is a denial
of their own reification.) Therefore, the workers must be put down. This is the
function of rectification. Since Deng has returned to the government, his policy
has been to restore one-man management,* entrust management to a few technicians, and reestablish rigid work rules for the workers (the "iron whip"). The
aim was to deprive the workers of their position as masters. The group has
studied the Mao line and his directives in the matter of industrial management,
going back to Liberation days, and particularly the Constitution of Anshan and
the struggle between the two lines in this area. It was noted that before the
Cultural Revolution the workers were not masters in the factory. One example:
prior to the Cultural Revolution, the supervisor of a casting unit once forced
a worker to make a repair without interrupting the operation; the worker's leg
was crushed, and he lost it. Workers were considered tools in the service of
production, as they are in the capitalist system. In the special-alloys unit, the
composition of the alloys was kept secret even from the workers, who had
simply to carry out passively the technicians' orders. In 1958, during the Great
Leap Forward, Mao made a tour of inspection in Shanghai, and praised the
mobilization of the masses in the steel industry. Then, the Constitution of
Anshan was published (1960), which opposed Soviet-style management and
supported the primacy of the workers. At the 1st Plenum of the IX Central
Committee of the Chinese Communist Party (April 1969), Mao said that management must be in the hands of true Marxist-Leninists and workers. In the old
society, we were like the grass that grows in the street, but Chairman Mao
considered us a treasure. The antiworker line of Liu Shaoqi is now Deng's line.
Let us carry the management of the factory forward in order to make the
principles of the Paris Commune a reality: worker management.

Some other answers to our questions:

The articles written by the workers of Steelworks No. 5 have been published in *People's Daily* and *Red Flag (Hong Qi)*, and they have appeared in
dazibao. (The workers were referring to the criticism leveled by themselves and

---

*One-man management, an import from the Soviets, had already been challenged in the fifties, and
the alternative of a collective leadership was proposed in the Constitution of Anshan (1960). The
trend against single management was widely publicized during the Cultural Revolution. For a
discussion of the substance of the question, see Franz Schurmann, *Ideology and Organization in
Communist China* (University of California Press, 1966).

other study groups against Deng Xiaoping's proposal for the reorganization of industry, which proposal appeared not only in the official press but also in the left-wing press, such as the journal *Study and Criticism*. The articles referred to are perhaps the only statements that go beyond abstractions and deal with the concrete. They refer among other things to "the three whips"—the "steel whip" meaning regulations, the "gold whip" meaning bonuses, and the "foreign whip" meaning the imitation of capitalist technology. Workers in the Shanghai naval shipyards write: "We are in our shipbuilding yards daily, yet what idea, even so, do we have of a Socialist shipyard? What difference is there between our yard and a capitalistic yard? If we do not solve this problem, the theory of productive forces will become lodged in our heads. In the past, when one talked about the factory, it seemed as if it just had to do with producing merchandise; in other words, of producing the material goods and meeting the quota. This was the poison of the theory of productive forces. If that was the way things were, what difference would there be between that factory and a capitalistic factory, apart from a change in ownership? According to Marxism, the capitalistic factory produces not only the material goods but also capitalistic production relationships. . . . With socialism, the factory not only must produce goods but also must establish . . . Socialist production relationships; it must produce intelligence and culture, it must occupy the superstructure, it must continually revolutionize the old production relationships. . . . We must . . . criticize in depth professionalism at the helm, and making profits at the helm. . . . Deng Xiaoping will bandy about the theory of the extinction of the class struggle; for our part, we will talk every day about class struggle. Deng Xiaoping wants management, control, oppression; we expose the boss. Deng Xiaoping wants material incentives; we curtail bourgeois rights. . . .")

The workers *do* have the text of the Program. The Program was not written personally by Deng, but elaborated on the basis of articles by him, and then revised and approved by him. In the course of the criticism, opinions differed. The majority of the workers, basing their position on their own past experience, rejected the Program; a few disagreed with it only in part; others were in favor of strict rules, with duties clearly established and individual responsibility for the labor performed in the single units. This latter position was opposed by some older workers who had had experience with capitalist discipline in the factory. Rules possess a class character; they cannot be the same in every society. The rules in force before the Cultural Revolution tied workers' hands and reduced their spirit of initiative. At the end of their general discussion, a few central points of conflict between Deng and the workers emerged; they were expressed in the form of questions:

Is the enterprise primarily a production unit or the basis of the dictatorship of the proletariat?

Should management be entrusted to the workers or to a few technicians?

Should production be stimulated by material incentives or by letting "politics take command"?

With respect to development, should one rely on one's own resources or tag behind foreigners at a snail's pace?

Is profit the goal of production or is it the satisfaction of the people's needs?

These points of conflict, they added, express the struggle between the two lines as it has been in the past and will be in the future.

Additional bits of information:

After the 2nd Session of the IX Central Committee of the Chinese Communist Party [held August–September, 1970, in Lushan; an open conflict developed between Mao and Zhou Enlai on the one side, and Lin Biao and Chen Boda on the other], the workers began to study Mao's selected works, Lenin's selected works, and—a few of them—*Das Kapital.* The study group was formed in 1974. Workers aren't against modernization, but they believe that there is not only one way to go about it, nor a single line that must be followed. They are against repeating the Soviet line, which goes against the interests of the proletariat. They want to support popular revolutions throughout the world; they do not want to "establish hegemony" over any other country. Workers have an enormous responsibility today. New cadres must be trained; Chairman Mao supported the study groups (in 1974, Jiang Qing came to talk with them).

I was familiar with the things these workers had to say, apart from the anecdotes. I had read them more than once even in their own published writings, where they were set forth in a fuller and more reasoned way than was possible in a conversation lasting only a few hours. And yet I was elated to hear these people speak, as was every one of us who was present. We felt as if we had emerged from a swamp of indifference, inertia, and falseness. It was the first group of Chinese this year who in a formal meeting impressed me as being normal people communicating in a normal way. Let's hope they do come back to talk with us, as they've promised. The experience confirmed what all the foreign students from various provinces have told me: members of study groups are the best people you can meet in China today, because of their cultural and political level and their critical, nondoctrinaire turn of mind. They talk intelligently and persuasively. Often they use the same expressions that at school are juxtaposed in a mechanical blah-blah. The terminology is still prolix, repetitious, and schematic, but the juice is to be found elsewhere, as it is with our Italian metallurgical workers, who express themselves in a mixture of shop and student jargon. Workers everywhere express themselves in inappropriate language they have borrowed indiscriminately here and there—from the culture industry, propaganda slogans, regional vernacular, schoolbooks, political-party and ghetto jargon. And with these clumsy linguistic tools they laboriously discover the road leading from the particular to the general, begin slowly to move beyond their reified situation, and become aware.

The people we heard from today realize what is at stake, and not only in China. Their problem is to master, and to help their fellow workers master, the tools for learning and for interpreting reality that will enable them to make independent rather than manipulated choices. They know that without this any form of democracy is mere talk. They know, too, that they are still very far from their goal—for all that they are a vanguard among the working class, not to mention all their fellow workers and the peasants. They grasp an essential point when they see the connection between their own problems and international problems. They have assimilated enough Mao not to exaggerate (except in a hortatory way) the difference between the workers in capitalist and in Socialist societies. They know that to call the Soviets "social imperialists" is an expedient, that the struggle is against something very present in China itself. It seems to me that their link with working-class issues in Europe—and in the world—is evident when they assert that "according to the revisionists, working-class criticism violates 'objective' laws." The "objective laws" are those of development, investments, markets, profits; they are the same laws that the managerial classes in the West —whether on the right or the left, whether the political representatives of capitalism or of Communist parties in or near power—invoke when they call for a sense of responsibility and for sacrifices. The story about the worker who lost his leg in the cause of production is illuminating. It lies in a tradition that goes back to the founding of the People's Republic and actually much earlier: the glorification of the indiscriminate sacrifice of the individual for the good of the collectivity, which too often is construed as meaning high productivity. To make models out of public heroes who sacrifice themselves in a spirit of insane dedication was a leitmotiv of the Cultural Revolution, which jarred on Western ears, as it should; I preferred to remember Lu Xun's splendid pages against appeals to sacrifice. These appeals, apparently unchallenged, still ring out in schoolbooks and in the official moral code. Workers dare not allow themselves to question official morality on pain of being branded heretics. They limit themselves to relating a well-known story but they reverse the point: the worker loses his leg not because he tries heroically to make the repair without interrupting production but because he is forced to by the supervisor who is a stand-in for the boss owner. The worker refuses to be a thing *the moment he realizes he still has bosses.*

One must be mindful of this in order to understand the anecdote about the chimney, the time required to build it, and Deng. In terms of hours of work, Deng's reasoning discounted too much. But for the workers, to measure success or failure in terms of working hours meant "to despise the workers." Once the worker refuses to be reduced to a component of capital, the fact that more people must work in order to achieve a certain result becomes irrelevant, whereas, whether they work or not, or work more or work less, all must nonetheless be fed and clothed and helped to survive. What mattered to them was that a job had to be finished by a certain date, and it was; they took into account its completion, not the hours worked. It is such an antieconomic way of reasoning as to seem illogical (even though it is the way we usually reason when we are working for ourselves and not to produce merchandise). It is a way of reasoning that recognizes only the category of things that are for use, but no longer merchandise (or the work force as merchandise); mistaken, no doubt, because those same workers maintain that the method of production under socialism is still market-oriented. But the worker who would voluntarily agree to build a system *based on his own labor being a type of merchandise would be a suicide. These young people know that workers in the "real" socialism are not free men, but that their condition as merchandise to be bought and sold is clearer, because it contradicts the principles proclaimed by those who govern. Thus these workers must and can be the bearers of an authentic instance of true Communist liberation within the Socialist reality, and against the party that calls itself Communist. The leaders of this party use the workers as instruments for increasing production and augmenting profits, forgetting that the purpose of communism is not profit, but the liberation of workers from the condition of being* things, *so that they may acquire fully the status of* men. *For this reason the leaders are accused by the young of "despising the workers."*

In the specific conditions that prevail in China, where there is an excess of urban *manpower, the proposal to make more people work for more hours overall in order to complete a job faster is valid on the economic level, and includes a class-based assertion of the worker's right to be protected against parasitism, which reaches quite a high rate in urban nonworker groups. In Western cities where labor is also in oversupply and the rate of unemployment and parasitism high, productivity is also relatively high because of the higher technological level. In the West, the analogous demand to that of Steelworks No. 5—on the practical level and from the Communist point of view—is expressed by the motto "We work less and we all work." In Shanghai, as in Europe, the motto of the bosses, however they may dress, is "Let fewer work to produce more."*

However, there is another possible interpretation of the "twenty-four hours a day" policy of work. It is possible that each worker worked daily more than the eight-hour norm. In this case, we would be back at the glorification of sacrifice, as exemplified in the Daqing oil-field ethic: we don't have the material means, we don't have the technology, but we achieve the same results through greater effort on the part of the workers.

In the construction of that chimney there was, conceivably, a combination of the two solutions: (1) more people were employed and paid; (2) the workers worked overtime without pay. Here we confront two contradictory situations— indeed a mass of contradictions—that tear the whole of Chinese society apart, and the Left in particular. Communist workers cannot fail to reject socialism as the basis for building the economy once their experience has shown them that the Socialist system eliminates neither mercantile production nor the division of intellectual and manual labor nor the reification of the workers. To build on that basis means to reinforce and stabilize it. This is what in China is called the "bourgeois line." However, the extreme poverty of Chinese society makes the struggle for communism impracticable without a prior material basis having been achieved. This was Liu Shaoqi's argument against the Left, and it is Deng's today.

On the other hand, a shift toward the Communist direction and the difficulties in the struggle to achieve communism increase rather than diminish when economic and cultural growth has developed and consolidated itself on assumptions of the market, division of classes, and the division of manual (not so much manual as repetitive and stupid) and intellectual (scientific, creative, organizational) labor. The urgent need for the Communist revolution was expressed by one part of Chinese society which was poor and backward. Mao's thesis—"China is poor and blank"—contends that because bourgeois assumptions have not been realized—within the international context of modern capitalism—in China more than elsewhere the conditions for revolution exist.

The contradiction is complicated because if one postulates an alternative economic system calculated to make the hypothesis of a Communist revolution meaningful one will be calling for the greatest possible expenditure of human effort and at the same time calling into question the very construction that effort is being invested in. The maximum effort and sacrifice, and the rejection of sacrifice as well, are motivated by and based upon the dual situation of workers in a Socialist society—they are both masters and slaves. Today the call is, We will achieve the best results if we rely on our own strengths, if we do without the foreigners and without the scientists and their culture and their technology. This choice makes sense if and insofar as the workers see themselves as "masters" of the factory, of the land, of the machines, and of the entire production process. The other stance—as men we do not want to be sacrificed for the sake of production—has its origin in the workers' having confirmed the fact that they are not the "masters" of the factory, the land, the machines, and the entire production process. "Who gives orders to whom," as the young members of the Beida and Qinghua study group used to put it, becomes the determining question. But in Chinese society, this question remains unanswered. Thus the continual oscillation between consent/sacrifice and countercurrent rebellion.

A Seeming Quiet
Evening, September 24

The new French arrivals are a young husband and wife who belong to the Franco-Chinese Friendship Association. Like many others, they married before leaving for China, to avoid offending the standards of morality that prevail here. They received their appointments directly from the Chinese and not, like the other French, "Bob" and Paule, through a cultural-exchange program. They will be teaching at the Institute. He is quite tall, blond, with a moustache, a typical Marxist-Leninist *gauchiste* of the '68 generation; his field is pedagogy, and he is indeed pedagogical in his behavior toward others, especially toward his wife. She is tiny and looks delicate but is actually strong. I like her; she's surely one who has her eye on what is essential and would be hard to lead astray. Neither of them reads Chinese, and they know almost nothing about China apart from a little propaganda. They have suggested to Uta and me that we join with them and some others (fellow teachers, plus a few French students) to study current events in a group. Uta has said no; she is against breaking the overall unity that has existed so far among all the foreign instructors, comrades or not; she is willing to belong to a study group only if it is open to all, without discrimination. (Years ago, on the fourteenth floor, little antagonistic groups had been formed. Anyone who was not a member of a little group was a loner. And everyone was miserable.) I go along with Uta's view. I gather that the French couple will form their group anyway, with Susan and the students; it's the only way they have to learn something. The students are well informed; it is hard for a program intended to withhold information to function well among people living on a campus.

September 28

Days of peaceful, concentrated work. I spend them mainly in my office at the Institute, preparing study materials for the second semester. I am trying to get as many language exercises as possible from the wretched material that has been provided—old trash that has been dug up who knows where. There is a kind of stingy tendency to hoard; they seem unwilling to throw away anything that has been stored in a closet, almost as if it were clothing or victuals. It would seem an odd concept of knowledge: sheets and scraps of accumulated paper, like the ants' grains of sand or Snoopy's dogbones.

Only Chen is with me. Zhang and Tang are off acting as interpreters for the Italians who are readying the exhibit. Zhang is living with students not far from the exhibit (whether he sleeps over or goes home at night I don't know). Tang is available to the Italians day and night, and accompanies them everywhere. I'd like to go see him in his room, but am afraid of disturbing him; I see how overtired he is in the morning, his eyes red from lack of sleep. He says himself that life is rather hard at the moment, but I do believe that neither he nor Zhang is displeased with what they are doing; it's a change, and they can learn a lot from being interpreters on the job and, in the case of Tang, also chatting in his free hours with different people.

I have finally bought a bicycle, the small-wheeled model, which is the least expensive. (Bicycles cost a lot here—from two to three months' median wages.) I will need mine for only a few months. I won't ride it to school in the morning, as the Germans and John do; I'd have to get up too early, the streets are very crowded at that hour, and also the cold weather will soon be setting in. A new bicycle comes with a license, and one pays a small yearly tax. We can leave our bikes in a little shed at the back of the hotel courtyard, behind where automobiles are parked or repaired. But to get to school, I'd rather take the bus with the Japanese, Susan (who reads), Olga, Aymin (who scowls), the French couple, Felicitas, and Alissa with Maya, hamper, and baby's bottle. . . . Felicitas must make up her mind whether to stay on for at least another year, or to go home now. She had a pact with her mother to wait at least three months before deciding. Now the three months are up. Dagmar prefers the Chinese school to the German, even if the children learn less—especially Felicitas, who doesn't understand Chinese; so far, her mother has not been able to get them to teach it to her. But at least there isn't the competitiveness among the pupils which is typical of the German school, and which Dagmar, who teaches at the secondary level, knows and hates. Dagmar also believes that the spartan life, far removed from consumerism, is good for Felicitas. We are all convinced, and we are trying to persuade the little girl that the opportunity to live for a year in China and go to a Chinese school is so extraordinary for a European of her age that it is worth her making an effort not to let it go by. Felicitas seems disciplined and willing, but she looks miserable.

Aymin, on the other hand, makes a real scene every morning when her mother gets off the bus with Alissa, Susan, and me at the entrance to the old wing of the Institute. She knows that once her mother has left, she will soon be deposited at the nursery school. Not an unusual protest among children, especially when they are very small, but Olga is afraid that in this case there may be something more serious. Aymin gets along well with the other children, but badly with the teachers. She senses that she is different from the others, and it upsets her, even although the difference nets her privileged treatment and much admiration. Aymin *is* beautiful. When our bus stops, people old and young crowd around to look at her and play with her. She pulls back; she wants attention, but she wants to be a prima donna, not a plaything.

Two men take turns driving our bus, and they are the most likable people among all the school personnel that has to do with us. They're excellent drivers, too. One man is thin and a bit wrinkled, although he's under fifty; his manner is that of the old worker who knows what he's about; he's thoughtful and patient, but in his wordless judgments, inflexible. Most of the time he's assigned to one of the Institute cars, which are used when there are only a few of us to transport. (The higher-up cadres, like Lao Bai, also arrive in the morning by car. I have never seen a cadre drive a car himself.) The younger man has a thin bronzed face and body, and is quite aware of how handsome he is. (There are two basic types of Chinese faces, one having an aquiline and the other a flattened nose; Chinese standard dictates that the handsome ones belong to the first category.) This man wears jeans—made in China, ergo the pants legs are a bit wide, but they fit his slim thighs snugly. He has the careless elegance of a French workman in a thirties film, even to a little beret that he wears at a jaunty angle. The professors and cadres, who imagine they're intellectuals, think he's badly dressed in his unbleached linen, and suspect nothing. He's quick and efficient, and understands things in a flash. He and young fellows like Tang get along like equals.

The weather is still mild, but it rains often. When I arrived at the Friend-ship Store to see the students, I was soaking wet. They hurried to meet me affectionately and were so pleased to introduce me around; in presenting the head clerk of his particular section, each would say to me: "This is my teacher." Normally, the clerks treat their foreign customers with disdain, but at this they softened slightly. They make a distinction between tourists and foreigners who are working here.

The students are out of their depth. Perhaps it's not only that they are unaccustomed to clerking but that they know little or nothing about the mer-chandise that is sold in Friendship Stores, which is for foreigners. Many of the things sold here seem neither Chinese nor Western but the fruit of invention; they may be things for "foreign" use as a Chinese would imagine them whose vague notions about the West go back thirty or forty years, and have been only casually updated. And if it is a typically Chinese item, the students don't know how to put themselves in their customer's place when he, in turn, needs explana-tions. For the rest, they react to this artificial ambience like healthy people.

The true open-door school must be an excellent thing, I think, if even this limbo turns out to be somehow useful. Their years notwithstanding, the students are youthful, adolescent—I'm unable to find the right word. They seem to have been brought up outside this world—perhaps like girls in convents once upon a time. And yet this young man has been a soldier, this young woman has led an agricultural brigade. . . . The most uninhibited are the city-born students, especially the daughters of cadre families. It could be that I don't see them right; I belong to a world that has lost the measure of peasant reality. (My friends in Emilia who farm their own fields are not, in this sense, peasants.)

In the evenings, the young foreigners play the guitar and sing old folk songs, or they listen to today's music on their cassettes—and this is the moment when I become aware of distance; I see myself as a woman who belongs to the era of their mothers, that period of prehistory when songs, serious music, light music, opera were separate and distinct and endured. . . . John plays his flute, alone in his room. Only Makita sits silently, evening after evening, in the TV room and for the nth time watches the funeral ceremonies and the mourning.

The mourning does go on; the ceremony on the eighteenth did not mark the end of it, and no one knows when it will stop. The black bands on everyone's sleeve seem permanent, something it would be an offense to remove.

Letters from Italy are slow in coming, and arrive in sheaves. It happens with everyone. When letters reach us, they have been opened and read, as are the letters we send. Once in a while, somebody protests. I don't. They would deny it, and there would be an argument as tiresome as it would be useless.

October 1, National Day, will be celebrated, but in a minor key. It's one way to put an end to this interminable mourning. Festivities will be decentralized, and held in local meeting places and city parks. We will not be on hand, since they have organized for us a trip to Nanjing for Friday and Saturday, which are the holidays.

I continue with my day-in-day-out routine. Three days a week I come back to the hotel at eleven-thirty. I wait for the bus, which has already gone by to pick up the babies at the nursery school and colleagues who work in the new section of the Institute. Outside the tiny porter's booth by the gate, a fat woman is generally sitting on a little chair; she invites me to sit down either on another chair or on one of the small benches along the wall by her door. The porters' "lodge" is both office and home; they prepare their food there, cooking up sauces in little pots, and they answer the Institute telephone. By the outer gate are some mailboxes, carefully locked. I don't know, and I've never asked, who has the right to have a mailbox. There are not enough for the students, or even for all the professors, but I have seen students open them and take out personal letters and instantly open and read them. During the hottest days of summer, when even the shade from the trees brought little relief, the woman used to let water flow from a rubber hose into a basin to bathe her feet. Every once in a while she would pour the water out and let it run over the ground. This woman and two porters, an elderly and a younger man, chatter with the hypervivacity that is characteristic of Shanghai people. Students and people who work at the Institute stop by the door or go inside for a moment, as one does in a country store. "It's coming! It's coming!" is my usual warning. Olga boards the bus, too, and Susan, who often waits apart on the avenue, chatting with some student or with her very private acquaintances. Back seats are always occupied by the Japanese and Maya's little stroller is stashed beside the driver. Off we go, rolling briskly along the outer boulevard, following the railway tracks as far as the square in front of Hong Kou Park. This square is the terminal for various bus services, and in the morning, there are endless lines of waiting people; in my early days here, I mistook them for a rally or a demonstration. Then along tree-shaded avenues, long walls, behind them, low peeling red-brick houses and laundry hung out to dry, then the canal—it's like an impoverished southern Amsterdam. Or sometimes, when there's not too much confusion, we go via Sichuan Road; it depends on the driver's mood.

These days, I lunch alone in the hotel restaurant; the others either have eaten at school or cook for themselves. After a short rest, I take a quick turn on my bicycle if it's not raining, and then set to compiling reading materials and exercises.

Three days a week I am at the Institute until four-thirty. I could go back to the hotel for lunch, or take advantage of a special mess for foreign instructors, but I insist on going with my bowl to the Chinese mess to fetch my meal. You go down a flight of stairs, on the walls of which are old Russian inscriptions now somewhat faded, and you make your way along corridors that wind around the outside courtyards; at first, I felt as if I were in a labyrinth. The wide windows, with lunettes, bring Yanan to mind, sometimes a convent. All objects and even the walls look as if they had long been abandoned; out in the courtyards, piles of rubbish stand among rachitic trees. Here and there you come upon a length of wall that has been repainted, and your impression is that some impulse of goodwill must have been interrupted. Along the way, blackboards and bulletin boards bear messages relative to daily life; these everybody reads; they are not slogans. The characters are always skillfully drawn. At one corner, you come to a closed door: "July Twenty-first University." It had been one of the workers' universities which were—or sections of which were—established in the schools. There is nothing behind that door now, but perhaps for appearance's sake the name must remain. Opposite are some parallel bars, likewise abandoned and now used by no one. On the other hand, along the ground-floor corridors and in the courtyards you often come upon boys playing shuttlecock. Bicycles lean against the walls at corners. You walk through the dark student mess hall, and come to a large room whose white walls look gray, as does even the light, which, come rain or come shine, sifts faintly through the dusty panes of big windows placed high up close to the ceiling. And the slogans, ideograms painted on or attached to the walls, seem gray and forgotten, too, although they were recently touched up for the mourning period.

Why I can't say, but I enjoy moving about among the scenery of this stage in a theater of an all-too-real crowd. Zhang is always the first to return with his bowl filled. When a person's turn comes, each can take two helpings, and friends share or swap in order to avoid standing in line. (Before the Cultural Revolution, professors did not queue up but took their meals apart.) The food is becoming less good and, above all, not always quite sufficient. I can't fill up on rice as the Chinese do, and I'd be ashamed to eat a double portion of whatever other food is served—that no one does. On my part it is an exercise in I don't know what idiotic virtue. Also, I am unable to drink the water, which here at the Institute is nauseating even when masked with tea or Nescafé. To avoid offending my colleagues, I pretend not to be thirsty. Some days it is impossible to wash one's bowl at the sink underneath the stairwell because it is clogged with food scraps and the water doesn't run off; luckily, it's half dark there, and one tries not to look. So I go with Chen to the men's room on our floor; no one pays any attention, and at this time of day it's not used.

After that, Chen goes off to nap, as most do. The midday sleep is a custom throughout China. (Tang rejects the habit, and makes a show of looking down on it.) I work, and stretch out in an armchair only when I'm very tired. First, I draw the faded old light-blue damasked cotton curtains that are strung on a string in front of the big windows by our desks. The silence is almost perfect, for the noise of traffic is far away, and I can rest until the public address system comes on full blast to awaken everybody at half past one.

In the evening, after dinner at the hotel, we almost always have coffee (Nescafé sent from home) in one or another of our rooms on the fourteenth floor, or on the fifth, where, for lack of rooms, Pascale and Roland have been put up. In this land of tea, to insist on drinking coffee is an affirmation of our cultural identity.

The teachers who don't know Chinese asked to be given some lessons. They have them now once a week, but are not at all satisfied with them; people who intend to study seriously, like Dagmar, actually do so by themselves; the weekly lesson is pro forma, just a way of showing that the foreigner's request has not been denied. At the Institute, they prefer that we not understand Chinese—that way, it's easier to hide things from us. They place their peace of mind before the optimum performance a professor can offer in teaching his own language when he also knows the language of his students. For my part, I asked to be helped in practicing how to read the cursive script, which is the one commonly used when writing by hand. An even more hypocritical solution has been found. Yesterday, an elderly professor came, for one time only, to explain a little about the techniques of abbreviations for my benefit. His advice—useful enough—was that I get some little manuals for myself, but these I could have found on my own in a bookshop.

My meeting with him was interesting, nonetheless. For a moment I felt as if I had returned to the old days in Peking. As he was explaining how one proceeds from the original complex character to simpler forms, and how these are then embellished with new elements, I happened spontaneously to remark how important this process is also in understanding the structure of the Chinese language, in which an analogous movement continually occurs in the phrase, sentence, locution—indeed in the entire discourse. The observation would have fallen on deaf ears had I made it to one of my colleagues, not to mention the students. The old man, however, understood immediately, even despite my imperfect Chinese. And I liked how he muttered when he noticed essential commas missing and characters incorrectly written in the student notebooks I showed him.

What relationship do scholarly people like this man have with the vast night school they wander wearily about in, dressed in their worn cotton jackets, bowl in hand if they are queueing up at the mess? The works of the ancient Legalists are published, with learned commentaries—full of distortions, it's true, yet not the work of the unlettered; seriously annotated editions of Lu Xun's letters, which up to now had been unpublished. . . . But where are these people, how does one get to meet them? We are permitted to have contact only with the bureaucracy; the night school is not concealed from us only because it can't be, since we have to work in it; the great curtain that is lowered to hide even the workers is only now and then fleetingly raised. What veins run through this country beneath the thin glaze? It is the common will that firmly seals this world against everything external to it; only infrequently is the seal broken by an opposition that can be from the Right or Left, but in either case has identical, reasonable tones and characteristics. That common will may be an artificial product, but it is well nurtured. For example, in the textbooks you read, "He was full of hatred for the enemy." . . . "The enemy forces were so close that you could see their big noses." When you go into a shop, they assume that you don't understand, and say to each other, "Here comes a big nose."

A few days ago, while I was chatting with Chen, I told her a bit about Nazism during the war, and about the concentration camps. She knew nothing about any of this.

It has rained all afternoon. The carillon in the clock tower on the Bund plays "The East Is Red" at six.

I went down to dinner and came back upstairs. Through the window the city, all illuminated, invaded the room and came to meet me. I stood open-mouthed like a child, and then I called Aymin to come look. The Bund, the bridges, the little park, the expanse of houses and palaces, the boats and the ships —hundreds of thousands of tiny lights traced their outlines against an already dark sky; here and there, luminous inscriptions in red and blue. This, after all that white and black.

Thus the period of mourning ended. A great production. By whom, for whom, against whom?

The workers' militia garrisons the city once again.

Nanjing
October 3

We got up at dawn, and left at six-thirty for Nanjing—the French couple, Dagmar and Felicitas, Uta, Makita, Ohara and his wife, John, and I. John had asked to go on his own for three days, to be with English friends who teach at the university in Nanjing. When the rest of us asked permission to make the trip, we made it clear that we wished to go alone, and for two not three days, and in any event, without interfering in any way with John's freedom of movement

—that is, his trip should be considered independent of ours. What happened was exactly the opposite, I think. We got permission easily because a group trip would make it possible to keep tabs on John without their having explicitly to refuse his request. We did not go alone; everything was organized by the Institute, and we had several escorts: John's interpreter, whose family name is Zheng, and an interpreter for the Japanese, and Uta's, from Fudan. The Institute and Fudan paid their expenses, and also for an employee of the Lüxingshe, the travel agency, who met us on arrival and accompanied us around Nanjing.

We went first class, "sitting down"—on long trips, one travels in first- or second-class roomettes. We "experts" are not allowed to travel second class, it seems, unlike foreign students. However, none of us was sure that this time it wasn't a case of Lüxingshe's abusing its power, for it is a powerful organization.

The trip lasted five hours. Trains in China are slow and comfortable, like the old British trains. Attendants are constantly on the move, tidying up, changing the hot water in the thermoses. Apparently the railroads have a plethora of employees. You can buy tea; you watch with interest as an unfamiliar landscape unfolds. The time passed pleasantly. I chatted with John and his interpreter, who comes from a poor family and is the son of the revolution; he's a man of modest education but with a certain sensitive intelligence. John would turn to me now and then to shed light on some philosophical or ideological question, but I consider him a master because his approach to things is positive. Apropos of the false relationship Chinese have with foreigners, John never talked to Zheng in generalities; he always gave him concrete examples of how, on the one hand, they are "servile" toward us—uncritically copying our products—yet how, on the other hand, they are presumptuous because they never question the foreigners who have made and who use those products (about design, specific qualities, uses, purposes) but assume that they can go ahead on their own without any guidance. And they're wrong. John brought up another example, a truck that is being shown now at the industrial exhibit. It was copied, he explained, from a recent European model but will perform less well on Chinese roads than some earlier models do. In order to know this, the Chinese would have to question someone who was both honest and experienced. Zheng put up a kind of semi-ideological, semipsychological defense, which was rather weak. We also discussed the term "bourgeois right," and what it means. Zheng agreed that the Chinese distort the sense of it, but insisted that, precisely for this reason, the Chinese locution is best: "bourgeois rights." Digressions on objective and subjective right (law and a citizen's right, etc.) with Roland chiming in. Zheng had trouble understanding, but in the end he did. The Chinese resist thinking in juridical terms, but can be led to understand single concepts by considering the ethical aspects of single case histories; the method is congenial to their passion for analysis.

The region around the lower Yangtze is among the richest in the country, and in summer is green and smiling. Buildings are of brick; the paddy fields, water buffaloes, and peasants do not betoken poverty and degradation, as so many country areas of water and mud do. It is a fluvial landscape, like the coastal areas in Italy. Here, too, there are boats and vistas and the same expectancy—yet not the same—of coastal plains foretelling the sea. Sand that is nonetheless fertile ground, plane trees growing side by side with pines. And the cassia that perfumes gardens and streets.

As if he had arrived at a vacation resort, John took off in a taxi with his friends—a free man. For us there was the usual Lüxingshe representative, the usual bus, the hotel where they oblige you to sit down to "rest" (which is to say, to waste time), and the speech outlining the already arranged program. You go along with all of it because it does correspond partly to what you have asked for, and you are not overdemanding, and because you want more than anything else a moment of release and rest. But an essential something has been taken away from you.

The dignified beauty of Nanjing, capital of the South, Peking's rival: You move through its streets, attentive and as if in a dream, and you concentrate on forgetting that you aren't *going* but are *being taken;* it is only by walking along a street in your mind that you are able really to see what you are looking at. Nature is happy here—river, hillsides, parks, the strong southern light. Thousands upon thousands of trees have been planted in recent years. Nanjing is Sun Yat-sen's city, where ancient history was translated into the Chinese National Republic. It is the mixture of the traditional and the modernized which that republic aspired to be without knowing how—except, perhaps, in these forms left as a bequest to what came after.

The hotel is agreeable; maybe it was not built by the Russians. At two in the afternoon, we went to the famous bridge over the Yangtze, a glory of the nation, with elevators that rise to the monument's own museum; guides point out every detail to you. It is one of the places where national pride is celebrated, for it is an engineering feat that succeeded despite the inherent problems, the lack of means, the inadequate technology, and the Russian intention to ruin China.

From the parapet, I looked out over a landscape of hills, private houses, industrial buildings, smoking factory stacks, canals and lakes and little bridges, and the green of fields and trees. Nearer at hand, well-designed sculptural gardens. The scene resembles one of those old engravings in which the perspective is from above, and which are dense with details; one finds modern versions in paintings and on posters. Then I looked at the river—slow, immense, yellow from the burden of sand it bears. Looking from so far up, I grew dizzy. In the distance, the clay along the broad riverbank is cracked; little waves lie in motionless curls, as if on a very calm sea. Infinite distance, and power. . . .

We were trundled by bus from one part of the city to another. As always when you are carried about like that, you cannot form an exact idea of the topography, which is so important if you are to take possession of a place, and which is so hard to reconstruct after the fact. As I habitually do when arriving somewhere for the first time, I had looked for a map. The Lüxingshe fellow told me there was none. A bit later, while we were waiting to go out, I saw a map on display in the hotel shop; summary indeed, but all the same somewhat more detailed than the one in the Nagel guidebook. I asked a clerk for it, and she answered, "Yes, there is one, I'll go get it," and walked toward the shelves behind the sales counter on the other side of the lobby. But her fellow clerks began to confabulate with the Lüxingshe man, then said something to her (I was too far away to hear what); the girl, minus map, tried to slip away. I called her back and asked for a pack of cigarettes. That she gave me, looking positively terrified. When I got back to Shanghai, I found that same topographical map for sale in bookshops where anyone could buy it. It's true, Nanjing is the headquarters of an important military district that has Shanghai as well under its control. But its inhabitants seem not to possess a sufficiently independent judgment to decide for themselves what can reasonably be an item of military secrecy.

We were taken to Yu Hua Tai, the Terrace of the Rain of Flowers Hill. The hill is famous for its monasteries and mineral waters. What our escort said to us was simply, "Now we're going to a place dedicated to revolutionary martyrs." Lüxingshe escorts have a tendency to consider, let's say, unimportant such things as the names and locations of the places one visits—indeed, even the places themselves, and one's visit to them, are unimportant. If they could, they would replace an actual visit with a highly edifying *baogao* that required no one to stir from the hotel. There are exceptions, naturally. However, the general tendency is to consider the words that accompany and comment on a given thing more important than the thing itself; and of all words, those that are politically and morally instructive are self-evidently more important than those that are descriptive. The function of instruction is to generalize; the concrete object and actual place are pretexts for the sermon. Specific explanations are given only if they are asked for, and then as though it were a boring extra chore. (When the thing in question does not lend itself to political instruction, it is dealt with in a hedonistic vein. The language of the presentation is erudite, more pertinent, and it expatiates and expands until it fills up the space all by itself.)

In a park of almost Syracusan beauty, four pavilions enclose a courtyard. They stand on the site where the Kuomintang used to execute Communists. More than one hundred thousand revolutionaries were shot here in a period of twenty-two years, between 1927 and 1949. The old building—all four pavilions —may once have been a monastery or private dwelling; now it is a museum dedicated to the memory of the martyrs. Photographs line the walls; they are enlargements of old snapshots of the Communists who were jailed and killed here; most look young, even very young. The photographs are accompanied by brief biographies, reproductions of letters or poems written by the martyrs, sometimes by enlarged copies of newspaper articles or documents. The installation has been done soberly and with care. People—and how many there are—who stroll about the park in a relaxed holiday mood also come into the museum and linger before these photos. (However, for more than two hours attention was focused on our presence.)

I looked at those faces, somewhat paled out and blurred from being enlarged, the wide, gentle, melancholy eyes, the hairstyles of the twenties. I read the boys' poems; the dominant theme was an ideal, sacrifice, the future—a future it was all the more necessary that they invoke because it was unreal. Names that have never been heard of, the story of a defeat. Irrecoverable time. This is not the revolution, but suffering and still more suffering. Is this, my anguish, an attempt to recover something lost? A lament, like that for the refugees from Spain who crossed over the passes in the Pyrenees at the end of the Civil War, and further back to the Paris Commune and the executions of Communards under the Wall of the Federals in Père Lachaise Cemetery.

However, here the revolution has prevailed. . . . No, the relationship between the sacrifice made then and the present result cannot be shown; the distance is abyssal. The future that was being prefigured then does not exist now; the history of then was and meant something different. (Gramsci's life sometimes appears in this light, but less sharply because he was a thinker, and his ideas live.*) The future as the locus of our having to be and the happiness of others, of the fulfillment of our hopes, is merely the illusory transfer of an impossible anticipation of the kingdom of heaven into a temporal dimension. There is no God outside us who conjoins past and future, and the present is not a point of passage. Action that produces results which are both consistent with our intentions and unforeseeable is compatible only with life and awareness, with the winning of the results; it is not compatible with self-sacrifice, because the continuance of one's own interrupted consciousness in others is an illusion. There is no way of salvaging eternity; and if eternity exists it is in the present of the self. The genuine passion to recall the past and to strain toward the future serve as subjective motivations. But there are no words that can unite us today with these murdered young men, only our distress and grief.

Inciting people to self-sacrifice is the greatest of all crimes. Lu Xun knew this very well, for he lived in the midst of all that bloodshed.

I needed to stand silently in the company of those faces, and to be alone

---

*Antonio Gramsci (1891–1937) was an eminent Italian intellectual noted for his literary, philosophical, and political views. He was a co-founder of the Italian Communist party. Imprisoned in 1926 by the Fascists, he died in 1937 while serving a twenty-year sentence. In Italy, his *Letters from Prison* are read even in the schools.

to read those old pieces of paper. But John being unavailable, Zheng turned to taking care of me. He talked and he talked, he translated every last word, he urged me to look at this and to look at that. I did everything I could to escape from him. I hated him. On the way out, they gave us each a little red booklet with biographies and a few words of the less obscure dead.

This evening the by now classic scene was played, in which the foreigners, confined to their hotel, attempt to get out and go for a walk by themselves. They plot it as children would: everybody is to go back to his room, then to sneak out, a few at a time, and give the slip to the custodians. But there's nothing for it; the guardians know what their charges hanker after, they sniff something afoot, and they forestall it. (This evening it was Uta's interpreter who got the assignment to accompany us—being the youngest, she has all the boring jobs unloaded on her.) And so the vision of strolling freely about vanishes. Presently, you no longer know what on earth you're doing out in the street, or where you're going, but on you walk, almost out of stubbornness.

Tonight, we had also to reject the feeling of guilt the girl would have liked to inflict on us, telling us, with a long-suffering air, about how she was positively sick from fatigue, how the night before she'd not slept a wink. . . . In any event, we left the wide avenues behind, and walked along small dark hidden streets (there was a moon), where it was a little like being in the country—people were sitting in their doorways or outside their houses, chickens meandered about. But none of us was relaxed, because it took real effort to ignore the resistance of our unofficial escort, who was full of apprehensions and reluctant to let us draw near even so modest a reality.

This particular interpreter, in all her sleeping beauty, takes Uta's hands in her own soft hands and stares into her eyes; Uta is her possession, exclusively hers. Added to the already abnormal relationship between the interpreter and the foreign woman she has in charge, there is a hint of the convent, of a jesuitical, overly sweet femininity. Anyone who does not come from a Catholic country does not readily understand that mandarin repression in China in recent centuries was a tremendous Counter-Reformation.

Dagmar and Uta don't understand why I am repelled by this girl and also do not trust her. "She's a child," Uta says. Or "They feel a need for tenderness, too." Uta comes from a country in which middle-class iconoclasm has reached proportions of total destructiveness. To this—the social equivalent of dioxin, job-related cancer, Vietnam, concentration camps, the bestial solitude and the ghettoization of much of the human race—the rebellious sixties strove to oppose tenderness, group and homosexual sensuality, the spontaneity of children and of the mentally ill, nonresistance, natural dirt, the vagabond life, and communes. Uta and Dagmar, who have shared in this revolt against the violence endemic in hypercapitalist societies, of which they themselves are products, have little under-standing of—indeed, they misconstrue—the jesuitical-mandarin and prebour-geois manifestations of repression here, together with all the hypocrisy that accom-panies it. For millions of Uta's and Dagmar's sisters and brothers, this difficulty has led to gigantic equivocations with respect to the Third World, and especially Asia, and in Asia, especially China.

Following the collapse of the Soviet-style model of progress that Europe's various Communist parties once accepted, progressivism in Europe has been replaced by political orientations searching for bygone lost paradises; they have indulged in an idealization and senseless exaltation of "the people," or in a Middle Ages they arbitrarily conceived to have been the realm of the "natural" (as opposed to bourgeois artificiality or a machine civilization) and the "cor-poreal" (as opposed to the rational). This misconception, which has a very strong ideological component, has been and is entertained by many young people and by the women's movement, too, out of simple ignorance. The Middle Ages did indeed impose its own totalizing rationality, and in terms far more repressive than the bourgeoisie later; it was the period when the great rationalist systems were fashioned, like that of Thomas Aquinas, before which all of the enlightenment pales. And if we want to move beyond bourgeois civilization into space rather than into time, in China we find in the Confucian system—and even more especially in the Neo-Confucianism elaborated by the great Chinese "scholastic" Zhu Xi, who was almost a contemporary of Aquinas—such a formidable tyranny of reason that it led one eighteenth-century scholarly opponent to write: "He who stands above admonishes him who stands below in the name of reason; the elder ad-monishes the younger in the name of reason; the noble admonishes the commoner in the name of reason. . . . They who stand below—the young man, the commoner —can deny the principle of reason, but even if they are in the right this is considered immoral. As a consequence, people of low estate cannot manifest their feelings and their desires to those of high estate; and these feelings and desires are the same for all. He who stands above binds the laws with the principle of reason, and the misdeeds of every individual of lower estate are multiplied into infinity. When a man dies at the hands of justice, there is still one who will feel compassion for him, but who will feel compassion for all those who have died at the hands of the principle of reason?"*

Perhaps again out of ignorance, many young people do not dream that they are fleeing to prebourgeois and extra-European earthly paradises (Typee, *not the Enlightenment's* Lettres Persanes), *the way the romantics did in the days of an earlier restoration. Demonstrably, what follows on a defeated revolution is a restoration, and that is what is running its course today, in various forms, through-*

*From "Elucidations of the Meanings of Words in Mencius" ("Meng Zi ziyi shuzheng"), by Dai Zhen.

out the world: a reaction against the rebellions of the sixties. It is senseless stubbornly to deny the defeat, but one would be well advised not to confuse restoration with a new rebellion of the oppressed; that rebellion will be possible, perhaps inevitable, in the future.

The Chinese Revolution—Yanan, the Cultural Revolution—disregarded or rejected the Soviet-progressivist model which European Communists did adopt. But where that rejection amounted to revolution was in the simultaneous attack on beliefs, traditions, morality, and deities of the people and on their temples. The educated Chinese governing class, agnostic and rationalist, did not believe in those deities. That in itself was no reason for the revolutionaries to adopt them. Mao Zedong never stated that the temples should not be destroyed; he said that the people must advance to the point of destroying them by themselves.

There is a difference between deities and reason. Reason is not a deity to be denied, for, were both gods and reason lost, nothing would be left to the people. It is a matter, rather, of discerning what *reason.*

Many Communist party leaders and old Chinese intellectuals extol the old habits, superstitions, morality, patriarchal prejudices, and all the folklore as authentic realities of the people; their preservation is fostered and they are presented to the outside world as the country's authentic treasures. Populist romantics in Europe who believe they have found the alternative where socialism converges with acupuncture, a macrobiotic diet, and even Tibetan Buddhism and magic practices do not know that that Socialist China is the same China that does not *reject the Soviet model; in that China, progressivism marches side by side with Socialist realism and national populism. To the people their traditions, to the intellectuals their academies, and to those who govern and who direct the* Real-politik, *science and skepticism. Everything comes together and is blended in the capacious belly of nationalism.*

So, inside the "new China" is there not still the "old China"? Surely it would be impossible for the Chinese not to be Chinese. But where China is its truest self, traditions are broken and beauty is profaned; and because everyday life is often inhumanly hard, there is no place for any populist idyll in social relations or in the various forms of culture.

There is complicity on the part of all leaders, up to and including the highest and excluding not one of them, in covering reality over with the colors of the idyll —this is carried to the point of the ridiculous with foreigners—and in presenting that idyll as the one and only truth; those who show they do not believe in it are considered not to be "friends of China." On this score, Chinese Communists stopped being revolutionaries long ago.

You travel eastward through this city of trees to reach the tomb of Sun Yat-sen on the Zijin Shan, the Purple and Gold Mountains, the culminating point of the triumph of the the first Chinese republic. You climb the hill via a double flight of white steps between white and blue buildings—white walls, light-blue majolica roofs—these being the colors of the Kuomintang. They are like Confucian temples, cold and bare, Chinese without chinoiserie; on the inside, an invisible, well-assimilated European influence. The military severity is appropriate for celebrating the man who tried, unsuccessfully, to build revolutionary armies in regular army garb.

The rich earth of an ancient erstwhile riverbed is covered with a wealth of vegetation; pagodas and temples stand among pine groves. You pass by the temples, for they rarely take you into them; they don't want to show them to you empty of the Buddha statues, which the Cultural Revolution destroyed. A pavilion library of brick and stone, with a barrel vault, has a strength almost equal to that of a Roman building, as is true of some Ming construction.

You reach the Xiao Ling, the mausoleum of the emperor Tai Zu, founder of the Ming dynasty, by walking the length of a long road flanked by the stone statues of animals and men. (The Ming tombs in Peking are of a later date.) The road is paved, grass grows between the stones, and a southern light lies over all. To one side, a stone arch, and beyond that another pathway, narrow and also paved, between grass and low trees, which leads who knows where out into the countryside where you can feel the nearness of water. The countryside is reminiscent of that surrounding Rome: the same streets of stone, the same luminescent landscape, with arches and the monumental ruins of a great empire.

Nanjing was also the capital of the Tai Ping. There is a Tai Ping museum housed in what was once the residence of one of the four "princes," the leaders of the Tai Ping Rebellion. The historical documentation is very rich and is carefully displayed as an educational exhibit. The subject is among those most intensively studied in the last twenty-five years. After earlier polemics, some prominent individuals—like the great Tai Ping general Li Xiucheng—had literally vanished, although they were by no means minor figures.* The past is being revised and corrected, as is the present. Some men seem to exist under a kind of curse. First, they are erased by their enemies, then they are exploited for ends all unknown to them, and then once again erased. . . .

*Li Xiucheng was one of the greatest generals of the Tai Ping Rebellion in its late period. After the fall of Nanjing, in July, 1864, he gave his own horse to Hong Fu, successor to the emperor Hong Xiuquan; he was unable to flee quickly, and was captured by the imperial troops of Zeng Guofan. The latter, before having Li executed, had him write his autobiography, which is an important source for the history of the movement and has been handed down to us in a version perhaps partly adulterated by Zeng Guofan.

In 1963–65, in both specialized and general readership magazines, as well as in the papers, there was a prolonged, fierce discussion about the proper evaluation of this man, who had been considered a hero until then. The dispute, which became increasingly heated, was part of a wider debate over peasant wars and revolts. It is also a typical example of how quite different areas—historiography, ideology, and current politics—are superimposed on controversies concerned with history.

As I was about to board the train for the return trip on Saturday afternoon, I saw John sitting on a bench. He had asked to stay in Nanjing through Sunday. Zheng came over and made me a little speech in confidence: John had wanted to stay in Nanjing for three days, but he had said so too late, when he was already in Nanjing, and nothing could be done to change the date of his travel permit since that could be taken care of only in Shanghai, his place of residence; however, John has not understood this and is annoyed. "John has great respect for you, he listens to you. You should talk to him, explain to him that there was nothing intentional about it, just a misunderstanding. . . ." And instead of a little holy picture, Zheng produced a small photo of Mao seated at a desk. "You like it?" he asked, and he gave it to me.

On the train, I sat beside John, partly because I was curious to know what had happened, and partly because I was tired of the French couple's chatter, however agreeable. John was gloomy and indignant—not with his interpreter but with the Lüxingshe people. He told me in minute detail about all the obstacles and petty sabotage that were set in motion to prevent his staying with his friends. As for the three-day permit, he had requested it in Shanghai even before the rest of us got in on the trip. I knew this was so, but I made a point of asking whether there could have been a misunderstanding. He gave me all the particulars. Everything had been explained clearly, and more than once; there could have been no confusion. You can believe there's been a misunderstanding once, twice, he added bitterly, but then you discover that it's a tactic, and you lose all trust. From long experience I know that he's absolutely right. John has the strength not to let himself be totally immersed in the ambiguity of the contest; he keeps his sense of who he is, and he finds it natural—although, as he knows, futile—to continue to defend his "basic human rights." He had talked to me the day before about the situation of the few foreign teachers in Nanjing—two English people, two French, one Peruvian—which is psychologically difficult because they are utterly isolated. The Peruvian speaks only Spanish and is unable to communicate with anyone; he has been reduced to alcoholism and may come to a bad end.

We talked on and on. I felt rather like the elderly aunt who, with all her experience now behind her, can suffer empathetically but without too great a personal involvement. I did make a point of saying to him that one must remain as detached as possible, must keep as integrated with Europe as possible. It's the only way one can manage to understand many things. The alternative would be a confrontation between an individual, on the one hand, and on the other, an enormous force that can crush with its mere physical weight.

Like many people in their thirties today, John does not believe in glorious destinies and has no expectations of an ideal future. Accordingly, all his values are invested in and related to daily experience. I formulated for him something on this point. "One cannot curtail one's own life in the name of history," I said to him. "That's how it is."

I was trying, with this advice, to help John be less vulnerable. I saw that he was truly disheartened. Zheng's attempt to make use of me had come to nothing, also thanks to John's resoluteness.

While the others dozed, we talked on, but about other things. John told about how, after finishing university, he had worked in Italy, and about some extraordinary places he knows in the hills in Piedmont. He's lived in Paris, too, and doesn't like it. He comes from Bradford, in the old industrial north of England, and you can sense that he loves it. But he's disgusted, too. In the last local elections in Bradford, he told me, the extremist Neo-Fascist party won 40 percent of the votes, the Labour party 38 percent. It's because of corruption among the Labour people, he says; those who vote for the extreme Right are disinherited protesters, who are growing in number because of the economic crisis. And there's no leftist element capable of guiding them.

Toward the end of the trip, Zheng, deeming that my persuasive mission must have been accomplished, came to sit with us. He launched into some involved, allusive talk about how we foreigners are set apart and "protected." There followed a spate of philological bickering with John, who corrected him: "Not 'protected.' 'Controlled.' "

"We prefer to say 'protected,' " Zheng insisted.

I intervened, using Chinese terms of reference: anti-individualism, pro-collectivism. (John kept quiet, wordlessly hostile.) I said to Zheng that one cannot submit to a collective society until one is by full right a member of it. I used his terminology, and he understood; he didn't concur, but neither did he offer any objection.

Then John tried to explain what elementary personal freedom is. Two worlds were set one against the other, as in a theorem.

I don't know whether right goes to the stronger, but certainly John was the stronger: a foreigner, isolated and powerless, who was speaking with complete sincerity. The other man—who represented the government of a great country, who was on his own home ground, and in a position of some power—was forced into being insincere and contradicting himself continually.

I have seen a documentary on Lu Xun—quite good, except that a few of those dreadful oil portraits were slipped in now and then. The biography follows the current outline that is found in cartoons and in textbooks. But the views of places—Shaoxing, Peking, Shanghai—are moving, and so are the old maps and the yellowed faces. Some newsreel clips are used, but they're brief. (It's bruited about that when Joris Ivens, the great filmmaker, was here, he gave people some pointers on how to go about making a documentary.) There are shots of May

Fourth demonstrations, young girls, boys in long coats, banners, flags. Also, the expedition to the north, soldiers on horseback, bundled up as in the First World War. The accompanying sound track plays the "Frère Jacques" refrain, which to Chinese ears has a revolutionary ring, since Zhou Enlai used it as a political song.

The images—the still photographs, locales, book covers, lights—make one think of Latin America or Italy or Greece in the nineteenth century. Before, out of ignorance about the culture of poor peoples other than Chinese, and because of the accelerated pace of history that in China makes one jump from the collapsing empire to the Socialist revolution, I had overlooked this affinity in reconstructing the figure of Lu Xun, and now it seems to me of the greatest importance.

People are saying that the Left has got the upper hand. That may be. But it's headed for trouble. Without Mao's prestige to back them up, the leftists won't make it. Their appeals are lucid and courageous. But more is involved than winning a political battle. They face an obstacle that will endure for a long time, a structural aspect of society that is reflected all the time, everywhere, and in every individual. You see it constantly in daily life, especially in a conservative school like ours. The revolutionary movement does not have its own independent channels.

5.

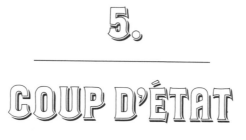

COUP D'ÉTAT

A Film
October 8

Two days ago, Wednesday afternoon, I finally got to see *Juelie* (*"Breakdown"*), the film I've heard so much talk about. It was shown at the Institute, in an auditorium that is a whole building in itself; it has a circular flower bed in front, but also, on seemingly permanent display, piles of pipes, bricks, and other construction materials. The interior is dimly lighted by weak hanging lamps and unshaded neon tubes. Rough cement floor, wooden benches, which like the ceiling beams are brown. You have almost to fight your way into the hall for, vast as it is, it is always jammed, not just with our students but with children from nearby schools, their families, little old women, babies, people from the neighborhood. Luckily, seats are numbered. There was much shouting back and forth before the show begins, and admonitions were flashed on the screen: "No Smoking . . . Observe Rules of Hygiene [which is to say, No Littering] . . . Quiet! [whereupon there is a twilight picture of flowing water, with a tree and moon] . . . Do Not Leave Personal Belongings." I like the place. The architecture, the way in which here the school is serving the neighborhood, the mixed makeup of the audience demonstrate that a relatively recent and drastic change in the use of things and in relations among people is already a tradition by now difficult to uproot, whatever the political evolution may be. But it is extremely rare for cadres of a certain importance to attend these showings.

    Breakdown is perhaps the best film produced here in recent years. The action is based on real events that took place in 1958–59, but the themes are current and directly concern the "revolution in education." It's the story of the founding and the troubled life of one of the earliest worker-peasant universities, which later became famous, in the countryside of Jiangxi Province. The characters are still "typed"—they unwaveringly support truth and right, their smiling eyes are fixed on some distant void; makeup is too heavy, lighting overbright, symbolism too pat, delivery rhetorical. But in other respects, tremendous progress has been made. The good guys are not battling bad guys and stooges and secret agents of the Kuomintang. The film portrays a genuine struggle, the characters' attitudes are often nuanced, and all sides bring their arguments out into the open. Concern for common people is genuine, and the dialogue is so authentic that at times one is truly moved. There are dramatic moments, for example, when the peasants and workers defy the examination requirement and demand to enter the university. The shooting script has been published in *Chinese Literature,* but it gives no idea of what the film is like. For one thing —and this is new—the ending is bitter. The worker-university experiment fails because the young people and the cadre who is helping them are silenced by the instructors—who want a high entrance requirement and, later, high-level, specialized certification—and by the provincial leaders, who in the end order the school to be shut down. In the very last scene, after the whole thing is finished, yes, a deus ex machina does appear; a car arrives with a counterorder from Mao personally. But this saving intervention comes from the outside, after the apparatus has already won. In this respect, the film reproduces an only too true reality.

It's finally been decided that teachers and students in the Italian section may read Italian newspapers. Before going to the film, Chen accompanied me to the ground floor, to the library, which is always locked—she'd got the key in advance—and in that abandoned room I leafed through piles of the *Corriere della Sera* looking for a few articles I can give as reading material.

A visit yesterday to the students who are "working" at the Italian exhibit. They seemed more alert, less timid. Italians are arriving en masse from Italy and from Peking.

"Good News"
October 9

This morning, Chen greeted me with a smile: "You've heard the news?" (She knows I listen to the radio in the morning.) The news is that the Central Committee has decided to publish the fifth volume, covering the years 1949–57, of Mao's works and to build a mausoleum for him in Tienanmen Square. *The People's Daily,* which I found when I got back to the hotel, has published the communiqué in such large type that it takes up the whole front page. Overplayed. The public announcement is incomplete, surely; there must have been other decisions, which would have been passed on to cadres down to some level.

There is a phrase in the communiqué: "The Political Bureau of the Central Committee of the Chinese Communist Party, under the leadership of Comrade Hua Guofeng . . ." The phrase is ambiguous, because Hua, as *First* Vice-Chairman, is the highest-ranking leader also of the Party, but until now his preeminence has not been couched in such unqualified terms.

It's as if something very important were happening. Not everybody is equally informed about what that is, yet wherever you go you sense a kind of excitement, mixed with uncertainty. Why was there no political study session yesterday? I spent two hours talking with Chen instead, in which I launched a full-scale attack on China's foreign policy. I also told her that I understand why the Chinese think it to their interest to divert an eventual war toward Europe, but that if such an eventuality were to arise, then I as a European would prefer that Europe be spared rather than China. Chen listened the way Chinese who are assigned to foreigners must listen to them. She was benevolent, understanding, said not a word, eschewing any discussion. Attentive. She must, in fact, report in writing what I do and say. (Everyone knows this, even if no one has ever spoken to us about it.) For that matter, I didn't expect the poor woman to answer me, and I was speaking precisely so that she might make a report.

In the afternoon, we went to visit the People's July First Commune. (When the political situation seems stirred up, foreigners are taken outside the city to visit communes.) It was a delightful end-of-week trip, in an intense yellow light that is like a long, long sunset. The countryside hereabouts is very gentle. Rice and cotton are already in blossom and vegetables look beautiful. No dust, no rubble, no crowds. Things are bright and colorful and fresh.

It is a small commune (seventeen thousand people), rich, with a program of semiurban land-use planning that breaks sharply with village practices and the clan structure. (Similar programs, also in an advanced state of development, are common in the Shanghai suburbs.)

By the sides of the cotton fields, peasant women were chattering and knitting as they rested; they were making sweaters for their children, but they also do finer work, which they sell to the government for export. The commune's primitive workshops produce electric motors and mechanical parts for large factories.

Our conversation with the people was disappointing. We knew that this is an advanced commune, which not only carries out town-planning experiments but incorporates them in an overall transformation of economic and social connections between city and country, carried forth by the leaders in Shanghai. The answers we were given to our questions seemed pat, following a fixed scheme that was the same in every commune throughout China, and devoid of significance. This does not coincide at all with what Susan heard in the same commune one year ago, however. (She wasn't with us this time, but I talked with her when we got back.) We speculate that these people are on their guard; they are protecting themselves against something.

October 10

Walls are covered with big strips of pink or red paper, inscribed with big characters: "We express our support of the Central Committee's two decisions." . . . These are semiofficial statements, posted by various units. A few read differently: "We express our support of the appointment of Hua Guofeng as Chairman of the Communist Party and Chairman of the Military Commission." (Both posts were previously held by Mao.) The mourning set is being struck and replaced by new *dazibao* in festive colors. Yet some people persist in going about wearing their black armbands.

I am off to the Institute every morning, in the bright autumnal light, our bus carrying everyone who does not go by bicycle; quite often Makita, he of the vague, only seemingly unobservant eye, goes by bike; Marcial sometimes. From the bus, Aymin spots them, for they stand out among the crowd of bicyclers who now wear blue jackets over their white shirts; visible first is Dagmar's mop of blond hair, then Makita, then the child's father. Each time this is cause for great excitement, shouting, waving. The whole bus waves; for the children, it is both a ritual and a game.

I climb to the second floor by an outside stairway, walk down the long corridor with a wooden floor that someone occasionally washes with rag brooms. The wide-open door to the men's toilet I pass by quickly so as not to smell the stink, the two small rooms with the tape recorders, a double classroom; on the other side, office doors with big windows, the glass very dirty, masked with paint, sometimes papered over; occasionally broken. Sheets and sheets of paper, small and large, announcements of plays and of tickets for sale, of foodstuffs available to the staff, minor regulations . . . for any place to be real, it must be invaded by ideograms.

The students in the Italian-language section are still away from school, and I am compiling study materials, feeling all the while that it's futile and absurd. Won't they simply be added to the heap? I've no assurance they will ever be used, or how, what with the orders and counterorders. . . .

The Italian ambassador, his wife, and some other embassy officials are at the Heping (Peace) Hotel, having come on for the opening of the exhibit. To meet them again made me feel comfortable and reassured. During the toasts at the reception marking the opening of the Italian exhibition, the ambassador offered congratulations on the appointment of Hua Guofeng as chairman. (He had been authorized to do so shortly before by the local authorities, of whom he had inquired whether the news was definite.)

The embassy people will be leaving tomorrow or the day after. Small-time industrialists, who have come from Italy with wives and staff, will stay on for two weeks, until the exhibit closes. They have been put up at the Dasha. I see them eating at round tables for eight or ten beside the windows at the far end of one of the restaurant's large dining rooms; you cross it to reach our small dining room, which is beyond the inner elevator and the doors to the rest rooms. Depending on the time of year, this large room is half empty or crowded with tourists. The Dasha, which is known in English as Shanghai Mansions, is used for long stopovers. As a hotel it is classed slightly below the Heping and the Guoji, which, in turn, is ranked below the Jinjiang. The Italian group includes technicians and workers, too. Why is it I feel no impulse to strike up a conversation with these people? And yet being cut off from contact with fellow Italians weighs on me—in token of which, my delight in meeting the ambassador and his wife. But they and others from the embassy live here, like me and like the students.

These Italians, on the other hand, are passing through, they are not much more than tourists, and we snub them. A hierarchically ordered society—above all, the hierarchy of knowledge—conquers and sucks you in without your realizing it, for you don't even imagine you have to defend yourself against it. And you play the role that you have been assigned. The few words I exchange with these Italians tell very little. *This is not because of any motive such as fear or caution.* It's rather out of snobbery, as is the case with all the foreign students here when they have any dealings with foreign transients. (The students, who are the most sinicized of all, snub the experts, the experts snub the embassy people, and all of them admit themselves to be miles apart from long-term residents, people who spend their lives here.) These snobberies are our superficial perception of something we act out because we are conditioned to do so and without our being really aware of it. One has only to think about this for a moment to understand that there is no need to fall back on nationalism or racism in order to explain the reserve of the Chinese toward us, nor need one invoke an authoritarian spirit in order to explain the reserve that Chinese who know more exhibit in dealing with those Chinese who know less. We are not accustomed to this coercive system because it has never existed among us in these terms. Or if it has, it has dissolved and now exists in more hidden and perhaps more insidious forms. The Chinese world, in comparison to ours, is as transparent as a Cartesian paradigm.

Coup d'État
October 12

Today, at six, Susan was standing by the entrance to the larger dining room as I came down to dinner. She stopped me and said, "According to the BBC, Wang

Hongwen, Zhang Chunqiao, Yao Wenyuan, and Jiang Qing have been arrested." The bulletin was described as unconfirmed. Later, John, who had heard the broadcast too, told me the same thing. (My tiny set brings in only Shanghai.)

This evening around ten, I saw truckloads of soldiers go by. It could be a coincidence. Yesterday Z——, a young journalist from the Italian news agency ANSA, saw a *dazibao* on the Bund with a title that read: "Where have the letters we sent the Central Committee ended up?" There was such a flock of people gathered around it that he could not read the rest. When he went back later, the *dazibao* had been ripped off. (The regulation is that a *dazibao* should not be torn off or covered over until it has been displayed for three days.)

This evening, it seems, the Xin Hua put out a news release on the dual appointment of Hua Guofeng. Today's *The People's Daily* had nothing of any importance: Some Papuans are here on a visit. . . . China, united as always, under the Central Committee, now with Hua at its head. . . .

October 13

The radio news this morning was more than usually negligible: the Papuans again were the lead story.

John told one of the elevator women what he had heard. Later, he overheard her and other hotel help asking each other in Shanghaiese, "Do you suppose it's true?"

I glanced at a copy of the Shanghai daily paper, *Wenhui Daily,* which I don't have the right to buy but which I can read on the bulletin board at the Institute. Like *People's Daily,* nothing. This morning, Lao Bai and a colleague were standing by the door to the Institute when we arrived. They shook hands with us as we went by. Unheard of.

In the afternoon, a screening of *Ode to the Mango,* a dull falsification of the factional struggle at the University of Canton in 1968. It was preceded by an old documentary exhumed from 1972, showing Mao receiving Nixon. In the background, Hua Guofeng.

The young Italian embassy people who haven't gone back to Peking play down the arrests. They're so used to the farfetched rumors which often circulate in Peking that they've lost their sense of what is real.

Today's BBC news: thirty people from among the top leadership under arrest; meetings of generals; troop buildup in Peking. Among those arrested is Mao Yuanxin, from the Liaoning Military Region, a nephew of Mao's. There's a rumor (among foreigners) that the Minister of Culture has been arrested also, and that troops have occupied Beida and Qinghua universities. A friend of John's has phoned from Peking saying that there are no visible troop movements.

Nobody can stand being alone, and we seek each other out for company.

This evening, we—the Europeans—had dinner in a little Beijing lu restaurant where you can sit without ceremony among Chinese. We consumed heaps of magnificent shrimp on a lacquered table with no plates and joked with the friendly waiters. Maya was in her stroller beside us. . . . Back at the hotel, we gathered in Susan's room, to talk, talk and smoke until very late. From outer space some news reaches us; even if not definite, it may be more than others are getting. But we are shut in a cage.

This afternoon, at the Friendship Store, the students were sweet and subdued. I have no idea what is told them, what is kept from them, what they know, or how many of them know it.

In this vacuum, I could not say what history is or who is making it.

The Chinese radio has dropped the Papuans. Now, over and over, like a refrain, one is called on to unite around the Central Committee under the leadership of Hua; the workers in the capital are studying Mao, criticizing Deng, and continuing to oppose the wind from the Right; they will struggle to the last against all those who oppose Mao's directive about the three "musts" and "must nots."*

Here we are. The enumeration of the endorsements coming from the base units, workplaces, schools, provinces, military units has commenced. . . . This will go on for days and days. Everything is presented in the guise of some grand democratic movement. Only, this time it's not clear what assent is being given to, or whether those who are giving their assent know what they are expressing, or how many of them know.

The only Shanghai unit mentioned so far on the radio and in *Wenhui Daily* as assenting is our Institute.

This morning, in the office alone with Chen, I explained to her why *Ode to the Mango* seemed to me false and contemptible. Then I told her the BBC news. (We had all agreed to talk about it with our interpreters, since we are officially permitted to listen to foreign broadcasts.) She was stunned. "It's not possible," she murmured, almost to herself. Then she added, "Power does not lie in the hands of one person but with the Central Committee, not with some against others, but with all agreeing together." My answer: "I am a foreigner, and I don't have the information with which to judge who is right and who is wrong. But 'unity' doesn't mean some against others. And neither Chairman Mao nor Premier Zhou ever agreed that power should be concentrated in the hands of a single person."

"Yes," Chen went on, "power lies with the Central Committee."

*"Practice Marxism and not revisionism; unite and don't split; be open and aboveboard, and don't intrigue and conspire."

She didn't ask for any more information, nor did she come back to the subject. She was controlling herself, but she was very much upset. When she left the office on some business of her own, as she often does, she was gone for a long time.

John's interpreter said that he would have gone to John's to listen to the radio. He also said, "If it's true, it will be terrible. And you people, you can count on being sent back home." Susan's interpreter knew nothing and asked for particulars. The interpreter for the French couple, who is the son of intellectuals from Xi'an and a dull-witted conformist, responded with slogans, but then he, too, asked for more details. According to Dagmar, her interpreter knew but only in a vague way. Uta's young interpreter knew nothing and was incredulous.

At least verbally, all of them are expressing faith in Hua, because he had the post of Premier when Mao was alive.

This evening I had dinner with the German women, at the round table by the window. We opened one big section that has mosquito netting; from the raised ground-floor restaurant one saw only the dark sky and the plants on the terrace—flowering oleanders and other southern bushes stirred by the wind that in Shanghai blows always. Tonight it was a caressing breeze (when it was not bearing bad smells), and it's not yet cold or too strong. Shinto, who had finished his meal at the small square table toward the back of the room, where he always sits with his wife, passed by our table and told us that the Japanese radio is talking about executions that have already taken place, but according to him the stories are exaggerated. The Japanese are very well informed, in fact, but the BBC's choice of news is more accurate.

The terminology of the Left—against Deng, about bourgeois in the Party, in favor of the Cultural Revolution, about the continuation of the class struggle, and so forth—is being preserved. A few little words, yes, are inserted, a few dropped; but these are merely signals, not a change in the discourse itself. *It means absolutely nothing.* Everything must be carried on as if nothing were happening.

Quiet everywhere; everything functions perfectly. The organizational machine is so designed that the rank and file do not start to move until someone high up pulls a few strings.

This goes against our democratic sense of things. But is it true only in China, and generally throughout the despotic Orient?

Attack on Shanghai
October 15

The radio continues to report statements of loyalty, which are multiplying. Articles by Beida and Qinghua professors and students expressing their loyalty are being read, too. The Papuans have reached Shanghai, and have been received by Ma Tianshui, secretary of the Revolutionary Committee here, who has made his statement in minimal terms—supporting the two CC decisions.

I was getting ready to go to school when Susan came by with the latest news from Peking, phoned by her friends: Beida and Qinghua have indeed been occupied by the army, and their joint group for study and criticism has been forcibly dissolved. (So the statements published in the papers and read over the radio are worth what they're worth.) Foreign teachers have been requested not to go to Fudan this morning.

At the entrance to the Institute, signs had been posted welcoming various representatives of the city—which meant that they were coming there to meet. Some of my students (the ones from the Friendship Store, who sleep at the Institute and take some lessons with me) were straggling along the avenue leading into the Institute. One of them told me, "This morning we won't be having a lesson because there's to be a meeting." Another one said, "Some people have a meeting, some don't." Chen asked me whether I had heard any more news. I told her what I knew about Beida and Qinghua. She played it down, and expressed her faith in the party. My answer: "Let's hope everything turns out for the best."

While I was working in my office, a student came in, fetching something or other. He's twenty-five years old, and has worked seven of those years in the northeast. He seems perpetually tired, as if he were looking for something with a stubbornness all his own. Chen assumed a professorial-authoritarian, almost contemptuous tone. He made nothing of it, but with a slight yet perceptible air of provocation half slumped into an armchair and started to leaf through a copy of *China Pictorial.* (The few old armchairs are a luxury reserved for us foreigners. When important cadres visit, they immediately occupy them as if the chairs were their property, and the foreigner becomes the host; everyone else always engages in a skirmish of compliments before sitting in them.) There was no apparent reason for the young man's remaining. Perhaps he wanted to talk, I thought. I felt as if I were not rising to some occasion, as if I should do something, and I didn't know what.

He stood up and came over to look at what I was typing. It was the translation of an excerpt from *Breakdown,* which I'd chosen as a text for class. He wanted to know what it was. "Ah, very interesting." And he read a few lines of the dialogue in Italian, understanding most of it.

Then we asked Chen what the words for glutinous rice cream puffs are—they're mentioned in the text. Chen relaxed, and, relieved, answered gaily.

This afternoon there was no political study. Chen gave me "to study at the hotel" the October 10 editorial published jointly by the three major official publications—*The People's Daily, Red Flag,* and *The Liberation Army Daily.* (These "study materials" are supplied to us as well as to the Chinese printed on minute sheets; they circulate in quantity, deal with all kinds of subjects, and vary in level from those intended for the masses to those for all eighteen grades of the hierarchy. The sheets are not on sale; your unit supplies them.)

After the meetings—obviously—the students put up also inside the Institute manifestos of support for Hua *zhuxi* ("chairman"), a title that follows immediately after the last name and that until now had been reserved for Mao. Rather than Mao Zedong, everyone says Mao *zhuxi.*

Going back to the hotel in the bus, I caught a fleeting glimpse of the four names written on a wall. The Fudan students who were on factory detail returned to school this morning for meetings. Shouts of condemnation chanted in chorus by the Chinese students. . . . Clearly, this is the day that has been chosen for somehow informing the people of Shanghai. There must have been meetings all over town. Squads of soldiers, unarmed, patrolled the Institute. We asked Bob, who was back from the factory, what was going on inside. "They could have been shooting up the place for all I would have known. It's hidden," he answered.

Nanjing lu: the crowd was even denser than usual. Some people were carrying posters. Many stood packed together, faces upturned, below the windows of the Revolutionary Committee on the Bund. There were also crowds in front of the glassed-in cases in which the daily newspapers are displayed. Rather fewer in front of the sheets that were just beginning to appear, on which the names of the guilty were written in huge characters, all distorted and crossed out with *X*'s. These signs have a terrible ferocity and cruelty; they are as pitiless as a beheading. One of the teachers has seen a *dazibao* that says Zhang Chunqiao is a traitor.

People are accepting what they are being told with no visible reactions; the tension notwithstanding, there is a kind of lightheartedness.

Feeling a need to be together, this evening we all ate at the big round table. Even Alissa and John came down to dinner, although ordinarily they cook for themselves. Afterward we stayed together in this one's or that one's room. People talked and fell silent in fits and starts. In a way, we kept up the usual routines, even to the songs and the guitar. But it was with a different rhythm, out of sync, as it were. As if everything we did had no meaning and we were only pretending to exist, we were seeing ourselves as phantoms. From an incommensurable distance we were reading a page of history. But we were also much excited to know about it, intent on our awareness as witnesses.

Now and then someone would look out the window. The gongs and the drums had commenced. One wracked one's brains to understand. Western shortwave radios were reporting satisfaction abroad. The Shanghai radio droned on with the bogus statements from Beida and Qinghua. It also said that the workers of Shanghai had resolved on a new high tide in the study of the works of Chairman Mao and the "three must's" and the "three must not's."

Although it was already dark, the street was jammed with people. We went out. It could have been daytime, there was such a crowd. We crossed the bridge and walked along the Bund, and partway up Nanjing lu. Little groups of people kept arriving in trucks; they would get out and post pieces of paper on which the four names were crossed out; also *dazibao*. The latter were directed against the Shanghai Revolutionary Committee—more precisely against the three top leaders, Ma Tianshui, Xu Jingxian, and Wang Xiuzhen. These three are the actual leaders, although nominally three of the four people arrested in Peking have headed the Shanghai committee. Wang is a woman from the textile union, which is being accused as a group of complicity, under the influence or control of Wang Hongwen, who was a textile worker himself. It is taken for granted that the four are guilty as charged, and everywhere their names appear crossed out. There is no discussion, nor are any proofs being offered. Instead, there is an attempt to show the local leaders' complicity with the Four, although in a few *dazibao* the local people are only being asked to take a position.

This is all rhetorical pressure. There's no apparent source of these initiatives—neither the authorities in power nor the opposition. The *dazibao* carry the group signatures of a few local units, but more often they are signed by subgroups of the units or are anonymous. The people and the cadres at the base are waiting to see; leaders and higher cadres stand accused; in that case, who is acting? The attack must originate in Peking. Someone in Peking has broken the legal chain of command and is making use of his own emissaries in Shanghai. It's impossible to eliminate the leaders here with a surprise attack, as was done in Peking, because of the organizational structure itself, which prevents it—every directive has the force of a directive only by virtue of passing through the Shanghai Party Committee and the Shanghai City Revolutionary Committee. Local leaders here stand accused, but they also have a base of support, especially in the factories, and the administrative and party cadres largely share their political orientation. It is the entire city leadership, as an ensemble, which is being accused. And yet, unit meetings were called this morning (by whom?) before there was any public announcement whatsoever either by the Party or from the central government, and an anonymous go-ahead for the *dazibao* was given before anyone in the local units in the factories, in the unions, in the port, or in the offices had announced a position. We must necessarily assume that a group of leaders in Peking, supported by someone here, wanted to mount a "spontaneous" revolt of the masses, a seeming overturn of power by the base. But it is impossible to find out who this "someone" in Shanghai might be.*

---

*Only later would we come to learn, unofficially, that in the beginning the *dazibao* had been posted by a certain number of students and professors from the Polytechnical Institute, those of conservative orientation. The resistance of the majority of citizens' units toward announcing support for the new direction (with the exception of a few higher schools) was overcome little by little by means of external pressure—leaders and cadres sent from other cities—and by military control.

The operation is not without risks. Contrary to appearances, the maneuver is predicated not on the rank and file being mobilized but on their inertia, and on the inability of local leaders to maintain an organizational tie with their own base, and to retain its trust. It's clear, however, that what we are seeing is only the outside, the theater. No question but that behind the scenes steps are being taken that have a "persuasive" impact.

There remains the question of who promoted the meetings this morning in many if not all units. Clearly, internal channels of communication within factions are more developed and efficient than one could have supposed. In any event, in the next few days something very big is going to be decided. It's doubtful that Shanghai is in any condition to offer open resistance, and one would have to know the balance of power in the rest of China. There are industrial centers where it won't be easy to impose this "order"—Anyang, Hangzhou, maybe Wuhan. Liaoning seems already to be in the hands of the military. But the main game is being played out here.

In the *dazibao,* the four arrested people are being called "the four plagues" (the flies, mosquitoes, mice, and sparrows of a public-health drive in the fifties) and "the Gang of Four," and so on. Big poster caricatures are also beginning to appear—fairly outrageous ones, and the more so because in this country by definition the caricature is an insult.

Later, around ten, a small procession from Fudan arrived with red flags and drums. There were probably two hundred in all. What may the group's size mean? Fudan student residents number about six thousand.

The crowd was tense but continued to react peacefully. People watched other people put up their sheets of paper; they laughed over the cartoons. It was impossible to understand what was going through their minds, to what extent they were in agreement or at odds. No one hindered the posting, no one lent a helping hand. People were watching a very interesting show. They were in no way the protagonists.

One sharp cleavage: we were not part of that crowd, which made for some embarrassment, also a sense of vulnerability. Yet the crowd was not hostile to us.

The Workers' Militia had vanished, even from locations it usually patrols, like the bridges. This is strange, given that the very purpose of the militia is to maintain order within the city. But perhaps the militia has been disarmed. On whose orders?

However, there are no soldiers to be seen either.

And now, back at the hotel, it is one o'clock. I don't know who lives in the room over mine. Whoever it is, he's awake, and pacing up and down. Outside, the boats and barges pass by continually; their engines sound even noisier at night.

October 16

The loudspeaker of the boatmen's radio below my window was silent this morning. The sound of another one reached me, from far off, maybe from a ship. Then, at 6:35 the men turned theirs back on: radio news rebroadcast from Peking. At seven o'clock, they turned it off again. This simply never happens. It must mean either that there are problems with the personnel at the Shanghai radio station, or the boatmen have refused to broadcast the party announcements.

The walls surrounding the Institute are splashed with the four names in big characters which have been crossed out; insults have been added, as in Nanjing lu, and signed by the Party Committee. Near the entrance, also on the outside wall, a long *dazibao.* I was late and didn't have time to read it. There are also inscriptions condemning the Four.

I asked Chen what was happening. Her answer was somewhat convoluted. In substance, the masses have decided to condemn the Four, who have been plotting. "The other day, I didn't believe the news because while I knew that there was a struggle within the Party I did not imagine that it had reached such a point. . . . We are all united with the CC under Hua." Et cetera. I said to her that when there is an open struggle each party can accuse the other of plotting; one needs proofs.

She: "The proofs are there. They'll be published later."

She asked whether we went out yesterday for a look around. She knew perfectly well that we had gone out. The floor employees at the Dasha carefully note down the times of all our comings and goings. When they see us waiting for the elevator, one of them comes out of their room at the end of the hall, where three or four of them are bivouacked among mattresses and white rolled-up quilts, and asks, "Are you going to eat? Going out?" The elevator boys and the porters on the ground floor complete the control. Actually, it goes further, extending to what one does in one's own room, what visits are exchanged. These operations are overseen, on our floor, by a "responsible comrade," a woman who is most solicitous about our health and welfare. All data are transmitted to the Institute, the paternal authority that owns us and is responsible for us.

Chen was concerned: "But there were so many people. . . ." I praised the population for being so alert. "It's a result of the Cultural Revolution. Before, nobody was interested in anything." Without asking in so many words, Chen wanted to know what we had understood: "It's good for everyone to express his own opinion. . . ." I set her mind at rest. People were talking among themselves, but quietly, I said, and they were friendly to us. They had even explained the *dazibao,* I added. Another flicker of apprehension.

Later, after she had read the *dazibao* on the avenue, she told me that they are criticizing *some* leaders of the Shanghai Revolutionary Committee who, unlike the masses, have failed to take a clear position against the Four.

"On what occasion did they fail to do that?"

"In a speech."

"The speech in which they welcomed the Papuans?"

"No, in a speech to the cadres at a closed meeting."

"If it was closed, how do the masses know about it?"

"The cadres report to the masses."

"Won't these leaders know more than any one of you?"

"No, the masses are the true protagonists, they know how to understand who is right."

"But the masses are made up of people, and until the day before yesterday they didn't know a thing, just as you yourself knew nothing. It's impossible for them to form an opinion in one day just on the basis of those manifestoes."

"The leaders are being criticized by the masses for not expressing their opinion clearly. When they were told to take a position, *they proposed putting documents and facts in the hands of the masses so that they could decide by themselves.*" (My italics.)

"But that's an excellent thing to have done. You said yourself a moment ago that it is the masses who must judge."

"No, the leaders should take a position at once, for one side or the other."

"Have the Shanghai factories taken a position—for example, the navy yards, Steelworks No. 5, the machine-tool factory, the longshoremen?"

"I don't know."

"To talk about 'the masses' doesn't mean much, it seems to me. One has to see what the workers really think. That counts for more than the opinion of this or that leader, to my way of thinking. . . ."

"Oh, certainly, certainly."

So, the only bit of information Chen has given me about the conduct of Shanghai's municipal leaders, contrary to what she intended, redounds greatly to their credit. And the speculations I was hazarding yesterday about how the "masses" are to be used have been confirmed. But it's still not clear who is conducting the action, physically, in the upper echelons: Shanghai people who are loyal to the winners? Or people sent from outside?

This intervention—however illegal an abuse it is—is relying on the fact that elsewhere the game has been won, and it is forcing the city leadership to the wall. There are two possibilities. The leaders may continue to be silent and to resist passively. In which case, no matter what support they may receive from their working-class base and from some groups of young intellectuals, that support will be effective only locally; it will be ineffectual with respect to the rest of China and the outside world because the only audible voice is the adversary's. Their defeat is complete, even if the main body of their forces has been saved for the future.

The second possibility is that the city leadership will mobilize its supporters and respond. That would spell the end, with the risk of extremely serious

consequences and possible carnage, including the intensified tyranny of centralized power, not only in Shanghai. It would no longer be just defeat; it would
be a total rout. ("It will be terrible . . ." as Zheng has said.)

If the Shanghai leaders were to follow Mao's tactic, they would have to
accept defeat for the moment, refrain from reacting, preserve what forces they
can for the future. And maybe that is exactly what they are trying to do.
However, in politics things don't happen as they do in a military campaign. The
opponents' victory is translated into the reinforcement and completion of certain structures that *by themselves* condition the future. When the day comes for
rounding up the forces one has saved, one may find that they have melted away.

This morning at school, the students were all very tired. Understandably.
They line them up, thrust a stick into their hands to which a paper streamer
with some slogan is attached, and make them walk, shouting, behind drums
(generally carried on trucks) for miles on end. The rest of the time, it's mass
meetings, rituals with no discussion yet enervating, "activities" such as writing
out posters, everything minutely organized. At the end of which, exhausted,
they go back to sleep in their overcrowded rooms.

Soldiers still carrying their travel kits, from who knows where, are patrolling work sites; they are like very young, earnest priests. The city is plastered
with inscriptions. They flashed by as we were returning to the hotel in the bus.
Not just "down with" but "slit his throat" and "let them burn." The name of
Jiang Qing was written not in brush strokes but in a design of small skeletal
bones.

For hours and hours, I have been watching and hearing the drums on
trucks that roll by beneath my window at the Dasha, and across the bridge and
along the far bank of the Suzhou; they are followed by endless columns of
people, three abreast, each person clutching his little flag. A few groups with
red flags head the columns. I have never seen such an overwhelming mass of
people—but organized and tightly controlled down to the last housewife and
urchin, as if it were an army. I should go down into the street to see what units
they're from, but I don't stir. It's remiss of me, I know, but I am too disgusted.

The workers in Milan who in 1969 streamed out of their factories more
than once to occupy the city against the threat of a Fascist coup d'état* . . . I
keep remembering that fraternal image, that confidence in themselves and in
each other, that faith in men's collective awareness.

Here I am seeing puppets manipulated by a string. Set against their leaders,
their unions, the Cultural Revolution, the Commune of '67. One day sufficed,
one order—who knows from where—and they responded with the automatism

---

*The so-called "Strage della Piazza Fontana" of December 12, 1969, organized by Italian Neo-
Fascists with the support of some government bureaucrats.

of the machine that functions even when the order is illegal. It doesn't matter who pushed the button, from where, for what purpose, toward what end. Down in the street, living flesh-and-blood puppets are shouting in hysterical voices— the women, especially—*"Dadao Jiang Qing! Dadao Wang Hongwen!"* And the answering chorus: *"Dadao dadao dadao. . . ."*

Facing my window, only five hundred yards away as the crow flies, stands the City Hall, the central administrative offices of Shanghai. The people inside must have exceptional courage and firmness.

I spent the late afternoon with the French students at Susan's. Everyone was weighed down by the same disheartened, disbelieving disgust. Maybe fraternity is a cowardly comfort.

In some *dazibao,* Jiang Qing is accused of having murdered Mao Zedong, and the other three of having tormented him during his illness. Which is to say, in a word, that they are responsible for Mao's death. To say, further, that Mao had been senile. (For how long?)

The farewell banquet for Paule Garçon, who is leaving for Argentina, was given on the seventeenth floor, complete with white tablecloth and almond milk. A parody of the banquets with Chinese cadres and interpreters was acted out by Bob (an expert) and Roland (a greenhorn). Someone told the story of how when a Chinese cadre saw the photograph of Lin Biao next to that of Mao in the French encyclopedia *Le petit Robert,* he exclaimed, "What's this! They've kept Lin Biao!"

"Well, you see," the Frenchman explained, "in our country we keep everybody."

Someone who had gone out late reported that the names of the Shanghai municipal leaders are now crossed out with X's. The accusations against them are mean and gossipy: Zhang Chunqiao allegedly bought something at the Friendship Store (reserved for foreigners), and more nonsense of that kind. In addition to the textile workers and the unions, the Office of Foreign Trade is also under attack. Among the misdeeds of Ma Tianshui, there is mention of his "ten points" concerning industrial management. Jiang Qing is pictured sticking out her tongue and holding lies in one hand and truth in the other. Wang Hongwen is shown with a fish, and issuing from his mouth is a balloon: "And you say there are no more fish in the sea?" There are two possible interpretations of this fish: persons to be recruited or persons to be attacked. Wang loves both hunting and fishing.

The infantile frivolity of the mob. Mao had warned of how easily China could "change color." At Fudan, the witch-hunt has already begun. Everybody is being questioned about every single thing he's said, etc. No, not everybody —some.

October 18

I sleep four hours a night. My throat burns from too many cigarettes, and whether the pain in my head is a headache or not, I no longer know. In my free time, so long as it is light, I walk and walk among the crowds, which are still unusually dense, and among the *dazibao* and caricatures that now cover all walls and shop windows—every inch of free space—to a height of two and three stories.

Sunday morning was sunny and mild. I walked toward the door, after dropping a card into the hotel post box, and there, nearby, was Zhang, typing. "You're going out?"

"Yes, I've got to get a little exercise."

"Where are you going?"

"To the Old Town."

"All the way down there? But that's so far, it takes an hour and a half." (Walking at a leisurely pace, it takes about a half hour from the Dasha.)

"I enjoy walking."

"Why not take a taxi?"

"That way I'd not be getting any exercise."

"But there are so many people on the street today."

"I'm not afraid of people."

"Well, no, there's nothing to be afraid of."

Southward along Sichuan Road, to where it crosses Yanan Road, Jin Ling Road, as far as People's Road. This is a part of Shanghai where a faraway, pre-automobile era of our cities seems to have been restored to life, where from the periphery one used to walk through shaded streets, passing small houses and villas, and all of a sudden find oneself in open country. Now it is a kind of urban countryside, inhabited, full of life and color: women sitting along the streets, laundry hung along the pavements, old quilted blankets brought out to be aired.

Today, people were clustered in front of the *dazibao*. Groups of marchers and trucks with flags and drums passed by. (When you examine these groups from close at hand, the marchers prove to be, in the main, very young—schoolchildren, even elementary school pupils, all carrying flags.) Adults were out strolling in large numbers, fathers carrying small babies, women pausing to gossip.

The Old Town: zigzag bridge; the teahouse with many old people; the soldiers, mere boys, who have themselves photographed on the small lake in martial or romantic poses; people who take care of all their affairs on the street, who are solidly together even in their disputes, perhaps in their hates. You go into the artisan shops, you wait in a long line until your turn comes to eat some dumplings. This is good and necessary, real and palpable. In the Old Town I saw almost no *dazibao*. Just some red streamers with the earlier, now old, inscription—the consent to the two decisions. Here and there, a small sheet like others pinned up elsewhere in the city. It's a copy of the telegram sent by the Central Committee to the municipal government inviting it, in a friendly, paternalistic tone, to support the CC, to carry out a propaganda campaign among the masses clarifying for their benefit the crimes of the Four, to encourage production, etc. The telegram was dated the sixteenth. This copy comes from an official source, like the endorsement signs. No "representative of the masses" has dared come here, then, to post *dazibao* and caricatures.

I left the Old Town, and walked north toward the hotel, amid vociferous scrawls and street noise. The walls of the Workers' Cultural Palace are blanketed with *dazibao,* as are those of the radio station, many union headquarters, and government office buildings. A *dazibao* can be long, as many as twenty or thirty consecutively numbered sheets. I stopped now and then to read them, and to look at the caricatures. They have told us at school that we may read the *dazibao* but not photograph or copy them, to avoid possible negative reactions on the part of the public. It's an excuse, dictated by their defensive caution; to whomever has devised this regulation, it doesn't matter one bit whether we know or don't know, read or don't read, so long as no visible documentary evidence of our doing so remains. The specific excuse chosen does have some basis, however, given the mercurial reactions of the Chinese. In relation to us, they have swung from the benevolence of that first evening to a don't-give-a-damn attitude to irony to an evident hostility, which is growing as the days pass. It parallels the crescendo of violence of the caricatures and berating of the Four. That violence is verbal and graphic only; otherwise, everything moves on in an absolutely peaceful way, no police are seen on the streets, there is not a rifle in sight, no street fighting. Anyone who was here during the Cultural Revolution will testify that the Chinese people have a capacity for extreme self-control; it is almost as if they were held in check by their terror of what could happen were they to lose it; if violence is unleashed, there is no curbing it, and it reaches a state of paroxysm. When they are unable to dominate themselves totally, they are totally lost.

Some Westerners keep the *dazibao* fresh in their minds, especially the names mentioned, until they can write them down from memory. I haven't the strength to do that, for I find I am overcome by disgust and boredom. I am falling short of a duty, I know; the writings that cover the walls of this city are important historical sources, more so than newspapers are elsewhere, and almost all of them will be lost, for there is no one who, whether officially or officiously, is photographing or copying or somehow recording them, except for a few private individuals who do so sporadically. Most of them are not hard to read, for they're almost always written quite clearly.

The caricatures have begun to show a certain sameness (actually, there is some speculation that prototypes are already in circulation, and identical or slightly varied reproductions): Wang Hongwen is shown with the fish; Zhang Chunqiao is represented various times at the top of a flight of stairs writing on a wall or exhibiting a piece of paper that reads: "Keep to the established policy." To have or not to have uttered this phrase is what sets good citizens apart from friends of the Four. If you ask for an explanation of the slogan, they tell you that it has to do with a distortion of something Mao said, "Stick to the policy of the past." It seems an idiotic argument. The incriminating phrase alludes to a brief "testament" of Mao's which the Four strongly espoused and which has been declared to be inauthentic. Yao Wenyuan is most often shown with pen in hand and a fan concealed behind his back. But it is with Jiang Qing that fancy runs riot. She is shown with a prominent display of thigh or with a siren's tail or with a rope around her neck (often the other three are shown thus), seated before a mirror, made up as for the stage, dressed in Western clothes, wearing a crown—in a word, a cross between the Empress Mother Ci-Xi and Snow White's evil queen.

The *dazibao* heap insults on the Four, but offer no critical arguments—their turpitude is taken for granted. Almost always their names are X'd out and often written crooked. The persons who are assumed to have been their friends or accomplices are, however, the object of criticism. Many attacks begin with the words "We should like to know. . . ." Then comes the demand that one take a position against the Four, or that explanations be given for the members of the City Revolutionary Committee's delay in informing the masses of the CC's decision when they returned from the meeting in Peking on October 13. Fresh charges are made against the textile unions. Certain "persons" in the city administration are castigated for defending the Four (by arguing that in the past they have done some good things), and, in particular, for showing sympathy for Wang Hongwen. "The City Revolutionary Committee of Shanghai is the committee of Yao Wenyuan, Jiang Qing, Wang Hongwen, Zhang Chunqiao." . . . "Let the city administration resolve to take a position [against the Four]." . . . "Take the lid off the class struggle in Shanghai." . . . The City Revolutionary Committee has allegedly expressed doubts about there being any plot. Many personal attacks against the two Shanghai leaders Xu Jingxian and Wang Xiuzhen. (The supposition is that someone is aiming to save Ma Tianshui, at least. In any event, it's the divide-and-rule tactic.) Allegedly Xu Jingxian made a speech on October 14 defending Yao Wenyuan. Contacts between the City Revolutionary Committee members and Peking—trips, letters, telephone calls —all constitute proof of plots. Events from various periods in the past, generally starting after 1972 or after Zhou Enlai's death, ostensibly point to conniving between the Four and local leaders. There are references to recent episodes involving clandestine activities in the factories, especially on the part of union leaders, and to obscure movements of the Workers' Militia. Newsmen on *Wenhui Daily* and at the radio station are reproved for having defended the motives or the guiltlessness of the Four (although not in public after the seventh day—the day Shanghai received official orders against the Four) or for being involved in "contradictions within the people." A whole series of incidents is set forth to sully or ridicule the figures of the leaders, detailing how corrupt their lives have been. (Among the "ten great misdeeds" of one, it is charged that he drank a glass of wine on the evening of Mao's death; other lapses are of a similar nature and gravity.) The leaders were *laoye,* the city government was a *yamen* (derogatory terms associated with the imperial period), and the leaders thought that they were the masters of the people of Shanghai. One spent too much money; another, a woman, used to attend secret showings of American Westerns and pornographic Soviet (!) films. The number of important leaders under public attack was three or four at the beginning, but has now increased to some fifty. The lists we read vary in length. Some names are written normally, others are encircled in red or black, and still others are X'd out. The same name is treated differently from one *dazibao* to another.

It is past midnight. Coming in through my window has been the noise of shouting groups—by now they have thinned out, and these may be truckloads from the schools. They've stationed themselves beneath the windows of the City Revolutionary Committee, and they're screaming over their loudspeakers that a spokesman for their delegation must be received. At one point, there may have been a reply from another loudspeaker, but I can't be sure. Tonight's performance has been the rebellion of a city against its leaders. And for once the leaders are in the right. In such circumstances, the crowd becomes a fearsome thing.

October 19

According to the BBC, the Four were arrested the evening or the night of the sixth.

There is a big Lu Xun revival in the papers. Yesterday, *The People's Daily* announced the publication of his diary and a fuller collection of his letters. Yesterday and again today, entire pages of photographs were devoted to him. The appearance of the two books is not exactly news. It's been known for some time that they were at the typographers, and if they're now available in bookshops, it's a sign that they were printed some time ago. (For that matter, the diary was published in toto in 1959, and has had subsequent reprintings.) Much ado about nothing. There is probably some good reason, which is not yet clear, why Lu Xun is being used. One will have to bide one's time. If a person could only manage to be completely detached, he could thoroughly enjoy watching as all these carefully concealed cards are brought out and laid on the table. Yesterday's *People's Daily* article emphasized that *all* of Lu Xun's writings will become available, and again went into his polemic against Wang Ming. Wang

Ming (Chen Shaoyu) was a major exponent of the Comintern line. Lu Xun's polemic in the thirties was not directed explicitly against Wang Ming but against Communist literary figures whom the Cultural Revolution later associated with Wang Ming's line. Connections that were never entirely undone are reemerging, especially in Shanghai: the network of political and literary factions in the thirties; the double face of the Left, by turns Stalinist and anti-Stalinist (dictatorial and libertarian), and of the Right (repressive and liberal). But the underlying conflicts will be acted out, as always, in the disguise of petty hairsplitting squabbles.

Yesterday afternoon I had a phone call from T—— T——, who had just arrived from Hong Kong. Unbelievable. We met later, and walked about the center of town to see the caricatures and *dazibao*. He had got a visa for Shanghai, using the excuse of the Italian exhibit. It seemed strange to me, all the same, that they gave him one at a moment like this. And sure enough, today, within the space of twenty-four hours, they withdrew it. So it seems that even in relation to foreign journalists different policies are being followed. Whoever let him into the country is not the same person who sent him back to Hong Kong. Naturally, the police authorities attempted to cover up the inconsistency by putting the blame on him, making it almost seem as if his position were irregular. Whereas, clearly, without a proper visa not only could he not have crossed the frontier or passed through the tight control at the airport but he could not even have gotten a room in a hotel. I urged him not to suppose there was something against him personally in this; it's just one of the chinoiseries they fall back on so as not to "lose face."

October 20

The papers continue to publish statements from various provinces and units supporting Hua, and today, finally, the radio has broadcast something about the plot of the Four. The seven o'clock Shanghai news program slipped oblique mention of it into reports on the positions taken by the city's upper schools. The names of local leaders are now X'd out in many places. Chen said to me this morning, "Who knows who will be coming to govern Shanghai now?" This afternoon at two, there's to be a big meeting in the Square of Culture. Chen went to lunch early in order to get there on time. I went out early, too, so that I could read a few *dazibao* on the Institute grounds before the bus arrived. One contained a list of articles meriting condemnation which had appeared in *Study and Criticism:* in No. 4 (1974), an essay by Yao Wenyuan ostensibly about the garden in *The Dream of the Red Chamber,* which in actuality deals with the internal Party struggle (probably this is *"Jia Fudi Da Guan Yuan he Lai Dadi Hua Yuan"* ["The Great Garden of the Jia Court and the Garden of Lai Da"], which is signed Fang Zesheng); also, in No. 8 (1975) *"Wuchan jeiji ziji peiyudi yingxionghua"* ("Heroes the Proletariat Creates Out of Itself"); and articles against Deng that appeared in 1976. The comments on the latter pieces are ironical, and they deny that the Four's position differed from Deng's. Another *dazibao* rejected Xu Jingxian's self-criticism before the masses, calling it incomplete and hypocritical.

We were not invited to the meeting today, but neither did anyone forbid us to go. I was dropping with weariness and stayed home. I slept until four-thirty, then went out and walked about the usual places. At this end of Nanjing lu, there is an enormous vertical canvas banner asking that someone come to govern Shanghai. Other inscriptions—unofficial—on red paper are beginning to appear: "We demand a new leadership for the city." The *dazibao* continue to lack any political substance; the accusations are gossipy trifles. It seems that every unit of the bureaucratic-parasitic type wants to demonstrate its goodwill by contributing to this tittle-tattle. No proofs of the alleged culprits' guilt emerge, and the circumstantial evidence is, if anything, in their favor. For example, a *dazibao* posted by the Dasha's housekeeping staff. I saw it as I came out of the hotel and, turning the corner of the enormous building, was assailed as usual by a burst of light and wind. A crowd of curious people had gathered to read it; it denounces a meeting purportedly held in the hotel. The employee who had brought the tea and various other service employees state the charge. One claims to have overheard somebody say, "If they want a fight, well, we'll give them a fight." Whether this is true or false, I've now learned that meetings of local leaders may be being held directly beneath my room without my having had the slightest inkling of it. You do see well-dressed Chinese in the elevator sometimes, but the role you are assigned here becomes so thoroughly interiorized that even elementary curiosity is taken from you.

The meanest sides of human nature are being appealed to: The taste for malice, prejudice, the notion that politics is merely personal or palace intrigue, the eye-to-the-peephole spying on private lives, the play on words, twisted meanings, loaded hints (I know a lot more than you do), envy, xenophobia. A dislike, perhaps contemptibly motivated, for this or that leader. The lie—the lie that is uncontrollable because no one dares deny it; berating someone as impotent because he tries to appeal to reason.

Mao Zedong is already disappearing, at least in some people's minds. Several *dazibao* refer to him as a poor old man manipulated by the Four Evil Ones. The huge billboard on Nanjing lu on which his two poems republished in early January had been copied has been completely covered with monstrous caricatures of the Four (Jiang Qing tricked out in a kind of Western evening gown) and a portrait of Lu Xun.

The exploitation of Zhou Enlai is beginning again, but it's muted. The device of repetition is already in play. Things are being stabilized, ritualized, becoming part of the daily routine. Everything is to be accepted. Yesterday was the time for meetings to mourn and declare support; today is for criticism meetings and shouting processions. Everything seems the same. What is real? The sameness? or the overturning of what until yesterday seemed to be true? A cyclical return, in which single events are lost. But, as they say in China, with sweat and with blood, with tears and with blood.

You, the foreigner, are outside it all; for you, a gentle limbo is set apart. Everything is so arranged that for you life is easy, that for you the acceptance of anything, everything, is easy.

A group of touring Italian doctors is staying at the Guoji. I heard about it by chance, from students working at the Friendship Store.

At the Xin Hua bookshop, on Nanjing lu, I asked for a book on Lu Xun that was displayed in the showcase of the little circulating library on the ground floor. The shop was almost empty, and the clerks seemed weary and dejected. They exchanged embarrassed glances and told me they didn't have the book. I persisted a bit, and to reassure them said that the book was on display on the ground floor. Perplexity. They asked me please to come back another time. For lack of precise directives, no one is sure what's all right to do and what's not. Most people carefully do nothing. Others take advantage of the confusion. Hotels often provide reading material for their guests. On the shelves at the Dasha, among the foreign-language publications available to the public, there is a pamphlet by Zhang Chunqiao, *Total Dictatorship Over the Bourgeoisie,* and another by Yao Wenyuan, *The Social Basis of the Anti-Party Gang of Lin Biao.* Who knows—are the people who put these pamphlets out for one and all to read the same people who attach *dazibao* that attack plots that are woven upstairs in the rooms of the Dasha? Chen says that the paralysis the Four have caused will end after a while—that is, the opposing factions will stop glowering at each other and stop fearing each other. I maintain that, far from stopping, the paralysis will be aggravated. A political and class conflict that extends throughout the entire society is not going to be eliminated by lopping off one leadership group, unless the intention is to establish an out-and-out reign of terror. For the moment, assuming there is a grain of common sense, this is unlikely, because it could provoke civil war. Everything is going to take time, and will be painful and full of strains. For years and years.

I'm always glad to talk with John. "I came to China because in Europe I had the feeling that I was falling asleep," he said. My answer was that here, whatever we may not be doing, we're not falling asleep. In these days, John is the person I feel closest to precisely because we do not share any ideological frames of reference.

Telephone calls from Peking. At Qinghua, it seems, posters and manifestos are now calling for someone to come to administer the university. Big public demonstrations are in preparation. The rumor there is that some Shanghai leaders have been arrested. This may be anticipating events by a few days, since the Revolutionary Committee here is still being besieged, and today's meeting seems not to have been conclusive. The warships in the harbor now have their cannon visibly trained on the town hall. A symbolic warning? Or the foreigners' mania to assign a meaning even to the fortuitous? One now sees many police, and they're dressed in blue. It's not clear whether the blue means they are already wearing winter uniforms or are navy patrols. The police on duty to date have worn white summer uniforms, and normally they are very few, more or less those who are assigned to regulate traffic.

People are tired, and they're beginning to look unhealthy. Susan and John had an unusual experience today when they, courageously, went to the meeting in the Square of Culture. (John goes everywhere on his bicycle. He even went to Textile Factory No. 17, which used to be Wang Hongwen's factory. He read the *dazibao* against city and union leaders, and tried to interview the men and women workers about them as they were coming off the job. He was gently eased off by a "responsible person," who intervened.) When Susan goes about alone, no one notices her because she is small and thin. But John is tall, and his face is so English as to be almost a cliché. Today, as they made their way into the crowd, they noticed people moving away and forming a circle around them, creating amid such a throng a narrow yet obvious space. People looked them up and down, from head to toe, in silent hostility. This went on for some ten minutes, until it became physically unbearable to remain there. But neither was it easy to leave, for bodies encircled them like a wall. Finally, Susan caught sight of a policeman. She said to him, "We want to get out of here." With some effort, he was able to open a path.

Uneasiness

The witch-hunt is on. It's now reaching down to people at the base. The number of leaders arrested to date in Shanghai is several dozen. It's the old, painful story all over again. After dinner, around seven, I met Tang in the elevator. His face was somber, his hair damp with sweat, and his eyes were red, whether from weariness or tears I couldn't tell. He said good evening very seriously. I knew that the Italians at the exhibit are leaving tomorrow, and that the students will be coming back to the Institute. So I asked him, "Will you all be back tomorrow?" "Oh, not I."

I recognized that bitter tone of voice; I remembered it still from my days at Beida in 1957, during another witch-hunt. It was so as not to hear it that I stayed far away from China for twenty years. The Cultural Revolution, for all that it has now ebbed, seemed to have swept away the reasons for that bitterness, even made it impossible to have brought the battle into the open, with, it is true, the evils of violence, but without the clammy oppression of individuals by bureaucrats. It came to me now like a reproof: remorse for being impotent here, unable to do anything to help these comrades. A principle of freedom—no matter how small, embryonic, contradictory—is being snuffed out.

October 21

From past experience I know how one makes oneself understood in these situations. This morning, as I was leaving the hotel to take the bus, I saw Tang standing some distance away, waiting for the Italians. I made a little detour, and went over to shake his hand, while for a moment I looked squarely, questioningly at him.

I have read the *dazibao* at the Institute. One of them quoted a letter written by the son of Wang Hongwen, in which the son insists that he does not believe his father is a counterrevolutionary. People are saying that it's a "black" letter —i.e., put together by third parties—and it seems that a professor and his daughter, who is a friend of the young man, have been charged with writing it. Other posters were vulgar attacks on the daughter of Zhang Chunqiao, with allusions to her private life. (She works at Fudan, where many people don't know she is the daughter of Zhang, and she hasn't been seen for some days. That can be one way of staying clear of unpleasant situations. Marjorie is acquainted with her, and even before knew about the family connection. But no one can learn anything from Marjorie; she's totally sinicized.)

There are lots of *dazibao* about the May Seventh school at the Institute. I asked Chen about this, too, and she was not reticent. Like almost all governmental and educational units of some substance, the Institute has its own May Seventh school, which is in the country just outside Shanghai. (The May Seventh schools have lost their original character, and are run by the individual unit for the manual-labor training of its own cadres, employees, teachers, etc.) Cadres and teachers go to the May Seventh school in shifts for their stint of manual work. Chen was there last summer. The municipal government of Shanghai, supported by leaders serving on the Central Committee, had organized the recruitment of the best students in the upper middle schools, to be sent to do their period of manual labor in this particular May Seventh school. (The same thing was set up for the May Seventh schools of Fudan and Shida.) Once they were there, the students not only performed their manual work but also attended some regular courses; in a word, they ended up organizing a duplicate Institute. And its pupils were fortunate with respect to students at the Institute because they were continuing their studies while still very young, immediately after getting their diplomas, and so they constituted a potential elite. It seems that the intention might have been to train local cadres quickly and give them a relatively high-level education. In the past, the regular students had protested against this system. Their criticisms: the May Seventh school was an annex of the Institute; manual labor was performed completely apart from the local peasant masses; the school served as a stage in the training of cadres; in this way, it circumvented the egalitarian system whereby, after middle school, all persons should go to work and candidates for the university should be chosen by their fellow workers. In the past, the protests had gotten nowhere. Now, taking advantage of the disgrace of the Four, they are being raised again.

It remains to be seen whether the practice is peculiar to Shanghai, or whether it is an expedient whereby everywhere, or in many places, the obstacle of the "obligatory" years of work after middle school can be avoided. I have the impression that things that have been done all over the country, whether good or bad, are all being dumped on the shoulders of the Four and their friends. People who are, or think they are, being harmed can vent their resentment in this way. In the case in question, the discontented people include, in addition to the students enrolled in the regular curriculum, the cadres and instructors who were, in effect, required to carry a double work load since they had to teach also during their period of manual labor—and what's more, teach in order to train cadres of the leftist faction, to which they were, in the main, hostile.

The same methods and objectives are used to criticize Xu Jingxian for having sponsored the program to send groups of very young people abroad to study foreign languages. He is being accused of servility vis-à-vis the foreigner (turning the Left's attack on the Right back on it), corrupting youth, etc. In point of fact, such groups have been studying for some time in London and Paris, they're not an invention of the Four, nor is the program limited to Shanghai. It is simply one of those initiatives that because they are undertaken quietly and without publicity are easily concealable. There are more instances of this than one might believe.

Today's news highlight is the arrival from Peking of the three men named to govern Shanghai (or, as it is phrased, to "help to govern"): Su Zhenhua (a political leader in the navy), Ni Zhifu (a young engineer with a working-class background, a figure to balance off Wang Hongwen), and Peng Chong, a "moderate" from Nanjing. We have been given no formal announcement of their coming, or why; the word has percolated from Chinese sources—greetings of welcome that are beginning to appear through the city, and now from loudspeakers circulating on trucks. It seems that early on control of the city was handed over to the military—that is, to the Nanjing Military Region, on which Shanghai depends. Now the military automobiles with Nanjing plates have disappeared. In Nanjing too, there is now talk about the Four and criticism of local leaders. It's not to be excluded that the military command of Nanjing is seen as excessively weak in controlling Shanghai. (That possibility would explain the presence, now, of the police that seem to belong to the navy.) Judging from the rumors that are going the rounds and piecing together bits of news from various *dazibao*—especially one posted at the Institute, which was promptly covered over—one might reconstruct the facts like this: Initially, Hua Guofeng was not against the Four but the position he took was not clearly defined. Following the Left's advance this year—that is, after the incidents at Tienanmen Square—a confrontation became imminent; at that point, the faction of moderate cadres (Hua Guofeng) allied themselves with the Right (ex-Liushaoqiists and technocrats, Deng). The Four, in accord with the Shanghai cadres, thereupon decided to arm the militia and to organize workers' resistance against the Right. The various contacts (by telephone and post, in addition to trips) that have been denounced in the *dazibao* as conspiracies probably refer to this phase, as did the mention of automobiles (loaded with arms?) which, according to accusations repeated many times in the *dazibao*, were supposedly sent into factories favorable to the Four, in order to arm the workers. According to the *dazibao*, the Shanghai leaders decided not to communicate their deliberations with regard to Hua's appointment as Chairman; to arm the militia and use the radio and the two local papers to attack the Right; and to mobilize the workers. But the others put the army on the alert and arrested the Four. After which the "peaceful" attack against Shanghai could begin.

Something in this reconstruction doesn't jibe, however. According to the *dazibao*, the local leaders' telephone contacts and trips, or at least some of them, took place *after* the sixth, the day the Four were arrested, according to Western sources. (And they are reliable if, as seems to be the case, at the moment when the "two decisions" were communicated to the public—about the publication of Mao's works and his mausoleum—the stakes had already been laid on the table.) Probably, taking advantage of the confusion in dates, the Right anticipated the moves the Shanghai leaders planned in response to the arrest in Peking of some thirty Party leaders, among them four at the highest level, to show that the Right was responding defensively and to justify its response on the ground of the Left's alleged plotting. It seems in truth that the Left, which was completely at a disadvantage since the majority of the army's leaders were against it, allowed itself to be caught off guard and was unable at the last moment, when it was already decapitated at the top, to muster even an elementary defense or any public show of resistance. To attempt that once the army had been mobilized would have been suicide, and irresponsible toward the workers.

At yesterday's meeting local leaders were present, and they spoke. They took the line of denying any connection whatever with the Four. After their more than week-long resistance, this was surrender. Now it will be easier to remove them (or worse). It seems that those at the meeting gave some support to Ma Tianshui, but not to Xu Jingxian or Wang Xiuzhen. Today there will be a meeting open to cadres and people will be able to follow it over the radio. Tomorrow a regular assembly is scheduled. A few foreigners—Bob, for one—

maintain that a compromise is still possible. This is what the various interpreters are trying to give us to understand so as not to traumatize us. (It's not to be excluded that the same tactic is being used with the Shanghai people, but its success, if any, would be only superficial; people pretty well know what's going on.) In my view, it is puerile to believe a compromise is possible at the point we have reached. Rather, the question is how fast they will be able to move on to the purge. If they move slowly, it will mean that the bond between local leaders and the people is fairly solid. (One must bear in mind that the local leaders are not only the three men at the top.)

Finally, an article in today's *People's Daily* gives a public explanation of why there's been so much mention of Lu Xun lately. (Some *dazibao* had already explained why.) In a short article he wrote in 1936, "The March Concession" *("San Yuedi Zujie"),* Lu Xun polemicized with a certain Di Ke about a book by a young writer. (Di Ke had expressed a partly negative judgment of the book; Lu Xun had championed it.) The Lu Xun text is reprinted, accompanied by a long comment. The article itself is unimportant, although, as always, Lu Xun's polemical style is very lively. However, it happens that Di Ke was the pseudonym of Zhang Chunqiao, who was then very young. Hence the deduction that Zhang Chunqiao must be a vile creature since even Lu Xun's article spoke ill of him. In a sense, Lu Xun's writings are being used the same way as Mao quotations—as oracular voices. Some more crafty maneuver is not to be ruled out; for example, the aim might be eventually to overturn the clarification the Cultural Revolution brought to political struggles within the Left during the thirties and to the diverse interpretations of the united front given by Lu Xun and by Zhou Yang, by Mao Zedong and by Wang Ming.* Today's article is anti–Zhou Yang but in substance could be otherwise. It is evident that it is in fact retaliation on the part of people who were attacked during the Cultural Revolution. Zhang Chunqiao would have seen to it that the one publication which revealed that he was Di Ke was suppressed. More details will surely be forthcoming, and we shall be able to judge better. But for Lu Xun, even forty years after his death, to be dragged into such a wretched business as this. . . .

I walked around midtown this afternoon for three hours. There were only a few processions with placards; the crowds were very dense. It was one of those stupendous days with a limpid sky, sun, and wind. The golden colors are autumnal, but shining, dazzling; when one faced into the light, it was blinding. To make one's way though the press of people was almost impossible.

By now their nerves are shot. They are working as they always do; they get up at dawn, return home late by long bus or bicycle trips, and, in addition,

*For a further discussion of this controversy, see pp. 306–309.

they cope with the unremitting meetings and the processions that march for hours amid an indescribable hubbub, which they augment with their drums, gongs, megaphones, microphones, and their shouting, singly and in chorus. What must the tension be among them, if it's so great among us? They sleep a few hours at night, their eyes are red from fatigue and lack of sleep, their faces are drawn—and aggressive, ironic, scornful, full of bitter rebelliousness.

Young boys were out on the streets in great numbers, hostile, a little bullying, showing off their brand of elegance with a provocative air, which is an admission of unhappiness—as it is among some of our young men in the south of Italy—for all their gentle Chinese pliancy they are dangerously unpredictable.

People were jammed together in front of the *dazibao,* but especially in front of the caricatures, which are gigantic, grotesque, and absurd (the city leaders are included now). Ah! Ah! Ah! People laugh, and point to Yao Wenyuan, Jiang Qing. . . . Plots upon plots are being disclosed; they are numbered, but I don't know what figure has been reached by now. Anyone who may have met with someone else to discuss or to organize something has been conspiring. Little boys copy not only the *dazibao* but also the caricatures rapidly and with great skill.

I was at the intersection of Nanjing lu and Xizang lu, near the big Store No. 1, when I realized that I *had* to get back to the hotel. Although I am small and today was dressed in half-Chinese fashion so that my presence scarcely stood out, I was nonetheless too much, I could no longer be tolerated. "What does this woman want?" "May she drop dead!" I heard these words repeated again and again; it was as if they were following me, stripping me of my security and my identity.

And yet I knew that they had no quarrel with me. I was simply an excuse to release a pressure that was directed against unattainable places, and therefore cried out to be diverted to other targets. Neighbors and comrades and others like themselves, first of all. Even to cross the street provoked quarrels, pushing, aggressive expressions. Violence deflected and turned against themselves.

Celebrations
October 22

Tang's story has had a happy ending, at least to this point. At the time we usually meet in the morning outside the hotel, he was talking with two other people, and I made no attempt to speak to him. I was already seated in the bus when he came over to greet me through the window, as he has done before. In a normal tone of voice, he told me that the others will return to the Institute on the twenty-fourth, but he not before the twenty-sixth.

"When are the Italians leaving?" I asked.

He said a little mournfully, "I am always the last to come back."

So I said, "Well, you're the youngest."

At the Institute, Chen reassured me, too: "You know, Tang's coming back, too." It's not to be excluded that Chen may have used her good offices in Tang's behalf, assuming that her word counts for something. But how did she manage to know what I had understood? They also play at gambling on what we know or don't know.

The city is now filled with red and pink paper sheets of official greetings: "Welcome to Su Ni [Su Zhenhua and Ni Zhifu], sent to Shanghai by the Central Committee." At the entrance to the Institute, there are soldiers on duty, unarmed. Inside, *dazibao* about yesterday's big meeting: "The meeting of the twenty-first is a big conspiracy. Why were the Four not accused?" "Today's meeting is a big conspiracy. . . . It is true that we must unite under the Party, but how is it possible to unite under leaders like Ma . . . who supported the Four?" (The second *dazibao* is dated the twenty-second, but probably "today" is the twenty-first.) Another says: "Let us firmly support the 10/21 meeting." The French have had a meeting with the worker-teacher of their section. In answering Roland, he said that Hua's appointment to the chairmanship was made by the Politburo acting on behalf of the Central Committee. When Roland objected that the Party statutes do not permit this, he changed the subject. He also informed the French that Ma and other municipal leaders presided over yesterday's meeting, but then someone had shouted that they should get out, and they were replaced.

In fact, things seem not to have gone so smoothly. The city's leaders, it's said, offered their self-criticisms. Some of those present did not accept them. There must have been clashes. Apparently the meeting was suspended before its scheduled close. I asked Chen, "Why do the *dazibao* say that the October twenty-first meeting was all a big conspiracy?"

She hesitated uncertainly, and then said, "I wasn't at that meeting. Anyhow, one doesn't have to believe all the *dazibao*. Sometimes they're personal opinions." Shortly before that, referring to the condemnation of the Four, she was insisting on the fact that "they were truly incorrigible."

I asked, "What's been decided about the Shanghai city administration?"

"Two comrades have been sent by the CC to help resolve the question." Then she got lost in Byzantine talk about whether or not the local leaders wished to mend their ways. With me, Chen plays the role of the moderate, of the person who would like, if possible, to save the Shanghai municipal leaders. Conceivably, she is even sincere in this, for that's what a great many Shanghaiese would actually like. On the other hand, her instructions are surely to minimize with foreigners, not to dramatize. In any case, Chen's line, whether it coincides or not with her own opinions, is in keeping with her instructions.

Yesterday's meeting chalked up a few points in favor of the municipal administration and at the same time, I think, signaled the official sanction of its end. Posted along the streets is the communiqué of the Revolutionary Committee, dated October 20, declaring its adherence to the popular will to support the CC and its decisions. The statement is signed by the eight top leaders. But *dazibao* have also appeared, albeit only a few, opposing them in more violent terms. In any event, it's by now public knowledge that the decision to replace the leaders was made at the top. It's not been possible yet to get the consent of the people of Shanghai.

Today, a big demonstration to celebrate the defeat of the Four. It was organized like a public holiday, with much color and noise. The cymbal, gong, and drum corps were all out on the streets (every self-respecting unit has its own, and some include genuine artists). I stayed out for a long time. People were much more relaxed than yesterday. They gave themselves over to the celebration as if it were an ending, a respite. Neutral—as is the sound of the drums and gongs, whatever the occasion. No question about the consummate skill in the production of this enormous happening. Four songs required singing, two of which were "The Internationale" and "The East Is Red." Trucks filled with soldiers rolled by in groups.

In Peking, a big celebration-demonstration is in progress, too. The Four have been named publicly, and the appointment of Hua to the chairmanship has been announced. He is now being openly referred to as Hua *zhuxi*.

Tomorrow there will be a meeting of the foreign instructors at the Institute, at which time they will be given explanations of the recent developments. I won't be able to take part, for I will be leaving in the early afternoon for Peking, where I have to give a little examination at the embassy.

The defeat of the Left was foreseeable. Starting with the events in Tienanmen Square last April, two opposing political battle lines were confronting each other openly—not two tendencies, but rather, on the one hand, a left-oriented composite group that was rife with inner contradictions; on the other hand, an aggregate of rightist tendencies that were heterogeneous but very strong if they could manage to cohere. Never as in these last months has the official press been so transparent, even if it did provide a distorted picture of the balance of strength as favoring the Left, which held many positions in the communications and cultural sectors but far fewer in others. In fact, notwithstanding the compromise reached at the Tenth Congress of the Chinese Communist Party in 1973, the aggregate of rightist factions has held a greater share of power at the top and throughout the Party apparatus for several years, and the Mao of the Cultural Revolution had been defeated in areas of policy as policy is played by politicians *even before the Lin Biao affair.*

We do not have the facts about the conflict at the top in any detail, and all the facts we will never have. But even from what we know now, it is easy to reconstruct the essential. After the death of Mao, in that interminable month of mourning during which the people were kept at their weeping, the final round must have been played out. The Left knew from the start that it was losing; Hua was not in the center but had gone over to the other side (one will recall the scene at the funeral ceremonies, and the use—and nonuse—of the notorious phrase "Keep to the established policy"). The Four had at their disposal the leadership apparatus in Shanghai and in a few other places; the upper echelons of the army were, in the main, against them. That the Four were preparing a putsch must be excluded. Not the slightest proof of such a thing is being supplied at a moment when it would be greatly in the Right's interest to adduce facts in support of the charges against the Four. (There is no doubt that later dossiers will, as usual, be assembled and circulated among the cadres which will prove nothing but on whose authority the cadres, in proof of their loyalty, will rely in reassuring the people.) Given the existing balance of power and what with the army adopting moderate positions, in the Four's situation only madmen could have hypothesized a putsch. (As for a "plot," the word, as we have seen, can mean anything up to and including an unofficial meeting between two people to discuss politics.)

The absence of political debate notwithstanding (the allied rightist factions cannot risk destroying unity at this point, and furthermore to argue publicly encourages discussion among the people, which for now is too dangerous), it is not too difficult to hypothesize what will be the substance of the present leaders' policy in the next months. They have been extensively criticized by diverse study groups (with workers and student members), which used either their own names or collective pseudonyms, and by individual writers both in the Party press and in big-circulation newspapers and periodicals.

(In recent months, the Left has had considerable visibility in The People's Daily and in Red Flag, has had its own periodicals such as Study and Criticism, Educational Methods [Jiaoyu Shijian], Dawn [Zhao Xia], Dialectics of Nature [Ziran Bianzhengfa Zazhi], and prominent exposure in several dailies, like Wenhui Daily, in Shanghai. The best-known study groups, apart from the one at Beida and Qinghua universities in Peking [which sometimes signed articles with the pseudonym "Liang Xiao"], are those of the municipality of Shanghai (with such pseudonyms as Luo Siding and Gong Xiaowen, among others) and of some big factories in Shanghai and other industrial centers. Among the People's Communes, the Xiao Jin Zhuang Brigade has made itself an outstanding spokesman for the Left.)

The policy is not a new one, for it has also prevailed during periods in the past. On the domestic scene, one may foresee emphasis on unity and against class struggle, on authority and on obedience, on order and productivity and against the preeminence of politics, on scientific specialization and against mass initiatives. How far they will go in this direction will depend on the balance of power within the rightist coalition between the old conservative leaders and the aspiring *technocrats, who are Westernized (or Sovietized, which is the same when it comes to methods if not to allegiances) and head the Academy of Sciences, and on Deng Xiaoping. (For the moment, criticism of Deng is being kept up, if feebly and only in the form of an occasional slogan.) There will be a show of liberalizing overtures to intellectuals and academics, a prudent, gradual dispersion of the revolution in education, suppression of the study groups and of the Workers' Militia in Shanghai and Peking (or their castration, achieved by making them dependent on the army entirely and not only, as until now, for the distribution of weapons). Factories will be reorganized to stress and augment production. A few more books will be published. Lastly, there will be a great opening, both political and commercial, to the West—its extent depending on the response it meets in these losing circumstances—and opposition to the Soviet Union will become even more pronounced. There will be a "modernization" of the army (reestablishment of rigid hierarchies, detachment from less strictly military functions, etc.), or this will be at least projected. In a word, whether Deng Xiaoping is present or absent, the alternative program to that of the Left is more or less his; there is no third way. The tone of propaganda will be paternalistic, Confucianist, and provokingly nationalistic. Nationalism will become aggressive—even if for the moment the aggressiveness is on the order of rather foolish wishful thinking—moving in the direction of power politics, and this will go hand in hand with the abandonment domestically of the option for a slow, comprehensive development that is not competitive with, but that is revolutionarily defiant of, the outside world.*

This is precisely what the Left used to call the "bourgeois revisionist line"; that is to say, the policy that is compatible with the interests of the managers, of those in positions of power in the scientific and cultural areas, and of the influential political cadres, followed by a large segment of the intermediate educated classes. Other social classes—first and foremost, the peasants and the workers— have a vital interest in a different policy to meet their economic and power needs. The convergence or divergence of these policy lines with capitalistic interests and policy outside China are direct and close. One need only note the sigh of relief heaved by the entire Western press (apart from extreme-leftist papers), which is kept well informed out of Hong Kong. The Chinese market will be opening up in conditions of relative inferiority as compared to the past; the "Chinese model" will no longer constitute a tempting alternative for workers in developing countries or in some heavily industrialized areas of the world.

In those places where the factions' resistance was measured in terms of their relative strength in the administrative, police, and military organs of the State, the elimination of the Four could be carried out like an operation halfway between bureaucratic routine and palace coup. In Peking and in other cities where the Left poses a problem only in a few institutions and centers of production, the people as a whole were not seriously affected; repressive measures were taken where necessary, and for the rest nothing beyond closed meetings was called for—little more than the usual activity, which over the past year has been very lively. This is how it has been at least during this initial phase, in which nonconformist cadres and individuals have not yet been affected on a wide scale. The leaders who have been eliminated are characterized as public delinquents and held up to the scorn of one and all. The possibility of identifying their crimes or supplying proof of them was not even considered. The Four do not face formal charges. If in the future there is a formal trial, it will serve merely to confirm the sentence already pronounced. The mere fact of their being exposed to public ridicule by those who hold power at this moment makes them criminals, and plunges people into the fear of being charged with complicity. Each individual is led to feel that he himself is potentially guilty, and to be on his guard against possible lapses.

What is more extraordinary—and new in China—*is the elimination of leaders who have had the support of about one-third of the members of the Central Committee (who sooner or later, in one way or another, will have to be taken care of also); in an attempt to make this less traumatizing, the proclamation of fresh replacements is slipped into the national repertory of slogans which serve to screen the fact that things have actually been overturned.*

The expelled leaders will be the targets of daily charges, the "down withs" hurled at them will become proverbial. Their names will be erased from the history books, their faces will disappear from group photographs, and their writings will be removed from bookshops and library catalogs. (Later, when what must be done has been done, accounts will appear, no matter how closely or how little related to reality, that will tell how things came about. . . .)

Some of this is beginning to happen in Peking and other cities, and in many rural areas, while the universities in the capital are occupied by troops in order to keep the students from speaking up. But everything is developing secretly. What China and the rest of the world hear about is the statements of agreement made by the students of Peking. The gigantic demonstrations now being mounted there also, and which are shown on TV, are the closing number, the rite in which the people's joy validates the legitimacy of the coup at the top.

In Shanghai, however, people are yelling in the streets, spilling their guts from morning to evening and all through the night. In this city, the group that has been overthrown included a large number of city and union leaders who not only controlled in part (but far from completely) the cadres but also, and above all, had firm bonds with the most active sectors of the working class and were closely linked to that segment of the educated young who came out of the Cultural Revolution. These elements formed a magnetic force vis-à-vis the whole city. Ergo, the destruction of the Four can be accomplished only by riding roughshod over the body of Shanghai. The base must be separated from the cadres and set up in opposition to them. The first step in widening the distance between the people and the Four is to vilify them and their followers by means of scurrilous personal attacks, to show them as being greedy for power, addicted to pleasures that their exhortations extolling patriotism and virtue denied to the people, bent on enjoying films forbidden to others, endowed as if by privileged right with those consumer goods the worker longs for (Wang Hongwen's motorcycle) although he is urged to suppress his desires for the sake of the revolution. In this way, everything the Four said and did publicly is shown to be false. In this campaign, all direct consideration of political issues is avoided; the aim is to strike chords related to general discontent, to heap the blame for many difficulties on the fallen or accused leaders, although the problems are ascribable neither to the one nor to the other group but rather to an objective situation. The presence of two leadership groups that hold opposed views and are virtually on a war footing has had some paralyzing effects on production, on education, and on the decision-making processes (although not as grave an effect as the exaggerations of the official propaganda would have one believe). Everyone has suffered therefrom.

The split leadership is a public political manifestation of the profound contradictions among the diverse components of Chinese society—its social and generational strata. To this, Mao's death has contributed a loss of orientation and of assurance, and a sense of being lost has seeped into public consciousness. In a country where daily life is hard, the need for "normalcy" is very acute, and one cannot tighten the screws for too long a time.

From on top—through semi-illegal channels since a putsch is in progress—the public is being mobilized, people are being forced to demonstrate, they are subjected to the bombardment of caricatures and dazibao, and pushed to spit out the poison they carry within them. Since the attacks are depoliticized and personalized, appeals are directed to the conservative elements in the popular mentality, which the revolution did not destroy and at times even strengthened. On the one hand, disillusionment with the new is aroused; on the other the wish to repossess the past, tradition, the old morality, and the old prejudices: against the woman who is active in politics; against the wife who does not remain passively dependent on her husband and wants to affirm herself in an independent way; against actresses and against "unchaste" women (chaste women were those who had one husband only and who did not remarry even after his death—indeed, did not marry in the event of a fiancé's death); against young people who are forward and do not obey their elders; against anyone who advocates "going against the current," who does not obey his superiors, and who is receptive to parts of a culture other than Chinese. The degree of virtue must be measured in terms of deference to conventions, such as to drink or not to drink wine in given circumstances, to weep or not to weep at funerals, to express in public proper sentiments. . . . A frontal attack on revolutionary principles is carefully avoided, and criticism of Deng Xiaoping is even continued. No one speaks out against the Cultural Revolution; on the contrary, the illusion is fostered, especially for the benefit of unknow-

ing foreigners, that some sort of new Cultural Revolution is under way, a revolt of the populace against bad leaders.

However, even if tacit or masked in humdrum verbiage, an attack on the Cultural Revolution is in fact in progress; it is carried out by the tactic of omission and of insinuation, and by establishing an implicit but sustained association between the groups that are discredited today and the political tendencies that have been identified with them.

Substance is never discussed; instead, the attempt is to besmirch and destroy all the new aproaches that are customarily subsumed in the term "Cultural Revolution": to act on the basis of reason rather than of authority in "going against the current"—and going even so far as revolt; to emphasize the class struggle; to demand autonomy at the base; to encourage cultural innovation and worker self-management; to foster the polemic of the young against the old, of women against men; to develop a collective economy in preference to individual self-interest; to promote egalitarianism; to oppose study conceived as a training of worker-as-merchandise at different levels; to recognize bureaucrats as a class enemy and the people's struggle to combat them as being "bourgeois in the Party.". . .

The decision to divide the people of Shanghai from their leaders is seemingly easy, but it can have serious and destructive results. By cutting the umbilical cord that unites the base to the leadership, by abruptly blowing up all local municipal authority, one creates a vacuum offering no more than an abstract reference to the Central Committee (which has not even been called into session). Leaders whom people recognize as their own (for better and for worse) and do not perceive merely as abstract images of authority are local leaders—here in Shanghai, the municipal leaders. Zhang Chunqiao was mayor of the city. For this alone, the people, who have been deprived of their frame of reference and freed of their immediate bonds to the organization—freed also of an ideology and a control— could erupt in a violent but vain protest, or they could sink into political apathy and indifference. But to force the people of Shanghai to disown the Cultural Revolution, offering them in compensation the chance to vent their impatience over material and moral conditions that are created partly by the country's objective poverty and partly by the struggle between bureaucratic factions runs counter to the political struggle they have lived through for the last twelve years. Willingly or unwillingly, every single individual was drawn into it. To destroy what the Left preached means immeasurably more than getting rid of the so- called Gang of Four. It spells the end of what for all those years motivated the actions of every individual—whether he acted in good or bad faith, partly out of free choice, partly through coercion: his sacrifices; work and production methods; the search for the ways and means to escape from being merchandised wage earners; the affirmation of a new meaning of life. Everyone glimpses the end of all this, more or less clearly; hence the intolerance he shows in rejecting the end becomes twisted and is vented against his comrades and, finally, against himself. The city is squeezed by such extreme contradictions and conflicts that in no way can it think them through rationally and without outbursts of collective schizophrenia. Passive resistance alternates with a sense of being lost, self-destructive outbursts are succeeded by infantile amusement over the caricatures and the impulse to stage and watch a dramatic show.

The substance of the contradiction seems to elude recognition because it is too all-pervasive. The motives for rebellion and obedience, for conformism and nihilism, the merits of conservation and of destruction emerge from accumulated layers of the past and surface on a terrain which offers no possibility for them to be expressed. All that has been superimposed and confused, all the knots that have not been untied, have been passed off as "solved" in the simplified jargon of socialism. One cannot express, much less study, these things rationally, because the objective and subjective terms of reference are lacking that would relate them to the systems of this or that historical period from which they come down to us —for in China the revolutionary acceleration our century has witnessed has overturned (without destroying entirely) successive civil structures that were in the first place either incomplete or already in a state of disintegration. This is most true of Shanghai, where yet another factor was added—the city's quasi-colonialization by the West. (Shanghai is the opposite of Mao's famous "blank page," unless by blank page one does mean the absence of an organic bourgeois-capitalist structure or rather—as is most likely what Mao intended—the formless mixture of heterogeneous elements.)

The people who work here are in a permanent state of protest and potential revolt. They are the working class as that class was in its primordial beginnings, when, as Marx said, "the rising bourgeoisie needs the State's power and uses it to 'regulate' wages, which is to say, to confine wages within limits that ensure the accumulation of surplus value, to lengthen the working day, and to keep the worker at the normal level of dependency." But the Shanghai working class was born of an already evolved capitalism, and therefore from its beginnings was the more deeply marked by the brand of the wretched of the earth. That once potent capitalism has now dissolved; there remains the gigantic monument to its collapse, which is the city itself, with its avenues and its huge buildings and its little villas —stores and skyscrapers covered with dust, cracked plaster, uneven sidewalks. The factories remain, and the men who work in them, and the old machinery that has been tended and endlessly repaired so that it may hold up beyond the limits of the possible. Traces of a frightful oppression are visible still in the bodies and minds of the old. An enormous accumulation of fragmented objects and ideas inherited from a destroyed past, now reused and further fragmented in hundreds of ways. A fabric rewoven with patience and intelligence from mountains of rags.

And a further part of that destroyed past is the revolution of fifty years ago, which ended in a massacre.

Liberation came to the city from outside, from a more remote past. Peasant soldiers occupied Shanghai; they wandered about in it, dazzled and lost, but they cleaned it up, they began to put the rubble in order, and suggested how it could be used. Everything was diligently restored. More than in any other place, what the peasants and their cadres brought forth has continued to present itself here as a Januslike reality.

The two faces are inseparable and irreconcilable.

On the one hand there is order and discipline. Which is to say, also an ethical order—taken over from the past and renewed: the total subordination of individuals to the collectivity—in the family sphere (the private nucleus as related to the public dimension), in the wider sphere of work and residential units, and, additionally, in the political organizations, which mark the passage from the private to the public realm. The public (national) interest requires that wages be "regulated" and confined "within the limits that ensure the accumulation of surplus value. . . ." It requires also that no unbridgeable gap be established between workers and peasants, who constitute the great majority of the population. Only a very rigid discipline, the preservation of traditional morality, and the control whereby not even the most insignificant individual is left one single moment to himself permit the workers to repress the impulse to object and to rebel, which is implicit in their class situation. Were that control to be lessened, the entire city would explode and set off on utopian adventures that would lead to its tearing itself apart.

In these conditions, Shanghai was liberated from colonial capitalist domination and led toward the recovery of its own identity and dignity, and to a voluntary, impassioned participation in building which even exceeded the limits of its strength. To share in the effort of rebirth meant to be involved in the dialectics between Confucian order and subversive violence that spread throughout the immense country. Obedience no longer to foreign masters but to one's Chinese cadres became obedience to the State (not a bourgeois State but one on the brink of being tempted by authoritarianism) which regulates the limits of original accumulation with a minimum of physical repression and a maximum of ethical pressure.

On the other hand, the soldiers of the People's Army who entered Shanghai in 1949 also carried the revolt against every owner and against the powers that be; the proposal to become "masters of the factory and of the State" restored to the workers the revolutionary ideology already spread among the peasants, for whom the term "proletariat" had come to have a purely allusive meaning. Only here did the long road traveled during the civil war reach its goal, returning to the place where it had begun. "The center of the Party's work has moved from the countryside into the city," Mao Zedong was affirming as early as 1949, and from then on this conviction and this necessity accompanied every resumption of the revolution. *

It is not by chance that the Cultural Revolution had to take off from Shanghai. (It was not only that the callous top-level bureaucrats in Peking were opposed.) However, as things turned out Shanghai was in fact too fertile a terrain for revolt, and the revolt that came could not be controlled or rationally led. The proletarians—in effect, peasants uprooted from their land and pillaged of their identity—are suspended in Shanghai between Confucianist despotism and communism. The hypothesis of an evolution from a premodern feudal epoch to a democratic-bourgeois society and from there to socialism has absolutely no connection with their history nor with their condition today. In fact those social strata and political groups that here offer themselves as promoters of capitalist construction (or "modernization") are not liberal bourgeois but heirs of despotism dressed up in modern costume. Either pathetically or hypocritically they ape the liberal bourgeoisie that affirmed itself in the West in the nineteenth century after the French Revolution and the American War of Independence, a bourgeoisie that for some time has no longer existed. In China old bourgeois cultural weapons are effective against despotism, but a liberation from despotism in the direction of bourgeois democracy is not to be thought of.

It is also true that the values on which the Socialist-Confucian bureaucracy is based can be identified in large part with the content of the Communist revolt —with, first of all, the insistence on the public as against the private interest. Repression and self-repression are based on, and meant primarily to serve, the public interest; without that, every class demand would be regressive, would amount to a defense of "bourgeois rights," and would become one with the search for the "bourgeois way" and end up in China's being made part of the international market, obliged to adopt and adapt to the market's prevailing mode of production. In a word, the country would be reduced to demanding a higher price for its work force in the universe of material goods.

The productivity of factory labor in China is incomparably higher than that of agricultural labor. The motivation to forgo a compensation for one's own labor based on its market value is egalitarian in spirit. But it must be universal, it must

---

*Prior to the Cultural Revolution, the high points of the continuing revolution in China were the movement to collectivize the land in 1955, the Great Leap Forward in 1958–59, and the movement for Socialist education in 1964. The first might seem to have been carried out exclusively in the countryside; in fact, it was intrinsically bound up with China's abandonment of the "Soviet model," which was urged by the workers, especially in the big industrial centers of the northeast. The Great Leap Forward was a movement that attempted to involve industry and agriculture simultaneously; originally, the establishment of the communes was a project to transform the peasants into wage earners, workers. As such, it failed in large part; its positive results—once the period of disequilibrium was over—redounded primarily to the benefit of industry. The movement for Socialist education, which attempted to overcome the rightist wave arising from the countryside, ran its course with no great results.

apply not only to the bottom but also to the top. To forgo defending individual interests is equivalent to capitulation unless it is accompanied by a class-based demand for political, economic, and cultural power, which so far has been in the hands of the bureaucrats, the managers, and the educated classes.

Following the Cultural Revolution, some cadres—those whom we ordinarily identify as the Left—pressed for an extreme form of antidespotic, egalitarian awareness among the workers. They urged the workers to express their deeply buried aspirations and to act in accordance with them. Almost always and almost totally these exhortations led to setbacks for the workers and for the educated young people who had joined with them. Such a setback had not, to this point, extended to the cadres. The most adept among them, those who had managed to keep or to recover a measure of influence even after the major retreat that followed on the Shanghai commune of February, 1967, * were often not the most principled or generous. The workers' dependency on them was not only hierarchical; they were also considered as their authentic representatives; they were among those who had power, but only so that they could represent the needs of the workers and guarantee a margin of freedom and the growth of "new Socialist things" introduced by the Cultural Revolution. The workers had wished that these cadres be solidly with them. They continued, instead, to collaborate with the vast corporation of mandarins, employ their methods in the power struggle, and enjoy the same privileges. They, too, were guan. *And so, because they were closer to the workers for all that they were radically separated from them, they were those the people most hated. It was the hatred workers often feel for intellectuals who express a truth in the abstract but cannot translate it into facts, although they do manage to preserve their privileges. But in this case it was more serious, because they were political leaders. Their behavior seems to have aggravated difficulties for the people, rather than lessened them. Immediate resentment is directed against those who are nearest, who have allowed a truth to be altered and have themselves altered it in a complex of empty forms and empty formulas.*

The evident contradiction between the commitments to sacrifice the private self and to rebel against public power was not allowed to deepen them and endow them with their truer meaning; instead, they were juxtaposed by competing factions among the leadership, each of which was concerned that it might be accused of heresy since each was part of the same corporation.

Given these assumptions, the fall of the leftist leaders has not made for solidarity; it has been received as one further proof of political inadequacy and incapacity. The leaders are held to be somehow responsible for the negative consequences their fall will involve also for the workers.

*For a discussion of what has become known as the "January Storm" (though the commune was proclaimed on February 3, 1967, and lasted only twenty days), see Neale Hunter, *Shanghai Journal* (New York: Praeger, 1969) or Victor Nee's chapter on the subject in *China's Uninterrupted Revolution,* edited by Victor Nee and James Peck (New York: Pantheon, 1975).

After concentrating the image of the entire Left in four individuals (never explicitly, as I have said, but allowing it to be understood in dozens of ways), the guan *who are managing the operation are now, with cynical shrewdness, directing the hatred the people feel for the* guan *against the Four. Nor do they seem overconcerned about the destruction they are wreaking not among their adversaries but in the minds of the people. They calculate that they can control eventual transitory explosions of violence. As for the people's awareness being the foundation and the moving force of socialism, this they do not believe in nor have they ever believed in it, just as they do not believe in "politics takes command" or in the continuation of the revolution; the latter they equate with disorder and see as an obstacle to the building of the country, which they want to do without having their power contested; they consider that the art of governing consists in a series of empirical choices which must be clothed in doctrinal veils that act as the spiritual food (opium) of the people.*

Peking
October 23

I am en route by train to Peking. It is a smooth journey, comfortable, and I have a whole compartment to myself.

The train attendants hover over me as if I were a great lady of bygone days. Upholstery and curtains of silk, embroidered cushions, a table lamp with shade, a small vase with either a succulent or flower. A fresh supply of water for tea arrives regularly. Soon after the train leaves the station, the cook comes, menu in hand, and you tell him what you want to eat. If you step out into the corridor for a moment, someone wordlessly sees to locking your compartment. You can turn down the volume on the piped music, relax in delicious, sheltered solitude, and immerse yourself in the long, long sunset; the light is still warm and autumnal, and it lingers over the fields of almost ripe rice in every tone of yellow. Water and earth, rivers and distant hills. . . . Then darkness comes, you light your lamp, you read, or, as I do now, write. You cross immense distances at night; a sudden jolt now and then means a station, who knows which or where, some place where many people live and rest, and life is never interrupted, and, as everywhere in the world, only the railway workers are awake. Landscapes and climates change—but men less so. From south to north, they have the same way of wearing clothes, of walking, of standing upright and occupying space and knowing themselves to be in this world. To cross China by train from south to north means also to learn what a unifying civilization is.

October 26

When I arrived in Peking, on the twenty-fourth, the final jubilee demonstration was underway—which is to say that people were flowing toward Tienanmen

Square to take part in the demonstration scheduled for early afternoon. The Italians were waiting for me at the station. The ambassador's wife's car got stuck in the crowd thronging endlessly in the opposite direction, toward Tienanmen. Traffic was completely disrupted; even buses could make no headway and ground to a halt. Pedestrians could move but slowly. People were in high spirits, like children; they played games with the stalled cars, pretending they were going to demolish them and of course doing no harm at all. A small group of students turned up, including two Italians, who had just arrived. "We're ashamed to be here," they said, "but curiosity. . . ." The school authorities had simply told them, "We'll explain later," and brought them along to "participate" in the demonstration. Participation was not obligatory, but neither had this been simply an invitation; not to go would have necessitated an explicit refusal. However, two Italian women students at Beida did just that. So here they are, foreign students and experts, holding little flags and duly organized to be part of the celebration. To be present at the festivities simply as spectators is not permitted, except in the case of journalists.

The Peking print shops had worked through the night to produce thousands upon thousands of big color portraits of Hua in the Mao format that were held high as Mao's used to be; sometimes they were alone, sometimes accompanied by Mao photos. The small paper flags attached to sticks were triangular here—in Shanghai, they're rectangular. In addition to slogans against the Four, occasionally you saw even a "Continue to Criticize Deng."

The Italians are affectionately welcoming and hospitable, and it is relaxing to live a "normal" life among them. In the evenings, we go to Peking's pleasant restaurants, which are full of both foreigners and Chinese; the service is excellent. People are orderly and serious, as they pedal along the broad streets; the external appearance of the capital city is programmed to give a sense of stability and security. (Peking is called not only Northern Capital but also Northern Peace; the words "peace" and "tranquillity" are frequent parts of Chinese city names.) It is still too early for the limpid weather Peking enjoys in the winter, but the light is beginning to be clear and transparent. This is a city of appearances—seen from the limbo that is the complex, flexible world of the foreigner here. In between the delicious meals, we have time for some bitter laughs and heretical toasts, by way of a futile, self-mocking revenge for the pressure of the omnipresent cadres, as unbearable to us as they are to the Chinese.

Return to Shanghai by train. A longish pause in the Nanjing station. The car I am in, for foreigners and cadres, is filled with men in army uniform carrying leather briefcases, and high officials. Slogans written in large characters on red and white paper ("We support the decisions of the Central Committee") had all been torn from the walls of the station—deliberately, from the looks of the remains. That doesn't quite jibe with Nanjing's reputation of being sympathetic toward the Right, but perhaps railway men are pretty much the same all over China.

The School

Developments in Shanghai and elsewhere: in Wuhan, it seems, a campaign analagous to the one in Shanghai is underway.

Last Sunday, city leaders were present at the demonstration here, but Ma Tianshui did not speak. The commander of the army garrison presided.

It seems that Hua may have tried to associate with both sides, but that the situation became too radicalized, and it was impossible for him to mediate. So he opted for one side, and momentarily won a little more personal power. But his position is delicate. Once the supporters of the Cultural Revolution have been defeated, there is nothing to do but await the public ascension of Deng once more.

As happened at the time of the 1976 Tienanmen events, propaganda is now concentrated on Zhou Enlai, also in the *neibu* text most widely circulated among the people. Someone in authority has decided that it could be used to inform us foreigners also, and the document was read to my colleagues during a meeting that took place while I was in Peking. When I got back to the Institute, I had a visit from Xing, the elderly cadre in my section, whom Marcial calls *"el calvito"*—"Little Baldy." He walked into my office, holding some papers in one hand and, with Chen looking on rather scornfully, sat himself down at her desk, opposite mine. He had, he said, to inform me of what had already been communicated to my colleagues during the meeting. Whereupon he began to read, without expression and without lifting his eyes from the papers before him, as if to say, I am transmitting what I must transmit, don't ask me for any explanations, I've nothing to do with it.

The body of the text was preceded by an admonishment: Do not take notes; do not report abroad. (The prohibition against taking notes or, conversely, the invitation to take them often accompanies group briefing sessions for Chinese at various levels.) Actually, there was nothing secret about this communication; it simply gave some news (and interpretations) that had not yet appeared in the papers but were to appear shortly. It is one way in which the authorities formally inform us about the whole Four affair. I am omitting here what had been repeated hundreds of times over the radio and in the papers—conspiracies, plots, "they wished to take over supreme power in the Party and in the State," they sabotaged production, etc. The actual news I learned from Xing was that on October 6, the Four had been placed under house arrest, that on October 7, Hua was unanimously named Chairman of the Central Committee and of the Military Commission by the Politburo (comprising the sixteen members who remain after deaths and the dismissals of Deng and the Four). The nomination will be ratified by the Central Committee at a plenary session to be held at a date still to be announced. (This point was made quite explicitly in order to minimize the obvious violation of the Party statute whereby the nomination of the Chairman lies with the Central Committee, not with the Politburo.) The Four repeatedly attacked Premier Zhou. They smashed the criticism movement against Lin Biao and Confucius by introducing a third element, criticism of the *hou men,* * which had not been provided for in Mao's directive, and their purpose in doing this was to create confusion.

Xing proceeded with his exposition: In the autumn of 1974, Wang Hongwen went to Mao specifically to denounce Zhou Enlai. Between late 1974 and early 1975, during preparations for the National People's Congress,* the Four carried out a frantic attack on the Premier, their ultimate aim being to seize power. Jiang Qing wanted Wang Hongwen to be elected one of the vice-presidents, but Chairman Mao was opposed; these maneuvers took place during CC meetings prior to the NPC.†

Furthermore, Xing continued, in many letters and in statements made before third parties, Mao criticized Jiang Qing for being ambitious. Also, the

---

Hou men—back door—is the secondary entrance to a Chinese house, and because it opens onto the rear courtyard it is rarely visible. "To go in by the back door" means to obtain a post through the recommendation or intervention of higher-ups, in a way that is neither clear nor public. Probably they intend a reference to criticisms made in connection with *hou men* which leftist leaders leveled against Zhou Enlai for having readmitted Deng Xiaoping to the leadership group. Deng made an unexpected reappearance at an official banquet in April, 1973, before any inkling had been given that his readmission to positions of political responsibility was even being considered. As for the original movement to criticize Confucius, it was aimed by the Left principally against Zhou Enlai and the old bureaucratic apparatus, which he had salvaged; in reply, it was used by the Right also against Mao Zedong. The movement criticizing Lin Biao and Confucius was promoted by Mao and then publicized by Zhou (Zhou had the means to render such a campaign meaningless if he administered it himself); this represented an attempt at a compromise meant to support the substance of anticonservative, antibureaucratic, antidespotic arguments but without attacking individuals by name. However, to a large extent, each person continued the polemic for his own purposes.
*The National People's Congress met January 13–17, 1975, following the second plenary session of the X Central Committee of the Chinese Communist Party, at which Deng Xiaoping was named Deputy Chairman of the CC and member of the Politburo. Zhou Enlai delivered the report on the government's program to the Congress, and Zhang Chunqiao presented a report on the new constitution. Mao was not present at either the Party or the Congress sessions. The struggle against the restoration, begun by the Left around mid-1973, was being counterbalanced by the slow, continuing reconstitution of the old apparatus, of which Deng's accession was one sign. The growing influence of the Left in ideological and propaganda areas, on the one hand, and the ever-widening takeover of key government posts by the apparatus continued up until the Tienanmen events in the spring of 1976. At that point the Left, worried by Mao's failing health, became more impatient in its efforts to seize positions of power—with some success at the top, but with limited success in the country as a whole because of the resistance of the apparatus, which sometimes went as far as sabotage. The campaign Mao launched for a study of the dictatorship of the proletariat proved helpful to the Left both because it explicitly raised the question of power and because it proposed to deepen the public's awareness and knowledge, without which the resumption of the Cultural Revolution would have been mere rhetoric.
†Mao was in fact in the south at the time, where he was receiving Dom Mintoff, the Prime Minister of Malta, and Franz-Josef Strauss, leader of Germany's Christian-Democratic Party.

Four revealed state secrets to foreign journalists.* The Four were like Wang
Ming's "twenty-eight-and-a-half" Bolsheviks.

(When Xing said this, I asked myself: Is this an attack on Zhang Chunqiao,
who was a young man in the thirties? Or on the foreign-policy line of the Four
for being insufficiently pro-American, ergo impugnable as pro-Soviet? Maybe
both, since the charge of "capitulationism" is now being dusted off again, after
having been batted back and forth by both sides during the criticism of the novel
Shuihu. Xing wound up his remarks with the familiar "Keep to the established
policy," repeating in this connection everything I had been reading in the
dazibao.

I asked who Liang Xiao was—he'd been mentioned as spokesman for the
Four. Xing smiled and answered, "at least according to his pronunciation, the
two schools."† He meant Beida and Qinghua, and their study group. With that,
he stood up, shook hands, and left. A weight seemed to have been lifted from
his shoulders.

Chen is much pleased by the fall of the Four. "The other day we walked
for four hours," she told me. "I was dead tired. But I went because I was so
pleased. Believe me, otherwise I wouldn't have gone." I've rarely heard her so
sincere. Then she talked to me enthusiastically about a film—*The Song of the
Gardener*‡—which was to be shown in the afternoon and which the Four had
sabotaged. "It's about educating young people. I'd like to know later what you
think of it." According to Chen, educators had liked the film, but the Gang of
Four had argued that it went against "politics takes command"; in point of fact,
the educators' job is not to let politics have priority, which means nothing, but
to see to it that young people study well; Chairman Mao, when appealed to, said
that this film should not be forbidden.

I believe there are two main reasons why the film is being exhumed now:
First, it was produced in the Changchun studios, which, together with the
studios of the People's Army, are considered "good" today, unlike Shanghai's,
which are not; second, it reflects the educational theories defended by teachers
who have had a Western training—i.e., between the pragmatic and the neopositivist—in distinction to those who support a class line. A debate between
the two groups was carried on last year in educational journals, with some
repercussions in the schools.

---

*The allusion was to the interview Jiang Qing granted Roxanne Witke. Probably this had been a
trap into which Jiang Qing allowed herself all too ingenuously to fall. (Witke subsequently wrote
a book, *Comrade Chiang Ch'ing* [Boston: Little, Brown, 1977].)
†The pseudonym "Liang Xiao" is pronounced in Chinese the same as the words "the two schools,"
though the expressions are written with different characters.
‡Likening the gardener to the teacher—the plant to be cultivated is for the one what the youth to
be educated is for the other—comes from Bertrand Russell. The allusion, possible because only a
few are in a position to grasp and understand it, is to the neopositivist tradition of the most advanced
Chinese teaching from the 1920s to forties, in opposition to Marxism-Leninism.

This evening there was a film on TV, a phony old Soviet rehash, *Lenin 1918*. How was this useful? It reaffirms the bond with tradition; it exalts Stalin at the expense of some followers of the Four, whose anti-Stalinist heresies were pretty explicit in the last year; it suggests a Stalin–Hua Guofeng parallel, each having been consecrated by the great dying leader's designating him to be his successor. (In the film, there's a scene in which Lenin, after the attempt on his life, lies on what was assumed would be his deathbed, and he summons Stalin to succeed him; here, the newspapers reported Mao as saying to Hua Guofeng, *"Ni guan shi, Wo fang xin"* ("If you are at the helm, I am at peace").

It's very funny to hear Lenin speaking Chinese (the film has been dubbed).

October 28

This morning I resumed classes at the Institute. I spent the afternoon alone in my office, since there was a school assembly in the film auditorium. When Chen came back from it, she reported that a communiqué from the Central Committee had been read, announcing that three persons sent by the CC had assumed the top leadership posts in Shanghai (replacing Zhang Chunqiao, Wang Hongwen, and Yao Wenyuan, who formally were the three top men; in practice, the actual city leaders were the dismissed Ma et al.). The new leaders, as everyone already knew, are Su Zhenhua, Ni Zhifu, and Peng Chong. Tomorrow we'll have a political study period in the section—in my case, with the teachers of Italian; the joint newspaper editorial of the twenty-fifth will be the topic for comment.

Later in the afternoon, Chen went with me to the customs office, which is in the port area, because I had to declare the temporary importation of my old Olivetti portable, which an Italian friend passing through Shanghai had brought me. To reach the customs offices, you cross an area east of the Dasha that is full of workshops and warehouses, the usual piles of material on the pavements, and both old and new houses, ranging from dilapidated hovels to recently constructed buildings with towers. Trees—full grown or sometimes rather stunted saplings—are everywhere, as are people, who are busy running hither and yon, carrying something somewhere. Within the walls of the port, it's like a quarantine zone, silent and deserted and gray. We were stopped several times at checkpoints on our way by car to the customs office, which from the outside looks like a little house except that the doors are barred. We rang a bell. They came to open and ushered us into a large room; two big portraits of Mao and Hua were already installed side by side on the wall. We were received by a rude, irritating young woman; her manner was peremptory (reminiscent of some Italian customs people) and she clearly saw herself as a guardian of public morality. A mini cadre in the making. She rubbed me the wrong way, for I'm not used to such manners. In China, you've only to go a little lower on the employee ladder to meet an altogether different tone. This girl treated me as if I had committed some infraction of the rules, whereas I was there on entirely routine business and on my own initiative. Since I came back to Shanghai, my nerves have been extremely taut from the effort to control myself. Today, my sense of surrender and apartness was such that I found myself no longer able to write the most common Chinese characters in order to fill out a customs form. False ignorance and false guilt, which put me—not consenting but by my own doing—into Chen's hands.

October 29

Political study in the afternoon, with Chen, Zhang, and Tang. I had decided I would say nothing. The text we were to comment on was awash in terms taken from the old Confucian language, especially words designating immorality, evil, and the craftiness of certain "bad public servants." It was all about plots and conspiracies and rampant ambition. Allusions to Jiang Qing as the imperial concubine who, upon the death of the emperor, would want to seize power. . . . (According to Chen, it was *her friends* who spread this rumor as a *way of supporting her!* I had read the identical things in articles by the most anti-Communist, anti–Jiang Qing of Hong Kong's China watchers.) I wanted to confine myself to taking note of the article, since there's nothing to discuss in a piece that talks only about conspiracies. And, in fact, I began by saying as much. Chen and Zhang started to talk in their turn, repeating the same thing over and over. Tang didn't say a word. His hands were shaking. Because he was there, I ended up saying a lot, and I believe I said it in the right way. I used their terminology. I said that what matters is not the conspiracies but the conflict between two policy lines and the class struggle. On this score we were being told nothing. In the West, I said, reactionaries have been contending for some time that the political struggle in China is nothing but a personal power struggle and a series of intrigues. Today, this view is being confirmed by Chinese sources, and the entire Right is rejoicing and congratulating itself. Unless we are given information related to the political content of the struggle, we cannot "defend" China. And can mandarins be divided into good and bad? In criticism of "Hai Rui Dismissed from Office," the answer was no. (This I said without thinking—without remembering at the moment, that is—that criticism of "Hai Rui Dismissed" had been begun by Yao Wenyuan.)

Chen and Zhang continued to insist that there actually had been conspiracies. All right, I don't question it, I said, but it isn't all that important. Intrigue is part and parcel of the struggle for power, which is always going on in politics. But in order to determine who is in the right, one has to see the substance of the struggle (for power, obviously). The winners will always say, no matter what, that the losers have conspired.

"But we must believe Chairman Hua because he was named by Chairman Mao—"

"Yes, named Premier," I said.

"Also *First* Vice-Chairman of the Central Committee," Chen said. "To prevent Jiang Qing's becoming Chairman after he died. Chairman Mao *knew,* and Hua is Mao's continuator. . . ."

"He'll be a good leader," I said, "but as for being a second Mao. . . . And then, out of eight hundred million people, who can say how many new leaders may crop up that Chairman Mao didn't even know—"

"No," Zhang said. "Chairman Mao *knew.*"

"Chairman Mao knew also which newborn babies in all of China will grow up to become leaders? You don't believe in God, but Chairman Mao would be like God?"

Chen got the point instantly, and corrected the silliness: "Yes, you're right, you'll see that soon the policy line will be made clear. . . ."

They insisted that the masses act spontaneously. I flatly denied it. I explained that spontaneous movement can also be a negative thing, and that the nonspontaneous does not necessarily mean the nonsincere.

This point they were very reluctant to grant. Naturally. Because it would be equivalent to admitting that intrigue is answered by counterintrigue.

As to the political line, I said that I see the gist of the earlier slogans being continued: yes to the Cultural Revolution and to the revolution in education; yes to opposition to a policy of hegemony and to both superpowers. . . . Will the criticism of Deng also continue?

Zheng, prudently: "Yes, according to the directive we've read. . . ."

I: "Well, then, exactly what are the grounds of disagreement with the Four?" I went on to say that I am optimistic, that I have trust in the Chinese people and in the Chinese Communist Party *because of their past.* But today it is a matter only of my subjective trust, not communicable to other parties. And unless policy is clarified it will not last indefinitely.

Then I asked suddenly: "Did the Four organize the Tienanmen incident?"

Tang had been sitting motionless until then, except that he was shaking, but now he could not suppress a sudden wordless no, signaled by a quick, almost terrified shake of the head. The other two definitely did not see it. They were vexed.

Chen: "It's not clear yet."

Paying no attention to Tang, I said, "I read the anti-Mao poems that were posted at the bottom of the Monument to the People's Heroes." Tang started to make notes in his notebook.

Chen: "A lot of people went to the square. It was spontaneous."

Zhang: "It was the Feast of the Dead, too."

I: "Don't try to tell me that. I know perfectly well it's been years since that's been observed with any public services."

Zhang: "But for the death of Zhou Enlai—"

I: "Yes, the masses came together spontaneously, in response to a simultaneous shared illumination, like the Buddha beneath the pipal tree."

Many people, I added, might find Deng likable as a person, and surely he was intelligent enough, but his policy line—his three programs—ran counter to the Cultural Revolution. And this much had become clear after all the discussion, all the probing, sharply argued, months-long discussion. I added that for the current line to be defined, I would think it essential that a discussion of related documents and arguments be continued.

Chen was put out. My insistence on the Cultural Revolution. . . . "The first important material about the Cultural Revolution was written by Yao Wenyuan. So how could you?" (Tang half laughed, to himself.)

We moved on eventually to some linguistic clarifications. A band, what is a jazz band? . . . Zhang wanted to know what pop music is. I gave an edifying little lecture on Western art today, not a word of which they understood. Zhang: "Painting that doesn't mean anything. . . ." I, maliciously: "Yes, that's what Khrushchev thought, too. He said that some painting was done by an ass with a tail for a brush." And about "The Demoiselles d'Avignon": "All the reactionaries were horrified." Although Tang didn't understand, either, he was listening with close attention. He believes I am more ingenuous about Chinese matters than is the case.

In the conversations that Dagmar and the French couple had with colleagues in their sections, the Chinese were more open on some subjects, more cautious about others, than the Chinese in my section. Perhaps because in my case they cannot be unaware that I know more, especially about the years past.

The street carousals continue.

October 31

Morning after morning the faces of these unprepared young people appear before me, for even the children of cadres and candidate cadres are simple people. And the effort to help them goes on because they are what they are, perhaps the final survivors of an extraordinary experiment: peasants and workers picked up just as they are and set down at the desks of upper schools throughout this country of 800 million people. The students of the preceding generation, those of the Cultural Revolution, were certainly more able than these, even in "making a revolution," for, within limits, they were little intellectuals. Today's students bring with them only an inherited traditional culture and an immense receptivity, which two things, taken together, put them at the mercy of the teachers and *of their methods,* which are still based on an old dogmatism only slightly corrupted by any pragmatic "modernization"—the China that the revolution found, not the China that it created. Study, and thinking, too, are based on authority and on memorizing. Literate people who have been made only more paternalistic by whatever modernization has taken place, and more ignorant by revolutionary tribulations, find these young peasants to be much more fertile material for the reconstruction of "eternal China" than were their own children, who lived through the revolution. But presently the logic that is now guiding the government will drive most workers and peasants out of the upper schools and humiliate the few who remain. It's inevitable that workers and peasants will be repressed outside of the school even before they are in the school. Perhaps this is how the road will be opened for a new cultural revolution—assuredly for a rebellion that will smolder until it finds a way to express itself.

Publications are disappearing from the bookshops in a hit-or-miss way. It's just that no one is sure what is and what is not "all right." Sometimes people gamble on the uncertainty and leave on sale material that surely is "not all right." At the bookstore for foreign publications on Fuzhou Road, you no longer find even Chinese grammars in French and in English. (Maybe because they're published by Beida?) I protest. "Sold out," they say. "But how can that be? Two weeks ago there were a lot in stock, and there aren't that many foreigners here who could have bought them." They laugh. In that same shop, however, Roland came on the two pamphlets that had also remained—through oversight or as an oblique comment—on the shelves of the Dasha: *The Social Basis of the Anti-Party Gang of Lin Biao* and *Total Dictatorship Over the Bourgeoisie,* by Yao Wenyuan and by Zhang Chunqiao. (In September, on their own initiative, the clerks had added these two pamphlets to a batch of books I had chosen.) Roland took the two pamphlets and handed them to a clerk, together with some other books, so that he could write up a bill and package them. Roland watched the man's every move as he turned the package over and over so as to wrap it well. When he opened it at home, the two pamphlets had vanished.

What the message may be or in what direction it is pointing I don't know, but quantities of little pamphlets are being displayed now which are reprints of two poems by Mao that appeared in *The People's Daily* in January. In the shops selling periodicals, *Study and Criticism* is no longer to be found. In one, however, I have found the magazine published by Beida still on sale, and the July,

August, and September issues of *Chinese Literature.* The Chinese public that frequents these shops doesn't know what kind of a publication this is, and secret denunciations are less likely. In a secondhand bookshop I have even found two issues of the leftist magazine *Educational Methods.*

6.

HUMILIATION

Dazibao
November 4, 1976

For two or three days, a rumor has been circulating that Li Xiannian has been named Premier. Three days ago, on Monday, A—— P—— telephoned from Peking to ask me whether there are any banners here to this effect. (In Peking, there's nothing but the rumor, which originated in Shanghai.) Actually, last Sunday, October 31, on my way home from the Jinjiang Hotel, on one corner of the huge intersection where Xizang Road crosses Yanan, I did see a large red poster, with the paste still wet: "We warmly applaud the appointments of Li Xiannian as Premier and of Ye Jianying as chairman of the National People's Congress. Long life to Li Xiannian and Ye Jianying!" The crowds are always dense at that busy intersection, but no one stopped to read. As I walked toward the Dasha, I kept looking around, but I didn't see any other such announcement. The next day both the French couple and I asked our respective interpreters for an explanation. Chen's answer was evasive: "One doesn't know yet," which, even so, suggested that she was not exactly hearing about it for the first time. The interpreter for the French also gave a vague reply. At the Institute, on the second, I saw a congratulatory banner that had been begun but not finished; the half already written was later covered by *dazibao.* Also some (very few) little jubilee posters have been smothered by *dazibao.* Today it is certain that the nominations have been withdrawn. No doubt it's had to do with an anti-Deng maneuver occasioned by the old leaders' rapid takeover of top posts. Some people, however, claim that Li Xiannian, who is pro-Deng, may prefer to keep the premiership for Deng and therefore declined the appointment. What the incident has confirmed is that each faction has its own invisible organizational channels, which are distinct from official Party channels, although they may be inserted into the same routes.

We see a veritable flood of *dazibao,* most of them against local leaders and cadres, who are accused of being accomplices of the Four, of having sabotaged the program to send educated young people to work in the countryside (this is against Xu Jingxian), of having been against Zhou Enlai, against the Dazhai Agricultural Brigade (read, "against Chen Yonggui"), of having branded all those who insist on the need to increase production "partisans of the theory of productive forces," of wanting only to play politics and of pitting politics against production. . . . Other *dazibao* against the *nü wang* (the queen). . . . An infinity of *dazibao* about an infinity of questions. . . . If their mere numbers did not suffocate me, and if I were not done in by weariness and disgust, I could collect a great deal of information. An entire "sinology" for the "sinologists." . . . People read the *dazibao* with curiosity; for them it's like a you-can-fool-the-people-some-of-the-time puzzle. And each person understands more or less, depending on his mastery of the communications code. A mandarin empire is coming to light, where long-lived gangs contend for power, join forces, split. Where power lies in knowing the secrets of those gangs. Where any opinion whatever is expressed, but only by allusion and metaphor. Where everything that is said or written on whatever subject can be twisted to convey a second, third, fourth meaning. . . . We've always known this, we've always been mindful of it. But to what lengths the ciphering of discourse can go was hard to imagine. And then there is always the problem of what the initial, surface reading may mean. Some meaning it must have, if only on the level of form.

Dazibao are pasted one over another in thick layers, and many are peeling off, shredded by the wind and rain. The weather is turning cold, dampness seeps in everywhere, the dust is turning to mud, the city is a dirty yellow. Radio loudspeakers squawk, processions with banners and little flags follow one after another through the streets—by now it is routine—and groups with gongs and drums roll by on trucks. These people are specialists in celebrations and criticism, even if often they have no clear recollection of which campaign they are playing their gongs and drums for. But they are happy to play them, and they give their all to playing well.

A maze of propagandistic sophistries about production and politics: Words are bandied about until they lose all sense, and people no longer have any criteria to help them decide which speaker belongs to which orientation. Some fogginess is essential since behind the Four the actual target aimed at is the Mao of the last eighteen years. Also, the discontent that arises from opposite causes ("too much work," "too little work") must be channeled against the Four. Everything is being expressed in its basest terms, the mud spatters everything, humanity is debased.

On November 1, the Workers' Militia reappeared by the thousands on trucks, and escorted by soldiers, they staged a parade. One of the assembly points was along the river by the hotel, so I could watch how men and women in helmets and overalls stepped down from the trucks carrying portraits of Mao and of Hua, how they were handed rifles by the soldiers, and how in rows (escorted by soldiers on either side), they marched off to their demonstration. When they got back, the procedure was reversed: Guns were handed back to the soldiers, and the trucks departed, still under escort. One of the accusations that we've been reading against the city administration—at first in the form of rhetorical questions but then as more and more explicit statements—is that city leaders attempted to arm the Workers' Militia in several of the big factories. Probably this is a put-up charge, but it is something that *could have* happened. The radio and papers have been exulting ever since over the militia's demonstration. We'll not be seeing any more of them for a bit, that's for sure.

Weariness . . . the wish to hear nothing, nothing at all. . . . And yet one must be orderly and active. So I get up at six-thirty, go to school, correct papers in which the students write that the situation is fine and that everybody is as happy as can be, pretend not to notice the somber, haggard face of someone who can't manage to follow the lesson and looks at me as if from worlds away. Listen, smiling and calm, to what Chen and Zhang have to say.

In one of the texts written in dreadful Italian which they gave me to correct, I read that, while Chen Geng was serving with the Red Army, he went to see Lu Xun in Shanghai, explained the army's situation in Yanan to him, and drew him a sketch of the area under its control. I asked whether Chen Geng was still living. Chen tittered, as she often does when asked about current affairs, and said, "Ah, ah, one doesn't know yet." I ask myself, Am I in a madhouse?*

Zhang is very much interested in fascism. I don't know whether this is because the Four have been accused of wanting to set up a Fascist dictatorship, or whether he is trying to understand what the Fascist danger really is, about which there's been so much talk in recent months in relation to China. I gave him a concentrated résumé of contemporary Italian history. I emphasized aspects that define Fascist policy, avoiding the equations fascism = violence, fascism = repression. I referred to what was "not a class struggle but collaboration," the corporate state, the totalitarian system (dictatorship of the bourgeoisie as the reverse of dictatorship of the proletariat), nationalism. But Zhang is a very poor listener; he is looking for and hears only those things that are immediately useful to his particular interest. Chen said, "If the leaders of industry move away from the workers, they can become bourgeois by speculating for their own profit." In other words, to be bourgeois is made the equivalent of being dishonest. Probably instances of Soviet-style speculation have been uncovered,

*Chen Geng died in 1961.

even if on a small scale and marginally. But Chen's ideas about capitalism are no clearer than Zhang's about fascism. "Leaders can become bourgeois and still remain personally honest," I said to her. And she corrected herself: "Yes, the main problem is the difference in pay between them and the workers." "No," I corrected in turn. "No, the main problem is one of power and of policy." Chen ate her words on the double.

Is it that they are impervious to a political education that has been going on for almost twenty years? Or do they reject it? When I answer their questions, I refer to matters of substance. For them it is so much empty doctrinal talk. If one rebukes them, they must heed what one says. Yet the conversation peters out because the parameters within which they judge daily reality are different, and they have never dreamed of questioning them. For example, the problem of pay differential is central in Chen's mind (she has never sincerely assented to accepting a salary lower than that of many workers), and the problem of power impinges on her only in relation to her search among preexisting unchallengeable hierarchies for a position for herself in society. Today she said clearly that the school should train "experts" and that education should not be politicized. "There've been cases of interference from higher up." Even more than an opinion, the remark bespeaks her rejection of any authority in the school apart from that of the teaching staff, of which she is a member. Chen would gladly do without the bureaucrats, too, but maybe she considers their presence an unavoidable evil, bearable provided everyone keeps within the well-defined limits of his own jurisdiction. Then, too, she feels that she and they are solidly akin because they share a concern for maintaining order—order of ranks and roles—and because, after all, in the main the same class supplies bureaucrats and teachers; the individuals in both categories have a common matrix. But when the worker teams came into the schools, power passed into alien hands. *These* cadres seemed parasitic and overbearing, not the others. What's more, they made common cause with the students, fostering a fresh threat to the power of the teachers. Politics, to the teachers' way of thinking, is the ideological chatter with which these intruders and the rebellious students mask their proposal to undermine the authority of the professors.

The films "of the Four" have been withdrawn, even if one or two continue to circulate by mistake. Of the other films now being shown, each is worse than the last. The curious thing is that if they are relatively recent, they more or less follow the same themes as those "of the Four," since evidently everybody had to hew to the directives that had been laid down. The inclusion or omission of a few elements here or there, however, does twist or reverse the message. For example, *The New Men of a Mountain Village (Shancun Xinren)* would seem to belong to the series about educated ex–Red Guard youths who are now living in the country and who partly submit to, partly oppose the restoration. The stock character that has been preserved is the poor peasant who sees things in the right way and who helps the young men. But instead of there being an authority—old or new—and an established political line that must be challenged, it becomes a question of fighting "the class enemy" in the guise of an ex-Kuomintang saboteur who goes around poisoning wells and people's tea. The brigade leader, who at first was drawn into error, in the end mends his ways. Chen tells me that the Four had forbidden this film to be shown.

November 6

In the few free moments I have at the Institute, I usually take a look at the *dazibao.* Now there are several against the Party Committee, actually singling out several members by name. My custodians are patently troubled that I read them. On the other hand, they are glad to give me some explanation about those that do not concern the school, especially if they are amusing and relatively unimportant. A case in point: there's one against *Wenhui Daily,* criticizing an illustration the paper published on October 31. In the foreground, a peasant is holding high a huge portrait of Hua. On either side of the peasant are the smaller figures of a worker and a soldier. Behind them red flags, some of which are flapping to the right, some to the left. Aggressive demands in the *dazibao* to know just what all this means. Interpretation: Hua, together with a representative of the peasants, Chen Yonggui, has turned his back on the red flags. That the flags are then made to flap to the right and to the left is a further bit of wickedness.

One would wish not to be involved, and yet inevitably one is, resist as one may. In self-defense, increasingly I refer back to Europe as the locus of my true identity. Even this can be dangerous, given the distance. There's the risk of Europe's being positive to me only because it is different, it is elsewhere—not too unlike the way China, seen from the vantage point of Europe, can be mythicized. There is also the risk that I may be disarmed entirely when I go back to my own country, when the excuse of distance will no longer be valid.

This referring back to Europe and to its values (all of them and mixed together) is illusory, but it is useful as a metaphor for the struggle that I know I have to wage in order to maintain my independence of judgment and to counterpose "something else" to the misery that tries to engulf me—even if that something were the future that we had believed possible for them and that today they repudiate.

Yesterday, Tang was typing an exercise based on a Peking Radio broadcast. I corrected only the spelling and a few words that weren't understandable; apart from that, I did not touch that hair-raising language. I told him there's no point in reading those articles. The Italian is bad, the accent is poor (if the students listen to a tape recording of the broadcast), and the material itself is too difficult

for them, given their present command of the language. The rest, which I did
not go into, he perfectly well understood. Chen was present, and she suggested
to me that I choose several fairly simple excerpts from the papers—"news
stories, even if they are old." I am too quick to look down on this woman, who
is obliged to keep in step with the central directives and on the right side of the
local cadres, me, the students, Tang. . . . This morning, she had to inform me
that a selection on the revolution in education, which, some time ago, following
an order from them, I had expanded from *China Reconstructs*, will not do
because the original had been written by the Steelworks No. 5 people. (Other
considerations apart, this is not even so; the material came from a report written
by Beida and Fudan students.) I answered that I could not interfere in their
decisions but that this is no longer a question of the Four: "And don't fool
yourselves that you are preserving the respect in the world which you earned
for yourselves in years past. You are acquiring the 'friendship' of the bosses and
their hangers-on. Of all the people I have met in China, the workers at Steelworks No. 5 are of the highest caliber; the interview the Qinghua group gave
to the *Wind from the East* Italians was very interesting. You invite ridicule when
you make all your trivial gossip public. There's not one copy of Beida's Chinese
grammar to be found in the bookshops. . . ." I was talking to a wall of silence.
The sole apparent interest of my noninterlocutors is to keep a minute account
of whatever I think. Tang and Chen Hongsheng were present during this (Chen
Hongsheng is a schoolmate of Tang's who nominally should be working with
him at the Institute, but he's been in Nanjing and came back only a few days
ago, perhaps because Tang's fate has not been decided yet, and they want to have
a replacement on hand). The two young men were embarrassed and pretended
to be busy with something else.

    "One must not say that Deng Xiaoping . . . was a counterrevolutionary."
. . . "With the excuse of criticizing Deng, they ruined production." . . . "Anyone
who was concerned about production had slapped on him the tag 'partisan of
the theory of productive forces.' " . . . These are things one reads in the *dazibao*
and that one is beginning to read in the papers. Rumors about Deng himself are
going about which can't be verified. For example, during the mourning for Mao,
he is said to have asked to visit the body, and the request was granted, but he
could not go during the hours of public ceremonies; it is also said that, after
paying his respects and offering the ritual expressions of grief, as he stepped into
a waiting automobile, another car bore down at top speed and crashed into his;
whether he has entirely recovered is not known. Perhaps these are just stories,*
useful in making a public figure look likable. The reason why so much attention
is concentrated on Deng, among both Chinese and foreigners, is that whether
he returns to power or not will be an index of how far the restoration will go.

---

*Which have since proved to be mere fabrications.

Houses

That minimal connection with the outside world which had been granted us now seems to be narrowing. They may no longer take us to visit factories. Since there are some cadres whose sole job is to organize "activities" for us, they've got to make us do something. So, they have taken us to visit Tianshan, which is a residential section, one of 138 that have been built on the outskirts of Shanghai since Liberation. The usual poor, decent houses, with two families sharing kitchen and bathroom, four people living in an area thirty meters square. This is, even so, a fortunate situation in a city where a large number of the inhabitants live piled together in a very restricted space and sleep in bunk beds. In this new Shanghai housing one senses a relative well-being compared also to the situation elsewhere in China. Wood floors don't make for the sense of squalor that gray cement floors do. Poor as the neighborhood is, it has a shopping center with walks reserved for pedestrians; those for little children are fenced off. Planting helps to make the extreme simplicity more attractive; there are the indispensable public facilities. After listening to the *baogao*, we visited the shops, the kindergarten, a worker's house, the housewives' workshop. You can always manage to learn something new, but only some special detail. Everything is preestablished according to a stereotype, the identical thing is repeated in Peking and in Luoyang, in Xi'an and in Shanghai. In Shanghai, the rents for workers' houses are slightly higher, but even so are extremely low. The same nursery schools with the same little children, the same little songs. . . . The first few times you are moved, but with time boredom sets in. Workrooms for housewives began as a revolutionary thing: get the women out of the narrow confines of the house, socialize their work, increase its value with a salary. Time passed, and the older housewives who had had no other opportunities were succeeded by younger generations of women who could work in factories or elsewhere, so that to continue to keep women in the workshops has ended up being discriminatory. The wages paid are minimal (equivalent to a starting apprentice's salary), thirty yuan, or about $17 dollars a month, and often the women work full time. They make small parts for factories, or they do needlework or some form of assembly work—workshop labor, off the books, performed for the State. Sometimes the surplus value is enormous, as in the case of wearing apparel and craft items produced for export. When we foreigners arrived at the Tianshan workshop, the women looked tired, but they were busy, and they kept right on with the task at hand. Now and again, curiosity overcame them, and they glanced up, but one sensed that they were too familiar with fatigue to be cordial. (In the older streets in midtown Shanghai, between two little shops there will be a window behind which you see so and so many sewing machines lined up, with a woman behind each, and little tables piled high with pieces of cloth, like rags.)

We used to admire this well-planned poverty, the universal capacity for sacrifice, the striving for a decent life, the ability to turn even the patches on clothing into ornaments. Should we now read these things in the reverse sense? Are these people not the same today as yesterday? The *baogao* has not changed: statistics, Cultural Revolution, the activities of women and of older people, the "three-in-one"* (here, where it concerned the upbringing of the children, it was to consist of school, family, and elderly workers), and the reminder of past sufferings. "Now the inhabitants of the quarter, under the leadership of the Communist party with Comrade Hua Guofeng at its head, study Marxism-Leninism in order to criticize the anti-Party crimes of the Gang of Four; faithful to the last wishes of Chairman Mao, they adhere to the basic line of the Party to bring the revolution to its completion."

We asked, among other things, what system is used in assigning houses. The application for a house—made by a husband and wife, say—is submitted to a municipal office; it may be presented in the quarter of the city nearest the then home of the wife. Older couples have precedence. The request may be made to the work unit of the husband or wife only if that unit has houses at its disposition. However, here in Shanghai, for example, there are many fine houses that are not of recent construction. Who lives in them? On the way back in the bus, Zheng, the English-language interpreter, gave John and me some further explanations. At the time of Liberation, a few houses were assigned, others were simply expropriated, and most continued to be inhabited by the people who had lived in them before. The most desirable residences are apartments in detached houses. Attractive or ugly, they are assigned as they become available, according to rank. The most highly placed cadres have precedence. The most expensive apartments cost forty yuan ($28) a month, but even those for fifteen to twenty yuan ($10 to $14) are very good. They are not easily come by, however, even by those who can afford them. "For example," Zheng said, "I would be able to afford one." Lao Bai, he added, lives in a villa.

The level of consumption is at once higher and lower than it seems, which is to say, the range is great. The quarter we visited today has 56,000 inhabitants. It has the indispensable shops, it's true, but they are, in all, the equivalent of an extremely modest department store, a food store with few essential products, and a shoemaker's shop. Quite a contrast between this and the kind of merchandise that is for sale in the special store where we go to shop.

A Young Man

I am grateful to my foreign colleagues for the mere fact of their existence. We represent for each other proof that it is possible for human beings to communi-

---

*A system of collaboration among three component groups, proposed as an attempt to put an end to factionalism; the three could consist of people, cadres, and soldiers, or youth, old people, and adults, or workers, technicians, and teachers, etc., according to the context.

cate. I can go to John's for tea in the afternoon; his living room has many windows, and sometimes a clothesline is stretched across on which Maya's clothes are drying, but it always has the nonaccidental disorder of a workroom. Here early industrial Shanghai meets old England to produce objects that John loves to discover and use—antediluvian typewriters, copying machines, radios, recording equipment, desk lamps, musical instruments. Among them, a flute, which he often plays; the notes sound faintly out in the hallway. Or in the evening, I can take refuge in the rooms of Uta and Dagmar, which are cozily furnished like homes. One closed door separates me from Susan, who grows thinner with the passing of time; I don't talk with her much, and yet her companionship is the most precious, informed, up to date, and discreet.

She, the French couple, and I have taken to eating regularly at the first round table in the restaurant; at a smaller adjacent table are Olga and Marcial, with Aymin, who climbs up and down her high chair; she can now say a few words in all our languages. These days, even John sometimes abandons his rigid economizing and self-sufficiency and comes down to have the evening meal with us. The boys who work regularly at the hotel take turns with students from Fudan in serving us; if the latter happen to be peasants, they are more timid and a little less ill-mannered but substantially the same. Shuffling educated young people to the country and workers and peasants to the universities has produced one effect in the generations under thirty-five, which is a homogenization of cultural elements. The "degradation" of advanced study is a two-faced affair here, too. One of the male waiters, who may be near thirty, is notable for his bizarre, theatrical wish to communicate. He comes to serve us only now and then. The system of rotation, if there is one, will always be beyond my comprehension. However, today at midday I found this man chatting with Susan, who was sitting alone at table with her usual pile of magazines. His face is thin, his hair slightly disheveled, his eyes at once lively and languid—the rather feminine beauty and seductiveness one often finds in Chinese men. In his flirtatious approach to Susan, he was saying, "How should I address you—as miss, madam, mademoiselle?" There followed an exploration, humorous up to a point, of the forms of address for Chinese and foreigners. For the Chinese, there is the universal *tongzhi,* but may one call every foreign guest "comrade"? Well, then, what to do? (The Chinese equivalents of Mr., Mrs., and so on sound disparaging, as *barin* and especially *barinya* did in Russia after the revolution, and do not correspond to the neutral forms in English, Italian, or French.) *"Il m'emmerde,"* Susan commented later in French, and she told me that last year, when she was still alone and had just come back from her summer vacation, this young man had told her how sorry he was for her, and said he would call her *meimei* (little sister). Centuries of reading sentimental novels reemerge here, but there is also a continuing irony directed against a factual situation and the restless search for indefinable good things that those books nourished, and that is sparked today by new stimuli—"material incentives," too, and above all personal gratification. The attempt to bend these impulses toward a revolutionary tension is finished now. It's not easy to foresee what will follow.

This same young man became involved, at dinner, in a bittersweet discussion with John about the "romanticism" in films. He declared that he does not like it, just as he does not like anything that is *fengliu*. (*Fengliu* means "dissipated," "joyously dissolute," with the suggestion of sex appeal; but it also had the connotation of style, beauty, nobility, and cultivation.) "But how is that?" I interrupted him. "Chairman Mao uses the term in a positive sense in his poem 'Snow.' " This he didn't remember, but found it the better part of valor not to say so. I went up to my room to fetch a copy of Mao's poems, and showed him the last lines of "Snow." "Oh, but here *fengliu* has a different meaning," he said. He took the little book and began to read aloud, with the strongly accented, almost singing tones that tradition prescribes as proper in reading classical poetry. He was pleased with his performance, poor as it was. He was merely playing his own character, as they all do in this immense theater.

John, the French couple, and I discussed what is going on. To this point, Roland is reacting in healthy fashion. (But I don't know how he will resist the future pressures to conform; I have more confidence in Pascale's toughness. Roland is disgusted that people keep avoiding any and all political discussion and busy themselves with minor matters. John, who no less than Susan follows and registers everything he can, on the one hand is beguiled by the news, the trivia, the secrets that come to light; on the other hand, he is inclined to put a positive valve to the emergence of individualist demands. It seems to him that people are finally beginning to come down to earth, that they are less entrapped in petty politicking and empty rhetoric. He is seduced by values that until yesterday would have been called petit bourgeois; to him, they seem worthy of respect, a sign of civic spirit. We talked about the housing problem; John says if only the municipality did not allow government housing to become run-down and then, from time to time, spend huge sums to have it badly repaired, but instead were to raise wages a little, making each person responsible for maintaining and improving the premises assigned him. . . . And, basically, it's a good thing that minor employees and teachers claim the right to live in a home of their own, as do at least some of their bureaucrat superiors; it's a move against privilege and proof that they don't despise decent living conditions, as they sometimes seem to. A good thing, too, that incompetent professors and do-nothing, inept master workers be criticized. . . .

The upper echelons are obliged to mime a cultural counterrevolution as if it were a spontaneous movement of the base: the fiction would not hold up unless it contained some elements of truth, even though polarized in only one sector of the population. All of a sudden, a quantity of information and ideas that until now have been restricted to X or Y level of the eighteen-tier hierarchy is being made public. The middle class is fascinated and excited but largely unprepared to cope. It cannot defend itself against, nor is it able to appraise and discriminate among, all the data pouring down upon it. This flood of information would seem to be a sign of mass democracy in action and at variance with the Confucianist hierarchical administration that has actually opened the floodgates; in some ways, it is more reminiscent of the Cultural Revolution, albeit in reverse. Blows are being dealt "politics" and ideology, and everything that is a protest against politics and ideology is being released. Individual feelings and resentments are emerging; the concrete and the personal are emphasized; a too undefined horizon is being narrowed; universals are rejected; the private and public sphere are being opposed to each other. This dimension had already manifested itself with the exploding of the initial uncontrolled freedom of the Cultural Revolution.

As the right emerges from ambiguity, it is provoking the emergence also of demands it will not be able to satisfy—demands not only for "material incentives" or for an increased consumption which are incompatible with the country's economic level but also for "bourgeois rights" to personal liberty that are incompatible with the Confucianist order on which the Right's own authority is based. And if indeed it were intending to support the creation of privileged mass sectors, as has been done in other Third World countries, what measures would it have to resort to in order to impose the related costs on the more than 600 million peasants? In China, it is too late to reestablish an absolute separation between city and country—the only separation on which a hypothesis that is simultaneously ultraconservative and replete with technological aspirations can be based in a country that is economically backward and that has a very low median income. Also, it is foolish wishful thinking to base the future of the country on the urban middle class. In the cities, the decisive component is the workers; the plan to join them to the middle class failed even in instances, in some Western nations, where "affluence" made a broad stimulus to consumerism possible. The workers are won or lost in the factories, at the workplace. This is a fact, as inescapable in China as in other countries.

Concert

This evening we were invited to a concert of Chinese music. At six-thirty, someone knocked at my door, and there instead of Chen stood Tang, who had been assigned to accompany me. Who knows why they sent him? Perhaps to reassure me and also to test him. I do enjoy his company. And at least I will not be subjected to Chen's chatter. Chen is scrupulous in carrying out her duties of persuasion with regard to the crimes of the Gang of Four. Tang was dressed very suitably for the occasion and had slicked his hair close to his head. He used to let his hair be shaggy and somewhat messy; it seems that even the way one wears one's hair carries a message. That's been so in the West, of course, but here the differences are less conspicuous, more subtle. While I was putting on my coat, he went over to glance at my books. He noticed that I haven't found the short stories of Hao Ran I've been looking for, only excerpts from his long novels. He promised to get me a volume of short stories from the library. We all set out together, except for John and Alissa. Again, the entire city was brightly lighted. "What is that Christmas lighting outside?" Susan inquired frostily of her interpreter. The woman answered a little uncertainly that she hadn't seen, she didn't know. . . . (She was being truthful. A moment before, she and the elevator girls were talking among themselves in Chinese, asking each other about it.) A soldier—I've no idea who he was—was sitting with us in the bus, and he said the lights had to do with shooting a film. My escort thought also that this was the case.

The theater we went to is an old one, *belle époque* in style, and may have been built as a music hall. Here it did seem a great luxury, and I found myself saying "beautiful." I had no idea what a concert would be like; this was the first I'd attended. Our seats were not all in the same row, as they usually are at the films—a sign that these tickets are in greater demand. I was fairly far forward, with Tang and the younger bus driver. The audience was not the usual cackling crowd munching on candies and nuts.

The usual girl—in Shanghai she is likely to be prettier than elsewhere— announced the numbers on the program. She was allowed a touch of rouge on her cheeks, and like all the other women who appeared in the course of the evening, she was wearing the one "elegant" woman's costume: a single-breasted suit, the jacket wide but nipped in at the waist, the skirt pleated. Nylon stockings, shoes with a bit of a heel—the audience craned its neck to see the shoes.

The piano was a concert grand. A thin woman dressed in dark-blue wool, wearing glasses, and with a permanent wave, played a Chinese composition of classic-Soviet derivation. Then she accompanied a male soloist, dressed in a *ganbu* jacket—flashing eyes, a touch of social realism, a touch of modern Peking opera—who sang melodic Sino-Soviet songs. He had a fine voice. (Chinese voices are now perfectly trained in Western vocal techniques. Their pianistic technique is also decent.) Then they brought a *zheng,* an instrument that resembles a horizontal harp, onstage. A graceful and serious young woman played a piece by a contemporary Chinese composer who, Tang told me, is very well known. I'm not competent to judge how conventional or academic his music is, but I found this piece very enjoyable, and certainly superior to the standard imitative "Westernized" music usually played by the Chinese. More singers, both men and women, followed. Familiar songs were alternated with new ones about the Gang of Four and the new Chairman. Response to that was chilly. . . . Apropos of one song, very popular, Tang said, "The content's been changed," and made a literal translation; he meant that the words had been changed. The audience applauded, which customarily it does not do; people liked the melody and, I believe, didn't care about the new "content." Another song celebrated Chairman Mao, who will live forever. . . .

The grand finale: a small Western-type orchestra onstage, with a chorus behind it. The members of the orchestra and the conductor, in a *ganbu* jacket, were elderly. They performed several (beautiful) poems by Lu Xun from the early thirties, which someone had set to noisy/declamatory music, again sub-Soviet in style. The words were projected on screens on either side of the stage, as is done here for opera. What meaning can Lu Xun have—even tooled up with social realist music and presented on an operetta stage—in Shanghai today? Every word, every sound is loaded with ambiguous meaning. This concert was the evocation of a fantasied cultural ambience fashioned of fragments of the twenties and thirties, a West that does not exist, the conflicting dreams of yearning people who are at odds with themselves and with each other. Obsolete Western models, false forms as they are filtered through the Russian transmission to China, and yet they seem authentic to these men, deprived of other cultural references, who are crushed between the big night school of their country and the fortuitous fragments of knowledge.

May Fourth, the thirties, the forties—every time still waters are stirred, so many things and problems surface once more, which are still not solved. The old groupings, the wranglings, their now dramatic, now obscene mixture with political events. And Lu Xun against now one now the other, still today understood only by a minority because he was too far in advance of his age and intolerant of the quarrels between political and literary sects. And yet, even today Lu Xun is exploited, distorted by these people, so similar to those of yesterday, as if resuscitated from another era.

It's like being in a dream, being taken backward into the remembrance of the past, though the colors are now faded. The memory of the youthful years of our fathers. Shanghai reminds me of some photos kept in my mother's chest, which I used to look at as a child, or illustrations from old magazines. . . .

Defamation
November 11

This morning the radio reported the surrender of the Shanghai railway workers in the form of an anti-Four statement. Earlier this month there had been a similar communiqué by the Peking railway workers and the famous locomotive works. It seems, however, that at several railroad junctions the situation may not be under control yet. Party contingents, supported sometimes by soldiers, are arriving, meanwhile, to establish order in all units. This reinstates a method of control from above that has made for so many difficulties in the past, and was so vigorously challenged during the Cultural Revolution (by attacks on the repressive use of such crews in the 1963–64 campaign for Socialist education, and in the period of the so-called "white terror" at Beida and Qinghua in early 1966, when many rebelling students were deprived of their personal freedom and criticized as rightist elements). Sending workers into the universities in 1968 was also a way to get rid of such bureaucratic-style intervention.

At the Institute, they are beginning to reap the harvests of the discontent they have sowed. The biggest headache—because it can't be concealed—is the arrival of the young people from the May Seventh school, who have come on foot from the country, and are demanding to know what their fate will be since the school has been attacked as a base of the Four. They traveled in a group for many kilometers on foot, and arrived at the Institute asking to be put up; they have begun to write *dazibao* complaining about their reception and the fact that the Institute doesn't want to let them take their meals at the mess. "What can you expect?" Chen said, when I asked her what she thought, since she'd carried on so about the May Seventh school. "The young people aren't to blame. And furthermore, the school exists, it's there, the students are prepared, they can't just be sent away." Some way will be found to fit them into the Institute. Separate classes will be set up for them, and there will be no trouble about keeping them all in line, because they are demoralized, and in spite of a few passing flareups, they're tractable.

From Italy, friends write that everything there is going to pieces. I feel profoundly alone. I listen to cassettes—Beethoven quartets, anarchist songs— to smother the din that comes from outside and to smother reality with familiar sounds from the past which are like a certainty of childhood or of centuries gone by. The connections that are allowed with the world outside are narrowing; even the mail comes late, and letters arrive in bundles. Things are rotting in a moronic repetitiveness. The sky is the color of mud.

We are reading an article suggested for political study; it has to do with the misdeeds of Jiang Qing while she was at the Dazhai brigade. She used to feed corn to her horses and she used secretly to watch *Gone with the Wind.* The title of the film is given only as *neibu* material, and everyone was intensely curious to know what it's about. If the book were imported, it would become a best-seller. The same curiosity and the same chatter, a few days ago, in connection with a poem Mao wrote for Jiang Qing, "Ode to the Plum Blossom." This led to a botanical/philological discussion with me about varieties of plum and about the wild plum.

I myself don't understand what makes me accept passively being caught in an ever-narrowing circle. In spite of the reasons I've given myself for why I have not insisted on going to the library, I really don't know why I haven't. And why do I avoid leaving the office during the fifteen-minute break after my second hour of teaching, and in this way give in to a request that Chen conveys to me only tacitly, that she would never dare put into so many words because

she hasn't the right? I am more disciplined and submissive than is demanded
of me. Some days ago, I became aware that Chen or Zhang or someone from
the administrative office comes to meet me at the Institute gate to hinder my
stopping to read the *dazibao*. If they do see me reading them, they try later to
cross-examine me about what I know and what I've understood. I'm getting into
the habit of playing the fool; I act as if I've understood almost nothing. I am
surrendering to the control. Every day, I retrace the same steps at the same
times: the obligatory route to the toilets (outside stairway, puddles, piles of
rusted wire to be clambered around); the obligatory route to the mess hall
(turning corner after corner along the gray corridors, washing the chopsticks);
the extra work during my leisure time, which is not obligatory (I do it voluntarily though I'm usually dropping with fatigue). I no longer go even to the
Institute's little bookshop. The incentives to acquire the "theoretical" knowledge that might be available here are fading. It is too obviously a jumble of
falsenesses. I could not offer any positive motivation for this behavior, but I
know that I am like a prisoner or a hostage. I don't react because, in actuality,
the only real way to react would be to leave, and I have decided, instead, to stick
it out and remain here for the duration of my engagement.

It seems to me that the truth is to be looked for in quite a different direction
from the one I have followed in the past, and that knowledge, far from being
withheld, is offered to me entirely—if only I will learn how to look around me
in the cage I find myself in, and to understand and interpret the data of the
limited yet very vast experience available to me. My personal situation will
become more and more suffocating, and things will become more and more
intelligible.

November 19

"The wrong that has been done by the Gang of Four is being examined analytically, unit by unit," Chen informs me. So that's why Party contingents have
come from outside. I had heard that the purge was in progress at the *xian*
(county) level, but obviously we have already moved beyond that. For a lot of
people, the torment is beginning, but also the true struggle; for in this country
of elastic resistances neither verbal consensus nor self-criticism necessarily
means a real change in direction—above all, not when the person who must
decide knows that he can count on explicit or tacit agreement in his own unit.

Chen's persuasive efforts are unremitting; her conversations are like the
little lectures on the radio or TV or in the papers. If she does not manage to
convince me, it will be a professional defeat for her. One moment, she professes
that she is supplying me with economic and political information I've asked for
—and at other times, she reverts to personal gossip about the Four. Either way,
she is boring me to distraction. Actually, one can now read articles that are
explicit about the economic line—for example, one in *The People's Daily* on the

fourteenth—and only someone who is ignorant of the precedents or who is a perfect idiot could fail to realize that we are at the point when the policy will be overturned that Mao carried forward for at least eighteen years, albeit with failures and backtrackings. Sometimes I feel they must take me for an imbecile. And then I realize that I'm wrong. Nothing is expected of me other than what is asked of the Chinese themselves: a verbal act of support, in my case, without self-criticism. It is not important that your support may be expressed out of ignorance or in bad faith.

"What the Chinese people have achieved is the fruit of great sacrifices. We must not slow down now. . . . We can work even twelve hours a day. . . ." The example of Dazhai is cited only on this score—labor that is unstinting of effort. Omitted is any reference to *how* the members of the brigade came to make such a commitment or to the fact that in the past Dazhai was proclaimed a model brigade because it had achieved good production results through Communist rather than production-intensive options. Today the Dazhai people are being metamorphosed into a kind of Stakhanovite collective, and Dazhai's original significance as a symbol is thereby altered. "It is not possible to consume and consume without producing more. . . ." China's population continues to grow, and increased production is a very real and urgent need. Today, this need is invoked in condemning worker demands concerning issues other than wages; such demands are represented as being the results of the Gang of Four's propaganda; the Four "intended to ruin the economy" in order to weaken their opponents politically and thereby "usurp" power, and therefore they "preached laziness" among the workers (and "ignorance" among students). Not only that. They also fomented disorder: "In Hangzhou, there were grave disorders, provoked by a leader who was one of their satellites [Weng Shenhe]; this man was criticized by Chairman Mao, but the Four removed his name from the criticism." . . . "Also among the railroad workers the Gang of Four caused many disorders." On November 12, *The People's Daily* stated that even after the earthquake in Tangshan the Four fomented disorders among the railway men, while the railroad workers in Canton, according to a broadcast on the thirteenth, are declaring that had the Four not been stripped of power, they would have caused the railroads and the country to suffer even more.*

This is not merely a question of individuals or of trends. An entire class

*The strikes in Hangzhou and other cities in Zhejiang Province, and labor unrest among railway workers throughout the country, were essentially spontaneous, the factional struggles being superimposed on them in various ways. It seems that, early on, Wang Hongwen was sent to Hangzhou to restore calm and was unsuccessful; whether this was because he was incapable or because he refused to resort to harsh repression of leftist cadres and of workers is not known. As for the railroads, the Four had no interest in fomenting disorder in the period of the earthquake, when a rightist Minister, Wan Li, had already been dismissed. Protests at the base were against the leaders of now this, now the other line. Several foreigners mentioned having seen at the time some slogans in a station: "Down with Zhang Chunqiao."

is gaining self-assurance, and demanding that *the others* decide to obey and to produce in disciplined fashion. At the Institute, there is a steady stream of erudite *dazibao* put up by the *raffinés* of the Chinese section: classical quotations, scholarly word play, allusions to literary characters from the past, references to Sima Qian, ancient China's greatest historian, and his *Records of the Historian.* This is the academy liberated. . . . At a gymnastics show in the big roofed stadium, I was sitting in one of the well-placed seats that are available to us; next to me was a young man with courtly manners who had with him a little girl dressed with true elegance. Surely he did not spring up out of nowhere. Why until today was I unaware that such people existed? And yet they are the people who are closer to us foreigners; perhaps, like us, they can eat mandarin oranges and lemons (which are not found in the fruit stores but are bought in the hidden shop for the privileged), and smoke the same expensive cigarettes as we. Yesterday, while we were talking about systems of musical notation, Zhang remarked, with a little smile, "Chen knows how to play the piano." She parried this like some eighteenth-century young lady: "No, no . . . once upon a time . . . now I've forgotten. . . ." Satisfaction on the part of both.

My Chinese colleagues are so much amused by the defamation of the Four that they cannot believe these stories do not interest me. Instead, they're afraid that I don't believe them, and so they keep piling details upon details that they find in their *neibu* leaflets, the *dazibao,* and the newspapers. "Wang Hongwen used to enjoy himself at night [doing what one doesn't exactly know; in all this talk among the Chinese, there is a hint of eroticism, and possibly here, as in other gossip about the Four, there's an allusion of this sort, but it's elusive], so during the day he was sleepy and didn't study. Once, in a single month he spent twenty-three thousand yuan. [How?] On the other hand, once when Zhou Enlai was offered tea, he asked the price because he did not want to accept anything without paying. Wang Hongwen truly was a bourgeois element!"

Even Zhang Chunqiao's daughter, who has reappeared at Fudan, criticizes her father. In the thirties, Zhang "was a KMT agent." He was scarcely more than a boy at the time and, living in Shanghai, followed the Party's directives of that period to collaborate with the KMT—ergo, he followed the line of Wang Ming.* Allegedly, he wanted to "modernize" the Party! (Actually, in those days the term was "bolshevize," but now they don't dare remember that—they would have to attack Stalin.)

---

*In actuality, Zhang Chunqiao was writing for a magazine edited by Ding Ling, which was anything but close to Wang Ming and Zhou Yang. The latter, a partisan of the Wang Ming line, is one of the elder bureaucrats attacked during the Cultural Revolution and now awaiting rehabilitation. Such confusion is being created in both political ideas and political tendencies that presently people will give up trying to make head or tail of it all.

But the person most libeled is Jiang Qing. Twice she "betook herself to Dazhai to plot. The Dazhai people, she said, had let themselves be taken in by revisionism and were politically backward." (When Jiang Qing said "Dazhai," she intended the reference to be to the Dazhai brigade leader, Chen Yonggui, with whom she strongly disagreed because she considered him a supporter of Deng Xiaoping.) People expatiate about her "bourgeois" behavior during her stays with the brigade: she used to dress elegantly, she made use of a car, she drank wine at meals. Even during the illness of Chairman Mao, she did not go into seclusion but continued to live her normal life, she was politically active, she even chattered and laughed. She was trying to imitate the (Tang) Empress Wu Hou and the (Han) concubine Lü Hou, who upon the deaths of their respective mates "usurped" imperial power. Even Chairman Mao once said that she was ambitious.

The image of the ambitious, conspiratorial, egoistic woman who, just like a man, aspires to power is reflected from Jiang Qing on all women. There is a wave not so much of antifeminism as of misogyny. Good, *nice* young girls feel pressured into jeering at recent films, in which a woman often appears as the heroine. In the old China, among the possible grounds a husband could adduce for divorce was a wife's loquacity and jealousy. One observes a return to the glorification of the submissive, dependent woman who claims no right to an independent personality. In the most recent version of the ballet *The Girl with the White Hair,* the protagonist flees from her master's house, taking with her another little servant girl. This detail is now to be eliminated, apparently because the girl is never a leader, much less can she be a leader if she has not yet been educated by the Party. The story of the successive alterations made in this ballet scenario could be the subject for a doctoral thesis.

Because Zhou Enlai is unassailable, he is the one fixed point around which propaganda swirls. "The Gang of Four were waiting impatiently for Premier Zhou to die," Chen says. Tied in with the exploitation of Zhou Enlai is the hoopla over a film called *The Pioneers,* which is about the Daqing "man of iron," a miner who goes to absurdly stubborn lengths in the search for oil, and who performs superhuman feats in the early days of the development of the oil fields. (The character is based on a real man.) We saw it a few days ago. It's a bad film and stupidly patriotic; to be reputed "an oil-poor country" seems to be a matter of national shame for China, and the search for this natural resource amounts to a battle for the country's honor rather than what it was—a desperate, dogged drive aiming at survival at a time of tragic economic difficulty, after the withdrawal of Soviet aid. The happy fact that oil deposits were found to exist is presented as a victory. There is the usual saboteur, naturally, who is discovered to have served time in jail and in the KMT. These idiocies turn up in a lot of Chinese movies. *The Pioneers* was made by a film studio controlled by people who are hostile to the Left, and it seems that Jiang Qing might have blocked the film's being exported. But this would scarcely suffice to make such a big thing of it, especially since it was not banned inside the country, although there are insinuations to the contrary; it was shown even on TV last summer, while I was in Peking. Apparently, it contains veiled allusions to major political figures—Zhou Enlai as the good guy, Zhang Chunqiao as the bad guy. Jiang Qing became aware of these allusions, and she is alleged to have tried, unsuccessfully, to have them cut. So, in order to relish such little games, there is now being spread far and wide this absurd glorification of dull-witted stubbornness—the idea that if you don't stop looking for oil, there's bound to be oil and you're inevitably going to find it. Next week, it seems, this film will be the topic for political study.

It continues to rain, with brief intervals of wind and clear skies. But the norm is mud and a penetrating humidity that makes one feel colder. They say that south of the Yangtze the climate is mild, and that to economize central heating is not turned on. But in Shanghai the temperature can fall several degrees below freezing. One makes do with little stoves—they're more like the handwarmers we had in Italy than stoves—that are fueled with bricks of coal dust mixed with soil. There are no stoves in the schoolrooms or dormitories or workplaces, but the heating system at the Dasha is first-rate, and my room is one of the warmest.

A People's Commune and a Party Among Strangers

On Saturday, we went to visit the suburban People's Commune of Huangdu. Heavy gray clouds were being pushed across the sky by the wind; but no rain. These trips by bus would be enjoyable if I could give myself up to my own thoughts or look at the countryside. Instead, Chen is always by my side, with her unsparing tutelage: "Shanghai consumes too much. One cannot expect to consume and at the same time slow down production. In the last years, with the pretext of making the revolution, too little has been produced. And then, not all of China is rich like Shanghai. The cities aren't enough, people can't eat machines. The other provinces don't like Shanghai—they ask why the city wants to follow the Four's line—and that's why they refuse to provision Shanghai. So the suburban communes have found themselves in difficulties, and they've had to change their plans and increase their quota for grain crops. In any case, their grain production isn't big enough yet for Shanghai. Things are being adjusted now, because the other provinces have seen that the people of Shanghai are not in agreement with the Four, and they are willing to send supplies. Nonetheless, Shanghai must increase industrial production and consume less."

This business is not clear. Chen's little lectures about how the other provinces do not want to supply Shanghai with food because it's been "bad" are so much foolishness. On the other hand, it is a well-known fact that Shanghai does have supply problems, but they are shortages of raw materials for industry and, to a lesser degree, of a few nonessential consumer goods, but not cereals.

In fact everywhere in the city one finds abundant supplies of sweets, biscuits, dumplings, and noodles, not to speak of rice. The rationing of these items is a means of controlling distribution rather than of limiting consumption. Often biscuits can be bought without a ration card in midtown shops. This or that item of fresh produce may be temporarily in short supply, but that is due to seasonal factors more than to anything else. It is a fact that to this point the suburban communes' productivity does not suffice to supply all the grain needed by Shanghai, but they have been working toward that goal; probably, there will now be a move to interrupt this program. And it is to this end that the little stories are invented about difficult connections with other provinces, no doubt generalizing from a few actual cases.

It's obvious that Chen is talking in line with directives that she has received; they have been transmitted to the leader of the Huangdu commune also, for later, during our talk with him, I asked a few questions on this subject and his first answers were identical to what Chen was saying. (The statements made to us at the places we visit are agreed upon in advance with the Institute cadres, who sometimes even supply carbons. Ditto for the replies to our initial, foreseeable questions. Only if we persist, framing the questions in different terms, do we sometimes manage to obtain a reply, or a partial reply, that is not preestablished. Success or failure depends mainly on whether the person to whom the question is addressed intends to communicate something or nothing that is off the sanctioned track.)

It seemed to me important to hear what this commune had to say on this score, for, like the other suburban Shanghai communes, it is one of the richest, technically most advanced, and politically most alert. I know that when one is dealing with some worker cadres in the schools it's relatively easy to show how vacuous it is to urge the primary importance of politics against the exigencies of production—but not with cadres of a unit like this one. This is the first production unit we have visited since the fall of the Four was made public. Who knows what criteria dictated the choice of this particular unit? Perhaps people here are in agreement and so there "aren't any problems"; or perhaps "things are being brought into line" and answering our questions is one of the tests that must be passed.

However muddled and childishly expressed, Chen's unofficial introduction seems to imply a radical reversal of the direction followed to this point. Self-sufficiency in cereals *at all levels,* from team to brigade to commune to *xian* (county) and to province, has until now been postulated as a primary, unarguable goal. Where it was not yet achieved, one worked to attain it. Not only has one read this for years in the press but also it was repeated at every opportunity when one visited communes throughout China. Self-sufficiency in cereals is basic in a country where they constitute the people's principal food. If this is now being put in question, it is the principle of self-sufficiency itself that is being put in question—the principle of "independence, autonomy, trust in one's own strength," which is the foundation of the theory of self-government at the base. Mao's plan envisaged that self-government would be extended gradually from small to larger units when and as improved conditions in production and communications and a maturing of the people's political and Socialist awareness made this viable. Basically, it was a process of growth: The power at the base would develop and eventually replace the authority of the bureaucracy. The bureaucracy's self-interest opposes autonomy and favors a system of centralized political and economic management whereby the division of all tasks is preordained above and communicated "from branch to branch" down to the base units. If the base units are deprived of their economic self-sufficiency, they will be left with no effective weapons of opposition. Once again the people will be completely at the mercy of a central leadership.

In his early remarks, the commune man also lamented the fact that, in the wake of the discord sowed by the Four, the suburban communes had been pressured to provide Shanghai's food supplies by themselves, something that lay beyond their powers. "In the past, China was like a single chessboard. The remote communes could supply the grains, the suburban communes the fresh garden produce, the city the machinery. . . . Self-sufficiency in grains is possible within the commune, but the commune cannot supply the entire city of Shanghai." No less disturbing than Chen's, these urgent prayerful statements had to be made for our benefit, like the ritual remarks that had preceded them—the masses are pleased with the victory over the Gang of Four; they have celebrated that victory; they are now engaged in deepening their criticism of the crimes committed by the Four. The man's remarks seemed to be oriented in favor of a return to a "before" (before the Great Leap Forward) when "China was a single chessboard"; they were also calculated to quicken the desire of the members of already rich communes eventually to grow richer by concentrating on truck farming, for fresh produce brings higher prices than grain. The aim of centralization is compatible with organizing production in marketing and profit terms.

However, when the commune leader went on to examine concretely the policies adopted at the outset of the Cultural Revolution, and their results, he presented both as excellent and offered no proposals for change. He said that one-third of the commune's land is planted in fresh produce, and a little less than two-thirds in grains. The commune supplies the city with fresh produce in the quantities sufficient to meet the quota specified in the State plan. Cereal production meets the needs of the peasants; also, grain is stored both as a food reserve and for future sowings; some is used as fodder; and the surplus, five million *jin* (three thousand tons), is delivered to the government. Before the Cultural Revolution, he added, they made only one harvest of rice a year; now there are two harvests of rice and one of wheat. In this way they have increased production by 40 percent. A further increase is planned through the application of methods of intensive cultivation, with a greater use of machines and fertilizers. To apply the principle that "production hinges on cereals," he added, "there is ideological work still to be done. It's a question of struggle between the two lines; in fact, with truck farming you earn more."

The man did not have to be urged, but talked on his own initiative. Obviously, he *wanted* to communicate something different from what was laid down by the carbon copy, or at least to offer an interpretation of his own, which is to say, of the commune's peasants and cadres, for had his views and theirs not been compatible he would not have dared speak this way. Underscoring the fact that yield could be increased by increasing productivity (the unstated implication was that it was not absolutely "impossible" for the suburban communes to supply Shanghai's grain), he was putting his knowledge as a "modern" peasant at the service of a nonprofit-oriented cause and in favor of local autonomy understood in comprehensive public-interest terms (the entire city of Shanghai) rather than in the narrow sense of group enterprise (the possibly higher earnings for the commune were it to concentrate on growing fresh produce).

This was a genuine lesson against the shift now in progress, and it was offered in a quiet, undramatic manner. When Roland asked the man what harm the Four had done, he replied (according to directives for the agricultural sector), "The Gang of Four sabotaged the movement to learn from Dazhai. It is essential to carry out ideological education among the peasants so that they may learn from Dazhai, as Chairman Hua has said." But then he added, "This education *should take as its pivot the class struggle,* but this has not been adequately done." It was a very clever response: While seemingly obeying directives, he was tacitly turning them upside down: "Learn from Dazhai"— the slogan which is now being twisted into a production-oriented sense—was brought back to its original meaning. What's more, the opportunity was seized to reaffirm another slogan that was not heretical because it has been repeated by Hua Guofeng but that has nonetheless been used in the criticism of Deng Xiaoping.

The commune leader showed a similar independence in answering questions about the system of keeping accounts—whether by team or brigade. He skillfully avoided taking a position against changing over to bookkeeping by brigade, as current directives provide.* Without expressing an opinion, he offered a positive evaluation of accountancy by brigade, and maintained that it was necessary to propagandize among the peasants on this issue; he voiced a proposal that throughout the commune one should shift over to accountancy by brigade relatively soon, thereby implicitly stating that here the conditions for it do exist if the level of the entire district is compared with that of Dazhai.

The question today is one of those for which, by definition, there is no answer, and indeed there may be none for years: To what extent will a policy rigorously programmed at the center succeed in transforming a people's way of organizing themselves, establishing relationships, thinking, being? How great will the resistance be, where will it have an effect, where will it turn back upon itself? And how far will the conditioning imposed by the so-called modernizing of the economy go? To answer that, one would have to be able to define the boundaries between what is transformation and what is not, between what counts and what does not count in people's lives.

I had to buy something at the No. 1 department store, and at 1:00, immediately after lunch, I went out, taking advantage of a clearing in the weather and

*The base agricultural unit (cadres plus association of peasants) divides among its members that portion of its own revenues designated for salaries according to the amount of work done by each; this is calculated principally on the basis of hours of work and a system of work points credited to the various jobs. The manner of division of the revenues among the peasants varies according to the level of the base unit chosen to do the accounts. If such accounting is done at the lowest level (i.e. the smallest unit, which is the "team"), peasants from the same brigade but from different teams performing the same job for the same number of hours would not receive the same salary if the per capita revenues of the two teams were different—if, for example, one team worked a more fertile piece of land, or was working land given over to crops that brought in more in the marketplace. If, on the other hand, the revenues and per capita distribution are done at the brigade level, those peasants doing equal work in different teams of the same brigade would receive an equal salary. Still remaining, however, would be different salaries between peasants of the same commune belonging to different brigades. If—finally—the reckoning is done at the commune level, then those belonging to all brigades within the same commune would be compensated equally. Differences would remain, however, from commune to commune.

High-level accountancy fits the goals of socialization and communization—but risks over centralization; low-level accountancy is conducive to some form of peasant autonomy, but risks an entrepreneurial development in the agricultural economy, with growing disequilibrium between rich and poor units (all the more pronounced given that in practice the "team" is made up of only a few families, who are often blood relatives). Mao's program was to start with lower-level accountancy (by team) and gradually change over to higher-levels (brigades, then communes), but only when the culture, technical knowledge, and political maturity of the peasants guaranteed that such a changeover was taken by their own free decision and that was still practically autonomous even at the higher level. Dazhai was one of the first to adopt accountancy by brigade, whereas in '76 the majority of communes were still using team accountancy. Yet in more advanced areas there were many examples of brigade accountancy, usually on a vanguard or experimental basis.

The Right was against passing over to brigade accountancy and accused the Four of attempting to accelerate such a changeover. After some reticence in the first few months, the Right has definitively settled on accountancy by team. Still it is probable that even today, in 1981, brigade accountancy continues, due to passive resistance toward turning back the clock.

the hour, for at that time the streets are a little less jammed, whereas by two the tide is at the full. There is a lot of blue now in the jackets people are wearing. I walked among the people on Nanjing Road as I did two months ago, and it seemed the same in every way. And yet this country is not the same. Where, in what is the change? I passed two young men who were looking at a caricature; they were pointing at it, and giggling: officials clapped into the stocks, the jokey political anecdote. . . . But there is nothing new about this. In Italy, we are so politicized and ideology-prone that often we lapse into the illusion caused by looking at reality through the lens of the political moment; if we then remove the lens, what remains is nonpolitical, indeed, completely disconnected from the political. Here Confucianism provides a key. Everything is a metaphor of politics, a dimension available to the few and withheld from the many; the individual life moves through repetition and tradition. But even in that life there is the constant, imperceptible presence of politics, which is nothing other than the morality that guides every action.

Foreigners who live here despair of ever being able to convey a sense of events to people in their own faraway countries, even to close friends. The pro-Chinese/anti-Chinese uproar is as meaningless as it is irremediably extraneous to what is tangible. . . . And here we don't agree, for each of us embodies the pro- or anti-Chinese stance he has known at home, and when we talk seriously together, we can even quarrel. But we share a homogeneity of experience that makes communication among us superior to any other. We are a ghetto in harmony with a universal trend of our society.

And in the warmth of exile and ghetto, this evening we found ourselves at Shida, in the residence newly built for foreign professors, with banisters and furniture of dark lacquered wood; after the long trip by trolley-bus through city streets and night-darkened trees, it was as comfortable as a private home. We were there to bid farewell to Paule Garçon, who is leaving for Argentina, where she will continue to teach French. Margaret, the tall, warm-hearted Australian, had prepared a cold supper. Everyone ate, drank, laughed, listened to music, and pretended to be alive. Finally, taxis were called, and everybody squeezed in—Aymin sound asleep—and back we went through the immense city now bathed in rain, the streets black and glistening—streets that are ours, yes, and that nonetheless for us will always remain unknown and unattainable.

The Mandarins
November 22

Yesterday—Sunday—an excursion to Wuxi. Our group included the foreign professors from Fudan and the Institute, twelve in all (counting Felicitas), protected by eight Chinese, plus a Lüxingshe representative. (Missing: two of the Japanese, John and family, Marcial and family—the expense involved for three people begins to be a bit heavy.) When we got up it was still dark, and we went out into the cold bundled up as if we were in the mountains, for a six o'clock departure. At the station, we found our railway car—first class with open seating, no enclosed compartments—full of foreign students from Fudan who were going to Suzhou. They'd asked for Wuxi but got Suzhou; several of us had asked for Suzhou and were bound for Wuxi. We swapped funny stories of how to go about getting what you actually want.

The train was moderately heated. The sky cleared and was crystal clear. In Wuxi there is sun and clean air, not like Shanghai.

What Wuxi may be like I can't say, for it was, in effect, off bounds for us. Every foolish wish to walk about unchaperoned was brushed aside. A bus picked us up at the station, and on this bus we circled around the city without ever entering it. We caught glimpses of narrow streets, rows upon rows of plane trees, as in Suzhou and some parts of Shanghai. French plane trees, they call them here, the kind with the peeling bark and big white patches. Lines were strung from tree to tree, and from them countless garlands of little Chinese cabbages had been hung out to dry—and here and there, clothing and blankets to be aired in the sun.

The small low white houses that we happened to pass by had neither the black decorations nor the nobility of those in Suzhou, nor the upper floor of wood that one often sees in Shanghai, but they do vary in shape, and they have windows of varying sizes at varying heights, their floors and roofs also at varying levels. There are canals, boats. The Grand Canal passes by here, with the dense web of natural and artificial waterways that are intertwined with it south of the Yangtze. Wuxi is an ancient city of water, a center for commerce, silkmaking, fishing. With a library that ranks among the most famous, the Nagel guidebook says. Wuxi used to be an obligatory stopover on a trip from Suzhou to Changan, and later from Suzhou to Peking, and it provided sublime retreats for the chaste and unchaste pleasures of the literati.

With firmness and foresight, the tranquil day of the mandarins had been reserved for the new foreign mandarins. With scant success, for we barbarians did nothing but chafe at the bit and complain and, in the end, giggle. Being older and less barbarous, I surrendered to a passing moment of repose and artificial happiness. And I was grateful, in the end, to our escorts for having made me wander all day long over and around Lake Tai Hu, which is immense and circumscribed by an infinite succession of hills.

On the Peninsula of the Tortoise's Head and on the lake's many islands the vegetation is conifers, laurels, maples, willows, cinnamon. At once lake and sea, like a more southerly Lago Maggiore. The water is clear and almost motionless, as is the sea in Holland, the reeds like those at the mouths of certain rivers on the Tyrrhenian Sea. The granite is gray and reddish as in northern Europe. But unerring artifice has given the landscape its form: contorted, perforated stone, pavilions, large and small, with pagoda roofs. Nowhere is there any excess, everything has been done with restraint. A few new buildings, hospitals or convalescent homes, have been skillfully introduced into the landscape. We boarded a small lake steamer, and took a long cruise among the islands toward the distant hills; we went ashore on one island. The boat was a fine new one, chartered for us. The crew put on a show of skill for us, steering the boat in pursuit of a pair of gloves that had been dropped overboard and that they fished out, finally, with a reed.

Most of the time I spent inside the cabin at the bow. The wide, clear windows allowed one to look all around as if one were standing in the open. Little by little, I surrendered, but in measured fashion. This natural-artificial landscape precludes any romantic appreciation. No immensity, no Kantian sublimity here. . . . For someone like myself, who is forever in search of synthesis, it is almost incomprehensible—at the very least, extremely enigmatic. On a shining plank against which I was leaning by a window in the stern, a pale-yellow cachepot, in the shape of a cup, held a vase with four large pale-pink chrysanthemums. Against the clear light of sky and water, it was a death image. Beauty and intense cold, surrender to death. It summoned up the intense cold of a winter long ago in Peking, which I had thought erased from memory. (This battle that the Chinese are waging against me today, to induce me to believe in their "truth" of the moment—that the revolution is a tale told for idiots, and that life is nothing more than the miserable daily effort to put each other down, plus an abstract doctrine, which is a thing unto itself. I say "revolution" by way of metaphor; I could say "freedom" or "reason.")

And yet the history of this country is full of other revolts: explosions, upheavals, *fanshen.* It is precisely that: overthrowing and violence, the other pole, that which is not. That which is the continuity of death, pleasure and intrigue and theory on high, above a people that is denied and without history. It is the dialectic of analysis, or of totality, as in the thinking of the great Taoists.

Then, as in that long ago gelid winter, love and compassion returned for this great people that labors hard and patiently in poverty.

Midday meal at the hotel in Wuxi, in a cold that made me drowsy. Then the ritual rest in a public room with armchairs ranged all around, the little tables with the tea, the rug, the central light fixture—a standard model seen everywhere. The afternoon program: a visit to the Li Yuan and Xi Hui gardens. The German women requested, with some insistence, a few free hours at least to walk wherever they wished. "Do you have to buy something?" was the reply. In the end, the request was ignored. We asked at least to make a tour of the city. They pretended not to understand. But it was not merely pretense. There was, as there always is, the difficulty of making them understand that a person can want to walk through streets by himself. They do not know how to define such a way of spending time. It is not part of the preestablished, standard visits and also plays no part in their own habits, according to which one walks along a street with the sole aim of getting somewhere—at the very least, going to a shop. We, as usual, felt like kindergarten children who yearn to rebel against the sensible teacher. Our reaction is rather like the impotent irony of the eunuch.

The garden of Li Yuan, on an island on a lake lying within the great lake, is a model of the Chinese garden, with a hill of stones, a labyrinth, a passageway beneath a wooden arcade over the lake. Poetry is engraved on stone panels as dark as slate, which form the walls along the passageway. Through one opening, you enter a small inside garden, with bridges over its own small lake; the lake is closed off by iron railings. In the distance, a strange little villa is visible, eighteenth-century European in style, graceful, maintained with care and elegance. It is a private residence. (The "second home" of whom?)

Before coming here, almost by way of granting our requests, we had been conceded a free hour to walk about the garden. As I was walking alone through the arcade, I ran into Uta. We grinned. In another part of the garden, there is a series of square pools separated from each other by narrow paths, allusions to the walkways that thread irrigated rice fields. The rhythm from one to the next is scanned by perfect square pavilions of dark wood. In the late-autumn afternoon light, it looks like a Chinese version of the garden at Marienbad.

The bus took us around the outside of the city once again. Before going on to the Xi Hui garden, we paused at a little shop where they sold the small clay figurines that are a typical product of Wuxi. Everyone had fun looking around and buying. The radio was on, with the usual rigmarole: *"Yi Hua zhuxi weishoudi dangzhongyang zhouwei..."* ("Closely united around the Party's Central Committee, under the leadership of Chairman Hua . . ."). The wrinkled little old man who served the customers, with the help of a woman, kept muttering to himself like some ditty: *"Dadao sirenban, dadao sirenban..."* ("Down with the Gang of Four . . .").

Chrysanthemums by the hundreds were displayed along the shady paths in the Xi Hui garden, and in the pavilions, where they were arranged in cup-shaped cachepots on little tables and black carved chairs. For an Italian, inevitably they have a funereal connotation. There was a spring—"the second spring" —a little fountain above ground. You throw coins into it, and they sink slowly, following a curious zigzag. I have seen this little game in so many places in China. They always tell you that the zigzag happens because the water is special. Perhaps it happens when the water has a certain specific weight because it is rich in minerals, or for some other reason.

"Alors, tu passes toute ta vie à faire des zigzag. ..." I looked up, and my eyes met those of one of our escorts, Bob's interpreter, from Fudan. He was older than the others—at least, he looked to be over forty—and had a conspicu-

ously ill-kempt beard (almost always a Chinese man's beard grows on the cheeks and on either side of the mouth, but sparsely), and he was wearing a light, faded cloak, old-Chinese in style (very much in vogue this winter among intellectuals). Once again from twenty years ago, there emerged unexpectedly a ghost that I had put away. Rightest elements, the ultra-Left. . . . Confused, pushed around from school to work, promoted and criticized and reeducated by this directive and by that counterdirective, by a revolution and by a counterrevolution, now serving the people, now obeying the hierarchy. . . . The tortuous path of yes and no, of the public and the private, the double meaning, cruelty and love. I know these drawn faces, the shining eyes, the prematurely aged faces, the gray hair, gray skin.

Here there are no Zhivagos. The Chinese do not as a rule liquidate intellectuals in camps. Rather, they absorb them into the cadre element. It is the great edifice of Confucian tolerance. "The great bloodless crime," Lu Xun wrote, half a century ago.

Love and compassion. Be careful of these feelings, I tell myself.

We went into a pavilion of dark wood, with scrolls on the walls, chairs of carved ebony, small tables, an exquisite tea. The Lüxingshe fellow, whom the others call professor and who does seem to know a lot (but may have no more than the professional guide's superficial knowledge) told old stories from the Han and Tang periods. He spoke distinctly, and I did not need an interpreter. (Earlier, in a pavilion on the lake, he had told us tales from the Warring States, Wu and Yue, bordering on Lake Tai Hu, taken perhaps from a popularization of Sima Qian's *Records of the Historian.*)

Bob was seated near me, with his interpreter between us, who appealed to me as he translated. The Lüxingshe man talked about the beautiful concubine Yang Guifei, and about the scholars who used to pass by here on their way to Peking. Almost in one breath, Bob's interpreter and I corrected him—not Peking, Changan. These pseudo-intellectuals are hostile to today's culture, yet falsely claim a classical culture of which they know not even the rudiments.

Tea was made of water from the "second spring." The Lüxingshe fellow quoted bits of Tang poetry. Behold, here were we in the coveted situation of being guests of scholars, promoted to the status of honorary scholars. . . . But my friends didn't even realize this; they were bored, they didn't listen, and snickered among themselves.

We returned to the hotel in near darkness, through long galleries of trees; it was a clear cold evening. Once again we sat in the lounge, waiting for dinner. Bob's interpreter took a chair by me. His eyes were gentle and expressed a kind of attentive, melancholy doggedness. A pro-Zhou man? Who and how many pro-Zhou men are there, and of what stripe? Many years ago, in a moment of protest a friend said to me, "I will turn to my government." (For years, people used to write to the Premier to complain of injustices, giving the letters to transient foreigners to post for them.) How many Chinese in these years have turned to their "government"? In defense of what interests, disparate as they might be?

Bob's interpreter asked me if this was the first time I have been in China. In turn, I asked whether he came from Shanghai. (He had a very strong Peking accent, even when speaking French. In fact, he comes from Peking.) He studied at the Institute for Foreign Languages "in the fifties." When? In 1956. What happened after that was not clear. He had been in Shanghai for almost twenty years. He spoke of Peking as of some fabled place. I know the old Peking he loves with such passion. Today it is almost unfindable for the foreigner, unless he has known it earlier through the feeling that the cultivated Chinese have for their city. I asked him where his family lives: his parental family in Peking, his own present family in Shanghai. It was the first time in the almost five months since my arrival that I was talking with a Chinese in a normal way. I said to him that I would like to be at Fudan rather than at the Institute. He understood this. He told me he speaks French badly, because he has been studying it for only a year and a half. Then he added that "before" he had studied it for two years at the Shanghai Institute. In Peking, he had been in the Russian section. So he must have belonged to the Party for a long time. Usually, it was Party members who studied Russian. Chen, too, had studied Russian. There is a whole generation of "progressive" intellectuals who have the Russian language of their youth behind them. Their biographies are studded with voids. "During the Cultural Revolution," my companion told me, almost as if to fill in those voids, "we did not pay attention to our [professional] specialization, and we involved ourselves in the revolution."

The Lüxingshe fellow was explaining how one raises silkworms. My neighbor translated a bit of it, with a touch of humor.

We had dinner in freezing cold. On the return trip, people dozed on the train.

On the way to Wuxi, Roland's interpreter, the one who comes from Xi'an and is a conformist of the young generation, was speaking of the Four; he said, *"Ils semaient le désordre et la paresse. . . ."* ("They sow disorder and idleness. . . .")

December 3

Every morning the radio—my little radio, which I listen to while I take a shower and the loudspeakers blare outside—repeats almost verbatim announcements, in which the phrase "the Central Committee under the leadership of Chairman Hua" is more than a refrain. It's rather like a "good morning," except that one hears it day and night and not only on the radio or on TV but when and wherever. There are many little marches, the music new or old, which boldly rap out "Down with the Four"; they are alternated with more tender motifs

about Chairman Mao and love songs for Zhou Enlai. The exorcisms against the
Gang are becoming a standard feature, like the grace Protestants say before
meals. The prodigious bravura lies in the speed with which the theme has been
made into a banality and a ritual.

The Girl with the White Hair in the ballet version performed by the Shanghai corps de ballet is the best I have seen. (It is still being performed in Jiang
Qing's choreography, in which the little servant girl accompanies the heroine
in her flight.) At the end, there is a scene of effective primitivism: peasants,
soldiers, and people together with the Girl with the White Hair and the young
hero-lover watch the round deep-orange sun rise from the horizon and climb
into the sky as the chorus hymns "The Sun is Mao Zedong."
    At the end of the performance, the artists regrouped on the stage and sang
a song that did not mention the Gang of Four. (Such mention inevitably came
in a mini-cantata done at the beginning, to general inattention.) Tang told me,
smiling, that this had been the most famous song during the Cultural Revolution. It was greeted with an ovation from a public that almost never applauds.
    They are still having me accompanied by Tang: the handsome, educated
young man, promising albeit slightly heretical, and the female foreigner of a
certain age. It's the new trend.

    I am witnessing the triumph of those who at the time of my first stay in
China used to be called "rightist elements."
    Since I am preparing reading materials for next year, the Institute profes-
sors have proposed I include letters of Gramsci and of resistance figures who
were condemned to death. (I learned later that back in the fifties, some Gramsci
material was being read in the Italian courses.) This, too, is a restoration, or a
cyclical return. In the history of Italy they look for stories of patriotism and of
the war of national liberation, rather than of any class struggle. There is fresh
talk of Yang Mo's *The Song of Youth,* a tearjerker love-and-revolution novel
that was a best-seller and then fell into disrepute during the Cultural Revolution.
    It is an internal drama within one class. Those in the process of thaw are
opposed by the applause of actors and public, at the theater, through songs of
the Cultural Revolution. But what are the real stirrings of the great body that
is China at its base? Everything seems fluid and muddied. Are the minds of
people unsure, or are this observer's eyes clouded?
    I will take advantage of things opening up to write to Italy for books. As
if I had the illusion I might make even make a tiny contribution toward their
not moving in the direction of Stalinist "humanism."

    I attended a poetry reading in the film auditorium. Topics are set in
advance; today they were homage to Chairman Hua and criticism of the Gang

of Four. It was a full house. A young woman from the Young Communist League presided, speaking at times in prose, sometimes in verse. For more than three hours, group followed group on stage and recited poems, collectively written, in chorus, or with solo voice and chorus, or in dialogue form. The Institute leaders were in attendance and sat together in a row, including those on the Party Committee who are being attacked in *dazibao*. Lao Han, committee secretary, wears glasses and has the plump round face of a good-time-Charley. Chen does not take him seriously. "A big mouth," she says. (Chen is now less reticent and more natural in her attitude toward these cadres.) Also present: groups of students from the various language sections as well as service and office personnel of the Institute. Many brought their own compositions, short or long. The same words, more or less, that one reads in the papers, but arranged in verse form. Dignified old men, paper in hand, read their little poems. The audience was jolly, laughed openly at the performers, whether individual or group, and pointed at the severe professors who became muddled and said *"Mao zhuxi"* instead of *"Hua zhuxi"* or made mistakes in rhythm or stress. Nothing of what they had to say interested anyone in the slightest; what the audience enjoyed was the comedy.

To conclude the program a chorus, accompanied by accordion, sang a series of songs celebrating the Long March. I asked when they had been written. "After Liberation, before the Cultural Revolution." They came from a film of that period, and were the work of a single composer, Xiao Hua, a general allied with Lin Biao and purged in 1968. This "show" in his honor is a signal that he must be about to be rehabilitated. No point in asking for explanations. The answer would be "We don't know yet."

Chen and Zhang wanted insistently to know "what meetings like this are called in Italian."

The Left had no concrete proposals for transforming this society. In opposition to the Left, the Chinese—or that sector of the middle class with which we have contact—seem to believe in a Sino-nationalist solution that is neither proletarian nor bourgeois. They refer to a Maoism that is not only earlier than the 1958 Great Leap Forward, but has been reprogrammed as a kind of socialist nationalism, which in reality could not be farther from Mao's ideas. This ideology, which they have borrowed from the West (and which has roots in the German romanticism and the Russian populism of the last century), preserves traditional values of the people, especially of the peasants. But these same values are those which guarantee the total and immutable dependence of the people upon despotic rulers. In China, the paternalistic power to which these leaders aspire is merely a new version of the old "mandate of Heaven."

The erstwhile mandarin scholars—the ambiguous mandarins of the Kuomintang and warlord period—are hardly distinguishable, even individually, from the great body of public officials and cadres. Following them, the petty bourgeois of Shanghai, who entertain the illusion that they constitute the national culture and national bourgeoisie, are the most pathetic victims of the return of the oppression of the past that purports to be the beginning of freedom.

The goal being followed is that of reestablishing the traditional system of order, plus "modernization"—a Westernization that preserves Chinese institutional forms and ethical values. Will they succeed where the Kuomintang failed, by improving the recipe with some Stalinist ingredients? All this belongs to China's past, and perhaps Mao's mistake was only that of wishing to move away from it too rapidly.

City and School
December 13

There are rumors of armed uprisings in Fujian and elsewhere, of serious unrest on the railroads, but, at the same time, of pro-Deng moves, which insist that Mao would never have issued a directive to criticize Deng. . . . Today, next to the big entrance to the city hall, on the Bund, I saw a *dazibao:* "Letter to Comrade Hua Guofeng." It was written by a worker who signed both his first and last name, and it criticizes Hua for attacking the Four without stating his own policy. A man came out of the door and calmly tore down the *dazibao* in front of people's eyes. Probably the "letter" came from the pro-Deng people; there is talk of a *dazibao* in his favor in Canton, which is a bastion of his. Meanwhile, there is an attempt to build a Hua mini-cult. An article in *Wenhui Daily* speaks of his good deeds in Hunan; three selections in the famous anthology *Socialist Upsurge in China's Countryside,* for which Mao wrote a preface, are by Hua. His writings and past actions are being collected and recast to create the image of a fine, devoted, modest leader who is bound to the people, the "ideal good public servant." Unlike the Four, who were intellectually aristocratic and had a modern mentality. (Bob and Roland evaluate Hua's traditionalist image as a plus. They know too little about the old China.) In all the schoolrooms at the Institute, there is now a large colored portrait of Hua beside the portrait of Mao; in some rooms and offices there is even, on another wall, a black and white portrait of Zhou. Not in my office; Chen, however, has gotten one for herself and put it under the glass on her desk.

Something about my resistance is mistaken. Why beat my head against a wall, stubbornly trying to find democracy where I know it cannot be? I would do better to keep my distance, and accept things as they are if I want to receive what little they are willing to communicate to me. It is becoming quixotic to reject the "method" in a structure where every possible contribution of mine is, by definition, excluded. I should play the observer. But a European observer who does not communicate is by this very situation made to feel in a "superior" position, and this I rule out; and to compound the confusion, the people I speak with distort and manipulate a language that I believed was also mine, and the people beneath them, whom they dominate, are deprived of it also.

In any case, one must be mindful that, in many instances, the first reading of a text is nothing; one must begin at least with the second and go on to the third, the fourth reading. . . . Our custom of refusing, on principle, to substitute the work of art or of culture for direct political argumentation must be set aside. That isn't the issue; here we are not in a Soviet dimension. Here it is a question of an ancient inherited tradition, in which coded discourse is the basic structure and the rest is pure convention. When a person begins to show signs that he understands this language, he will notice how even halfway cultivated Chinese, of whatever opinion or persuasion, are truly pleased. Which is proof that even the exclusion of the foreigner from communication is ambiguous.

To reach this understanding is equivalent to measuring a distance that is immense and, at least today, insurmountable.

I have to get out, not stay shut up in a hotel room. The streets speak, and as I walk, my mind is freer to reflect and wonder. Mud and rain and rotting bones are miraculously erased by a sudden splendid sunset—the light of southern climates. The slanting rays of the sun shine in my eyes and I walk blinded. The streets and the people are so lacking in form; the perfection of Peking, its wordless enchantment, its great spaces belong to another day. Here the degraded buildings bring back the London of Herman Melville—"Paradise of Bachelors and the Tartarus of Maids." Imitations of imitations of Kensington in ruins. Big erstwhile churches, with double- and triple-mullioned windows and brick annexes, among piles of gravel and rubbish and dust. Bank monuments, hard, disbelieving people, close-packed together, laughing harshly and coughing and spitting.

(At the hotel, students from Fudan and some of my colleagues talk and talk and talk; day after day they theorize, they discuss the latest news. It is a sickness. At the moment, the Dasha is full of Chinese officials, civilian and military, who come and go and hold their meetings, having arrived from who knows where to work in the city and keep control of it. We people on the fourteenth floor are the only foreigners left in the hotel.)

Today I walked for a few hours, feeling happy. On my way back to the hotel, I took the route along the Suzhou. It was already night, and the sky was both dark and luminous, the air touched with pink. Pavements were heaped high with bags, baskets, piles of wood, scraps of iron, bales of straw. Dust and slow-moving bodies everywhere. Work. Boats. The port. Waves from the ocean travel up the Yangtze, and then up the Huangpu as far as this. The workers who do all this producing and carrying and fetching are immensely more fortunate than their English brothers of a hundred years ago. It would be laughable to talk to them about heavenly harmony. There's no cause to wait for the people to destroy the temples; foreign capital and degradation have already destroyed them. The old repertory will never be put together again out of the fragments, not for a people that has been deprived of its identity.

The short young man with glasses in the bookshop smiles in a friendly, not hypocritical, way. I buy magazines published in the past inauspicious months which, no matter whether by mistake or out of ignorance, are still in circulation. They say that by mistake, films of the Four are still being shown even at the Institute. So, heretical films and books still circulate. Routine can still play with a chance to win against the harmonious order. Chen lied about a film which was announced to be shown a few afternoons ago. "That was being shown during the Cultural Revolution," she said scornfully—actually, it was made only last year—and she didn't go with me to see it, leaving this chore to Zhang. (With hindsight, I now deduce that her sudden indispositions shortly after I arrived were perhaps an excuse so as not to have to act as translator on certain subjects.)

The film was another one about relaunching the Cultural Revolution; in all of them, the main plot is always the same. The protagonists are groups of ex–Red Guards now living in the country or working in factories who are leading the fight on the spot, going against the current and attacking the restorers. Some waver or give in, others persevere, seeking to ally themselves with the poor peasants or with the workers. The symbolic constants are the carefully preserved Red Guard armband, the waves of the sea (the Cultural Revolution that resurges), and, at the decisive moment, a flashback to Tienanmen Square, with the crowd of Red Guards and Chairman Mao.

None of these films is a masterpiece, and some are not even bearable—as when Mao appears as a heavenly vision to a young man or woman who stares into the distance, wide-eyed, while revisionists make attempts on people's lives. Others are not too bad; they have some lighthearted moments and even a touch of humor. They were mass-produced for propaganda purposes, and also for wide TV viewing.

The People's Daily is singing the praises of Mao's first wife (who was, in point of fact, his second), the true wife, the woman of his youth, the revolutionary martyr.

The Power Station

Finally, they have taken us to visit the Xiangpu power station, behind the port area. It is a famous workers' bastion, almost a symbol of past struggles. Our visit is a sign that order is being restored. To get there, the bus drove through the section of the city northeast of the hotel, which I had already crossed on my way to customs. Spirited confusion reigns here on the city's old industrial outskirts. . . .

It was the first time I ever stepped inside a power station. The sense of physical power was overwhelming, as we walked by antiquated but solid installations, and an occasional silent worker within the enormous blackened walls of the plant. We climbed up to a terraced roof, and then to another higher still. Below us lay the river, ships, junks, and the pier where they unload the coal and oil that fuel the plant. One of the young union men who were guiding us about —he had a very intelligent face, of the kind you don't encounter in educational circles—said to me, "This plant used to be called 'the red fort.' Wang Hongwen would have liked to use it for purposes of his own." A moment earlier, he had pointed out to me rows of sheds flanking the building: Textile Factory No. 17, "the one where Wang Hongwen—" at which point Chen had intervened, but I interrupted her. Between the power station and Textile Factory No. 17 there are "cooperative relationships."

After the old British- and German-built installations, which are still in operation (the station dates from 1913, and it passed from British into American and then into Japanese hands), they showed us one of the enormous boilers designed and built in China during the Cultural Revolution. (Chen attempted to translate this "during the Great Leap Forward" but I corrected her.) The public reception room displayed all the prescribed portraits, but in the control room of the new plant I saw only a small one of Mao. The work areas were immense and bare, none of the usual flags or posters or banners. Outside, next to a one-room shed used for meetings, the official glass-covered bulletin board by the door had a few caricatures and *dazibao*. Not a sound in the room, nor any workers either. One big solitary red banner: "Take the class struggle as pivot."

The power station still has a Revolutionary Committee and even, they say, theory study groups: "They are carrying out criticism of the Gang of Four." We were received by a "management representative," together with the vice-secretary of the Revolutionary Committee, a few union people, and a few members of the Young Communist League. A management representative is a new kind of official, or has a function that has been reactivated after a lapse of many years. The man had a round intellectual face, in a characteristically Suzhou way. He made the usual address, while the others listened in silence and watched us. He outlined the history of the power station: the workers' struggles almost from the outset, the 1927 uprising, the nine-day strike in 1946, the armed fight for liberation in 1949, the Kuomintang bombing in February of 1950. Trust in their own strength, autonomy. . . . We let "politics take command," but we know how to increase production. During the Cultural Revolution, the workers criticized Liu Shaoqi, who thought the revolution originated in production. Workers share in management at all levels—top, department, squad—in line with the Anshan Constitution and following the example of Daqing. "Three-in-one," a July Twenty-first school patterned after the example of the machine-tool factory, young workers sent to the university to return later to the plant. Out of the twenty-one hundred workers, four hundred are women. The workers have shared in the criticism of Liu Shaoqi, Lin Biao, the Gang of Four, influence of the Gang of Four. . . .

Specifically how they have collaborated in that criticism or to what, concretely, that influence amounted remained nebulous. Answers to our questions on these points were kept to generalities. When he was actually talking about the plant, the management spokesman, who had probably been assigned from the outside, presented a picture not truly different from what it would have been months ago. He did speak explicitly against the single-management system and against the work regulations in effect before the Cultural Revolution, while injecting the equivocal notion of "post–Cultural Revolution regulations," about which, in point of fact, no one has ever heard a word. It was obvious that the "return to order" is being effected gradually and with extreme prudence. In the months and perhaps in the years ahead, it will be very difficult to understand what really is taking place in the factories. There will be a complex backing and filling that either will be kept entirely concealed or will be glimpsed only in ambivalent allusions.

Nausea
December 24

Wenhui Daily carries daily attacks against Wang Hongwen and his activity in the Shanghai factories. Among their other crimes, the Gang of Four encouraged the struggle against followers of the "capitalist roaders." Meanwhile, *The People's Daily* is lauding whoever it was who wrote that *dazibao* in defense of the film *Zhuangye,* and thereby went "against the current"—this in the summer of 1975, when, on the contrary, the current was turning precisely in that direction. Lenin's famous phrase about socialism's being collectivization plus mechanization is being quoted and underscored, and a widely diffused slogan is reversed: "Satellites in the sky need not mean the red flag on the ground."

Ten days ago, *The People's Daily* published a first-page violent attack against Zhang Chunqiao for something he wrote (half in prose, half in verse) which has been found among his personal papers. The document is to be included in the dossier on the Gang of Four. It reads:

Thoughts on February 3, 1976

Another No. 1 document.
Last year, there was a No. 1 document.
Success truly does drive them mad.
So swiftly, so brutally: but soon it will be over.

The misguided line does not work. They will have a momentary success; it will seem as if the world belonged to them and a "new era" were beginning. They always overestimate their own strength.

The people are the decisive factor.

To represent the interests of the people, to act in behalf of the interests of the most, and in whatever situation to stand on the side of the masses and of the vanguard means to prevail. The contrary means inevitable defeat.

Thus:

Among the bursting of grenades a year ends,
The wind from the East brings warmth to the new year's wine.
The rising sun illumines millions of gates,
New messages of good wishes replace the old.

The reference is to the lunar New Year, which falls in early February. The No. 1 document is one from the Central Committee. Directives and communiqués of the Central Committee are numbered consecutively through the year, year by year; they are not published in the big newspaper's, yet usually they are widely diffused and known in whole or in part. According to the comment in *The People's Daily,* Zhang's impatience was owing to the fact that the document in question announced the appointment, approved by Mao, of Hua Guofeng as Acting Premier. The paper's deduction was that Zhang's "Thoughts" were directed against Hua and against Mao. It was not explicitly said, but the rumor is being circulated that Zhang wanted the post of Premier for himself, after Zhou Enlai's death. Presumably, this version of the matter is oversimplified and partially falsified. In fact, before Zhou died, Deng Xiaoping seemed certain to be his successor, or at least Deng's supporters gave that out as being for certain, and leaked abroad a statement to that effect, which Mao was alleged to have made to President Gerald Ford. It is likely that the Left's opposition blocked Deng's appointment but not the compromise solution of leaving the post empty and entrusting the vice-chairmanship to Hua. Hence Zhang's dissatisfaction, aimed at Deng and his people rather than against the person of Hua—not to mention Mao, who not only was ill but whose hands were virtually tied.

This was not written for publication, and it is almost incredibly honest. The fact that it is disclosed to invite the opprobrium of the people is alarming—unless you include among other possible conjectures the intention of the journalists (or whoever gave them this text) to make it public. When Chen started in with her little propaganda modeled after the article in the paper, I didn't answer directly but asked a question instead: "When will the public trial of the Four be held?" She was wordless. I added that Stalin at least held public trials, even if they were not believable because people were tortured. . . .*

The students are working on compositions in Italian that will be read on December 26, the anniversary of Mao's birth. They're pretty much all the same: "Eighty-three years ago, in Shaoshan, the red sun arose in the east, the infinitely loved and respected Chairman Mao, the splendid red sun that lives in our hearts. From that moment, there has been hope for China. . . . Revolutionary experience has shown that only he who follows Chairman Mao will win, and that he who does not follow him will fail miserably. . . . Chairman Mao personally named his worthy successor, the respected and beloved Chairman Hua. . . . Under the leadership of the Central Committee of the Chinese Communist Party, with Chairman Hua at its head, we have shattered the monstrous counterrevolutionary crimes of the Gang of Four. . . . This is a day of great happiness, for the country and the army have their own leader, the beloved and respected. . . . Be at peace, Chairman Mao. . . ." Zhu Yuhua has asked me if he could entitle his "article" "Rest in Peace, Chairman Mao." One girl has written, "Mao Zedong-thought is our spiritual food." My time is spent correcting these compositions.

But there are intermissions. Like going with the students to dig ditches. They were like children on a picnic, and all intent on their lofty task. The characteristic Chinese attentiveness and kindness toward the guest came back: I must, no matter what, take their gloves to protect my hands. They talked with me in a simple, direct way, asked me the words in Italian for everyday things and actions; for one moment everyone was quit of doctrine. How much more they would learn if we could do lessons every day in this way, and how much more relaxed and happy we all would be.

Through these exchanges, I've discovered that some of the students play one or another musical instrument, and they've promised to play for me. Even Zhang seemed a different person—he, rather than Chen, accompanied the students; she was not well and went, instead, to the library to put "the books" in order—what books who knows. She kept Tang with her, and he must be savoring the advantages of being co-opted to the status of scholar. Everyone knows that the teachers despise *laodong*—manual labor. (This work detail was not open-door instruction but simply physical work with an educational purpose, such as that the students go to perform periodically in a rubber-goods factory here in the neighborhood.)

I do ask myself whether they will manage to destroy Tang's wholesome, happy attitude toward physical work. He's told me about his life in the country after he finished middle school—the hard work, the swims in the river, the little

*As noted earlier, such a trial was eventually held, it being concluded in January, 1981. It is probable that Jiang Qing was not tortured, though not unlikely that the men were.

trips with friends. "There were three of us men, and in the evening we would bicycle into town. . . ." He boasts about being able to lift seventy kilos with a bamboo balance stick. Nothing about Red Guard films, no apparitions of Mao, no harking back to great principles, but joy in a daily life lived with dignity. This is what I believe the priority of politics in the slogan "politics takes command" should mean—work and everyday personal doings fused with their intelligence.

"The Gang of Four confused the students' ideas, so that they wanted to be political activists, and they didn't listen to their professors, and they didn't study," Chen says to me. "Why don't you talk with Tang about it?" With this in mind, they leave Tang alone with me in my office, they send him along as my escort to the theater, and so forth. I want him to keep his self-respect, and by keeping silent myself I help him to do the same. However, will my *not* being reeducated make trouble for him? What will he write about in his reports on our conversations?

There's beginning to be talk about reinstating examinations. No one knows yet what criteria will be used in recruiting new students. Cadres come and go from Peking, but apparently so far they cannot reach a decision. Meanwhile, Chen and Zhang keep after me to know which students seem to me the best; clearly they have in mind the idea of making a selection. I avoid answering, or get some small amusement out of praising the intelligence of the ex-soldier Zhou Shiliang, or the quick, direct intuitive understanding of Wang Min, the brigade leader. Chen and Zhang are looking for different qualities; a taste for the complicated appeals to them—they mistake it for subtlety—and indeed it is one prerequisite for making a good *guan*. They also know that the children of cadres of a certain rank will be admitted no matter what, even if they are utterly incompetent. (To come from the family of a leading cadre brings other privileges as well. When an Institute librarian recommended some edifying books to one young girl, she answered scornfully that what interested her were modern American and English novels, and that she had books sent to her from Hong Kong through an uncle. This, then, is a norm. It made me think again of Jiang Qing's being charged with corruption because she dared watch *Gone with the Wind*.)

Political study of Chairman Hua. . . . A fairly detailed biography, even if less so than one published months ago in a Taibei magazine. The windup was a series of uplifting anecdotes: Chairman Hua eating with workers, Chairman Hua going like any other citizen to a meeting of parents at his daughter's school. (What, then, are the usual habits of these leaders?) One hour out of three was given to an expository account of how Hua loved Shaoshan, Mao's birthplace, about how he had worked to have the museum built and to honor the memory of Mao's first (second) wife. Jiang Qing, on the other hand, hated Shaoshan, and she never went there. (Shaoshan the place stands for Yang Kaihui, Mao's wife, who was hated posthumously and jealously by the "perfidious concubine" Jiang Qing.)

It's cold. I have a little stove in my office. Even before it was installed, Zhang and Tang had moved in with two small desks. I'm glad they have. The pretense of work done in common is never totally gratuitous. Also, my status of being different and privileged is less pronounced by the fact of their being here. Zhang's desk is on my right, adjoining my own and Chen's. Tang sits somewhat apart, usually at the big conference table, and he works silently on his own, preparing his lessons or a glossary that he then gives me to correct. The other two interrupt me continually asking for explanations, so that I no longer manage to do my own work during the hours spent at school. I am a tool, as I've said, and I don't mind being used. I do prefer answering Chen; she couches her questions intelligently and is trying to deepen her knowledge of Italian. To make Zhang understand anything is usually hard, because he cannot differentiate between what qualifies as a fact and what is an opinion open for discussion. During work breaks, I roast chestnuts, which aren't to be found in the fruit shops but which I can buy in my little hidden store. My colleagues toast *mantou.* We sit around the little stove to warm ourselves, and eat our chestnuts and *mantou.* Every morning before ten, a fat elderly professor comes in, says, "Good morning" in Italian, and distributes whatever printed matter is due each of us; occasionally I receive some little sheets, generally reprints of articles that have appeared in the newspapers or in *Red Flag,* in addition to *Pékin Information* or *China Pictorial.* Zhang tells me the old man knows a little of all the romance languages—his mother was French. He must already be on pension, but he would rather go on working. I believe that to go around delivering papers to Institute colleagues is considered a commendable act of service, or, at least, I've heard a student of mine praised by his comrades for doing the same.

The sheets of paper are immediately tucked into each person's drawer—no one must read those belonging to anyone but himself. Often they are long sheets of various individuals' self-criticism. At the moment, the statement by Wang Xiuzhen, the textile labor woman on the municipal Revolutionary Committee, is being circulated all over. Even the elevator boys at the Dasha are passing it around among themselves. An excerpt from it was later plastered over many walls in numbered *dazibao.* I have the satisfaction of reading material that is forbidden to others, too. Usually, there are copies of the *Corriere della Sera* lying on my desk, and when a student comes in to ask something, Chen, in a flash, pops them into her drawer.

For the midday meal, between eleven-thirty and twelve-thirty, Tang goes off to his mess. He despises the traditional noonday nap, and in the same spirit does not wear padded clothes or wrap himself up in odds and ends to keep warm; he wears just a T-shirt, washes his hands often, swims, and rides his bicycle four kilometers every day. (This is the hygienic enlightenment of Yanan, plus traces of the noble life style of the scholars—do not go early to bed but remain awake late to study or to converse with friends.) Sometimes Zhang stays on in the office instead of going to sleep elsewhere; he crosses his arms on his desk, leans his head on his arms, and dozes; at such moments, when I see him weak and vulnerable, like a child with its tiny cunning, I feel tenderness for him.

And there am I, wide awake during all that time, watching other people rest, with my baggage of knowledge serving no purpose. As a foreigner, I may receive only the lowest categories of information, a restriction that, according to the prevailing criteria, is appropriate to a presumed lack of culture, unpreparedness, and even stupidity. Yet I possess more adequate tools for understanding than do my tutors, sometimes even in specifically Chinese subjects. In these circumstances, how can the workings of my mind be defined?

Sometimes official steps are taken to break my isolation, and during rest periods I will receive well-organized visits from students, who take advantage of them to practice their Italian. There is the kind that immediately preempts an armchair, stretching out his legs and sitting so low that his head is sunk between his shoulders, like the peasant who comes as master into the gentleman's house, also aping the arrogance of some cadres; and there is the kind—like Liu Fenghua, the class prefect, he of the plump, oval face—who overflows with compliments, and if I say to him, joking, "Come, come, sit down, you're the class prefect," he parries with already typical *guan* manners, "Oh, no, professor, we are all comrades. . . ."

Yang Qingbin is a frequent caller, a thin boy with a long face and half-closed eyes—a solitary, tense with ambition. I've discovered that he knows how to play the two-stringed Chinese violin, with its long-drawn-out, obsessive, captivating lament. Yang comes from far away—Ruijin, in Jiangxi Province; when the others go home on their brief vacations, he cannot because the distance is too great, so he buries himself in old novels—*The Investiture of the Gods,* by Xu Zhonglin, for example. When I am with him, I feel a perhaps baseless (but reflected) diffidence; it seems to me that we move around in a maze, and I can't decide whether at bottom it's a question merely of shrewdness on his part or whether it is insecurity and an instinctive self-defense. He is able to offer opinions rather freely, but his overanalytical intelligence defeats him where others less gifted readily understand.

As for the girls who come, I classify them either as young ladies or peasants, and my sympathies are with the peasants, though a few of the others and I quickly come to understand each other. Their abilities were hidden and repressed at first, but now are becoming more and more clearly defined as the political turnabout is more surely delineated. It is simply astonishing to watch now how the confident intelligence of the peasant girl Wang Jianhua sometimes falters, almost as if she is daunted by a complexity that she feels confronts her.

On the other hand, Fan Jianping, who wears the same common clothes but manages to be elegant, is becoming more assertive; she seems to be shaking off her old somnolence and to move ever more quickly along an ever surer path; things once known but buried are returning to sustain her and reinsert her in her proper but until lately lost dimension.

Back at the Dasha, we warm our frozen feet, and that at least is a good thing. But it is becoming unbearable to live here with the cadres, who take over the hotel in toto—including us, who are here like a foreign body, set apart like hostages. Contacts with these co-residents are strictly forbidden, and although we would not dream of seeking them out, the system of controls becomes suffocating. We meet them as they go up and down in the elevator, when they are on their way to meals or meetings or to visit each other, often with their elegant infants ("cadres' children," Susan whispers to me). Their arrogant faces are ridiculously like their caricatures. "International" characteristics melt away into a Chinese specificity, levels differ and are well marked. Some play the detached intellectual, sometimes wearing their hair very short in tardy imitation of eggheads; but the more frequent is the *Animal Farm* type who sucks on the last bits of food between his teeth and with a benevolent-paternalistic snigger asks his inferiors, "Have you eaten, ah ah?" They look at us sometimes with an air of complicity, sometimes with unconcealed scorn.

In the evening, I go down to the restaurant because I feel hungry, and when I find myself faced with some greasy mess, or tofu, I can't manage to get it down. (Now that the tourists are all gone, the food is poor and also the Western menu has been discontinued.) If I ask for a sandwich and egg to take to my room, the serving people, who are increasingly rude, say that there is none—that's part of the Western menu.

But I must resist. Must keep as closely in touch with Italy as possible, not care if letters arrive late, if they have been opened and resealed, if I am not permitted to have relationships of my own even outside these boundaries. To resist means to affirm something, here as anywhere else.

And I must let the city speak, must walk and relax when the cold lessens and the air condenses into a light smog and the smoke stagnates, when this could be Milan or any other place in the world.

The end of the year is near, and a general cleanup is in progress. Squads of people, with cleaning tools and ladders, are scraping the walls clear of *dazibao.* Something has been decided. Perhaps the definitive interment of the city's legitimate Revolutionary Committee. But legitimacy is a vague concept —nonexistent, actually. These days, there are big meetings in all the units. Sometimes, looking embarrassed, they send us home from school. There is an attempt to launch a "Socialist emulation" campaign, but apparently it's not getting off the ground. An occasional truck passes by with flags and drums, and that's it. This time, they don't succeed in making the people rejoice.

The Port

A breath of fresh air: a visit to the port—a week later than the date first announced, and not, of course, to the famous No. 5 Zone, which was too closely connected with the Gang of Four to be "in order" yet. They took us instead of Zone No. 3, which is reserved for domestic shipping. It was a gray day, and the ships, cranes, and tugs were a matching blue-gray. We stopped for a bit on the quay. Men and women bundled up in very heavy quilted clothes, all wearing some strange sort of big apron, were passing back and forth hauling loaded hand trucks. Like all big ports, the light and the river evoked the anxiety felt in another century about travel over water, the anticipation of distance and of separation.

We went into a rather dark reception room on the ground floor of the building; only one portrait, Mao's, with swags of mourning streamers. (Now and then on the street you see someone who is still wearing his black armband.) Present were the representative of the Revolutionary Committee of Zone 3, the vice-secretary of the Party Committee, several well-dressed people who looked like cadres but were identified variously as "electrician," "driver," etc., and several workers. On benches in the rear were seated young workers and students from Fudan and the Institute who are attending open-door classes here. The Revolutionary Committee man, rather elderly, made us what is called a "brief introduction," which is everywhere identical except for the numerical data and some historical details. (For the school, I am translating drafts of these presentations that include visitors' observations, which are anticipated and "packaged" in advance.) It was suggested that we ask questions. Almost all were answered by the workers with cadre faces. What they had to say—for example, in answer to questions about the union—was an incoherent superimposition of details they don't yet have the courage to eliminate upon others that are new and incompatible. There was a frontal attack on positions that these workers had made famous throughout the world. "The Four maintained that the workers must not be slaves of the tonnage" (an allusion to the *dazibao* of the Zone No. 5 port workers in which they said, "We want to be masters of the port, not slaves of the tonnage"). The Four opposed Socialist emulation, insisting that it is a revisionist method, and so the movement was blocked. Today, instead, it is the duty of the union to encourage it. Model workers must be singled out among those who produce the most. The Four were opposed to this, and defended absurd views, such as that workers can study during working hours, that "one must not hold back the revolution in the name of production." The Four used to say, "Better be late with socialism than on time with capitalism." . . . "Better Socialist weeds than capitalist shoots." The Four wanted the union to be independent of the Party.*

They were against regulations based on individual responsibility. (The collective responsibility of the squads is being dismantled through an ambiguous formula of individual responsibility at the workplace. The intention is to assign responsibility individually, not only to workers but also to supervisors, beginning with those at the base. It is not yet a single-management pattern, but it seems to herald the return of that system.) Workers influenced by the Gang of Four had protested a blackboard on which the comparative figures of tonnage loaded and unloaded were recorded; they claimed that this signified giving priority to production.

I noticed the distance between the workers (cadres) who were answering our questions and the elderly man who had spoken first, although, in conclusion, he had come out in favor of chartering foreign vessels (a policy which the workers of Zone No. 5 had opposed). This man is a worker-manager who had grown up in the port area, and for him the zone is a reality that has its own history, its accomplishments, its ways of doing things, and its struggles—a continuity not to be marred by directives from the outside. But between the team's cadres and the young people seated at the back of the room the separation was total. The latter were watching the encounter as if it were an entertainment. When I asked whether worker study groups still existed, they burst out laughing and looked at me curiously. And their hilarity peaked when, in response to a question about whether there was any continuing opposition to Deng's proposal to restore work regulations, the "electrician" answered that they had never heard of any such proposal. (The port workers have written articles against this, as everybody knows.)

It was evident that these men who had come from outside to establish order had nothing whatever to do with the workers. But the terrain has been conquered step by step, and unless there were to be some explosion, I believe there are no possibilities of serious resistance in the short run. Passive resistance could be very strong, leading to a slowdown.

At the end came the high points of the show; with consummate art, a little

---

*The workers' demand for power has repeatedly been voiced through non-Party mass organizations —for example, between 1963 and 1965, in the rural areas, the associations of poor peasants (organizations from the era of agrarian reform, recalled to life). More recently, the Left sought to strengthen the labor unions, at least in Shanghai, and women's and youth organizations. Before the Cultural Revolution, the central agency that coordinated all activities of the unions was one of Party apparatus (Liu Shaoqi's) tools, and therefore was attacked. In general when it comes to the unions it's necessary to make the distinction between the central organization (Pan-Chinese Federation of Unions), which is part and parcel of the Party's control over the workers, and the individual unions, especially in some locations, which in greater or lesser measure actually reflect the desires of the workers.

old man (retired) told the story of their life in days past, all suffering and travail, and of life today, a bed of roses, to which he added a topical note, a satire based on the Four which only a few months ago surely would have been aimed at Deng. The form and motifs of this standard variety number are always identical. Now and then professional folk singers appear on TV, with Chinese violin and mandolin accompaniment, to perform it solo or in a group. I saw them several times last summer, during a festival put on in Peking. At that time, they were singing criticism of Deng; now, with the same imperturbable irony, they are singing attacks on the Gang of Four. Voice, motifs, and the extraordinary miming and musical bravura are all identical. They could just as well sing a joke about two lovers or a hymn to shit. For them and for their listeners, equally, the theme is utterly irrelevant—what counts is the witty exchange they can improvise on it.

The form is pure abstraction; it not only fails to make people think but fosters their not even forming opinions, because whatever the surface content may be—a love song, a hurrah for Mao or a hurrah for the Left or a hurrah for the Right—everything is always identical. The formulas used in the past are preserved and used today, with the details updated. The people cannot escape from a servile situation on the sidelines of history where one element, the folk format, remains permanent, but built into it are topics that vary and develop in response to changes in a world that is external to the people; when those changes are presented in an unvarying format, they are perceived by the people to be an unvarying mess of pottage, just as they sense an unvarying sameness in their own situation vis-à-vis the position of the leading classes, of those who have, of those who know. Through the lips of the singers, the people are telling us one truth—that for them everything works out to be the same; they revenge themselves by saying the only thing they can say; your stories mean nothing to us, and our strength lies in our knowing that. A moral victory all too like that in Lu Xun's story "Ah Q."

Celebrations, Holidays, and Ceremonies

A color documentary has been put together on the last honors paid to Mao. It's a montage of bits and pieces, most of which have already been seen on TV. In one short sequence that I had not seen before, Joris Ivens' lesson had been learned after a fashion, even if academically: a series of scenes of people standing motionless during the three minutes of remembrance, in factories, aboard ships, out in the fields, on mountainsides. An instant configuration of the whole country, its vastness made palpable . . . Now absent is the wreath with the huge sunflower offered by Jiang Qing; likewise, the voice of the announcer which softened in pronouncing her name (and this I heard repeated so many times that the sound is still in my ear). Where they could not cut they've cropped. At the final ceremony you now see Hua Guofeng and, behind him, Ye Jianying. But Wang Hongwen had been so close by that it was impossible to eliminate all traces of him; of Wang you see still a portion of one sleeve. The effect is nightmarish. You end up wondering whether factual reality exists, or ever has. But there was also evidence—astounding—of a canceled message. We saw the film in a big theater, and it was jammed. Everyone there was looking at *what was not to be seen* in the documentary, looking behind the abrupt, violent cuts in the sequences. During the moments of greatest suspense, there was silence; only here and there you heard the "z-z-z-z-z-z-" sound that Shanghai people simply cannot help making at the most exciting points of a performance. You also heard some "ah ah's," which is a kind of laugh.

So all of those people whom I see once again weeping and weeping became a primitive yet aware image of despair over something that has ended. The powerless ones in that long month when the jockeying went on behind grief's back.

At the end, a few documentary bits were added in which Mao appears alive: an immensely attractive physical presence, a free man in this country so little capable of being free. For a second, you saw him with Zhou Enlai and Zhu De; also, a glimpse of him greeting the Red Guards from Tienanmen.

December 30

They told us at the last minute that if we didn't want to, we need not go to school on Christmas. I went anyhow—what would I have done shut up in the hotel? But we had bought gifts for the children, and in the evening we all gathered in Olga and Marcial's living room, and later in Dagmar's room. In Peru, Marcial and some other university people had formed a folk theater, and he mimed some scenes for us. Aymin is stagestruck and she acted as his "straight guy." She was very serious, and the rouge she had rubbed on her cheeks so changed her expression that she looked strangely adult and fierce. Maya sat on the floor among all the toys and colored paper flowers that had been made for ornaments. We all felt extremely depressed. John had brought his flute and played some sublime sixteenth-century music.

In class on the morning of the twenty-sixth we celebrated Mao's birthday. The students had pulled the benches into the middle of the room, making one large table. We sat around it, and each read his composition. They had asked me to say a few words, too. I tried to recall, briefly, what had made for Mao's greatness, which today is being methodically destroyed.

I have no stomach anymore for reading the *dazibao,* which they continue to put up inside the Institute, and I don't even want to read the newspaper. What I would like is a rest, a good long sleep. There's an attempt, not very successful, to stir up enthusiasm for production, using the slogan "Learn from Dazhai!" —a few trucks with the usual drums. No one pays any attention.

Sudden, short attacks of homesickness for, inexplicably, a specific place on a street in Milan or in Florence. Why, from all of Italy, only those two cities I can't imagine.

They have published "The Ten Big Relationships"* with some changes from the unofficial version. I don't know how many people there might still be, even among the Chinese, who aren't familiar with the material. The other meaning of the publication may be merely the reference to the pre-1958 Mao, or perhaps it is to herald the fifth volume of his selected writings.

Concerts of Chinese music are sometimes telecast. Quite beautiful compositions for *pipa* or flute. . . . Naturally, the Gang of Four prevented this music's being played. It remains a mystery how in the short time that has elapsed since their fall entire orchestras of very young girls have been able to master the *pipa*. It would seem that the Four prohibited a great many things that everybody went on tranquilly doing. Now a hundred flowers bloom. But a great deal of what was produced in the entertainment area after the Cultural Revolution is vanishing, especially films.

It is also being said that this year the harvest has been good thanks to the fall of the Gang of Four. In the old days, the emperor was the mediator between Heaven and Earth. If his actions were wicked, Nature did not respond.

The few papers I receive from Italy carry comments about Chinese affairs which are very approximate. Whatever role the lack of accurate and abundance of false information plays, it is clear that Westerners are assenting to the restoration and quickly willing to form an alliance with the restorers. In favor of which sectors of society and against which others, in Europe no less than in China?

January 1, 1977

Last evening, we and the other foreigners living in Shanghai were invited by the City Revolutionary Committee (the *new* Revolutionary Committee). (Foreign residents in Peking were invited by Vice-Premier Li Xiannian himself.) A high-ranking cadre was present, who had made a speech two days ago before the new National Congress on the theme "Learning from Dazhai."

Everyone was properly dressed, and we went by bus to the International

---

*A speech made by Mao in 1956 whose contents were widely known in China but never officially published until now. Its subject was the various relationships of paramount national concern; foremost among these were the relationship between industry and agriculture and the relationship between heavy and light industry.

Club, where we were offered a sumptuous banquet. In addition to the above-mentioned cadre, there were present the official in charge of cultural affairs, a member of the Foreign Affairs office, and several women, one from the All-China Women's Association (I don't remember what posts the others hold). Seated at the head table were the older Japanese, the French, and elderly residents, like the eighty-year-old T—— C——, whom I should have called on long since, but haven't been able to make myself. I don't feel like meeting the ghosts of "the friends of China" of another era, who are surrounded now by aides and nurses, and having to listen to exhortations against the Gang of Four. I sat at a table with Makita and a young Japanese couple who have arrived recently at Shida, plus several Chinese and our interpreters. As always happens on such occasions, everyone sat stiff and embarrassed, not knowing what to talk about, groping for some way to break the silence. The formal, hypocritical aspects of our relationships with each other have become more apparent recently.

Both the leader's toast and those offered by Chinese at the various tables repeated the same refrain: The past year has been a year of great joy because we have had two great victories, the defeat of the Gang of Four and the appointment of Hua Guofeng. This whole ceremony had one purpose only: to get us to take a stand in public against the Gang of Four. They did oblige us to raise our glasses in honor of the event. We had been informed earlier that anyone could reply to the toasts if he wished. It was a way of inviting us to do so. It was not easy, short of being rude, to offer a toast without making some response to those of our hosts, which were all keyed to "the great joy." Bob had intended to offer some criticisms about teaching methods, and he inquired of his interpreter about the propriety of doing so. "Provided you put it on the Gang of Four, you can make whatever criticism you want" was the answer. Bob admits that, cravenly, he added mention of Hua. Dagmar and Uta got out from under by having Felicitas make a childish little speech. Ohara, Marcial, and Mohammed (the Egyptian) serenely echoed the Chinese refrain. An Australian woman, a teacher who just recently arrived at Shida, did more or less the same. John was the most serious (he had talked to me earlier about what he would say); in perfect Chinese, he offered a toast that dealt with educational problems and ignored specifically political questions. I should have followed his example, but in comparison with him I am too weak. Also, I would have had nothing to say because I do not believe, as he does, in honest "bourgeois" reform programs for Chinese schools. So I said nothing, which was boorish. Still, I felt the moral violence being visited on me gave me the right to be ill-mannered. I will not forget the hard face of the cadre when he shook hands with me as we were leaving. One of the most repulsive, internationally shared characteristics of bureaucrats of the CP, whether in power or out, is their finding it absolutely inconceivable that one could oppose them.

Back at the hotel, we waited for the New Year in Dagmar's room—we

Europeans and the Egyptian; the Japanese went off on their own or to sleep, and presently the Peruvians left for bed. In a blue wool *ganbu* jacket, John played drunk in a nicely humorous way. He repeated his toast, fracturing it into bureaucratic jargon in which the words made no sense and the whole speech curled back on itself endlessly. In a drunk's vacant fashion, he was making fun of himself; he then translated the toast into pseudo-German for Dagmar's benefit.

She has made her room inviting, but it isn't very big, and we were crowded together on couches and footstools; it was hot. At one end there is a wall almost entirely taken up by one dark window, and visible through it the city was like an apparition. Not for us. We were in a place apart, a patch of nothing, a space for nonbeing. But within this small square of room we had a sort of boundless freedom. There are so many ways of being prisoners. I had had a bit to drink, too, and I was seeing colors heightened—the green upholstery of the armchairs, the red sweater of Felicitas, and her yellow hair pressed against Uta's brown head. Seated on the floor, John was miming a man's attempts to reassemble a little bench that had collapsed beneath him. Without seeming to, what John was expressing, with grace and measure, was the awareness of us all of being manipulated and insulted.

Here they know nothing about the sacred privilege of sleeping late on New Year's morning. I was up this morning at eight to receive the ritual calls from the leaders, which began at nine and lasted the entire morning. Chen lives far away, and she must have got up disagreeably early on what is one of the few holidays the Chinese have. Honors are done at the price of everyone's discomfort, but they legitimate the function of the people who must preserve the rites.

Xing, *el calvito,* unlike the cadres in the other sections, did not appear together with the Institute leaders but came alone to see me first and then Marcial and Olga. He repeated the refrain that will not, lackaday, abandon us for the whole year since it is the propaganda programmed for 1977. But his remarks were somewhat more human. He conceded that before the great joy they had had a few misfortunes—the death of all their major leaders, the earthquake. . . . Lao Bai had come today in the company of a military leader, who is new at school, and something of a lout—he asked that his cup be washed before the tea was poured.

I did not sleep in the afternoon because Aymin began to knock at my door, shouting, *"I—ta—li—a—na!"* She came in and stayed until evening. I love Aymin very much.

The explanations Chen gives me about how the university degenerated after being opened to "the masses," and how necessary it is that admissions to schools be selective, are identical, down to the last comma, to those of many well-to-do people of various persuasions, from Christian Democrats to Italian Communist Party leaders.

Peking Opera
January 3

Last evening, we went to see *Taking Tiger Mountain by Strategy*. It's one of the best of the modern Peking operas, and the production is fine, with truly outstanding performers. We're hoping that they continue to present it, and that it doesn't get banned as a Gang of Four production.

Every time I see a Peking opera* performance, I am astonished afresh by its radical diversity from Western art. In this one, the commander of the People's Army, the bandits in the mountains, and the splendid sequence of the assault itself are incorporated among the traditional mime, dance, and acrobatics. Although an element is introduced which has roots in romanticism, the work as a whole is essentially abstract, and is immeasurably removed from realism. There is no relationship—none is intended, I would say—between word and action. As the words, in verse form, are sung, they are projected onto two screens, one on either side of the stage. At a certain point, although I didn't remember the story line, I stopped reading, because I realized how pointless that was; instead, my attention should be concentrated on something quite else, exactly the way one listens to a musical passage. On something that has a line of continuity, a very precise meaning, and observes stringent forms. Once one has had a theatrical experience such as Peking opera offers, one understands why cultivated, un-Westernized Chinese may be so utterly uncomprehending of our Romantic and realistic art, and why they may look on even Renaissance painting as realistic.

It is only partly true that the evolution of twentieth-century art forms has brought us nearer to this China. We have moved in the direction of what one might term progressive elimination; our sensibility finds that the nonfigurative is almost a necessary premise of abstractionism. It is a perfecting that even when sublime entails loss, that is a transition toward emptiness.

In China, a process of destruction which is to some extent parallel has taken place in very different terms. The cultural revolution that began in 1919 with the May Fourth Movement and that is far from having been completed was directed not against imperialism but against tradition. Western—especially European— culture functioned as the catalyst: from the Enlightenment to Romanticism to realism to late-nineteenth-century decadent and on to avant-garde (cubist, futurist, surrealist) art (little of the avant-garde, and far from the best). The introduction of bastard elements of European post-Romantic and veristic origin into the purity of the old Chinese art answered a cultural-revolutionary need because it supplied a tool for fracturing that purity. In one sense, the result was a disaster.

*Peking opera is a term denoting a form of theatrical entertainment. Peking opera companies are found in many places other than Peking, and one of the finest is the Shanghai company.

But continuity would no longer have meant even conservation; it was simply not possible. Probably there will be an attempt to preserve old forms, but it will be counterproductive; at best, it will yield no more than an increasingly weary, stale multiplication. Paintings of birds and horses and bamboo, Peking operas with masks and costumes—all these things will be produced as export items that will find favor. They have their place today in the world market beyond the parameters of the Chinese universe. But the culture market outside China has reasons that are interiorized in the works it deals in, which are both merchandise and non-merchandise since the producers and the exploiters belong to the same milieu and see things with the same eye. The unity of these non-Chinese works lies in the putting together of a contradictory and fragmented reality. The Chinese producer will remain ignorant of this, and in his output he will continue to refer to a (harmonious) Chinese universe which is extraneous to the culture of the world market. His awareness of the "outside" will be inferior, like that of the trader who does not grasp the laws of the market. Within China, meanwhile, the use value of his products will be illusory because the unitary ambience that generated the originals no longer exists.

The Chinese were once apart from the rest of the world—they formed a universe sufficient unto itself versus an out-thereness. As the barriers fell, they fought back with absurd stubbornness, even defending what had already been utterly destroyed. As they saw it, to give in would have meant ignominy and colonialization. Joseph R. Levenson, in his book Modern China: An Interpretive Anthology *(New York: Macmillan, 1971), has reconstructed the reasons which prevented China from finding a "nationalistic-bourgeois" way out of the anachronistic totality of its late-Confucianist system; to tear down the barriers, to accept the relative, to agree to communicate, to make itself into a nation became real and possible only with the struggle against the colonizers in the period following the October Revolution, the revolution of May Fourth and of the Communist party.*

Levenson's masterly analysis does not attach sufficient importance to the distortions that ensued in the development of the Third International, and to the resulting repercussions in the Chinese Communist party which became fully apparent only later.

While the May Fourth Movement ambiguously combined a defense of national identity with an iconoclastic antitraditionalism, it nonetheless opened a way for laying bare the contradictions in Chinese society rather than pretending to annul them. *

The loftiest moment of liberation was attained by Lu Xun, almost in isolation; read today in the perspective of time, his writings reveal a consciously chosen

---

*Among other relevant writing of the period is Lu Xun's splendid essay "Looking at Things with Open Eyes."

discordancy and an ironical assumption of the role of the colonized. The internal and external, the Chinese and the foreigner could finally communicate because the rupture had been moved into the political area.

However, the Communist parties rejected the distinction between politics and culture. The political struggle against the imperialist colonizers was then trans- lated into renewed resistance to European culture's exercising a critical or de- structive function, *which might be a sequel to, and completion of, the process begun with the May Fourth Movement. Overturning Lu Xun's position, the Com- munists (like the Nationalists) retired to defensive positions; they believed they were fighting colonialism by refusing to admit they were colonized; in opposition to world culture, they reverted to affirming national characteristics, against which Lu Xun had inveighed so fiercely. They adopted the national-people's garb newly arrived from the Soviet Union. Contributing to this tortuous response was a sense of inferiority, fear of succumbing to cultural shock, fear of losing identity, and mistrust of their being able to be independent while at the same time they were protesting in extreme terms that indeed they were.* *

China's entrance into the world as a nation, as an equal among equals, had been mediated by an anticolonial International born of the October Revolution and led by the Soviet Union. Any other route would inevitably have led back to colonization, as the Kuomintang experience demonstrated. But the directive that came from the U.S.S.R. in the early thirties did push China backward onto the Kuomintang route, to conservatism and cultural subordination. On the one hand, inferior traditional forms were again taken up, thereby locking the people into a contented acceptance of second-rate products; on the other hand, Western literary and art works were introduced, secondhand, chosen not in their country of origin nor by the Chinese, but by copying criteria that had been adopted in the Soviet Union, as examples of other people's national-popular art and "realistic" and juxtaposed to Chinese products in the peaceful eclecticism of an all-embracing

---

*Intellectuals in the thirties were fully aware of the multiple conflicts. Opposing Lu Xun and his friends were Party bureaucrats of the Muscovite persuasion. From then on and up until after Liberation, the cultural world of the Left was profoundly divided; divergences of principle were interlaced with power struggles and personal hostilities. Some basic questions found expression in a series of polemics among writers grouped around, respectively, Hu Feng, who had been close to Lu Xun, and the Party bureaucrat Zhou Yang. Eventually, Mao Zedong took a position against Hu Feng, who in 1955 was arrested as a counterrevolutionary. He had directly dealt with the question of "national forms," which had been debated during the war, partly in Zhongqing, partly in Yanan. Hu Feng opposed "popular literature," which he termed "feudal" and "reactionary," and favored May Fourth Movement literature, arguing that if the social base is solid, one can employ even imported forms in creating a national literature. Zhou Yang took the opposite stance. He characterized May Fourth literature as "alien" and "Europeanizing," and maintained that a na- tional literature must have its origin in folk literature. In a 1951 essay, "The Road of Realism," Hu Feng again argued against a vague, uncritical assumption of a folk reality—almost as if it were free of "obscure aspects"—and against unquestioning patriotism and "national forms" frozen in formulas. According to Hu Feng, writers and artists must "advance policy" and not be its marginal tools.

"united front." Many misunderstandings that prevail in China about the West result from this selection, which covered not only the arts but philosophy, history, science, and sociology. Moreover, the people who enjoyed these imports belonged only to the educated middle class, whose remoteness from the mass of the people was thus renewed and perpetuated. Works that should have led the Chinese conscience toward a difficult confrontation with other cultures were, instead, amalgamated in a false harmony. Soviet mediation was often even more heavy-handed. In advance of reproductions of European painting—carefully chosen from the fifteenth to eighteenth centuries and excluding contemporary works— there arrived second-rate imitations of socialist realism, from which have come those oils of brawny peasants heading into the wind, marching toward the sun of the future, but with their hands in a pose taken from the Chinese theater repertory. This pollution continued on into works done after the Cultural Revolution. In Taking Tiger Mountain by Strategy, *the backdrop for the splendid dance of the soldier-phantoms at night is a Swiss Alps scene painted by a Soviet artist. This is the very colonization which the Chinese have been running away from for more than a hundred years.*

Soviet influence was devastating in the first years after Liberation, but the terrain had been prepared during the civil war. For a long time Mao Zedong himself favored directions in the cultural field which he fought on the political front. While in Yanan, he used to praise Lu Xun—and not without a particular motive—but then and until as late as the mid-sixties he left leadership in the cultural sector to the enemies of Lu Xun, and more than once he intervened in support of their policy, even very harshly, as in the case of Hu Feng. This is not a matter only of Mao's being influenced by power relationships within the Party or of choices being forced on him for narrowly political considerations. In Mao, as in Lenin, a totalizing ideology was grafted onto a populist heritage. On the one hand, there was the odious image of the scholars, old and new, and their cliques which had to be put down for the sake of the liberation of an oppressed people; on the other hand, there was the aim to establish such an intimate unity between leader and people as to exclude any intermediaries who were not reduced to the status of tools. Professional cultural activities and the role of intellectuals were obstructed; no consideration was given to the fact that in the process of eliminating the division of labor, this role should be attacked not first but last, or the process itself would be gravely compromised. In the case of both Mao and Lenin, their choosing the short cut—to eliminate the intellectuals as an independent category —tended to increase the influence of a class of bureaucrats and mandarins. Principles adopted in the political area were extended to the cultural sphere. Here, too, there was to be autonomy and independence (from foreigners). Especially*

---

*Stuart Schram, author of *Mao Tse-tung* (New York: Simon & Schuster, 1967), has noted in Mao a tendency to return to Zhang Zhidong's thesis: "Chinese culture as substance, foreign culture as tool."

in Mao's later years, after the break with the U.S.S.R., he reverted to under-estimating the value of foreign cultural contributions; they were accepted (and only verbally without restrictions) *as elements in a universal repertory and not as challenges to the autonomy and unflawed completeness of the Chinese cultural edifice. It was the old pan-Sinicism cage all over again, plus the introduction of a foreign culture without any interchange, any dialogue, so that it was, in effect, subservience to foreigners and* guan. *One rejected Beethoven but composed in imitation of Khachaturian, or accepted the classics and "democratic" and "pro-gressive" works within the perspective of the 1934 united front of mandarins. The Cultural Revolution delivered blows to many artists and writers—unjustly, since the creation of a culture cannot be laid as a fault to any individual. The* persons *deserve respect and compassion. But to lament over the* culture *that was destroyed does not make sense, since in actuality there was little to destroy, where "culture" meant merely a compromise between the sterile repetition of the Chinese past and the anachronistic imitation of outworn Western works.* Any *alternative—be it even, for a period, the negation of it all—offered for the future more hope than that blind alley.*

Mao, Zhou, and the "Old Cadres"
January 23

The purpose of mobilizing old cadres (who are numerous) against the Four is to produce a current of opinion favorable to reinstating the old leaders in positions of power. (Among these leaders are those who really were attacked by the Left, unlike the great majority of cadres, toward whom the Left's attitude was much more flexible.) Theater productions are being utilized for propaganda purposes, and even more so films exhumed from years back which deal with incidents in the civil war and the war with Japan. A case in point is *The Soviet of the Red Lake,* which has been shown on TV and in movie theaters—a little melodrama with some very tuneful songs, high-spirited rebel peasant-fishermen, fatherland, mama, and Party, done in color that is reminiscent of old-time postcards. In the first part, the action and choreography are lively, even if copied from three or four standard recipes. Then the action winds down to a standstill, and there's a tearful finale, with mama in jail and partisan-daughter singing the famous song of the Red Lake outside her window. The film harks back to guerrilla activities in 1930 and is being shown now in homage to He Long, who came under criticism during the Cultural Revolution. (Indeed, it was produced to honor him.) To hear Chen tell it, this was one of the six films the Four opposed.

But behind the cadavers, living or dead, of elderly marshals, from Zhu De to He Long to Liu Bocheng, there emerges the by no means cadaverous face of Deng Xiaoping, together with the men who are close to him. The various forces that contributed to overthrowing the Four are certainly not in perfect accord among themselves. In Peking, Deng's followers are putting up *dazibao* describing him as an eagle and asserting that he must become Premier, whereas Wu De, the mayor, who helped restore order at the time of the Tienanmen incidents, is called a chicken, and even Wang Hairong, Mao's young niece, is being harshly attacked.

The propitiatory figure that is being employed for restoration purposes is Zhou Enlai. No one would dare challenge him, and therefore a double, even triple, game is being played around his name (as happened at times in the past, with his consent). Zhou Enlai is not the same thing as Deng Xiaoping, and Deng Xiaoping is not the same thing as the old guard. Hua Guofeng keeps in with all and sundry (as he used to know how to keep in with both Left and Right, when Mao was still alive), looking to reap just as much personal power as he can, which is based only on this uneasy equilibrium. The situation can go on for a long time, since the moderate-conservative group is both successful and unsuccessful—it is meeting with no opposition from the base, but an elastic yielding, a resiliency. The general situation is souring. There are shortages of food supplies, in Peking queues for some necessities, in Shanghai queues for cigarettes and fresh produce, disappearance of some types of merchandise. These are day-to-day phenomena, not important on any large scale, but they prove that great enthusiasm for work is lacking, and the people are showing none of the activism that, according to the propaganda, the fall of the Four was to have brought about.

Everywhere great celebrations have begun to mark the anniversary of Zhou Enlai's death. Zhou's photograph is being shown next to and on the same level as Mao's. This is based on reality. What Zhou has in common with Mao belongs, in a certain sense, to the past and to that part of the past which survives and goes on still: the revolution in its early days and its heroic years, the rewon dignity of the Chinese nation, the resistance to the Soviet Union. But for a great many Chinese, and ever more explicitly in recent years, Zhou was also so much the image of what Mao was not that he became his opposite. Mao's pan-Sinicism notwithstanding, he had an anarchic streak that, to many people's way of thinking, prevented his being that guarantor against the disintegration of the state, ergo of resistance to foreigners, which they did recognize in Zhou, notwithstanding his being partially Westernized and clearly "open-minded" toward foreigners and their culture. Zhou was also the stabilizing force in the continual earthquakes of class struggle, he was government versus Party. He represented administration, continuity, order. And he was also the guarantor of the people's civil rights.

If he became the rallying point for bureaucratic and intellectual groups that in the last years were substantially hostile to Mao, his popularity extended far beyond that. For very many people, he represented their refuge from ultimatums to which they had no answers. He was a figure who was essential to an unexpressed, universal need for freedom. Not so much freedom from the domination of authority as freedom from the unceasing struggles, the omnipervasive politicking—for something else, some alternative that was not clearly recognized and not definable. "If Chairman Mao was a father, for us Zhou Enlai was a mother," Chen has said to me. For the Chinese, the father stands for authority, the mother for affection. But one must not forget that Mao's was the authority that derives from "thought"—motivation that is entirely internalized, and therefore at times all the more intolerable, whereas after 1949, it was Zhou only who constantly held the power in his hands. "Chairman Mao gave the directives, yes, but the person who had to take care of things was Zhou Enlai."

The bureaucrats, who are aiming today first to make Zhou a counter-object of devotion to Mao, then to make the two interchangeable, and ultimately to destroy Mao, are being obtuse. They do not understand that while Zhou's exercise of power was a determining factor in his popularity, people did not see him as the incarnation of power but as an image complementary to that of Mao. If the one is destroyed, in the end the other will be destroyed also, having been exploited as a tool to mask quite other interests.

A film in memory of Zhou Enlai is being shown repeatedly on TV. It's a good documentary, far superior to the patched-up one about Mao. It ends with some short but extraordinary bits from old documentaries. The funeral ceremony is shown with the usual cuts, and a beautiful sequence of the urn being borne through the immense, gray city. A long portion of the soundtrack is the funeral oration delivered by Deng Xiaoping; his name is never mentioned, and his face is not shown, but everybody knows who it is. The film ends with a long shot of the Monument to the People's Heroes, that huge obelisk that stands in the middle of Tienanmen Square; the base is covered on all sides with flowers. It is an evocation, a reproduction of what happened on that famous day, April 5, 1976—I've seen photos of that demonstration that are almost identical with this view. What was left unfinished then has now been completed.

The Tienanmen events have been repeated, this time with a positive result for the followers of Deng, who during the ceremony called for an immediate restoration. Today they no longer need write poems against Mao and can plaster their *dazibao* on the fences surrounding the area where the mausoleum is being constructed and on the great gate—*dazibao* against Wu De and the others who did not take a position in favor of Deng at the time. The targets of the attacks do not belong to the Left, but this Thermidor, like any other, will run its course, even if everything should have to be settled by an apparent compromise, rescuing the largest number of people at the top.

At the Institute, as in all other units, Zhou Enlai is being honored. We foreigners were called together, too. Our meeting was for foreigners only. Once again, the purpose was to oblige us to declare ourselves, ostensibly on the subject of Zhou Enlai but actually not on that score at all. Each person was virtually forced to speak. What on earth is the sense of sitting for three hours around a little altar with a big photograph on it (and above, side by side, photos of Mao and Hua facing the four fathers of the revolution (Marx, Engels, Lenin, Stalin)? It's getting to be like a Catholic church, full of saints and popes.* And what sense in mouthing over and over the same long, wordy, stupid remarks in praise of the dead statesman? "Idiotic nonsense!" John observed in exasperation as we were leaving. And yet there is a sense to it—i.e., the foreign experts also extol Zhou Enlai. But this means that the foreign experts join us faithful clerics, while we make a certain use of the celebration of Zhou Enlai and, without their knowing it, they say things that are useful to us. To what extent are the people similarly exploited, the more so the nearer to the base?

One of the "Chinese professors" present at the meeting told of having seen Zhou Enlai eight times! He pulled out a little piece of paper, which he said was a card of invitation from years back to a meeting of newly graduated students, of which he was one, at which Zhou had made a speech. "It's only a piece of paper, but for me it is sacred. . . ." Such things happen often in private life, too; one must bear that in mind before dismissing them as so much buffoonery. If someone dear to you dies and that evening you go to the movies, you are some sort of delinquent; ditto if at a time of mourning, you drink a glass of wine. Lu Xun has taught us how to evaluate all this. The misanthrope who does not weep at his grandmother's funeral is considered a monster. (Lu Xun also wrote that, in China, even to move a table from here to there calls for shedding blood.)

But my students have not read Lu Xun. Perhaps this year, their second at the university, they will read a few of his short stories in their Chinese class. Also, not only do they not have the vaguest notion of the writings and ideas of Marx, even in simplified terms, they also know almost nothing about Mao. This in itself is no scandal; it is better to have a school for workers who at the outset are, of necessity, ignorant than the Marxist academies one finds in some of our universities in Italy. The true scandal lies in the fact that these young people, who are studying to the best of their abilities, are required to use their time memorizing an endless series of stock phrases about Lu Xun and Marx and Mao, and edifying anecdotes and distorted biographical sketches; they spend hours "studying" articles in *The People's Daily*, which is to say, learning a synopsis that they then stupidly repeat aloud. I have learned that it is a great privilege to have access to the complete works of Lenin.

What little ground I had managed to win in my struggle against mechani-

---

*These small altars are more or less copies of the ones for the dead that people used to keep in their homes (and perhaps still do in some parts of the countryside); now, rather than a small tablet or nameplate, a photograph of the deceased is customary.

cal, stupid rote learning I am now losing in disastrous fashion. The students no longer want explanations; every time I urge them to reason, to think things through for themselves, they balk; they ask for hard-and-fast rules they can commit to memory. If I point out that there is not a rule for everything, they demand lists of "right's" and "wrong's," which they then proceed to memorize. Things that have no interconnection whatever are associated simply because they have in common a sound, a particle, a phrase. What accounts for this rapid deterioration? They have found out that they will have to take examinations. For them it will be the first time, but they belong to the country that invented examinations, and they're familiar with the machinery. Weaknesses and shortcomings that were undetectable and even nonexistent before are becoming apparent, as are their insecurity and competitiveness, lack of interest in knowledge for its own sake, concentration of all their energies on succeeding. Knowledge is becoming synonymous with acknowledgment of an outside authority, dependence on others is respected and sanctioned, whether it be cadre, professor, or foreign expert. In these circumstances, a selective screening that ideally would be "modern" and based on merit amounts to a return to the authoritarian principle, the extreme conservative degradation, the loss of intelligent independence.

If they are troubled by the prospect of examinations, these young people are even more deeply alarmed over a huge swindle they see looming ahead. They know that the system which brought most of them to the university is being challenged, and they feel the rug slipping out from under their feet. The attitude of their teachers aggravates their apprehension, because the faculty tends to support the success of the more aggressive climbers and the children of cadres. I do what I can to restore some balance in this situation, but I know that I carry very little weight.

Chen thinks in terms of competitive schools; if the students know they will have to take exams, she says, they will work harder. Which is true, if you can call work the frantic, futile activity to which they have been giving themselves for days.

"We'll be giving exams now that the Gang of Four has been got rid of," Zhang says triumphantly, for all the world like some petty Fascist official. He of all people. If he were to be given a serious exam in Italian, he'd be the first to be failed. I like him better when he is being human—when he forgets to remember he's a professor and tells me about his childhood, how he and other little boys used to run through the (now closed) Buddhist temple in the old city, and how they would hide from the furious monk in pursuit; or when he pokes fun at the unhappy lovers in *The Dream of the Red Chamber,* saying, "Those two idiots!" At other times, he will forget all the big problems and talk about everyday things; without realizing it, he conveys a great deal about life as it is lived in Shanghai, and how hard it is. Zhang's meanness lies in the art of "making out," which he practices like a street urchin who tries to slip unscathed through the intricacies of a gear system that is essentially alien to him, even if he knows the workings of it well enough. And his occasional malice is one version of that curiosity about foreigners, mixed with envy, which you often find in the people of Shanghai.

People like Zhang can be taken in by those who fool them into thinking that they can be little squires, and they don't realize that by lending themselves to this they contribute to their own ruination. The great majority of the Chinese middle class is too poor, even culturally, not to be utterly lost if it were to try to join up with the powerful in China; they would become one huge "I'd like to and I can't" group, with no choice left for them but complicity in "sucking the blood of the workers," as Mao said. The only way they can know themselves and make the most of themselves is to become integrated with the wretched of the earth. In education, a selective efficiency-oriented criterion presupposes a reasonably adequate level of mass instruction, especially in elementary technology. On the other hand, funds available for schools are too meager to finance both the development of mass education and a selective education at middle-school level.* Here, the selective method can be successful only for a very limited number of people and only on the upper academic levels. For the others, it is nonsense, or, as in the old university system in Europe, selection will be made primarily on the basis of class and privilege and only marginally on the basis of merit. What's more, insofar as merit is taken into account, it will be defined in terms of a high and median culture that is in toto imported. (If you don't have the soil in which to make a given tree grow, you will be forced to transplant it.)

The educational petty bourgeoisie—teachers and assistants—are prone to look to their own particular interests; they take a shortsighted view and opt for selectivity because they think it will upgrade them socially.

In the schools, but not only in the schools, the choice of the "capitalist road" risks leading China into a decline. A regression toward a colonial status is entirely possible, given the country's still great poverty. It's doubtful that there is a capitalist road that will not place the middle class in a situation of inferiority vis-à-vis foreigners, and the great mass of people in a situation comparable to that of the "marginals" in capitalist societies—only here not comparable to but worse than. Today the people who, behind the screen of the struggle against the Gang of Four, are doing their utmost to upset the policy of Mao seem not to understand that to conform to the logic of the world's masters and to adopt profit and power as fundamental values is to choose an inferior position for their country internation-

---

*One reason for making base units responsible for managing elementary and middle schools was to lighten the financial burden on the government. The number of students in the universities shrank after the Cultural Revolution. Now, however (1976), contrary to the situation in the fifties and early sixties, all students are supported by the State.

ally, and to increase and extend inequality and abuse at home. Behind Mao's directive "Do not seek hegemony"—that is, do not seek to become a great power among great powers—there lay no utopia but, rather, stringent realism. It was the only directive compatible with opposition to class power within the country.

Solitude

It's been raining for some days. The world is drowned in water and fog, and dampness penetrates everywhere. It makes me feel the cold more. Going up and down in the elevator, we see a great many cadres, both elderly and middle-aged, also civilians, including women and children, military people, police. (A lot of police are now coming to the Institute mess, chopsticks in hand, in addition to the regulars.) The cadres fill the hotel, but they are not always the same people; there is a rotation. It's said over and over that one of the misdeeds of the Four was to keep people busy with political campaigns instead of leaving them in peace to attend to their work and their own affairs. But now people are much more taken up than before with meetings or political study, on which they spend hours and hours every week. Whether, apart from the usual repetition of set phrases, an attack is in progress against base cadres I don't know. It's common knowledge that at least two of the city's top ex-leaders have been arrested. A few days ago, crowds of students gathered by the Institute gate, waiting to be picked up and taken by truck to the stadium nearby in order to salute young people from other schools who were leaving for the country, it was explained to me. That is unlikely. It is too early, since no one has been graduated yet this term, and that kind of farewell is ordinarily a street affair. It's more likely that the students—a chosen group, for all that there were a lot of them—were taken to attend a criminal trial, if not to witness the execution of the condemned, for sometimes executions are carried out at the stadium. The young people did seem somewhat stirred up.

The term is coming to an end. I am still preparing reading materials for next semester and the year after, and helping Tang translate a glossary. It was compiled in Chinese and in French by the Foreign Languages Institute in Peking, and covers a range of subjects. It is a little *neibu* list; so is the tiny Chinese-English dictionary of political terms, which Zhang has left on his table so that I can use it if I need to. In the sections dealing with policy there are listed, one by one, the slogans and quotations that are usable for the various alternating policy lines. For his Chinese-Italian list, Tang has eliminated some that go too far in one direction. This is one part of a manual of multiple uses that the *ganbu* put together for purposes of self-protection and survival whatever the circumstances may be. It also helps to simplify the job of passing the word to the people. The *ganbu* is the custodian of orthodoxy, which is defined not by content but by formal canonicity.

This helps one understand why, when it's a question of translations, they are unwilling to depart from an established version (which is canonical if only because it has the sanction of print); why they are horrified if you propose variants; why they are adamantly against any suggestion that a person express in his own words the ideas behind some commonly held position. (I once told Zhang that in our schools the person who does not express himself in a non-repetitive, fresh way can expect a negative comment. He seemed utterly unable to grasp that.) You also come to understand how, within the space of a few days, the same people can affirm conflicting views in all seriousness and with no sense of shame.

To make some recordings, Zhang or Tang accompanies me to the small sound studio down the hall from us. I sit in the little room, which is lined with some sort of soundproofing material—it's makeshift but effective—in almost total darkness, with just an old desk lamp. The room's as cold as an ice box. A very pleasant technician signals to me from behind a glass that I am to start or stop. He knows a little bit of every language taught at the Institute, and he never fails to thank me when I've finished and am about to go back to my room. Who knows whether he's always been a technician, or whether he had more prestigious functions before getting into this line of work. I wonder the same thing about the typist—a man, very efficient and intelligent—whom I can judge only from his work, since I've never met him; we communicate through Chen. He's no longer young, and this I know from seeing him a few times when he has knocked softly on the glass pane to call; he has never come into the room. Is it that direct contact with me could be risky for someone who is not authorized? Or is he timid because of shame for a personal disgrace which is known and discounted by others but rekindled by the presence of a stranger?

I keep asking myself what my relationship with these people is, what I can communicate to them when they ask me to talk about my own country, now that the so-called opening up is beginning. Hundreds of millions of persons who behave as if they lived on an island suspended above the world. . . . Until they give up this assumption, they will never be able to learn anything outside that island, no matter how many notions they manage to catalog. However, notions have their limits, too; and in fact, the Chinese are inclined only to add details to an existing picture. But the moment one begins to talk about the most insignificant fact, it turns out that that fact cannot even be added as a detail because the picture is false.

They resist knowledge about other people, for it challenges them, yet they are prepared to accept the moribund values of the capitalist market as a universal model, to sell their workers as a low-cost labor force. This paradox can lead to a tragic shrinking of awareness.

From *The People's Daily*, January 4: "In many Latin American countries, justifiable alarm is aroused by the fact that the Soviet Union, intensifying its contest with American imperialism, is extending its reach, expanding on all sides, and has openly attacked Angola. Governments and public opinion in many [of these] countries continually denounce these moves, affirming that 'today the Soviet Union is the country with the greatest imperialist and colonial characteristics.' "

My usual walks through the midtown area: on Nanjing lu I saw a small pro-Deng *dazibao,* with the name partially scratched out. I came across a bigger one on the same type of pink paper, barely affixed, on the Bund just beyond where it crosses Beijing lu. (Earlier, occasional pro-Deng posters had appeared in the outskirts of the city.) A few days later I saw, again on Nanjing lu, a poem entitled "Deng Xiaoping Is Good," which opened with "Old Deng, old Deng. . . ." People gathered around tranquilly to read and copy it, like spectators curious about a drama that does not involve them personally. En route to the Institute, I also saw a *dazibao* about the Tienanmen incident that held the Four responsible for it.

Some foreigners who had gone to a restaurant for Peking duck saw Deng there. They said to him, jokingly, *"Pi Deng, pi Deng!"* ("Criticize Deng.") He laughed, too.

I had a dream that I was in Russia during the Stalin days, and, later, that I had a long conversation with Jiang Qing.

I've slipped under the glass on the table in my room all the postcard art reproductions which I've received, plus other reproductions that I've cut out. I've had a friend send me cassettes of *Aida* and *Il Trovatore.* I mind the cold, I would like to eat one piece of honest-to-God bread, hear a concert, and see a good movie.

I'm tired of never being able to stop, no matter where, without people looking at me as if I were some sort of strange animal, of never setting foot in a private home, my own or someone else's, and not even in a public library, of being surrounded by people who tell lies or who clam up in order not to tell lies, tired of having forgotten what spontaneity is, of having the blare of loudspeakers forever in my ears, of being without good music and good art yet not amid silence and quietude. And all these things notwithstanding, I am greatly privileged because I eat better than other people, live in a hotel where it is warm, am able to buy many things for myself, and have enough money to travel a bit.

A Film and a Factory

The municipality has invited us to the International Club for a showing of *The East Is Red.* The film was made in early 1965 and is based on a musical of 1964. It is being given tremendous publicity: one whole page of photos in *The People's*

Daily, and a spate of articles. Also, since we could have seen the film quietly in any movie theater, the special invitation extended to us is a token of special solemnity—the "liberation" of an important work from the Gang of Four's censorship is being celebrated. The film is being associated with Zhou Enlai, and is part of the celebration of his anniversary. Raised to the status of patron saint of conservative intellectuals, he is being presented as someone who shared personally in the preparation if not in the production of films; this one is said to have actually been filmed according to instructions from him. It does seem that involuntarily they are doing their best to obscure the great dignity this man attained in his public service.

The idea in *The East Is Red* was to produce a screen spectacular: a cast and crew of three thousand along with who knows how many dance groups, orchestras, etc. It was supposed to be, in ballet form, the story of the revolution, from just after World War II to 1949. The model to which it aspires seems to be the American musical comedy; the spectacle is interspersed with bravado acrobatics/choreography and with sentimental ballads. But there are other ingredients in the hash as well: Romantic painting (livid colors and groups of hungry men and bodies in chains); social realism (lucid faces and vigorous bodies); and even—the only really good element had it been taken out of context —authentic songs of the era. The result is crazy. The actors in chains, all decked out in social-realist tatters, run after their liberators, who are represented by robust worker and peasant types accompanied by an intellectual in a suit; hurrying along in a sort of Broadway rhythm, they throw out their behinds and shake about from right to left. They are caricatures of themselves. In fact, the element of caricature dominates to the point where, swept away by astonishment, one begins to see all this as some sort of Chinese version of *Nashville*— or, perhaps better, as the footage served up at the cutting table of some Chinese Robert Altman. The thing grows and keeps growing until at the end, in front of a tiny Tienanmen constructed of yellow cardboard that is entirely out of proportion with the actors (as if we were at some sort of puppet play), the various minority groups follow one another in their Sino-Sovietoid dances while in the background, on the steps, rows of humanity, dressed diversely but predominantly in Western style, sway together from side to side.

The East Is Red has been well-received by foreigners in Peking and Shanghai, as it most certainly will be in Europe, where it is soon to be shown. This once again proves how deep and unconscious is the attitude of implicit superiority of Europeans in their dealing with Africans, Asians, and Latin-Americans: they always seem to find beautiful that which, if produced at home, would be considered substandard.

We are factory visiting again in lieu of political studies. Everybody's got bronchitis, Chinese and foreigners alike, and many people stay home. Even Lao Bai is ill, as is Chen; John, too.

We drove halfway across the city by bus. I took the seat beside the driver and held Aymin in my lap, so that we could see better where we were going. The Bund, Yanan Road, Huai Hai, and then due south along Zhongqing Road ... then again in the direction of the river, through mist and rain the color of mud. After passing by the elegant residences in the ex–French Concession, we plunged into a maze of streets and alleys, lined or not with trees (at this time of year, tree skeletons) and with houses and shacks, some two-storied but most having only one floor. Dwellings alternate with shops, storage sheds, small workshops, larger ones to the rear. This is an older section, older and more poverty-stricken than the port area to the north. People were moving about on their bicycles, dressed in hooded semitransparent gray raincoats; a few wore brownish-yellow rain gear. They looked like monks in a faraway Holland; the colors were early Van Gogh, earth brown, dull yellow (the yellow umbrellas of Shanghai), clay gray. . . . The street was long, storylike. We heard the river and the boats nearby.

Our stay in the factory's cold reception room so reduced me that I feared I might have gotten pneumonia, but then I slept for twelve hours, and now everything is all right.

The plant produces structural steel pipes. It's well known to travelers, for at one point it was a showplace for every foreign delegation passing through Shanghai. In Italy, I had heard workers protest and intellectuals comment ironically on their return: "Lousy. . . . Some working conditions. . . . They call this a model factory!" etc., etc. This is a little bit the fault of the Chinese for not explaining why they had foreigners visit this particular plant; maybe the interpreters were not well prepared or did a routine job. The factory is not a standard either in Shanghai or anywhere else in China. The reason for showing it has been precisely that it is so inadequate. It is a "red flag," a symbol, an example of how without means, without adequate plants, with untrained labor, and amid the greatest poverty it is still possible to manufacture sophisticated products, objects of high precision and prime quality such as any technician in his right mind would think could never be produced in those conditions. Even today sections of the roof are sometimes missing so that it rains in, people work crowded together, there is emergency backup electrical equipment. Your escorts will point to a new machine standing beneath some straw-mat roofing with a hole in the middle, and they will tell you, "Some people think first of the temple and then of the Buddha. We think the Buddha comes first, and then, if there's time, the temple will be built."

The manager, a man no longer young, told us at length about the history of the factory. He is vice-chairman of its Revolutionary Committee and had with him a woman from the union as he talked. The enterprise had passed through four stages: from being a store that in 1953 was selling knickknacks to today's factory that has an annual output of nine thousand tons of twenty-two hundred different types of pipes. Some are for the defense and petroleum industries, others now are designed for medical and sports use.

The man did not speak the usual jargon. He related, simply, the story of a revolution: the repeated struggles, year after year, not only to arrive at the point of producing what seemed to be the impossible but also to do so despite opposition and/or scornful skepticism. He told about how when the engineer in charge prior to 1965 was faced with the stubborn persistence of the workers in wanting to carry out a task requested by the petroleum industry, which he considered too difficult, he abandoned the factory for six months, and how they then formed a three-in-one union of workers, technicians, and cadres, how after thirty-one attempts to work out a satisfactory design, they succeeded in manufacturing special cooling pipes needed by the petroleum industry. There were similar experiences with material needed for national defense and laboriously designed in collaboration with soldiers. At first, the factory personnel were utterly unprepared but gradually became more competent; workers were trained to become technicians; products became more diversified and specialized. The factory's leap forward was achieved with the Cultural Revolution, when it no longer had to fight an isolated battle, often against its own top management, but found the road ahead free and clear, after which production quadrupled and the range of products was much enlarged.

Pipes of five-gram structural steel were ordered. Because the factory had no experience with this, it was obliged to make trial tests and was incurring losses. No matter, since other units were showing a profit; profit must not be calculated unit by unit, the manager said, but on the basis of overall utility. (He knew perfectly well that to exclude the aim of making a profit at the level of individual enterprise was the opposite of the thesis that now will come to prevail.)

When the speaker tried to smile, his mouth curled in a grimace, like a tic. He knew he was playing a role that no longer made any sense. Notwithstanding that, he made us understand that they—he and the eight hundred workers—have sturdy shoulders. He made numerous statements contrary to the orthodoxy of the moment. Among other things, he referred to direct contacts with other factories in Shanghai and in other provinces, which is to say, to one of the points of conflict (together with the principle of self-sufficiency) between the Left's line and Deng's. "We will be faithful to the last wishes of Chairman Mao," he said, "and we will go forward, whatever the difficulties, with our duty to the proletarian revolution." Several times he said, "The workers are tremendously steadfast." Yet he was aware that if foreigners are still being brought here it is that he and the factory, and others like it, are being used in the same way as is Daqing. Hard work and unremitting effort are to be the norm for workers. He said that the bases of their work are twofold: Marxism-Leninism and worker self-sufficiency. (He also quoted the slogan that today is under a cloud: "Independence, self-sufficiency, reliance on one's own strengths.")

The man did not mention the Gang of Four, and no one was so foolish as to ask him about them.

Roland wanted to know how they study Marxism-Leninism. The man then began again to describe what the people working at the factory were like in the early days. Illiterates and rickshaw boys, picked up haphazardly here and there, were little by little, in a way, transformed, and gradually became able to produce new things. In the evening classes, the young people have had a general education, the old have experience, with the result that young and old stay united. Every week, the worker-teachers give three lessons, two on political questions and one on matters having to do with job training. The workers themselves maintain the equipment, and they repair the machinery themselves. (Nonetheless, the man added, we should learn techniques from the industrialized countries.) The workers had found in the writings of Mao the strength they needed to solve their problems, and also to manufacture the sophisticated products that some people, influenced by Liu Shaoqi's line, had not wanted to make before the Cultural Revolution. . . . In those days, the workers were not able even to enter the experimental laboratories. Then they took over the management for the production of small structural steel items; there had been four hundred discussions in which everybody had taken part, including the cooks. "The masses are the real heroes."

We told the man that what he had said and showed us was a model of socialism. In spite of himself, his mouth again twisted in the same grimace.

The Persecuted
January 28

At six o'clock on an evening like this, a heated room is a welcome thing, and to be enfolded in layers of clothing is welcome, too. Outside, the world is like a vast Nativity scene; it's been snowing, this time for real, and all roofs on the boats on the river and on buildings are white. It is almost dark, and the colored lights make the scene quite Christmaslike.

Today I ate alone in the restaurant, which was all topsy-turvy because tables had been moved about and prepared for a meeting. In front of me, I had a cleared space, one window, and behind it the bright reflection of the snow; a soft, dull light poured into the room.

Now my colleagues are all off to see an opera about the revolt of a secret Qing-era group, called the Society of the Little Knives. The dances are said to be quite fine, and I'm sorry not to have gone, but I have a mild bronchitis with a touch of fever, and I don't want to catch more cold. Scenes from today's meeting in the restaurant, which began shortly after I had lunched there, keep coming back to mind. I attended it with Chen, who had come to fetch me in a state of some excitement.

We were all on hand, together with the interpreters and the cadres, Lao Bai included. The program was a very unusual interview—theater about theater —given by the singer Yuan Xuefen, the actor Liu Jue, and Zhu Jingduo, the youthful *kung fu* master (*kung fu* is the form of boxing in Hong Kong films). All three are members of the local opera in Shaoxing, a small city in Zhejiang Province, which was the home of Lu Xun, and is famous for its wine. The actress and the young boxer are widely known today as symbols of persecution at the hands of the Gang of Four. Indeed, Zhu Jingduo is by way of becoming a public hero. He dared to write to Mao to complain about Zhang Chunqiao. The papers have already talked about all this, but the important thing about today was the live performance.

Yuan Xuefen is in her early sixties. I had seen her in old films and heard some of her recordings; her voice is pitched in the Chinese manner, and on the caterwauling side. She looks her age now, but—so they tell us—she nonetheless sings opera excerpts, and she is always warmly received as a consolation for all she has suffered. (This morning, when Zhang learned about the forthcoming interview, he said jokingly: "That singer used to be famous, you know, but a lot of people didn't like her because her voice is too sugary. When she would sing *The Dream of the Red Chamber,* all the old women used to cry to hear her, but not me. I had to laugh." Now that Zhang's no longer afraid of the leftist censors, he sometimes becomes a kind of conduit for me, letting me hear the voice of the common people of Shanghai. From the tone of his comments, it is evident that, despite official directives, the actress is not taken seriously, and that her performance is an object of ridicule.)

The woman had gray hair, cut short, and she was modestly dressed in a little blue cotton jacket, but underneath, barely visible, was a silk blouse. The face was that of a once pretty goose-girl type, but now it is drawn and anxious —the face of someone who has indeed suffered unjustly and carries within a sense of the outrage visited on her. The *kung fu* master was unreal—a poster image of the robust, handsome, frank man of the people. The actor seemed young at first glance but is actually past his forties; he was wearing a Chinese jacket (this is currently high style among intellectuals, rather than the Sun Yat-sen *ganbu*), and a blue wool overcoat; he was thin and pale, with a Pierrot face—a Barrault out of a Chinese version of *The Children of Paradise.* He spoke first, and told the story of his theatrical company.

From his remarks: The Shaoxing opera came into existence only some sixty years ago. It sprang directly from village opera, from performances put on by the peasants. In these only men acted, taking both male and female roles. However, in the Shaoxing opera, with professional actors, only women performed, taking on also the male roles.* In the old society, actors were despised. However, after Liberation, the Party interested itself in them, and actors feel great gratitude to Chairman Mao and to the Party. In the years following Liberation, the Shaoxing opera, which even before used to perform in Shanghai, was divided into four groups, three exclusively of women, and the fourth comprised of both women and men, he being one of this group. Zhou Enlai repeatedly took an active, personal interest in the work of this company. He met with Yuan Xuefen on several occasions, criticized the weakness of the old style of theatrical performance, and indicated the directions that should be taken to renew it. Zhou was the true interpreter of the line of Chairman Mao: Let a hundred flowers bloom. . . . The company used to perform old things from the past about mandarins and beautiful women; Zhou criticized these productions, and the actors tried to improve and to produce shows with modern themes. A group of women went to perform for the army. Zhou pointed out that they should co-opt some male actors, since military themes do not lend themselves to being acted out by women only.

The Cultural Revolution had been well received. The actors had willingly practiced self-criticism for having, under the influence of Liu Shaoqi, put on old works. At the same time, they knew that the Shaoxing opera was popular in Shanghai, and they wanted to continue to serve the peasants, workers, and soldiers. Before the Cultural Revolution, there had been more than a hundred separate opera companies in Shanghai. The people were satisfied with the great variety of entertainment. But at that point the Gang of Four and their accomplices launched their attack. They wanted to have only one flower bloom—which is to say, the Peking opera, supported by Jiang Qing, who was opposed to Mao's line. In Shanghai, the number of opera companies was cut down to ten (today there are thirteen). The result was monotony. The people are bored to see the same type of entertainment all the time. Not only that, but few new works were produced. Even films were too much alike, and there were too few of them.

*In Lu Xun's "Village Opera," the author, who habitually ridiculed traditional Chinese theater, instead recalled nostalgically the performances put on by the peasants in which he himself, as a child, had taken part. To associate himself with Lu Xun and thus win the foreigners' approval, this actor was making a somewhat forced association between the female opera of Shaoxing and village opera, which was an entirely different thing. In this instance, there seems to have been no direct derivation, although there is no doubt about the connection between folk performances and elaborated theatrical forms, even if it is not immediate. But this has nothing to do with the Shaoxing opera in particular. The Shaoxing opera must originally have been a women's activity which the common people, who despised actors, looked on as bordering on prostitution. (In the course of the conversation, the actress was to say that there are historical reasons for women having chosen the theatrical profession: "They had no other way out.") Rather than candidly facing the problem of restoring dignity to a despised profession, the actor was trying to hide it behind a false folk character. In this context, the reference to Lu Xun was grotesque, since he had taken an almost diametrically opposed position.

The Shaoxing opera was sabotaged by actors being sent into the country-side to do manual labor. They were entirely willing to be integrated with the masses, but if numerous members of the company were sent into the country for years at a time, the corps that remained in the city was inadequate, and members who were in the country, being unable to practice, forgot their craft. Thus, there was waste and destruction of talent. At the same time, the musicians, the stage designers, and the best actors were urged to transfer over to the Peking opera. Dominated by Jiang Qing and supported by Zhang Chunqiao, the Peking opera enjoyed all privileges: its own headquarters, rehearsal space, gymnasiums, higher salaries (the directors were salaried on a par with high-ranking cadres). Other companies, on the contrary, sometimes had to rehearse out of doors for lack of accommodations. In such circumstances, naturally the best among the young actors were drawn to the Peking opera and abandoned the other companies. (In response to my question: no steps had ever been taken to dissolve the Shaoxing opera, but for a certain period—nothing more precise was offered as to the date or duration—the group had been reduced to seven or eight members, who were too few to be able to organize performances.) Leaders lost interest in the Shaoxing opera; once, when Zhang Chunqiao was asked how the company should go about rebuilding itself, he answered that it was not his business and that the members should work something out by themselves.

The accomplices of the Gang of Four organized a cultural group to attack the masses, belying Mao's directive to struggle with words and not with physical violence.* The singer Yuan Xuefen was especially persecuted, almost as if she were a counterrevolutionary.† She was subjected to five hundred criticism sessions, at which more than a thousand people were present.‡ One day, several persons, claiming to be sent by the Central Cultural Revolution Group, made a search of her house on the pretext of investigating who, prior to the Cultural Revolution, had issued orders that the company should perform in Peking. (It never became clear whether this involved a given number of performances or an actual transfer to that city.) What they were actually after was to get her to name Zhou Enlai. They sequestered photographs of her with Zhou and also personal diaries. But they found no proof. For seven years, she was kept in isolation. (In response to a question of mine: not in prison. She was under a kind of house arrest in her own home, but was not permitted to be in contact with

---

*Actually, Mao's directive came during the Cultural Revolution, at a time when no Gang of Four existed.

†Contrary to what the speaker was implying and what Yuan Xuefen wished later to convey to the foreigners, she was not merely a singer, and therefore attacked in a crusade against "intellectuals"; she was also an active and somewhat prominent political figure, a Party member, and a delegate to the National People's Congress.

‡We were unable to find out what the charges against her were.

people, even her own daughter; she first saw her grandson, who was born in those years, when he was seven.) And yet she recognized her errors; she attended a May Seventh school (whether before or after her house arrest never became clear). When she was released, it was only on probation, and every week she had to report everything that she was doing. (It eventually became clear that this persecutive treatment ended years ago; ergo, it had occurred before the Gang of Four existed. Counting up the years, it would have been in the period of the Cultural Revolution.)

The actress herself took over from there. Unlike the actor, who had been rather dry and factual, she wasted most of the time in long, pointless rigmaroles about her love for the masses and for the Party, for Chairman Mao and Premier Zhou, about her hatred of the Gang of Four, etc. She added almost nothing factual. Last year, Jiang Qing had sent to ask that she sing for her the arias of *Xi Xiang Ji (The Western Chamber,* or, *The Story of Ying Ying,* one of the masterpieces of Yuan theater, a thirteenth-century drama of romantic love). She had replied that she had lost her voice and that Jiang Qing should, if she wished, listen to her old recordings. She had not wanted, she said, to sing for Jiang Qing, who was a liar when she pretended to be a revolutionary, since she also loved this feudal theater repertory. That being so, why had the Four criticized the singer for performing *The Story of Ying Ying?* The woman's pale face burned with hatred, and as she spoke, she seemed to vomit hate. It was repellent, and also proof that she must have been injured in some unendurable way. People like this woman want only revenge. (But she is not the ordinary citizen they would like us to believe she is; she was once in the game.)

The young hero's speech was entirely political. Party member (in this case, so stated), model Communist. Came out of the Cultural Revolution. Son of poor peasants. Praised in his May Seventh school. Like his physical image, his biography was a manifesto. Through Deng Yingchao, Zhou's wife, he had addressed a protest to Chairman Mao about the sabotage of which the Shaoxing opera was victim. This letter and others had been intercepted by Wang Hongwen, the young man had been subjected to an investigation and had spent eleven months in jail before he was cleared of all charges; the acquittal statement, however, affirmed that he had committed grave political errors. (This relatively recent incident was reported on at length in the newspapers.) In Shanghai, four thousand people were arrested. (It was not clear when the arrests began or ended, and how long the individuals remained in jail.) The Gang of Four attacked Chen Yi, Liu Bocheng, He Long, Zhu De, Li Xiannian, Tan Shengbin. But the main target of their attack was Zhou Enlai and his foreign policy. (The Gang of Four, in the words of the young man, meant the "Left" or ultra-Left during the Cultural Revolution. In fact, however, the attacks upon leaders which he alluded to, and the occupation of the Ministry of Foreign

Affairs, occurred in 1967 and were the work of ultraleftists who were well known and who were also cleared from the political scene a few months later. Not only did no Gang of Four exist at the time, but none of the "four" was implicated in those incidents. Only Jiang Qing was suspected of any sympathy for the ultra-Left—and it is still unknown whether justly or unjustly.)

The young man was, clearly, a political cadre. Unlike the other two, he appeared neither anxious nor vindictive; he was composed, like a person who knows he is strong.

As usual, the three accounts took up all the available time, and at the end there was no possibility of asking questions. The few I had managed to raise I had forcibly interjected in the course of their statements.

When the young man said that his arrest was ordered by the Ministry of Public Security, I asked Chen whether at that time Hua Guofeng had not been Minister. She promptly said no, but then she consulted the others. The conclusion: "The arrest was ordered by the Vice-Minister."

Today's meeting was well planned, both as entertainment and as a means of communicating several things to us.

For the first time, we were present at an open attack on the Cultural Revolution, in which the Gang of Four became a pure metaphor. With the exception of the business concerning the young man, everything we were told harks back to a period much earlier than the date of the presumed formation of any Gang. The years 1965–76 were spoken of as a single wretched period. It would have been pointless to ask for specific dates; they don't answer, they deliberately sow confusion with a partial tactical retreat; in fact, the attack must be made in depth and unmistakable, but not put into words.

Manifestly, the idea was to portray the present moment to foreigners as a kind of de-Stalinization and a return to liberalism. Therefore, it was forcefully reiterated that "the Gang of Four had set up a Fascist dictatorship." The ploy is fairly feeble, since the repression carried out against the Right by the organs of government (without which there is no dictatorship) was rather bland, when it existed at all, if for no other reason than that state power was never in the hands of the Left. (If someone tried to overthrow Zhou Enlai, he certainly did not succeed. The only sector where the Left enjoyed any real power of any duration, although it was not theirs exclusively, was the press and the performing arts. As for their power in Shanghai and several other cities, we know how laughable it would be to assert, for example, that Italian Communists have established a dictatorship in, say, Emilia.) The case of the innocent young man held in preventive arrest for eleven months must be truly exceptional if such a scandal is being made of it throughout China; certainly, it will not impress people from the France or Germany or Italy of today. It does seem that here no one has any notion of what fascism is. * *People know only about civil war—the hot war against the Kuomintang, and the cold war that for more than a decade has been waged to gain control of the whole country, sweeping into it many people who, persecuted by one side or the other depending on the time and circumstances, react with hatred for, and a desire to be revenged on, one or the other side. The only thing there has* not *been is the dictatorship of one group over the other; in fact, the apparatus of both the State and Party was manned by an assortment of members and supporters of opposed tendencies; this was true especially of high administrative posts and of certain cities. Both groups made use of the apparatus to increase their respective power in a struggle as ruthless as it was covert. To assess how deep these hatreds are one need only reflect. People who go to great lengths to conceal the smallest defects from foreigners and maintain an often futile system of secretiveness do not, at a certain moment, hesitate almost masochistically to unveil how the country is going to wrack and ruin, how production has ground to a halt, how the most absolute arbitrary power has supplanted the rule by law, and finally, how in the last twelve years and up until Mao's death in the People's Republic of China there has been room for a Fascist dictatorship.*

So fierce a struggle cannot be only among factions. It is fed by very profound contradictions in society itself, even although they are not clearly reflected in the struggle, indeed are not only not expressed but rather suffocated by it.

Innovations at School, Police at the Dasha
February 4

This afternoon, there was a meeting at school on "the revolution in education" —which is to say more accurately, on our experience in teaching. (The locution

---

*As in the West, the incorrect use of the word "fascism" gives rise to a series of misunderstandings that are more than a mere matter of terminology. Today in Europe, one often hears the word "Fascist" used with no reference at all to what fascism and nazism really were in historical reality. The first thing forgotten is the essentially nationalistic character of both movements. (The Kuomintang of the thirties, with its nationalistic one-party regime, borrowed much from Italian fascism.) Mussolini invented the slogan of "the proletarian nation" (Italy) against the "demoplutocracies" (America, France, England) with an orientation very similar to that of many of today's Third World leaders who are considered semidemocratic or semisocialistic. That the character of these regimes is very similar to that of the historical Fascist state (single party, police state, power concentrated in a bureaucratic middle class, nationalism) is hardly ever noted by the mass media. "Fascism" and "Fascist" are words used only in a generic way to devote violence and repression, and have the value of insults when used against governments or the leaders of factions opposed to one's own, or against the satellites of either of the opposing imperial powers. Thus we see disappearing from the historic meaning of fascism the socio-economic-political reality on one side and on the other the memory of the extremity, the monstrosity to which the Nazi-Fascist violence and repression eventually led. This failing is even more accentuated in China, where opposing factions find it easy to define as "Fascist" acts of repression of modest scale, not comparable to those of the historic Fascists; when on the other hand they fail to recognize true analogies between the current Chinese regime and the earlier Fascist one.

is being deliberately retained, as are many others that denote policies in the process of being abolished.) The cadres must have received an order from the top to consult the foreign instructors.

We had all got together before in John's room for a preliminary exchange of ideas. We found that our opinions on almost everything were unanimous, and we agreed on several points that should be interpolated among general observations and proposals, which would leave each person free to take up topics of particular interest to him.

As usual, at the meeting they gave no sign that they were either accepting or rejecting our ideas. There were the customary thanks and some useless palaver. It will all come to nothing, but if some suggestion is accepted now or at least within a year, it will be a coincidence, for the decisions will have been independently made at the top. We are pawns in their game.

And yet nothing is ever totally useless, since human beings cannot completely abstain from communicating even when they have resolved to. What does not get through via public channels—since here we exist on the margins of society—does in some measure get through thanks to the small range of individual contact that cannot be withheld from us, even if only questions of language are involved, I now know that Chen and I can take up problems together and that she listens to what I say, as I listen to her.

Some days ago, we had a little meeting at the hotel. We were assisted by two representatives from Fudan and the Institute, respectively (the latter was John's interpreter), who helped us defend our objections to some sort of policeman's having been put in charge of the Dasha's safety system. The discussion concerned our petition to have a certain door opened. The doors that give access to three stairways from the hall on our fourteenth floor are secured on the stairwell side by locks and heavy chains. The doors themselves are rather heavy. For all practical purposes, then, one can enter or leave our floor only via the elevator. The moment we became aware of this, we were all understandably alarmed. In the event of an emergency, we are in a cage; especially if a fire were to break out, when elevator service would be halted, even members of the hotel staff, who have keys, could not get out onto the stairs from the floor above in order to open the door. The hotel management is aware of the danger; last year, during the months when the earthquake alarm was in effect, the central door in our hallway was left open.

After we had stated the problem afresh—and Zheng did his utmost to explain it well—the police character behaved in standard fashion. He ignored everything we had said, and he insisted that (a) the door in question has always been closed; (b) it may not be opened "for reasons of security . . . there must be no interferences between one floor and another" (i.e., any contact between us and cadres living on other floors must be physically impossible); (c) you are not to worry about anything because we are responsible for your lives and in case there were any danger we would certainly save yours, even at the risk of our own; (d) you say that there are safety standards which all civilized countries have adopted, but the existence of a standard does not guarantee safety.

Given the man's arrogant and even offensive tone, you would never understand why he had not simply ignored our petition instead of calling us together unless you knew that invariably the goal is to extort your formal consent to whatever is being imposed. Your declaration of consent is the one and only purpose of the contest, while the original point grows more and more abstract until it becomes mere pretext.

This time not only did the policeman not obtain our consent but found himself cornered by our arguments. We even got some fun out of suggesting solutions that would satisfy our request without compromising his "security" requirements. One proposal was that the key be enclosed behind glass at our expense. Peremptory questions were asked: Granting your good intentions, we would like to know concretely how you would go about sacrificing yourselves for our sake and saving us. In a word, it was a tiny triumph for the West and a demonstration of the fact that we are not such barbarians as not to know how to play and win a game of sophistry.

Satisfaction over having penetrated and been able to maneuver within the system? The fact remains that we are in prison. We ourselves are turning into Ah Q's.

Nothing has been decided for the moment. The policeman said that he must give the problem some thought. But they will open the door, perhaps not for a little while and then on the QT. Their only alternative would be another meeting, to try to get what they did not get the first time round. Too risky for face saving. Also, we have the support of our units.

When foreign residents in China meet, someone is always telling a story about how he is "struggling" for or against something. They're struggles of this kind.

Xie, the new "political leader" of our section, came into my office. "Go ahead and talk," Chen said to him, "because that one doesn't understand." (She was talking Shanghai dialect, heedless that I understood this one sentence.)

One of my students has written, "The works of Lenin and of Chairman Mao have been translated into almost all the foreign languages in the world" —meaning "almost all languages in the world."

Basically, the Chinese are right to treat foreigners who live here as if they were idiots. For years, they have been keeping them in certain conditions—not literally the same people, obviously, yet all foreigners end up accepting what they are told as if it were true; they submit to living under a system of controls, and to being treated as if they were objects. They protest only now and then, and only over material questions—the only things about which there would be no well-founded basis for protesting. If one objects, "You don't inform us about what is going on," they are dumbfounded. "But what do you mean, so much is being written and published.". . .

Why, then, "foreign friends"? Simply because without the qualifying "friends," "foreigners" signifies "enemies"; otherwise, considered simply as themselves, they are nonexistent.

Young People
February 7

Of the generation of '65, the educated young people who have spent some years in the countryside are more balanced, more mature than our twenty-year-olds in Italy—just as young workers used to be more mature than students when there was still a clear demarcation between the two categories. And more candid, too. Now, in addition to Tang and Chen Hongshen, I often see a friend of theirs, Liang Chongwen, who works in a machine-tool factory (No. 1, I believe). He comes to the Institute now and then to translate technical terms. At the moment, he has a long list to translate, and will be living here for a week. "He's as happy as the day is long," Zhang remarked the other day. Like anyone else, Zhang becomes likable the moment he talks straight and stops playing the pious man. And the boy does smile; one surely is better off at the Institute than in a factory. I advise him in his work, but with difficulty because I am not familiar with machine tools or with how they function. He knows a little more than I, but not much; he's been at the factory only a short time. So we try to help each other. Liang worked for three years in the country in Jiangsu Province, after getting his middle school diploma, and then attended the Institute, from '72 to '75. Counting backward, this means he is one of those who went to work in the countryside between 1967 and 1969, all of whom remained there for a fairly long time. (Most of my students belong to the next generation, which has done a shorter stint of manual work, in some cases only one year, although I do have a very few "oldsters," who have spent a long time in rural areas.)

Today the students had exams, translations, and dictation. In my office, I was working on the glossary and had gotten as far as the section on metallurgy, about which I know precisely nothing. Luckily, Liang was there, so I could ask him for help. When we are alone, he takes Carlo Ginzburg's book on the geography of Italy from my desk and leafs through it slowly. Also, the other day, again when we were alone, Chen Hongshen asked me a string of questions about Italian cities, how we live, and so on. They are hungry for information, and while frightfully repressed are yet capable of an open smile; also, they have an inner strength that does not come from the old values but is hard to define.

They have found the knack of carving out for themselves minimal moments of freedom among the interstices of a false life. Yesterday afternoon, Tang—again, when he was alone with me—played a tape of several Italian folk songs, very low so that they could not be heard out in the hall or in the adjoining room. The paradox of years ago at Peking University is being repeated: the only people the Chinese can trust (the only ones who in no circumstances will play the spy) and who—this they know—can understand them are these foreigners who live among them, half-imprisoned and kept as much as possible in the dark about everything.

"The students are taking exams, the poor things," I said to Liang, to see what he would answer.

"I believe that taking exams is useful for one's studies" is the obligatory reply. But then he asked, "What do you think?" Yes to exams, I told him, but only as a test of what is working or not working *in the teaching* and not as a way of grading students. I did my best to outline for him a realistic picture of a school based on competitiveness, like the modern German school.

I asked Liang which he liked better, working in the field or the factory. "You work less in the factory, and it isn't as tiring." Working in the country is very hard, he said; the hours are long, and almost everything is still done by hand, although the Jiangsu countryside, where he was, is not one of the most backward or poorest areas.

"But you educated young people, in addition to your regular work, did you do something to improve the education of the peasants?"

"Professor, when people work twelve hours a day, they're too tired to study. But we used to explain the papers to them a little bit, and the three articles by Chairman Mao that are the most read. . . ."

Mostly, they lived together, in collective housing for young people. "But sometimes the peasants would give us individual houses. Their idea was that we might get married and settle down among them for good." (He lived in a house by himself.)

House. Family. The center around which everything continues to revolve, the one nonpublic moment that every Chinese vigorously claims for himself, the safe place where tension is relaxed, the counterbalance to his troubles, his labors, the political struggles. "In France, people have few children because they know that after they've worked hard to bring them up, they will abandon their family and go off on their own." So says Li, Chen's husband, who is head of the French section and an intellectual of some pretensions.

Zhang played a tape, a recording of a song dedicated to Zhou Enlai. It's tuneful and sentimental, like most of the songs now in vogue; actually, they are real love songs, but they celebrate leaders both living and dead, Zhou above all.

I asked whether this habit of treating public leaders as if they were beloved women is old or new.

"It's new."

I say that at home such a thing would be inconceivable, etc., etc.

"But Zhou was not simply a leader," Zhang observed.

"He was also a father and a mother, is that it?"

"Yes, yes," they replied quickly, happy that I seemed to have understood.

"You relate everything to family feelings," and as I said it, I knew that I was wounding them deeply, that I was touching them on some very private spot. I wouldn't do it if I weren't against the pretense that the ancestral cult of the father is more Socialist than our bourgeois disintegration of the family.

Yesterday, in class, I found everybody gripped by great excitement. They were laughing, their faces were flushed, and they simply could not pay attention. During the break, four or five went out and came back with a handful of caramels for me, almost dragging Zhou Shiliang with them. "His brother's getting married this morning! He brought the 'happiness' caramels, but he didn't have the courage to give them to you." Zhou, all red in the face, defended himself: "These are really bad children, they won't leave me in peace." And he fairly fled from the room, with the others at his heels, still making jokes. And it wasn't even he who was getting married! "People's attitude with respect to marriage is inhibited. Relatives and friends make so many jokes that one feels a kind of shame; to a point where, when a child is born, they are still frightened . . . yet in relation to the child everyone is full of authority. . . . From now on, men who are awakened to self-awareness must cleanse themselves of this turbid mentality, which is characteristic of the East. . . ." Fifty-seven years have gone by since Lu Xun wrote those lines.

The heterogeneous factors that hindered one's comprehending the many faces of China in the twenties have been further complicated by elements of mass culture, the growth of a proletariat superimposed on an agrarian world with an unrecorded past, Soviet influences, political conflicts, and contradictory definitions of each of these components. Nothing will be so revolutionary in the China of tomorrow as the destruction of the family. (I do not mean revolutionary in the political sense.) For nothing is so profound or so widely shared, or constitutes such an ancestral defense against society, as the family connection. It is the maternal realm where neither repression nor order penetrate. This is all the more true today when the function of the father, the representative of outside political power, is diminishing.

Among the many paradoxes, Zhou Enlai, the beloved father-mother, repeatedly criticized the ties of the Chinese to their past: their universalist presumptions, their xenophobia, their lack of a sense of the relative. He was reproving them, in a word, for not being "modern" enough. He broke their hearts by leaving instructions that his body be cremated and his ashes scattered. He had the least patriarchal of families, living with an independent woman who had been a revolutionary from her youth.

One must not forget that the majority of the country's inhabitants live in mud houses, work twelve hours a day unaided by machinery, and with effort read an occasional paper. And outside the houses of newly married country-women, it is not all that rare to see displayed the clothing that attests to a lost virginity. Only if one bears such things firmly in mind can one bet on the other proletarian China, battered and despoiled by history.

Western Dining Hall—Sentences and Suicides

Since the food at the hotel has gotten to be so bad, I've not been able to make up at dinner for the meager food at the Chinese mess at the Institute. The French couple, who've gone to the Western dining hall for foreign professors from the day they arrived, have been urging me to do the same. After some hesitation, I decided I would.

It is in the newest section of the Institute, two or three hundred meters from our building, which houses the French, German, Japanese, and Arabic sections, with other space allocated to baths and dormitories. This part of the Institute was designed in a more modest style and at least so far hasn't the decrepit look of the main section, although even here the garden is seedy and sad.

Three times a week, after a four-hour morning stint, I go back to the hotel at noon. I wait by the gate for the bus, which has already gone by to pick up the children at kindergarten and colleagues who work in that area, so that when it returns it is full. Sometimes it is late, too, and to wait in freezing wind is disagreeable, especially since I am already numb from the cold in our rooms at the school. In this weather, the porters invite Olga, Alissa, Susan, and me into their little lodge, where they have a bench, a telephone, and a little stove. The other three days, when I stay on at the Institute for the afternoon, I walk to lunch with Tang, whose room and mess are in the new section too. This short walk is a kind of vacation. Sometimes Tang talks about his family—they live in a small city near Suzhou—and about how they all get together for New Year's, and each person prepares his own special dish. Tang boasts of being a very good cook: "That's not so usual with men here." Other times he speaks of his girl, who is studying medicine, or of friends who have just arrived: "We talked and smoked until very late, and now I'm awfully sleepy." Friends from school, from his *xiafang* ("sent to country") years, and, later, the university keep in touch with each other from the most distant places, and despite rare vacations and lack of money, they manage to travel and meet occasionally. I don't know how strongly knit the bonds are among these hundreds of thousands, perhaps millions, of young people who are still sentimentally close to their families but who are also divested of worldly goods and impedimenta, like monks in a vast lay community. If the ties among them are a closely woven fabric, surely it is more important than the thousand and one petty political quarrels among the various factions.

Tang and I bid each other good-bye at the door, and I go into a huge barracks, with a kitchen and two small rooms adjoining. In the middle, beneath large ceiling fans, four little tables are set up in a row. No napkins, but silver place settings (as at Oxford), which come from who knows what foreign colonial source. You pay very little for a quite decent meal (the cook is a young man who was trained by a man said to be a master chef); you can even have bread —a bit soggy and not of pure wheat, but just the same, bread. The one drawback is the water, which in this part of the city has a nauseating taste; some people get around that by drinking orangeade. In the kitchen, besides the cook, there is a woman who helps him, and sometimes several Chinese seated and eating. Why in the kitchen, I don't know; are they for some reason in isolation, or is it a privilege, or are they simply on familiar terms with the cooks? The woman waits on tables, without great ceremony, or you can go to the kitchen and fetch your own food.

When schedules coincide, at the table there will be Pascale, Roland, Olga, Marcial, and Mohammed. The latter comes every day because for at least one meal it solves his pork problem; here the only meat served is beef.

There are also other guests, foreign professors who live in Shanghai permanently. Of these, I've so far got to know only Kieu Duc Thang, a Vietnamese who teaches French here; he is married to a Chinese woman and has lived in China since 1946; after 1949, he worked for Peking Radio for a long time. Susan introduced him to me one day, when he arrived on his bicycle, pedaling along the little entrance path at school. He is a tall, solidly built man, with a rather dark complexion. From the moment he shook hands, and looked at me with his gentle, grave eyes, I felt certain of his unconditional solidarity and, at the same time, his unsparing judgment. "He's a real Communist," Susan said to me later. "He does a lot of manual work." He doesn't call me by name, as all the others do, but addresses me as *"camarade,"* a form of address the Chinese deny us. Kieu has chosen to live as a Chinese in every respect—salary, work responsibilities, housing. He has the status of foreign resident, a status somewhat different from ours which at times entails genuine humiliations. He comes from a family of intellectuals, which for Vietnamese means possessing classical Chinese culture as their own; he has been living here for so many years that he is supremely well-informed about Chinese affairs. He asked permission to do his political studies at a somewhat more serious level than is generally permitted to foreigners, but he has managed only to become associated with two or three resident professors who have been reduced to semidotage by age and idleness; every week, he must give them a report on current events.

None of these things have I learned from Kieu himself, nor have I ever heard him complain about the way he is treated. Sometimes, when he is confronted by my impatience, he urges me to understand more, to put myself in the position of simple people, and to do everything so that China may be better understood abroad. *"C'est notre devoir internationaliste."* One encounters such breeding among many of the older Vietnamese. Within the limits allowed, Kieu is also our source of news. He does everything he can to make us feel less cut off.

Today, our Chinese colleagues ate their lunch with more dispatch than usual, because the "political officer," Xie, had said something to them earlier in an undertone which had put them in a state of great excitement. "We're going to a film," they told me, "but there's no ticket for you." Tang left the office with me, so evidently he also was excluded.

On my way out after lunch, I asked Kieu, "Is there a film today?"

"Yes, but we foreigners are not admitted." (I heard later from another source that his wife had a ticket, but not he.)

"Why not, what is it about?"

"It's a film that was shot according to directives from Jiang Qing, and there's a young actress in it who is said to resemble her. . . . It would be very interesting to see it. Unfortunately, we can't. It's a shame."

"And so," I added, "we know nothing about it, and when we take part in the criticism, we'll have simply to repeat what we're told without knowing what we're talking about."

"Aveuglement," he said, and he laughed.

The newspapers are lamenting the fact that the campaign against the Gang of Four is moving too listlessly. "Some people believe that only a few people are involved who were cut off from the masses." Whereas. . . .

As far as we are concerned, the anti-Four propaganda has tapered off. Zhou Enlai is celebrated, we are taken to visit workplaces where some "order" has been established by now; having noted our impatience, they may be aiming to fetch in through the window what they cannot get in through the door.

Suicide: four days ago, at Fudan, the vice-chairman of the Party Committee.

The other day, when I saw the students who were going to the stadium, my guess was right. Twenty-five criminals were executed; an announcement to that effect has been posted. Until now, according to what we have always been told, death sentences were not carried out for a year or two, during which time efforts were made to reeducate the condemned person; in practice, for the most part such sentences were never carried out. Perhaps they are changing the system.

Perhaps. Among many cloudy things, one of the least understandable is the administration of justice. I asked Chen whether the "solitary confinement" imposed on the actress Yuan Xuefen is a punishment provided for by Chinese law and who has the right to impose it. The only answer she could give me was that "in Shanghai, the Gang of Four used to be in control of all police units." She was not being reticent; she truly did not know. She asked me a lot of questions about our penal system and was very much interested in my answers. She found it very hard to understand the distinction between judiciary and police.

7.

NEW YEAR

Travel
February 11, 1977

Another snowfall, but the snow is melting. The semester is over, vacations are beginning, and I am leaving for Vietnam. Despite the snow, the cold is already relaxing its grip, tension is easing, the students are happy and distracted, because soon they will be going home; for the moment they've forgotten about the threat of exams. The few whose families live too far away for them to get home, and several others, will remain here, masters of the Institute.

We have had one last meeting with some of the ranking cadres: Wei; Han, representing the Party Committee (he has come in for some criticism but will probably survive since he is certainly not the overbearing sort but rather like a rubber ball). Profuse thanks for our work and for the opinions we've offered. Many of our proposals will be accepted, or so they said; others will be studied further. Openness, collaboration. . . . A wider knowledge of foreign countries is essential, there will be more conversation and wider reading, the number of books permitted the students will be increased, more texts will be made available in their original languages. The recommendation that *pinyin* be used in transcriptions has been accepted. Comrade Zhang has accepted the English-language instructors' proposal that they conduct an experimental first-year course. Nothing says that the experiment will work out, but it is right that it be tried. Foreign professors must be kept informed about curriculum plans and must work together with the Chinese professors. The Gang of Four has greatly damaged the school, because they distorted the directive of Chairman Mao about "Red and expert." Practically speaking, the Four were against specialized study, etc., etc.

It is clearer than ever that precise directives have come from above calling for a change in methods and for a gradual transition to what they would like to think is an imitation of the American high school. Our cadres are not at all equipped for such a changeover, partly because they are too uninformed and partly because they are too much in a rut. There will be a series of new and, judging from the description, more or less useless activities. For the mass of the students, the content of their work will not change greatly, since what does not work well depends neither on the fact that there are political study sessions (they are to be continued but will be devoted to criticism of the Four) nor, much less, on open-door instruction, the only truly modern thing about this school. The real changes will be gradual, and they will be made in the recruitment system and in the mandatory requirement that recruits perform one to three years of work after finishing middle school. A minority among the students who are fortunate because of family situation or individual ability will manage to carve out for themselves a somewhat larger area of freedom; thus the embryos of the future middle-upper class, which the new direction in education cannot fail to produce, will be developed. This will come about with difficulty, however, because it will be hindered by a covert underground class opposition and by the obtuseness of the bureaucracy. Very likely what we will end up with will be a misshapen reproduction not of America, which is an unknown quantity here, but of the Soviet Union, including perhaps the concept of liberty held by dissidents within the Soviet Union.

As far as we are concerned, all the talk notwithstanding, things will go on as before. Susan and John will begin to work on their proposal for the experimental first-year course amid the resistance and sabotage of most of the cadres and Chinese instructors who want them to fail. But no matter; we're all happy for the interlude awaiting us; when we return, the cold will be past, and we will be moving into another season.

Tomorrow I leave for Peking, where I will get an exit visa from the Chinese and an entry permit from the Vietnamese. Both have already been arranged for, and there should be no problems. For the Chinese visa, everything was done to facilitate the matter for me, and I have a letter from the Institute for the police in Peking.

Kieu has given me several small New Year's gifts for his family, which I am to deliver to his nephew, who teaches radio technology at the Polytechnic in Hanoi. The nephew's sister is an officer in the army and fought in the war against the United States. Kieu is very homesick for his own country, which he has not seen for many years. He has suggested I ask his brother to accompany me about; the brother was a provincial governor, but is now living in retirement in their native village. "He is a frank, open person," Kieu said, "and he will be able to explain many things to you." Kieu is much concerned about how Vietnam will seem to me. "They are a little overwrought today, there's a certain

influence. . . ." While almost ashamed to do so, I indicated the lesson Vietnam
has taught us. "You know," he replied bitterly, "even the most miserable
conditions in Europe cannot be compared with the poverty in my country." And
in very simple terms, he talked to me about their enormous difficulties, not the
least of which is the great number of demobilized men from the Saigon Army.
"They have to be fed, and they all have big families. . . ."

What is it that makes even the best among the Chinese incapable of such
sincerity and simplicity? The Vietnamese lived the colonial experience to the
full, they squarely faced their colonizers, and in driving them out appropriated
for themselves something of the colonizers' culture. Today we can know each
other, we are equals.

February 12

On the train, traveling toward Suzhou. Late afternoon, sunlight, beautiful countryside. . . . The little cubelike houses are limed an intense white, and, with their
black roofs, they look like pieces in a construction set I had as a child. A tiny
exultation is stirring inside me, not only because I am traveling through great
spaces but also because *I am alone* and know that I shall be able to move about
on my own for two whole weeks.

February 15

It is six in the evening, and now I'm on the train going from Peking to Hanoi.
After the confusion of the last two days, it is restful to be alone again.

Peking was in its full splendor of winter air and light. The wind was so
frigid and violent that when I was walking along Donghuan Boulevard the short
distance from the Italian to the Swiss embassy, my face ached so that I had to
turn around, bend down, and wait for a moment. But my tiny exultation had
become full-blown joy over simply existing in that light and among those spaces.

In Peking, I was the guest of a young ex-'68 Italian CP member, now a
diplomat, and of his wife, who is studying at Beida. (The ambassador is in Italy.)
The couple generously run a kind of open house which, especially during
vacation periods, becomes a student encampment. A tension in me was asking
to be released, and I found myself caught up in the young people's orgy of talk,
meals of pasta and wine, and outbursts of anger and agitation. Upset and
ultimately ironical, they are fiercely determined to destroy what remains of a
vision of hope. It's frequent enough to feel at twenty that one is old, that one
has already lived a whole lifetime, and has now reached the final moment. The
events one has lived through have been illusions and delusions, the more painful
today because they are no longer experienced with the simulated innocence of

the romantics but with a transparent mask of snobbish indifference. Here they give vent to their feelings in silly, childish battles with the Chinese bureaucracy over a travel permit, a small heater, a lamp, an opened letter. In *Panorama,* they read that allegedly Jiang Qing pinched the nose of the dying Zhou Enlai to torment and offend him. Their comment: "If she did, she's a genius." They play with one of the many huge colored photographs of Hua Guofeng, which was left lying on a table. Each person tells, in detail, about his own little experiences. The Chinese girl from Beida who was operated on for appendicitis in the surgeon's consulting room, while wide awake and strapped to a table: "Because you're young and you must be brave." Only now, like people who have endured torture, she suffers from nightly nightmares. The people whose *ayi* are not permitted to have their children meet the children of their foreign employers; this is a standard restriction, but with Italians, of course, familiarity and something akin to friendship are inevitable, and the prohibition is got around by "chance" meetings in public gardens. Someone reports that the psychiatric hospitals are filled with young people, especially women, with sexual problems.*

Suicides for the same reasons. . . . Complaints: How the Chinese lie. . . . How foreigners living outside Peking face continual control and isolation. . . . Anecdotes: About the little European boy who repeats insults against Mao in Chinese which he has picked up at nursery school. . . . About the elderly Swiss woman who is married to a Chinese and whose purse is inspected every time she leaves the embassy by the soldiers on guard duty. . . . "We make China into a problem of our own because we are people without a country," M——— F——— said once. These young people are lost not because of China; they are lost the way their comrades living in Rome or Milan are, who know nothing about China.

At the home of Swiss friends, I saw the issue of *China Pictorial* in which the photographs of the funeral ceremonies for Mao Zedong were published. It was the Chinese edition, which is no longer to be found in the bookshops; the foreign-language editions either have not yet been printed or have been removed from circulation. (It's just a matter of being a little patient; sooner or later, they will be available.) Eliminated leaders have vanished from the photos, but no tricks have been played to conceal their existence; in their place there is simply a blank—a black or white empty space, depending on the background color. And in the captions where their names would normally appear, there are X's —three X's for names composed of three ideograms, two for those of two ideograms, like Jiang Qing.

*Perhaps this is why my students have asked me insistently whether in Italy the psychiatric hospitals have many young patients.

February 17

I've been traveling for two days on the international Shenyang-Hanoi train. As far as the frontier, the railway cars are Chinese, and regulations are somewhat less rigid than on domestic routes. I am in a car occupied only by foreigners, including Vietnamese.

As we were leaving Peking, the moment the Italians who had accompanied me to the train left, a very young, rather plump girl came into the compartment I occupy by myself. She sat down and began to chat. She is eighteen years old, she told me, lives in Shenyang, and is going to Vietnam for a three-month vacation. She asked me what country I come from; she wanted to see a photograph of me (perhaps so that I would give it to her, but I have only the photo in my passport). She was so unusually communicative that I wondered who on earth she might be, and the suspicion even crossed my mind that she might belong to the security services. The explanation is simple, however: she is half-Vietnamese. Her father, Chinese, died some time ago. Now she is traveling with her mother. Not long afterward, when I came back from the toilet, I found the door to my compartment locked—they always lock your door when you go out, for the traveler's protection—and for the moment there was no one on hand to open it for me. The girl realized what had happened and invited me to their compartment. Seated among luggage and packages and pots—including even a sewing machine—was her mother—a thin woman, dressed in black and wearing glasses. She welcomed me with a warmhearted friendliness that reminded me of our South Italian peasant women, but this was no peasant; there was a modicum of culture behind the poverty. She offered me hazelnuts and caramels, which here are not inexpensive. (Here in Asia, where I am richer than almost all the people I meet, not one person ever fails to offer me some sort of gift.) We talked easily, as if we had known each other always. The woman was quite intelligent, but she treated her daughter like a child. In reply to the usual question—how many children do I have—I said I was not married. The girl reacted as the Chinese always do, with distress and concern. She clasped one of my hands between both of hers, as if to comfort me in my appalling situation. The mother asked, "Why have you never married?" To see how she would react, I gave her the answer that the Chinese are quite unable to understand: "Perhaps out of love of freedom." The woman thought about that for a moment, and then her face was illumined. "Very good," she said. And after a bit: "Ho Chi Minh, such a great leader, never married out of love of freedom." Without knowing or intending it, I had referred to what for every Vietnamese is the supreme good. For them, the struggle for independence is also a struggle for freedom. The concept is very different from what the Chinese mean by "liberation." We were speaking in Chinese, since after living so many years in China, the woman had almost forgotten the French she had studied when she was young. For "freedom," I had to use the word *ziyou,* which has a negative connotation today—somewhere between "license" and "bourgeois rights." But at that moment the Chinese language was only a small obstacle that could have no adverse effect on an idea shared by us both and, to our shared way of seeing things, by the entire human race. Ho Chi Minh and the other Vietnamese Communists carried this concept back with them from France; it enriched the meaning of their traditional spirit of independence, and made the very struggle against the colonizer a form of communication. Because they fought unyieldingly against French colonialism, the Vietnamese feel no shame that there are French components in their culture and do not conceal them. It is Chinese culture they are afraid of. They are so deeply imbued with it that they can no longer distinguish it in themselves, and are in danger of being swallowed up by it. (Later on, during this trip, I was talking with a Vietnamese cadre about my work and about the Italian language, and made some reference to the Latin origin that Italian shares with French. He added that Vietnamese also has elements in common with Latin. This is an evident absurdity; it was born of his wish to displace the more obvious analogy, which is the closeness between the language in the north of his country and some dialects of South China.)

The woman did, however, share her daughter's concern for me: "Don't you find it hard not to have a family, to be all alone?" I answered that one is not necessarily alone, one has friends. . . . She shook her head. "Friends. . . . One can't count on them." She was thinking of her own situation.

The girl did not leave me for one moment. On this trip beyond her own borders, I became the tangible incarnation of everything outside which was barred to her. Anything belonging to me struck her as extraordinary, even the by no means expensive cotton blouse I was wearing. "It's so beautiful," she said. I pointed out that it was quite like her own. "Oh, no, it's not the same thing." She showed me the little necklace she was wearing. "What do you think?"

"It's lovely."

She shook her head. It was already unusual and contrary to the rules that she should be openly wearing a necklace. She wanted me to describe what necklaces are like where I come from; I didn't know what to say.

I asked her what she did. She was finishing the last year in the upper middle school. Her mother works in a factory (perhaps not as a blue-collar worker). Her name is Yuehua, which means Vietnam-China. "Do you love China?" she asked.

"Yes, I love China."

And she: "I love Vietnam." She is as immature as a twelve-year-old, and of a transparent innocence. In a few hours, she opened up with total trust to a stranger, and with even a physical abandon, settling down to sleep on the berth opposite mine until her mother called her. She saw in me something that was dimly desired and would surely elude her. "We must stay friends," she told me, "for always. Promise me that you will write to me—but no, I know you won't, I know we'll never see each other again." This was not a sudden adolescent infatuation, but something more profound and motivated, like her love/longing for Vietnam, which was an alternative to her daily life, a permissible yet slightly heretical difference setting her apart. But what she was looking for she would not find in Vietnam, which is so much poorer than China.

In the primitive way in which this girl was able to express herself one perceived the restlessness and discontent of a whole generation. The desire for freedom and for good things—good things like freedom. I began to feel ashamed of the way in which for so long so many of us in Europe have demanded of the Chinese that they stand firm in all their perfection and virtue and their ongoing uninterrupted revolution, insisting it is their duty to renounce everything that for the poorest among us is a comfort we take for granted. For years and years we let the Vietnamese shoulder the burden of our intransigent anti-imperialism. When the most humble working people demanded the right to enjoy those very good things of life—starting with the daily steak—which we would have considered it degrading to give up, we good intellectuals, imbued with anticapitalist virtue, deplored the consumerism, the surrender to the affluent society, and the corruption of the working classes. Never had I seen so clearly how hypocritical it is for the rich—even if rich only in culture—to oppose freedom and revolution to the demands of the poor for material goods.

It can be disagreeable when the Chinese withhold brotherhood from us, but they are right. When one travels through this endless countryside, through landscape that becomes ever more gentle and luminous and green as one moves southward, one sees men and buffalo diligently, doggedly, unflaggingly at work; it is a landscape of dignity and orderliness, of human bodies and tilled fields, of houses in mud, of legs perennially immersed in water. And it has been thus for hundreds of years, an enormous cumulative labor, as in that long process of which the plundering of the peasants in Europe was only the traumatic and final phase. From the mid-nineteenth century up until the First World War, China was despoiled of the fruit of the labor of its peasants and craftsmen.

If a little Chinese girl looks at me today and wishes that she were like me and knows that she cannot be, it is because of what I, too, have robbed her of. This is why the Chinese throw their nonfraternal feelings in our faces.

We have an equal right to resist the aim of their *ganbu* to classify us as so much merchandise, which they, adapting perforce to the prices on the international market, can acquire and use as such. And we are wrong to give way when it seems to us that a fundamental political solidarity is lacking between their leadership and the opposition we claim to constitute in our own countries. Kieu Duc Thang is an example of right and of resistance. For him, the task is both easier and harder. He comes from a country that is poor, ex-colonized, and certainly without historical responsibilities in respect to China; yet it is increasingly doubtful that the relations China entertains with his country are marked by "proletarian internationalism."* Most Europeans tend to give in. I, too, allow myself to be protected by my embassy (and I know that this offers several material privileges), or I stop eating at the Chinese mess. The surrender is more serious when people little by little get into quarrels over the prices of merchandise and services—rail and air travel, excursions, salaries, and the thousand and one conveniences they lay claim to. When I have pointed out that, if nothing else, these squabbles are immoral (for example, on the part of German students who, even if they are not individually rich, nonetheless benefit from their country's immense wealth), my colleagues reply that when you are held as semi-prisoners, isolated from society, frustrated in your work and in your relationships with the people around you, a minimum of extra comfort and the brief escape offered by a trip become necessities. And it's true, even if exacting this compensation is equivalent to accepting a logic whereby even unhappiness can be assigned a monetary value.

In point of fact, it is a deception for the Chinese bureaucracy to claim that it can neatly separate the treatment of foreigners from the treatment of its own people. Whoever considers that he is authorized to treat three-quarters of mankind—all the non-Chinese—as commodities is going to behave the same way in relation to his Chinese compatriots. The term "internationalism," threadbare as it is, still means something to the foreign Communists living in China. They refuse to be discriminated against by the Chinese *because they are foreigners,* although they know that to object will be nothing more than the affirmation of a principle, and utterly futile. "Three worlds" are recognized in statements of theory; in practice, in the treatment of individuals, members of the Third World are less discriminated against than the others but often are more looked down on, and sometimes priced as cheaper merchandise.

The people of Peking and the people of Shanghai, who have known foreigners as colonizers, look on us with diffidence and envy so long as we remain remote and wrapped up as a group in our privileges. But if one moves a step in their direction, if one looks like a specific person with a face and a body and a recognizable age, after an initial movement of curiosity the Chinese is immediately inclined to see the foreigner as someone like himself, who also has troubles and worries; the duties of host toward guest become a sincere sharing with this person who is far from his own land and his own family. If the person is here to work, the Chinese are grateful to him, and without there being any need to speak of it, they are aware of the unhappy isolation that is forced on the foreigner by the masters he and they share, and they feel sorry for him.

*Kieu's position would become more and more difficult over the years, as the relations between China and Vietnam deteriorated and eventually led to war. Still, he attempted to retain his love for both countries, though with ever deeper anguish.

"How is your little friend?" The man who sells fruit and biscuits in a shop opposite the post office, not far from the Dasha, was inquiring about Felicitas. "I haven't seen her for a long time."

Felicitas enjoys shopping for all of us, and here, as in the other little stores and even, I believe, in private houses in the neighborhood, people know us, know who works at the Institute and who at Fudan, knows that she is German and I am Italian. I explained that she is now a boarder. "At the school attached to the Institute?" he asked, and he seemed rather concerned. He asked me to give her his greetings, and to tell her to stop by on her free days. I think of the friendly terms on which the elevator boys and girls and the service people on our floor know Aymin—it's a relationship of a visceral equality that the child does not have with any of us, even if her mind loves us much more. Or the customs and postal employees, whom I should find disagreeable since every package of books I am mailing I am obliged to take, open, to the post, and let them leaf through each, page by page; at first, I would laboriously put the package together again as best I could; now, since they recognize and know me, they take care of my things better than I could ever do. The customs man, short and thickset, middle-aged, gray-haired, with the respectable face of a worker, always calls his woman assistant over; they weigh my packages, figure out the charges, tell me I should make two packages into one and advise me how; they weigh and reweigh, discard something, rewrap, retie. They go about this in a direct, friendly way. It is not a special attention offered the foreigner; to help someone who is in difficulties is as obvious here as with us among members of our own families, but it is a sign that the foreigner is a person like any other except that he deserves a little more sympathy. Simple people reserve the right to offer this sign or not; it's a matter of their choosing.

Yesterday morning, in the stations of that immense triple urban and industrial conglomerate that is now Wuhan (Hanyang, Hankou, and Wuchang), people stuck their heads inside the train, even, to get a good look at me. This often happens in places where few foreigners pass through, and one does finally get tired of it. But behind the infantile curiosity there is something more: our isolation is the mirror of the isolation imposed on the Chinese, which is far more severe in their case, for they are isolated from the whole world. And so, in the aftermath of colonialism, the so-called people's xenophobia is nourished.

Changsha, Hengyang, Nanning. . . . We are crossing province after province. The air is growing milder, the light more intense. Rivers . . . mountains . . . the rice already quite high, the vegetables fully grown. . . . At each station, typical items are on sale; the train attendants alert us over the public-address system, and one may get off to buy wine, eggs, rolls, tea. . . . The loudspeaker is the traveler's constant attendant and aide. It tells him how to behave, admonishes him to go wash up, not to make a mess in the toilets. And partly because they are urged on by this voice, partly because they've acquired the habit, every morning the Chinese travelers, glazed tin cup in one hand and box of soap in the other, go wash their faces.

When we stopped in Hengyang, Yuehua came to ask me to take a turn around the station with her. Ordinarily, foreigners are forbidden to leave the train, or at least so I believed, and I was afraid of breaking a rule. The girl laughed. "You may," she said, seized me by the arm, and dragged me off. We both enjoyed the mild air and I, an unexpected small freedom. I was on a journey, it was no longer cold, I could talk with people, I could get off a train. Yuehua and I circulated among the food vendors, all of them surrounded by a press of people, and among travelers hurrying about with their luggage on their shoulders, and we ended up at the booth where they were selling wine.

By now there are several Vietnamese on the train, some of them cadres returning from Europe, where they had gone to study—agriculture mostly. They are very communicative, they talk confidently about future projects and the potential wealth of their country; if, however, any reference is made to the destruction their country has endured, they change the subject, like survivors of the Nazi concentration camps in 1945.

I have chatted with the Vietnamese woman in the corridor, while we were waiting to wash up. Clearly, she is happy to be going home. (During the long vacations, many Vietnamese do go home with the unexpressed hope of remaining there, but they find conditions very hard and almost always return to China.) When she said, "The Vietnamese are stupid," I told her that, on the contrary, they've shown that they are very intelligent. "But they are not well educated," she objected. My comment: this is not their fault, and if they do have many problems today, that is because of colonialism and the war they endured, whereupon she was as happy as if that self-evident fact were something unbelievable, and she thanked me. "You are wise," she said. I laughed. They must be despised by their Russian "protectors." I remember how the Russians were treating the Chinese in '57.

The compartment beyond the Vietnamese woman's is occupied by a Bulgarian couple who come from North Korea. He—I don't know whether he is some kind of "expert" or on the staff of his embassy in Pyöngyang—is a round man of a certain age, with a round pink face and round blue eyes. She is the director of a school, the once-pretty Slavic blond type, neat and unassuming. Each is so typical as to suggest a caricature. They invited me to stop by their compartment. She likes Italian songs like "Mamma." But then she sang old Bulgarian songs in a charming voice. The compartment was full of Vietnamese speaking French or Russian. Bottle in hand, the husband was offering drinks to everybody—Korean vodka with ginseng. Even Yuehua and her mother got involved. Group singing, from "Santa Lucia" to the "Internationale." One little Vietnamese cadre delivered himself of a long rigmarole about friendship among peoples. Yuehua, who understands only Chinese, was rather ill at ease. But they urged her to sing, too. She didn't want to, but then she did, and quite well, sing "The Red Lake," which is the most popular song in China at the moment. At the end, fraternal embraces between the Bulgarian and a Vietnamese, both of whom had had their share to drink.

On occasions of this kind, I do profoundly appreciate the Chinese inability to be overfamiliar, and even their raising certain barriers.

From the far north to this south, the dignity of the Chinese, the forms they have been able to impress on nature, on the earth, and on growing things are the same, despite the diversity of the natural surroundings. They have wrought the miracle of making this immense country homogeneous.

The sensation of traveling through unfamiliar space awakened me in the middle of last night. I looked out. It was very dark—we were in a new-moon phase. The land, which had been flat until a short time ago, began to assume strange outlines like pinnacles. They were the famous mountains of Guilin, I realized. Fantastic shapes that continue southward until they enter the sea in the bays east of Hanoi. All day long, Yuehua and I have watched them; they were so close that I felt I could touch them—the train was following the level valley floor—each sharply separate from the next until, in the distance, they merged in a succession of what looked like stage sets against the horizon. These are limestone mountains, and the sides and tops are covered not with trees but with low, thick shrubbery, or else they are exposed red-yellow rocks. I was stunned; this to me was an aberration of nature, and I could take no pleasure in it. To Chinese eyes, this landscape is most beautiful, because they identify with the strange and the beautiful, as when nature manages to distort itself and somehow make itself unnatural, as if it were imitating the intervention of man. The tormented, perforated rocks in Chinese gardens—which are, partly, at least, the work of the human hand—and the bound feet of women both derive from this taste. As do the forests which from ancient times have been leveled by cultivators engaged in erasing the traces of the untamed world.

A pause at the frontier, before reaching Friendship Pass, which you cross by Vietnamese train because the railroad gauge changes. To leave China is to lose a system of secure order. From the Yanan era, a dignity and simplicity of style has extended to include everyone; today it is corrupted by the bureaucrats but not destroyed.

When I stepped down from the train and walked along the station platform in the silent, gentle sunlight, the void that is peculiar to every border locale widened until I felt at once anguished and slightly exalted. Very soon I would be losing that cloak of protection and control which weighs on me and integrates me, and once again I would be exposed, and alone with myself. It was like emerging from an immense belly.

Luggage had been unloaded and piled in heaps; travelers were going to the customs office and to the bank. Formalities were held to a minimum, except for Vietnamese who are residents of China, like Yuehua's mother. She and the girl were taken to a special room (a Frenchwoman who walked toward that room was firmly but courteously led away), with all their shabby luggage, their bundles, and the sewing machine. They were there for a long time; the mother must have had to open and show everything, the way emigrants returning to Italy from Switzerland must do.

On the Vietnamese train, which was decent enough, we sat wherever we liked. There were only a few carriages, but also only a few travelers, and there was room for everyone. By a combination of chance and spontaneous mutual choice, I was in a compartment with a young Frenchwoman, the wife of a diplomat. She had come down from Peking, too, but as often happens on Chinese trains, we had been glancing covertly at each other from a distance in the dining car or corridor, without daring to approach each other and speak. "Who is that, I wonder?" each asks himself about the other, which means also "Why is he traveling alone? What is his status? Would it be permissible for me to talk to him, or him to me?" The distance between one foreigner and another is like the gap that divides both from the Chinese. There is no physical obstacle, although everything is so arranged as to preclude meetings. Compartments are separate, table places in the dining car are preassigned, etc., but the psychological impediment is so strong that even the least sensitive people are aware of it, and a conscious act of will is needed to overcome it.

I got along with the Frenchwoman very well from the first, and her company was restful. Like all generous-spirited people, her feelings for the Chinese include solidarity and impatience. As the physical distance between them and us increases, the impatience tends to dissolve but the solidarity remains. She told me about a trip to the Soviet Union, and about seeing officers flog soldiers with knouts.

I've lost sight of Yuehua. She and her mother have been taken up by a group of Vietnamese. The girl had made plans for us to meet in Hanoi; I let her talk on, but even if Vietnam is not China, it will not be easy for her to come find me at my hotel. Actually, she knows perfectly well, too, that our meeting is an episodic thing. Would it have been different had she met a person of her own age rather than me? In substance, no. One limitation of youth is that the young cling to the present, they won't concede that things do not go on and on forever but remain within a defined time and space.

Friendship Pass leads into a long, tortuous corridor of hills and mountains. Many armed soldiers, both Chinese and Vietnamese. . . . The countryside is an extension of the southern China landscape, drenched in light, the colors bright and fresh.

The green of the vegetation and the water becomes ever more intense. The moment we crossed the frontier, people looked different. The women—many more women than men are in evidence—wear wide black silk trousers, and kerchiefs rather like those of our Sardinian women. All the girls have splendid hair, which they wear long and unbound even under an army cap. People are slender and seem very gentle and fragile; they almost tremble because of their all too meagre diet. After the little border station—where I was reminded of the orchestrated confusion of a postwar station in South Italy, except that this was far less noisy—the countryside we passed through was under cultivation. The bomb craters, some huge, are so densely placed, perhaps thirty feet apart, that no attempt has been made to fill them in. Where the earth is firm and dry, the inside walls of the craters are planted; in the paddies, they form tiny lakes. The burned and rusted debris of trucks and locomotives, and fragments of aircraft are scattered here and there.

I began gradually to forget my personal tribulations, and I would have forgotten myself had it not been for a sense of guilt that gripped me, for all that I didn't want it to and set about summoning up the rational wit to reject it.

Hanoi
February 23

I arrived here on the seventeenth, at eight in the evening. As the train moved over the long, long bridge across the Red River, crowds of people on bicycles, a few trucks, and even motorcycles moved along lanes on either side. It was already almost dark, so that the surrounding landscape was shadowy and vague —but vast, like some further body of water lying beyond the river. At the station, R—— and C—— S—— were waiting for me, with a car they had borrowed from the ambassador. This was a blessing, because there are no taxis, the streetcars do not serve all points, and one must make out as best one can. My head was in a whirl from the fatigue of a more than two-day train trip, but once I had deposited my luggage and coat at the hotel, without even stopping to wash my hands, I went out with the two young men. It was the Tet holiday, and the entire city was out in the streets. I was engulfed by crowds and deafened by firecrackers which were being thrown constantly at street level, from windows down onto the streets, and under your feet (this brings luck). The hundreds of street lamps that encircle the lake in the center of town had been turned on in a public display of light and holiday joy. It was a necessity of a kind, after the years of blackouts. (At the end of the war, they put on a great festival of lights, which some foreign idiot found a foolish expense amid such poverty.) All the temples, large and small, were open and illuminated. Groups of young people, in costume, kept arriving on the run from the Chinese quarter, and one after another, whirling torches, they went through the streets performing the dragon and the serpent dances (the first for the departing old year, the second

for the new). We crossed a small bridge over the lake leading to a small island
with a temple where a nun, on her knees, was chanting in singsong. Women,
their hands pressed palm to palm, made little bows as they knelt. One was
permitted to walk up among statues and splendid offerings of fruit to the lighted
altars, even at the heart of the temple; I noticed among the offerings other quite
ordinary eatables of today, like boxes of cookies, which somehow did not strike
a false note. We were clearly foreigners, presumably not Buddhists, but people
invited us to come close and look.

Out on the streets again, I observed small buildings mixed in among houses,
with doors that made them look like dwellings (and so they are, for often the
monks have beds inside). Later, in a tiny temple that we entered, asking ourselves if it could really be a temple, an old woman—the sex was uncertain; it
could have been an old man whose bald head was covered by his brown habit
—pointed out the beautiful objects one by one; she gestured in silence, like a
deaf mute, and kept smiling to encourage us to go closer, nodding her head yes
yes.

People's holiday celebration consisted of walking about and looking at the
lights, the flowers, the peach branches, since their poverty allowed for nothing
more. There was not even a street stand selling nuts or dumplings or a toy. Yet
rarely, perhaps never, have I been caught up in such a collective abandonment
to joy. There were no organized parties; each group did what it wanted to do
by itself.

The image of Hanoi that is imprinted in most people's minds is of a city
that has resisted beyond the limits of all human expectation barbarities and
destruction, a colonization amounting to genocide, and American bombs. In the
mornings, I go out alone, and under a light, fine rain I walk along wide streets
that are well paved and maintained and spotlessly clean. (The Vietnamese do
not spit, and they use street sprinklers they have obtained from Eastern Europe.)
Great trees cast a green light over everything—but when the rain stops, the sky
turns violet. River, lakes, temples. . . . At this time of year, a mild climate.
. . . Throughout the central sector of the city, which is actually vast, the houses
are two- or three-storied, creamy white or pale blue, late neoclassical in style;
all are in excellent condition, with framed windows and green Persian blinds.
French colonial style. . . . The horrors of the last years made us almost forget
that Vietnam used to be a French colony. I walk through a French colonial
cityscape among gentle, polite people dressed in American style. Also, everything is so Chinese without this being China, which makes for an image of how
men may be crushed in ways other than the horrors of war.

This is the first time I have ever been in a colonized city. A few hours were
enough to give me this idea, which I hadn't had before arriving.

A defeated America has returned, via Saigon, in the form of left-behind matériel, and in the traces of itself that one sees stamped on the people—colored windbreakers and motorbikes, boys with long hair and narrow pants who may have come up from the south for the holiday and look for all the world like Hong Kong Chinese. Windbreakers mix in with the Chinese-mandated blue or green jackets. Some of the girls, who wear their hair loose and free, look like some of our southern young women, modernized and a little sexy. In the bookshops that carry foreign-language material, I've seen a large number of Russian books, technical and scientific ones for the most part. The TV and movie theaters offer sentimental, sub-Soviet films. In the service employees and minor cadres one notices the slovenliness of Russia or Eastern Europe. (The Swedish presence is better; the Swedes work in groups on construction projects; their life is hard, and they bring with them materials and whatever else they need.)

A Chinese colony. . . . A French and an American colony. . . . And now by way of becoming, perhaps, a Russian colony. . . . If the Vietnamese people continue to exist, it is thanks to the tension of resisting heterogeneous aggressors who lead it toward the obliteration of its own way of living and even the loss of itself. One talks all too easily of another people's bravery. We used to say, "The Vietnamese will be able to hold out even to the point of total destruction." They held out. It is now that they are defeated. There is not enough to eat in a country where the land is fertile and abundant but has been reduced to such conditions that years will pass before it can be cultivated, if indeed it will be possible ever to reclaim all of it. (The part I passed through on the train is, they tell me, among the relatively less stricken areas.)

The country is living on international aid. It perseveres in seeking such assistance because it knows that there lies the only escape from the pressure of the new colonizers. To this point, the Vietnamese have yielded to the Russians in nothing that puts their independence at risk. But today, unlike during the period of American aggression, they are alone and destroyed. It is impossible to say against how much they will be able to hold out; the playing off of China against the U.S.S.R. is no longer enough to guarantee their independence.

There are no available hotel accommodations, and the embassy is kindly putting me up in one of the rooms it keeps on reserve in a most elegant hotel in the center of Hanoi. Like a large part of the city, it was built by the French. A three-storied building, it has green venetian blinds on all windows, doors, and balconies; the floors, as the ambassador's wife made a point of bringing to my attention, are of rosewood. My room looks like storage space; it will presently be occupied by an official who is expected shortly, and meanwhile other embassy people have stashed luggage and other paraphernalia in it. The windows open onto balconies that are enfolded in the green of trees lining the street. When I first threw them open, I was flooded by a memory of out-of-season arrivals in houses by the sea; there was now, as then, that slight swelling of the wood from dampness, the tiny flaking of white paint, the faint musty odor, a light dusting of sand that soils nothing, the reassuring softness of the air. Opening off the hallways are wide square balconies with handsome balustrades which one can lean over and look down at the floors below and the back-and-forth of multilingual blond- and black-haired children. On the ground floor there is also a back-and-forth of mice; however, in the spacious, well-lighted dining room, with white drapes at the windows, dark furniture, and straw-bottomed chairs, they serve an excellent coffee.

As you walk down the corridors of this hotel, you read on the doors: Embassy of Mexico, Italian Embassy, International Red Cross, Embassy of the German Federal Republic, United Nations, Belgian Embassy. . . . When men and women—they may be wearing jeans or evening dress—meet on the stairways, they may bow or exchange jokes, and later your companion says to you, "That's the wife of the Cuban ambassador. . . . That's the Dutch ambassador." . . . The hotel service staff is, to say the least, elusive, but you may go up to the storage area and take extra beds down to your room. . . .

My first glimpse of the Italian ambassador's wife was as she was walking down the stairs, wearing a white wool coat over a black gown—extreme simplicity. She comes from a great Nanjing family and has been married for many years to an Italian. She is no longer young, but she preserves and perfects a style that you cannot call beauty for it is too pure. Last year, she coped all alone with the hardships and difficulties entailed in helping her husband through a grave illness. Even now her life is not easy, living in two rooms in a hotel, getting up at dawn to shop in a market far from here (as all foreigners do, although they are privileged in that they can eat as they like), taking care of all the daily necessities in a city that is poor and lives almost on a war footing. "How fortunate you are that you are in China," she said to me once when we were alone, and for a single brief moment she relaxed her reserve. She maintains the cool external appearance of the well-to-do woman who has no cares and who devotes herself above all to the care of her own person. It is a moral obligation that the ugly things and the burdens of daily life not be visible. This, too, is a form of Chinese dignity.

I accompanied her and the ambassador on one of their evening strolls. In the center of town, they showed me a temple with splendid statues, and later the Catholic cathedral; it is the usual caricature of Notre Dame, but that evening it was filled with people who were seriously intent on the service. They suggested places I should visit. (Museums are closed for the holiday, which is a pity since here you can go into any and all of them without obtaining prior permission.)

For one whole morning, I bicycled about with C—— S——. Expanses of water and of green, where very new building has been carefully designed to stand adjacent to the French city. Thus, in the immense square where the tomb of Ho Chi Minh is located, the monumental is attenuated by discreetly neoclassical palace/villas, which are the headquarters for ministerial and other governmental bodies. We went from there on foot down to the lakeside, where trees were about to burst into flower; on the far banks, also a distant flowering of groups of old low buildings with sloping roofs, as in Holland (the connection may come via Indonesia). I was amazed not to see traces of destruction. C—— explained that some less central quarters of the city are totally destroyed, but one doesn't see them because either they are surrounded by low walls or else the peripheries have been rebuilt so that the rubble and huts are enclosed. We passed by the embassies of countries that enjoy independent quarters—France, the U.S.S.R., Cuba. . . . On one large lake, the Cubans have built a ridiculous, ultramodern hotel—tropical-vacation-paradise style—which has a bar where the cocktails are made according to the instructions of Cuban bartenders. The dining room operates on a partially self-service basis, and here the men and women moving about are blond—Swedes or East Germans. The distance between this and the people is chasm-deep, but not underscored and thrown in one's face as in China.

I stayed in Hanoi five days. For the first three, all places of work, museums, and schools were closed for the Tet holiday. Furthermore, the tourist office was rather inefficient, and at least during that period was being run by an employee who was, shall we say, uncooperative and inclined to attend to people already part of an organized tour, turning a deaf ear to the rest of us. Therefore, I made none of the visits that have become ritual "must's" in Socialist countries. I simply had a vacation for myself. It was a "nonvisit" according to the parameters of some misguided overpoliticized views, according to which a visit to China, say, must consist in shutting oneself up in rooms to conduct an exchange of ideas that the Chinese have already diligently mapped out in their manuals. My "nonvisit" to Hanoi was satisfying and rich and relaxing; my one serious disappointment was not to find Kieu's nephew. I had only the address of the institute where he taught, which was closed. So I also missed meeting, through him, the old father.

February 26

I made the return trip with M—— P—— and the baby as far as Hengyang (R—— has taken off for Laos); she continued on to Peking, but I changed to make the connection for Shanghai. I had to wait for twenty-three hours, because the train coming on from Canton en route to Shanghai had left only a little before I arrived. I asked a policeman for help, and he directed me to some women who also belonged to the police. One of them took me in custody. She made me leave my luggage in a small locked waiting room, despite my protesting a bit, seized me by the arm, and took me to a Lüxingshe hotel nearby. A two-storied Chinese building, white and pale green, which was divided into pavilions with small garden-courtyards and rooms that opened out on long narrow terraces. Hengyang is not open to foreigners, and this hotel is for Chinese and Overseas Chinese—and how much more agreeable than the ponderous buildings the Russians left behind them.

I stayed in the hotel, under the eyes of soldiers, until the following morning, without being able to obtain either my baggage or my passport until the moment before departure, and being held carefully apart from the Overseas Chinese who were guests at the hotel. I was also forbidden to go out; but following my refusal to stay indoors for twenty-four hours, I was granted the right to visit the city's public gardens, accompanied by a Lüxingshe guide.

Return

The Hunan landscape: hills, broad plains under cultivation, water, houses, huts, groups of farmers with red flags. . . . Red earth and green rice. . . . Vapors rising from the earth and on the horizon, as in their paintings. A total nonconnection between this and the radio lecturing about the Gang of Four, to which no one listened. The distance between this China and Shanghai. . . .

I got back to Shanghai this morning, feeling guilty because I was two days late; and if by any chance I had not felt guilty, they would have seen to it that I did. Chen was waiting for me at the station, for I had wired ahead the time of my arrival; she came back to the hotel with me, and we worked here together for the entire day. Tomorrow, Sunday, I will have to work, too. (Classes resume on the twenty-ninth.) But no matter; the vacation has given me a respite, and I can look at things and at myself with more detachment. Spring is in the air, and I feel as if I have got through the darkest stretch of the tunnel.

I find that my colleagues are relaxed and in good spirits also. Some of them overcame all obstacles put in their way and went to Canton by themselves. They even managed to travel second class, this thanks to Susan's special skills.

8.

SPRING

Questions Cultural and Scholastic
March 21, 1977

I've been twice to the exhibition of the Gang of Four caricatures, which are said to be the work of Shanghai artists. Some reproduce recognizable models and are identical to ones we have seen several times along the streets. The show includes both paintings and drawings, which occupy several rooms. Forms and styles are very varied. Most of the works are mediocre or conventional, but others are bona-fide paintings by real professionals. The best works are by well-known elderly artists. They had been put down and silenced and had disappeared. And now here they are, tranquilly emerging from the shadows as if nothing had happened.

On my second visit, Tang went with me, and he filled me in on quite a bit of the background. With time and patience, one could get a great deal of information from this exhibit, which would take years to filter through the press.

The only person who is pictured often with real hatred is Jiang Qing; occasionally Zhang Chunqiao, too; the caricatures of Wang and Yao are conventional. Much of the work expresses the most vulgarly reactionary prejudices. Jiang Qing once said that a society dominated by men is not the only one possible; so, here she is represented as the queen of the monkeys (humanity in its prepatriarchal period). Or she and her associates are shown propagandizing through the countryside in favor of the changeover to accounting by brigade. Zhang Chunqiao is unfurling scrolls with the motto "Keep to the established policy," and so forth. Wang is saying, "One can't trust old Hua." "Who's that?" I asked Teng. He shrugged. "Hua Guofeng."

Old films that are never seen or have long been forgotten are being exhumed and given serious attention. The fact that they are being offered once again, while at the same time all those works that tried over the last twelve years to find new and different paths are disappearing, says much more than all the political directives or the newspaper articles. The revivals go directly to the point, with no detours or contortions or maneuverings.

One significant example is the 1962 film celebrating Ding Ruchang, a "good" mandarin at the time of the 1894–95 Sino-Japanese War. It is typical of the works challenged by the Cultural Revolution.

"My daughter was stunned when she saw actors wearing tails and long [mandarin] gowns," Chen told me. "Children like her know nothing about all that, and it's useful for them to see such things. They must know about the past, too." Right. I don't doubt that the success of the revival is owed partly to the amusement people find in seeing a costume play—something a little different, at last, from the "all alikes" Zhang used to complain about, which in one way or another tried to imitate British and Russian historical films. But neither Chen nor her circle of friends and acquaintances is so ingenuous as to take a stand for such superficial reasons. For those who "know the past," the Sino-Japanese War hurts even today; it is one of the sharpest wounds to their national pride. For the authors and now the distributors of the film to hark back to that painful experience is an excellent choice to rekindle the spirit of nationalism and to appeal in its name for the unity that was shattered by the long class struggle. Admiral Ding Ruchang is a "positive hero"; the film presents him as being in favor of the war and against the hesitations and the casting about for compromises of Li Hongzhang.*

Long before the Cultural Revolution, Left-oriented groups had opposed the celebration of past glories and failures in these terms, which implies that the policies and actions of past governing classes be inherited in toto; and they also criticized the presentation of historical events from the perspective of those who held power ("the history of sovereigns and ministers"). The liveliest polemic had developed around the traditional concept of the relationship between the "good ruler" and the people, according to which the ruler interprets the needs of the ruled, and the ruled see themselves mirrored in the ruler. Almost all works for the theater and films which dealt with the imperial period used to be based on this assumption. It was the only one that allowed for an apologia on behalf of the governing class, in the person of one or more of its representatives who were morally estimable for reasons of rectitude or altruism or patriotism.

In the film, the sailors and the people generally see Ding Ruchang as a

---

*In the film, Li is a weakling vis-à-vis the foreigners, whom he supports when they refuse to supply more financial aid and military equipment to the fleet, and he is also associated with the stupid policy of the Empress Ci-Xi; therefore, he comes into conflict with the heroic and intransigent Ding. This does falsify history, at least in so far as Li is concerned. Li was, in fact, aware of the Chinese fleet's inadequacy, which resulted from a lack of funds, and aware, more generally, of the weakness of the Chinese armed forces. For that reason, he did his best to avoid a ruinous war in which China stood to lose much more than its supremacy in Korea, which was the original issue at stake. His prowar opponents were headed by Weng Tonghe, who at that time was most conservative and very close to Ci-Xi.

father; they legitimize his being lord and master by electing him their protector; the two sides trust each other, their mutual confidence being based on an unshakable relationship. An essential component of that relationship is the difference in status and in functions; he is the gentleman, the commander, the wise man; they are the children, the ignorant ones, who ask for protection and offer obedience, and to this tacit accord each party is committed to the death. Not every ruler merits such dedication, but only he whose conduct is in harmony with the function assigned him—the good ruler, who follows "the way of the kings," in distinction to one who follows "the way of the tyrants," and who is therefore, by definition, a usurper. Certain things are expected of the ruler: it is his duty to be literate, to behave and to dress in a certain way. The people esteem him for his independent wisdom, and they choose him to think for them.

Zhou Enlai followed "the way of the kings," Jiang Qing followed "the way of the tyrants." The Chinese are analytical; they do not abstract concepts from individuals, which accounts for the personalization of the struggle against the Gang of Four.

Our inability to understand this area of relationships derives not so much from a different tradition as from our present-day experience. In the West, we deal not with individuals but with corporations, holding companies, multinationals. Our public figures are ITT, the Rand Corporation, FIAT, the Communist party, the CIA. The public figures offered the Chinese are sovereigns and ministers, scholars and leaders; the mass of the people must be anonymous and be able to find expression only through sovereigns and ministers, scholars and leaders.

The revolution that began with May Fourth (from Lu Xun to Mao Zedong) overturned the oppressive lie within this reality. Not entirely, however, since the lie continues to be a reality. Its overthrow did not affect all parts of Chinese society, and it is these sectors that the conservatives are aiming to reach today. But the result will be the opposite of what is sought. If this road is followed, the entire Chinese people will come inevitably to the point of believing in no leader whatever.

The films now being shown deal also with the modern period, the twenties, the civil-war years. *"Hai lang taoqing" (Wave of Cleanliness)* was produced in 1965, in Canton, and "was blocked by the Gang of Four." The mini-intellectual and professorial circles are agog over its revival; Chen is sure that the film will interest me greatly. In fact, some of the less knowledgeable foreigners are carried away, and think highly of it. Finally to see young "modern" post–May Fourth women, youthful revolutionary intellectuals dressed in long mandarin gowns, rickshaws, the re-creation of streets and interiors of the China of those years— all this satisfies a taste for the exotic. It also represents the years of "alliance" between the Kuomintang and the Communists, between the national bourgeoisie and the proletariat. A crucial moment—1927, as the alliance between the two parties collapses—is used as background to the personal stories of four youths. But the political events are represented confusedly and are incomprehensible to someone who does not already know them.

More teaching aids useful to the people: articles, slides (I have to translate the captions into Italian), films, posters, epigraphs and slogans written by top leaders, living and dead—in praise of Lei Feng, a little soldier in the People's Army who served the people with all his heart and soul. "Learn from Lei Feng," the interpreter for the French says. "Once upon a time everybody learned from Lei Feng, and everybody was polite and disciplined, and everybody helped everybody else, especially the stronger helped the weaker. And then everybody stopped, and nobody worried about anybody else anymore."

So, the people are being reeducated with tales about Lei Feng. Lei Feng is an orphan (his parents were victims of the old system) and a true son of the Party, who never thinks of himself and does everything for others. Boy Scout stories, intended to teach people to be kind and unselfish—virtues of the people (but also included in the behavior required of cadres). Anyone who performs good deeds in imitation of Lei Feng receives honorable mention—for, say, helping old women onto trains or steering them along the street when it rains. Wang Jianhua, a student of mine, has been cited for some such good deed.

The actor who plays Lei Feng in the film does quite well, and he looks the part, being small, boyish, wide-eyed. A man-child of an innocence verging on idiocy, in a word, utterly good. A Saint Francis sentimentalized into a little Counter-Reformation pious paragon, a good example for a pure and obedient people. They knew how to invent this character, for (at least according to the CIA) Lei Feng never existed. However, his biological existence has no importance; a character is always a created thing.

If someone in ordinary conversation associates the behavior of a real person with the name of Lei Feng, it makes people laugh. The effect can only be comical when a detail from a ritual context is introduced into such a heterogeneous thing as everyday speech, as, for example, when peasants are referred to as "poor and lower-middle peasants." Lei Feng has been so discounted that even foreigners may be included in the joke. It happened that my Egyptian colleague was feeling ill, and I had to go with her to the hospital; the next day, one of the young men in the office said to me, laughing, "Ah, ah, we saw you last night. . . . You've learned from Lei Feng!"

I feel positively grateful every time anyone speaks to me in the language of real life rather than in political jargon. On Sunday, I left my bicycle in a parking area without locking it; it was near the big stores on Nanjing Road, where the crowd was so dense you could scarcely breathe. When I went back to get my bicycle, I found it secured by a heavy chain. As the parking-lot woman was unlocking it, she gave me some friendly advice: "Never leave it unlocked. There are thieves about!" I could have hugged her. It was the first time that this idea was not expressed to me as "Pay attention to your things because the class struggle is still going on." Had I said to that woman that there is a class struggle, she'd have laughed.

That same day, right by the big Store No. 1, on a side street so jammed with pedestrians, buses, and small trucks that one could hardly move, I noticed a rather confused group of young people coming toward me. Surrounded by this group, although a few steps ahead, were a young man and woman. She was distracted and disheveled, and she was clasping the man tightly around the waist, the way one might desperately, abjectly, cling to a tree, to any secure object. He was striding straight ahead, trying not to notice her. All of them were almost running. They appeared and disappeared like the sudden apparition of another reality. People paid scarcely any attention to them, and I did not go after them because the intervention of a foreigner would have done them more harm than good, even risked their being arrested. Even as filled with pain as it was, an apparition like that was for me a comfort.

According to the American radio, Deng is already Premier. This is surely not so. However, in Peking, word has been leaked that "he has returned to work." The power struggle among the various groups in the coalition still goes on, but by now the overall orientation is clear.

Zhang and Chen have informed me that the excerpt from the film *Juelie,* which was chosen as reading for this semester, has not been approved by the students (it's the film one of them was so pleased with at the time of the fall of the Gang of Four). "Why do you say not approved 'by the students'? What you might better say is that on the basis of directives, the film won't do."

Zhang: "No, no, it was the students themselves. They read the title and asked that it be removed." Chen stuttered something or other. They have already chosen a substitute piece, an article written by an Italian woman on open-door classes in the Hongqiao commune two years ago; they have also tidily cut the article to remove any reference to class struggle, and from the history of the commune as told by the peasants only the pre-Liberation period has been left in.

On the whole, the foreign teachers fluctuate in their reactions to current political trends, and for a complex of reasons they resist recognizing the real nature of the developments now taking place. However, when any attempt is made at school to involve them in the new policy, all hesitations disappear and they act with confidence. Their refusal to take an active part in either the examination or the grading process was nearly unanimous; no one felt that the question need even be discussed. Their ideas are always clearer when they must take a stand not on general matters but in the area of their own work. But there is something more. For the first time, they are measuring themselves against contradictions analogous to those they know at home, and here the conflicts are so obvious in substance as to dislodge the various equivocations that intrigue us in Europe. For years, a group of leaders here, pushed by popular protest, has understood that even in the cultural field there exist irreconcilable interests among the various social strata, and in educational policy has chosen to favor the most humble and least cultivated, to facilitate access to culture to those social groups which up to now have been kept ignorant. Meanwhile another group of leaders, in collaboration with the majority of the old party apparatus, stubbornly attempts to reconcile the irreconcilable in the interests of unity. Today, the partisans of interclass unity have the upper hand, and they are openly arguing their case, but it is too late for their arguments to escape scrutiny by millions of people for whom criticism has become second nature. Furthermore, no room is left for the new leaders to misrepresent the options they have chosen as serving the interests of the workers and peasants, because their plans necessarily entail the physical expulsion of thousands upon thousands of young workers and peasants from schools they have been attending. It is possible to induce workers to give up a part of their wages in exchange for other and future advantages, but the proposal that they give up their already won right to an education is too obvious a deception.

The counteroffer to the people is the "flowering" of traditional artistic and literary products. This is the ultimate version of a scheme introduced into China by the U.S.S.R. after Liberation. According to this scheme, culture in the U.S.S.R. was to be absorbed in the implementation of politics, even if this meant the physical destruction of the bearers of culture. The result was the appearance of the pseudoculture of the thirties, together with the concession of an elevated status to obedient authors and artists; the progressivist scheme in its national-popular version was reproduced and stabilized.

The attempts by friends of Lu Xun to resist this were defeated. On the basis of a hierarchical concept of successive social orders occurring in the course of history, and of culture as an enormous museum inherited from the past, it was proposed to transmit wholesale to the people the culture of past eras, on the pretense of educating them in its traditions. On the one hand, they again took up the Romantic concept of popular culture and behind a mask of autonomy spread among the people the culture of the old ruling classes, in which "the people" were valorized with a specific dignity so that they would remain within their assigned limits in an immobile and "harmonious" hierarchy. On the other hand, they adopted the progressivist ideology whereby the victorious ruling nations and classes at the peak of the pyramid are privileged, while the defeated and the governed are, by definition, inferior. Two contradictory bourgeois inheritances were combined, any dialectic among them was eliminated, and through the use of totalitarian methods they were made one. Even more so than under the bourgeoisie, the people were consigned to an inferior status. For the benefit of the new ruling classes, the "engineers of minds" (i.e. writers, according to the definition of Stalin and Zhdanov) held the people in thrall with the national and popular culture and under the tutelage of a power which was based on another—a scientific and international—culture which alone was recognized as being lofty and authentic, consciously and critically addressed to the ends of production.

The Left made repeated attempts to resist this cultural policy—in more explicit terms when it could circumvent obstacles by discussing it in terms not of China but of the Soviet Union. But the Left itself was mired down in contradictions and ambiguities, and, in the end, was unable to propose alternatives since, in common with the target of its criticism, it held to the principal assumption: the political instrumentalization of culture and science. Notwithstanding many illusions—entertained not only by the Chinese Left—a political revolution is not sufficient to turn illiterates into literates or to transform a culture of slaves into a culture of free men.

In China there was a political revolt of the subordinate classes against the uses to which the dominant classes put science. *But the Left in China (no less than in Italy) created confusion between politics and science. The political revolt was allegedly clothed in a* "scientific" *garb; this proved to be a baseless claim that worked only to the advantage of the dominant classes and their claims. When the rejection of* "bourgeois science" *was carried over into the schools, it fueled attacks against the Left for promoting a do-nothing policy, glorifying ignorance, and destroying education.*

The rejection of scholastic knowledge has nothing to do with science; what is being rejected is the school, which, within a class system, is dedicated to production—i.e., to the dual, parallel functions of producing a labor force and training scientific and managerial elites. Inevitably, workers will resist being cast as the labor suppliers, reduced to being tools, and likewise it is inevitable that they will oppose the creation of elites with a monopoly on knowledge.

Conflicts that explode in the school are not solvable unless they are at the same time solved at the workplace. The interdependencies between school and production, knowledge and power are increasingly accentuated in modern societies, creating a knotty dilemma that has so far proved impossible to disentangle. The experience of Socialist countries, or of countries with a strong Socialist component, has amply shown that unless illiterates stop being illiterates and

---

*The revolt of peasants against academically trained doctors who don't cure them, of workers against the engineers who use ideas as tools to gain power, and against production-oriented technocrats, and so on.

unless a slave culture is transformed into a culture of free men, the political revolution itself is caught in a vicious circle, which leads to the generating of class power. Mao Zedong's Cultural Revolution sought to break this circle, but it was unable to propose viable alternatives.

The conditions to which the second-class citizen is condemned seem increasingly like the sentence that cannot be appealed, especially in categories that have been subordinate since the beginnings of civil society—the young and women, who are not even given the alibi of power exercised by delegation, which is offered today to the working classes. The absence of any visible escape has produced in the West a kind of Luddism directed against the whole educational machine, and a desperate nihilism about the very hypotheses of liberation. Because it seems impossible to escape from the vise of power without making oneself the master of others or the accomplice of one's own masters, these second-class categories accept as positive, as something to be exhalted, their subordination and all that defines them as slaves. Luddism overturns and neutralizes the Cultural Revolution in a suicidal movement. The cultural deprivation that has been endured is assumed as a value. The first, indispensable move toward political revolt and the recovery of independence despite and against *the given condition is confused and annulled by the acceptance of that condition as a positive value.*

In China, the nihilistic ideology has not yet appeared, largely because of a singular circumstance. At the top of the Leninist party in China there were those who challenged Leninism in favor of the Cultural Revolution. It was a minority, albeit an extremely powerful one, that chose this option which remained conflicted to the end; and the Cultural Revolution was defeated because it was impossible to direct it from the center and from the top. However, powerful intervention helped it to spread widely and in depth throughout society, and, most important, helped clarify its character as a struggle of workers and young people against the owners of capital and science within socialism.

The power of the interclass conciliators is such that this heredity could be eroded and lost. But the program of economic development that the conciliators intend to carry forward will tend to sharpen class contradictions, one consequence of which will be to define the workers as independent subjects. The face of Chinese society in the years immediately ahead will depend in large part on the speed with which the inheritance of the Cultural Revolution is eroded in relation to the speed with which the workers will mature in the course of modernization.

Socialist Rivalry and Problems of Freedom

At the No. 3 machine-tool factory, which we visited on the twelfth, we were received not by a leader of the plant's Revolutionary Committee but by the "head of the office" of the Committee, together with another member of that office. This may be a sign that the purge was rather radical, despite what these officials said to the contrary; or it may mean that the Revolutionary Committees are being replaced by management offices. There was also a man from the union, a woman technician, and a woman introduced as a "vanguard worker," meaning, according to the rulers' new criteria, one whose production output is high.

The person who related the factory's history stated that this factory had had no cadres connected with the Gang of Four and that, at most, the Four's influence had been felt slightly.

When we walked through the various sections, we had a sense of emptiness and remoteness. I remembered the factories I visited in 1974, and the documentary *Open Factory*—filmed independently in China in 1971 by Italian workers and technicians. The freedom enjoyed by the workers then was incredible—scandalous for those managers accustomed to our factory system. The workplace seemed to be a continuation of the personal world of the workers. In Luoyang, in the famous tractor factory, a worker's family came and went during work hours without the slightest inhibition. On the assembly line, workers would shift and switch duties by mutual consent without awaiting directions from on high. I saw once again those frank, open faces—a bit ironical—with which the workers at the No. 2 watch factory in Shanghai would then watch us. Even last summer, in Peking, in the automobile factory, I remembered the Italian diplomat who was stupefied to see coming out of such a madhouse cars produced perfectly down to the last bolt. The vivacity and joy, even in such confusion or during hard work, in the food processing factory I visited in Shanghai shortly after my arrival last fall and the unrestrained participation of so many men and women workers during the *baogao* given us by the directors. . . . But now the workers had become silent and disciplined—they seemed absent, changed into hard-faced shadows. The factory was plastered all over with spanking-new, handsome manifestos extolling production. On large scoreboards the names of all workers were listed, and beside each was entered the percentage above or below the average output which that person had achieved. (I have heard that in other factories the name of each worker is accompanied also by the notation of his absences or tardinesses. When these exceed a given figure, the person's wages are docked.)

Sporadically, trucks with flags and drums are still circulating around the city, praising Socialist emulation. The people pay no mind. They actually underscore their indifference. For example, at a political meeting at the Institute, while the directors recite their *baogao*, I have seen girls serenely read novels; from time to time, they absently raise an arm to share in the collective *dadao*. People's interest is whetted more by attacks in *dazibao* against this or that unit cadre and, sometimes, in what reply they make in self-defense, but it's a gossipy kind of interest.

April 2

A big refinery, one of China's largest, is located on the other side of the Huangpu River, almost out in the country. For us, a spring excursion by bus and ferry, and on the return trip a long detour to take still another ferry. . . . Greening willows, their new leaves small and tender, stand among the gray shantylike houses, the dust, the spit. The part of Shanghai lying beyond the river, however, is different. Here, industrial plants and dwellings are scattered among cultivated fields. Huge barracks, small private homes. . . . Yellow colza flowers and the green shoots of grain. . . . Canals and swamps. . . . Across the flat countryside, the outlines of ships and cranes along the river, which is invisible, rear up as if they were growing out of the earth. On the return trip in the evening, moving southward were public buses and huge tractors, little carts piled high with cauliflowers and bunches of celery stalks. The carts were heading for the city's food stalls; girls pull these carts, grasping the shafts in their hands, and pressing against the leather strap that runs from shoulder to waist. When the traffic was slowed, people came out of their little houses to watch the show; the children held their supper bowls close to their mouths, and, their eyes glued to the scene, with their chopsticks they accurately stuffed the food into their mouths. This show had an added attraction—a busload of those strange animals, foreigners.

At the factory, we were received this time by the vice-chairman of the Revolutionary Committee; the "representative of the manager's office" contented himself with standing beside the other man. There were three more people, among them one with a job new to me—"salary manager."

The refinery employs a thousand workers, divided into four shifts, but overall, the personnel number four thousand, most of whom are assigned to auxiliary jobs. In the history of the factory the period that the manager remembers best is that of the Great Leap Forward (when all worked and discussed together—"seven hands, eight feet, seven mouths, eight tongues"), and then the discovery of the Daqing oil deposits, and the Cultural Revolution. "The struggle between the two lines has been very sharp."

"There has been the Gang of Four's negative influence," the youth representative added, "but also a positive element, which is the workers' will to apply the revolutionary line of Chairman Mao."

The vice-chairman went on to say, "One must distinguish between what was negative and what was positive through mass criticism. There is no organizational change in direction. One must deal correctly with the contradictions in the bosom of the people."

Criticism of the Four imitated the well-known clichés: They were opposed to technological knowledge, against the drive to produce, etc. But everything that was said was quite removed from the reality of the factory as they themselves described it. Confronted with data about modernization and the sharp increase in production during the Cultural Revolution (from 1.5 to 4 million tons of refined oil, plus new ventures—production of gas and manufacture of various by-products, Makita asked, "So the influence of the Four here was slight?"

"Er, well, yes," the vice-chairman answered, "their influence was quite slight when production was growing."

"Since when was their influence felt?"

"Since just after the 'January storm.' "

Question: "What difference is there between regulations in effect prior to 1965 and today's [i.e., after 1976]?"

The answer to this was confused, something about a difference between regulations that are not well defined and not reasonable and those that are reasonable.

Question: "For how long have there been no regulations?"

Reply: "Since 1965, or thereabouts."

We then went out and, walking among the enormous installations and the pipeline system, went into the buildings where the remote-control machinery is housed. Some of the electronic installations were built by the refinery's workers. "Isn't that uneconomical," Roland asked, "when you could buy the equipment at less cost from specialized factories?"

"We do it for reasons other than cost," the engineer replied. "We do it because it's good for the workers to know and understand the tools they use. Also, that way they're self-sufficient when repairs are needed." Probably investments to build this equipment, which is a separate operation from the refining of oil and is not included in the overall State plan, may be among those that factories must no longer make.

Despite the addition of the Gang of Four to the list of those supporting the wrong line, and despite the endless repetition of generalized accusations, the logic behind these men's actions contradicted the recent switch, and the contradiction was evident even in their language. Our questions were intended to bring out the contradiction, but before answering, they would snicker, almost as if they found it a joke that these ignorant cretins should unknowingly be touching on real facts. Or maybe they were merely trying to hide their embarrassment. (We don't know to what extent the people who talk to us during these visits may be under the control of the reorganizing teams.)

The reintroduction of rules didn't seem to be very significant for the moment, since it amounted only to notices listing obvious provisions such as that an employee in a given department must report any equipment breakdown, must wait for his shift replacement to arrive before he leaves, etc. More onerous was production control, which goes by the name of Socialist emulation. On the lists of workers' names, beside each there was a red, yellow, or blue slip (norm surpassed, met, not met). I asked in vain how it is possible to establish norms for individual performance in an operation that is almost totally automated. It's always hard to distinguish between what is done simply to blow smoke in people's eyes or to make bureaucrats shut up.

From all the fuss that was made about rules and controls, one fact emerges which we underestimated. Throughout this city and in many places elsewhere in China, for ten years factories functioned without even the routine rules we saw today; there were no controls, people could stop work to carry out some cultural activity, groups took time out of the working day to study; there was a true rejection of supervisory authority. For the first time in history, workers were for ten years without bosses in the factories. Perhaps an increase in production was a little slowed with respect to what—an unprovable hypothesis—it might possibly have been otherwise. However, it was certainly not slowed down in absolute terms, for starting with the Cultural Revolution there was, on the whole and everywhere, a notable increase in production,* which now people find themselves hard put to account for. How to reconcile the factual evidence and workers' evident pride with complaints about the nefarious influence, etc., that allegedly ruined production? In any event, workers continued to produce, and nobody died of hunger.

The true difficulties were to be found not in the economy but where millions of peasants entered an educational system that previously had been reserved for the privileged strata of society and was run by petty intellectuals who were busy with their internal disputes, and acted either repressively or stupidly.

From Deng's program: "The technical personnel of enterprises must be considered productive. Technicians cannot be included in the category of cadres who are separate from production or nonproductive personnel." This is to be construed as meaning, among other things, that technical personnel are not obliged to do manual work.

During the study of Mao's essay "On the Ten Great Relationships," the Institute professors had long, seemingly Byzantine discussions about one sen-

---

*The affirmations, with which the Chinese press aimed at the general public, and especially the foreign public, alternately inflate and deflate economic data, are of no account, and must be considered either pure propaganda or for or against a specific political conviction. Based on serious studies made in the West in recent years (gathered from Chinese sources, but specialized ones), it seems safe to say that from 1964 to 1978 the indexes of gross national product and per capita income are more or less constant and scarcely influenced by political ups and downs. Specifically, in the period between 1966 and 1975 one notes a notable period of growth, particularly in certain sectors —for example, in chemicals. See for reference purposes the documentation (with commentary by well-known scholars) gathered for the U.S. Congress by the Joint Economic Committee for the years 1969, 1972, 1975, 1978.

Signs of economic difficulty—admitted to even in the daily Chinese press—are to be noted for 1980, and rather grave ones in 1981.

tence at the end of the first paragraph: "We must mobilize all forces, direct and indirect. . . ." The problem was to determine whether they, as educators, were a "direct" or an "indirect" force. They even asked my opinion. To me the problem seemed meaningless and not pertinent to the text (as indeed it is not). The instructors meant to establish the fact that they were productive personnel, on a par with workers and peasants. (How does this matter? I asked myself ingenuously. In a Socialist system, isn't it the same thing, provided one is doing useful work?) What concerned them was that they should get themselves out from under any dependency on, or dictatorship of, the workers and peasants. To be on the same level? Given the existing power relationships, for them to be formally on the same level was equivalent to being above the workers and peasants.

One day I was looking for an administrative cadre, but couldn't find him. "The cadres are doing manual work today, like every Thursday," Zhang explained. And he added triumphantly, "Not us!" So apparently they were recognized as being technical personnel—or principal force.

In these terms, manual labor is reduced to a mere payment ritually paid to the piper in order to enjoy a political or administrative function. With many exceptions, etc.

We will see developments and extensions of the area of "principal forces."

On the lists of those who have been condemned to death, which are posted beside the People's Court, the names of several very young people appear who have been convicted on political charges, and one explicitly for having supported the Gang of Four. Several others were found guilty of rape. There is some uncertainty among the foreigners about these sentences; the most recent conjecture is that they might concern members of youth gangs of the "new bourgeoisie."

In Nanjing, too, there are fresh lists of persons who have been sentenced to death. These death penalties seem to be based not on explicit political charges but, worse yet, on flimsy grounds, frequently group rape. In full daylight, in the center of the city, eight young men allegedly close in on a girl and force her to undress! Such a thing is inconceivable in Shanghai, and even more so in Nanjing.

The laws concerning rape are very severe, but in practice, there is great latitude in defining the term "rape." Often it is applied to two unmarried adults who have voluntary sexual relations. Some days ago there was one of those mass meetings from which foreigners are barred; what it was about was a mystery. In due course, we learned that it had been a criticism meeting on the subject of rape among consenting adults. A man and a woman, both adults, both unmarried, had had sexual relations, and someone had taken it upon himself to inform against them. So, they were to be criticized; the charges were brought by members of other units. Obviously, in this case there was no crime, the absurd use of the term "rape" notwithstanding; however, in such cases, administrative measures are taken to deal with the persons who have come under criticism. Generally, they are separated and sent to work in provinces remote from each other for a period of several years, after which they are permitted to marry.

A young foreigner who has a serious infection goes to the hospital. (Foreigners go to the best and most modern hospitals.) His testicles are swollen, and he is unable to move. He asks a woman nurse (there are no male nurses) to help him urinate. She refuses.

A young Western woman goes for a medical examination. No examination takes place, because not only must the girl not remove her undergarments, but she must not take off even her sweater. (Of course doctors also often behave in a completely normal way.)

Some university students are convinced that a man's heart is on the right, and a woman's on the left—or vice versa, I don't remember exactly. If a girl wears a sweater, it is obligatory that she wear a jacket over it.

A French professor is explaining the use of *monsieur, madame, mademoiselle*. He adds that in today's usage a woman no longer in her first youth is also addressed as *madame,* irrespective of whether or not she is married. The students consider this usage insulting for an unmarried woman.

On March 8, a foreigner asked some girls how they were going to celebrate International Women's Day. Answer: "It's not being celebrated, because among us there are no women." . . . Some young men are asked why they are not attending birth-control classes. They reply that a person who is not married must not be informed about such things. (I wonder how the barefoot doctors, who often are young and unmarried, will go about teaching the peasants.)

Twenty years ago, at Beida, there was nothing like this. It's an argument in favor of those who oppose peasants' going to university—advanced in how much good faith? These young people are living in a big city, and for years they have been taught far from their families and places of origin. Had there been a little goodwill, would it not have been possible to educate them? And not them only. Millions of young people have gone back to the countryside after their schooling; if the cultivated elite had wished, there could have been not only education for these peasant students but, through them, mass education on a vast scale.

Noneducation is not confined to customs and sex, but is even more grave in the political area. "Does the class struggle exist in Europe?" a student will ask. Or, "What does a peasant in Italy do when he has to borrow money from the landlord?" (These young people believe that the landlord-shark who existed in China at one time is typical of capitalism.)

A fresh opportunity for mass education was offered by the Confucius criticism movement. However, the middle-range hierarchy fiercely resisted it with political arguments, claiming that behind Confucius the real target was Zhou Enlai, and so forth. This may even have been true, but people of goodwill would have stressed the valid points in the campaign, aiming also to thwart its secondary anti-Zhou objectives, instead of using the latter as a pretext to oppose the campaign's valid substance.

As a joke, someone showed a Chinese teacher something Mao had written, but attributed it to Zhang Chunqiao; the teacher read it and said it was disgusting.

There are those who are very aware, students who are preparing to resist the probable "bourgeois dictatorship." And there are also confused people who would like to understand.

The Bourgeoisie in the Party

The comedy of political study was performed a few days ago, during discussion of an editorial in *The People's Daily,* March 14 issue: "Radical Overturn in Relations Between Us and the Enemy." There were only a few of us; the English, Peruvians, and Japanese had escaped. Instead of the usual time-consuming *baogao,* the professors with political expertise gave a résumé of the editorial and asked us to express our opinions. Roland made some intelligent comments, but did not attack it too hard. In the article, the Four are accused of having stated that the bourgeoisie was in the Party—a social class, that is—whereas, according to Marxist doctrine, it can only exist in society and have representatives in the Party. Allegedly, the Four then identified this bourgeoisie with the old Party cadres who had an old-fashioned mentality, appropriate to the previous phase of the revolution—the "democratic-bourgeois" one: ergo, capitalist roaders. Instead, the old cadres are excellent people; even during the democratic-bourgeois era they favored the Socialist revolution, they have been tempered by past struggles, they have a wealth of experience, etc., etc. Conclusion: a few bourgeois have infiltrated the Party, but even if quite dangerous they are few. Today they are, precisely, the Four.

The aim of all this is to clear Deng Xiaoping (who was never mentioned by name) of the charge of following the capitalist road and of representing the bourgeoisie in the Party, and to make the self-interest of the old cadres polarize around his person. In answer to our questions about Deng, they said: Before and during the early years of the Cultural Revolution, he was partly a capitalist roader. Then he recognized his errors, and he was again allowed to work. After that, he committed further errors, but he applied the directives of Chairman Mao. He has good points and bad points. Every time he committed an error, the Gang of Four would charge him with it, for they did not want "to save the sick man" but to belabor him to death, to beat him down so that they could seize power. Our question: Was the exoneration of Deng after the Tienanmen events the work of the Four, or did they have Mao's assent? No direct answer: "That will be cleared up in the future." In any event, "it's a question of contradictions within the people."

I wanted to have a little fun by embarrassing these political professors a bit, so I asked who was the bourgeoisie in China's Socialist society.

They spent two hours answering that, mainly trying to dodge this way, then that. Roland backed me up in the question. Lao Bai was amused, like a man watching embarrassed little boys or farm lads shuffle their feet. Today, it wasn't up to him to answer, and for that matter, he never answers anything. In the end, they concluded that the bourgeois class, apart from survivors from the past, is comprised of *workers* who are interested in their own welfare, who do not obey the Party, who think only of their self-interest, who have been corrupted. In a word, in China the bourgeoisie is a bunch of hooligans and rebellious workers. "Bourgeoisie" has no meaning; the term is used because these people must cling to doctrinal jargon. But what they mean is "the enemy." And in their confusion, they ended up confessing who their enemy is.

When the meeting broke up, and we were standing in small groups for the customary leave-taking, one of the professors—the thinner one, who wears glasses—came over to me and asked, "Well, according to you, who is the bourgeoisie?"

This was to be our first and last chance for discussion at a political study meeting or anywhere else. Before the preordained, endless *baogao,* they would ask us, sometimes insistently, to voice our opinions, not so that they might respond to them but in order to record them. Susan, on the rare occasions when she came, and I would answer with a "no comment."

The Fudan students have been in factories for several days, also talking about the bourgeoisie in the Party. They polemicized, the cadres answered them sharply, as did a few workers, too, although the latter were more uncertain and, on the whole, seemed perplexed.

And so it is that the defense of the "proletarian line" is left in the hands of a little group of foreigners, students, and a few teachers scattered here and there in Chinese schools. But the situation we will find on returning to our own countries is not so different. The big parties and the parties of the old Left will be as one in painting the figure of a young worker as the hostile outsider, until they have made it a criminal act to dissent from "interclass conciliation."

"At this point, one no longer understands why they criticize him," a pro-Deng man has said to Pascale. "After all, the economy has got to be rescued." The reintroduction of Deng occurred even before his public physical reappearance, with this use of his arguments in attacks on the Four. For example, among them are phrases such as "to strike down the good cadres in the Party and the model vanguard people," "to speak only of politics and not about the economy, speak only of revolution and not about production," "to create chaos in management"—all taken textually from his programs.

The only way to cope with this accumulation of contradictory juxtapositions would be the simple, modest, understandable step of referring to facts of daily life and to what actually happens at the workplace. To see things from below.

Concrete, specific facts and daily reality are counterposed to a host of ideological falsifications in the East as well as in the West. Everywhere those who hold power speak a language that is dense, monolithic, rational, national-popular, and civic-minded. The unitarian values are the nation, democracy, socialism. Daily reality demonstrates, minute by minute, event by event, that there is no nation, there is no democracy, there is no socialism.

In China unity is achieved and contradictions are removed through the simultaneous use of all available ingredients, juxtaposing ideas and programs that are, in fact, irreconcilable. The meaning of words is literally turned upside down. The bourgeoisie made up of workers or the muddle over productive work and manual work are merely two extreme examples. A dense fog is laid down over real problems, everybody finds his views confirmed, no matter how widely they vary from the next man's, because absolutely everything is stated. It is not only dialectic that is destroyed but also the possibility of employing theoretical thinking in order to express anything whatsoever. Ideological language is reduced to total vacuity, and at the same time the people in power employ that language exclusively in addressing the masses. In the upper strata of society, reality lurks in the wings; in the lower, on the periphery of the private sphere. Counterrevolution flourishes in the guise of a hymn to the hyperrevolution. *

Behind a screen of unitarian values, the detachment of thought from language proceeds apace. The antipeople mechanism of the powers-that-be shatters ideology from within.

The operation could not succeed if the presuppositions did not exist, and if theoretical discussion were not already undermined by the misuse to which it has been put. The ganbu *have controlled this discourse for a long time. It comprises set phrases, in which identical words follow one upon another in an identical order. Variations consist only in their presentation. Some people are able to marshal them in such a way that, taken as a whole, they seem to make sense. Others are either less skillful or indifferent, and jumble them together so that the cumulative result is nonsense. However, between the two extremes there is no difference in*

*The chorus that will accompany the ditching of democracy in Italy will be hyperdemocratic.

substance. In fact, in no case is this discourse meant to have integrated meaning.

The repertory of set expressions is enormous, and they have been compiled in lists and glossaries. Often they have been taken from Mao's writings, also from editorials and from slogans of one or another post-Liberation period; some date from even earlier. Political lines compete, neutralize each other, slaughter each other. But the phrases endure—all of them. They no longer have any intrinsic meaning, but they are part of the political patrimony. Of course, depending on which political tendency is ascendant, a provisional screening is made, and some phrases are even banned, like the well-known "keep to the established policy." But such cases are few and far between; for a term to be definitively struck down, it must never have made it into the repertory.

When one says "we count on the people" ("people" here in the sense not of "nation" but of "working classes"), "we have faith in the masses," one means: The people are sufficiently aware to resist attempts to shatter ideology, or to divorce language from concepts, and concepts from things. However, the people cannot resist, for the shattering has already taken place; it is a fact. The subject classes can begin to resist only when they realize that they have been deprived of the ideas that served them as weapons in their struggle, and of the words that expressed their antithetical positions. This expropriation has been the work of their own organizations. And not only in the spheres of thought and words.

And not only in China. An awareness of having been dispossessed is beginning to spread through Europe, but again in ideological forms. People are drawn to anarchism with its myths of immediacy and popular spontaneity, to ideologies of negation; to negate the significance of history and even of human reason, even into the flight into mysticism and magic, which has penetrated even into workers' circles. Once again there are world visions, universalistic solutions, almost as if the point were to look for philosophical alternatives to Marxism. And the essential purpose is being lost sight of, which is to reestablish the relationship between every individual's everyday life and conceptual and political categories (the bond between the particular and the general); for example, modestly to set about finding out what, in daily, down-to-earth terms, has changed in the life of a worker or of his unemployed son so that it can be said of them by the leaders of their Communist parties (whether in "actual" Communist countries or in those West European ones where they are near the power center) that they are the State and must assume the responsibilities of the ruling class; first of all, what has changed in the work context, since in our societies production is primary. This search is not a "discourse," it is merely the preparation of the terrain. It is the initial and necessary job to be done when the terrain has been destroyed. The repression that obtains everywhere is aimed to prevent men from seeking spheres of communication that elude the institutional, ideological, and market conditionings imposed by those in power, from circumventing the law of separation between production and thought, existence and thought.

If China's economic development proves to be relatively rapid, the old arsenal, including the verbal weapons, could become obsolete and be swept away, dissolving into dust before it is replaced with other tools modern mass culture disposes of for expropriation and mystification. Chinese workers would thereby be offered a greater chance than their companions in the West during this interval, during this period of temporary linguistic and conceptual impotence on the part of those in power. For the Chinese workers to be able to seize on such weakness and take advantage of it, it will not be enough that the tempo of development is relatively rapid; they will have to move in time to organize themselves.

Beethoven

On the evening of March 27, virtually every foreigner at the Dasha was in the TV room for the great event. We knew that all Shanghai and certainly all Peking were glued to their sets. Contrary to what we had been given to understand, the program included Chinese compositions, although written for the Western orchestra. One selection was for *pipa* and Western orchestra.

But in conclusion the Fifth Symphony was played, announced merely as "Symphony No. 5 in C Minor," with no mention of Beethoven. It seems that this was the first time since the Cultural Revolution that a Chinese orchestra has performed Western classical music in public.

The performance was quite good, even if the reduced size of the orchestra was compensated for by a bit too much volume. The Chinese tendency to give our music an over-romantic reading was checked by the orchestra's concern to play well; the result was a little noisy and inexpressive, but perfectly acceptable, at least to my unprofessional ear.

The tense faces of the players, the elderly, fat conductor, the thunderous applause from the audience at the end (and also, from inexperience, at the conclusion of each movement)—most unusual on the part of people who habitually do not applaud theater or music performances. But this was a great moment of liberation.

I listened unmoved to music which was as familiar as day and night. A certain irony flickered among my young colleagues. For the Chinese, players and listeners alike, it was the celebration of their return to the human community.

In his own right, Beethoven signifies one thing, but in the culture of today, he is an ingredient in the multidecker sandwich. My colleagues were right to poke fun. It is ridiculous to take him up in this way, as did the U.S.S.R. and the Popular Fronts and the youth festivals of my twenties. But there was no point in rebelling. The real meaning of this performance lay in what it symbolized for those who took part in it.

I've said that the Chinese felt liberated, which is to say, they were expressing a sense of being liberated in this way. *Which Chinese?* Even people who are visibly so pleased (pleased to turn toward us in this way; this morning at the Friendship Store, the symphony was being played either over the radio or on a gramophone) hadn't suffered any great privation from not being able to listen to Beethoven—except, perhaps, musicians. The Chinese among whom I live are some of those who are rejoicing the most, and I know for a fact how little, not to say nothing, they understand of Beethoven; actually, they enjoy "Mamma" and "Come Back to Sorrento." If they listen to "serious" Western music, they will get to Tchaikovsky or Puccini long before they get to Beethoven.

For the Chinese who feel liberated, Beethoven represents "humanism," which in their country has been so much contested, or, to put it with fewer circumlocutions, Europe. (The more unlettered call Europe "England," convinced as they are that our countries are all English counties and even that we all speak English as our native tongue. Zhang, yesterday morning: "Beethoven is an English composer?") These people represent a well-circumscribed group. It does not include even those with a certain level of education, although the upper-middle class proposes to extend this interest far enough to include them, at least. The great mass of Chinese are completely alien to European culture. My students burst out laughing if one mentions Christianity. The Egyptian teacher is a believing Muslim; he never speaks of religion to avoid being offended. The students also laugh if you try to get them really to look at Leonardo's "Gioconda." That the portrait of a woman could be so important sends them off into peals of laughter.

China has never been colonized. For colonized peoples, these cultural complications are not so strong. Whereas analogous difficulties do exist for the Japanese—though not so exacerbated and often not apparent—despite the fact that they are not sealed off against Europe, are integrated into the world market, and are not in a position of inferiority.

For the Chinese who enjoy modest economic means and middle school to university education, Europe is the upper-bourgeois locus that is hated and envied the way one hates another people's freedom. The present leadership gambles on this hatred and this inverted love. In the association Europe = bourgeois civilization = freedom, the last, freedom, is identified with the advantage (if only cultural) some enjoy over others. And there is a reverse complementary association —socialism/tyranny. The claim to equality on the part of the uneducated at the bottom level of society is felt to be an abuse. "Fascist dictatorship" is the accusation made by ex-victims of the Gang of Four. This concept of fascism is like that of the anti-Fascist fraction of the Italian petty bourgeoisie, which was put off more by fascism's vulgarity and brutality (today we say "by violence") than by its substance.

Although Mao Zedong was very much isolated at the top, he tried to break

*up these associations not with abstract value judgments but in "social practice,"
and he addressed himself to revealing the "nonfreedom" that exists in the "bourgeois" order, and showing how the only possibility for democracy lay in the revolt
of the common people in order to attain self-government.*

*Apart from the seeking of personal and group privileges, of class power, this
was the only possible strategy. This strategy was spelled out in one of the places
in this world where at the time it was least feasible. China had not experienced
the leveling effects of the capitalist market; social stratification there was more
profound than that based on mere differences in income; the inferiority complex
of the Chinese educated middle class with respect to its (real or presumed) opposite
numbers in the West led it, as I have said, to cast its democratic aspirations in
a European-bourgeois form, and to link them to a sense of superiority in relation
to the rest of the population and to pretensions of cultural authority. (Meaning,
in many cases, power plain and simple, in the context of a mandarin heredity and
a socialist social order in which factors that are not directly economic weigh
heavily.)*

*Although party factions were influenced by Mao Zedong's vision and by the
fact that some groups of the population identified with that vision, the leaders and
cadres had a fundamental caste interest that led them to reproduce in the main
in China the same conditions which in the Soviet Union had led to the alternative
democracy/tyranny in its false, antipopular form. And not unlike the policy
proposed by the Eurocommunists in Spain and Italy, which is the ultimate expression of one authoritarian concept of power, today they are choosing freedom for
the few and fobbing it off as splendid democracy for all.*

*But what happened in China between 1919 and 1970 means that the unani-
mous heavenly harmony has been smashed beyond possible repair. The condition
of the lowly in day-to-day life, which was essential to the heavenly order but was
predicated upon their being deprived of the full use of language (other than the
local, the vernacular), was denounced as "mute China," and language, in the
same order of things, denounced as a tool of the "four thousand years of cannibalism."* Mao Zedong was defeated, but he sowed small seeds of freedom sufficient
to unveil the cadaverous aspect of "the eight-legged essays"† and the false sound
of the heavenly harmony; sufficient, also, to make it clear that the one truth is
to be found in the mutual relationship and the words of ordinary men who are
no longer mute, who are living simultaneously in the dual order of hierarchy and
equality, of submission and independence, and who are irreversibly present in*

---

*"Mute China" is the title of an essay by Lu Xun, which deals with language and much more
besides. "Four thousand years of cannibalism" is an expression Lu Xun employed in the short story
"Diary of a Madman."
†Stereotypic form for essays obligatory in State examinations in imperial China. But the expression
"the Party's eight-legged essays" was already being used by Mao in the thirties to denote the dead
use of political language by many Communist mandarins.

places from which they used to be barred. Rough peasants in the universities, workers who cannot be made not to spit on the ground and who cannot be brought to say "down with the Cultural Revolution," either—by now they are everywhere, they invade everything. Obedient, full of prejudices, prepared to observe the ritual, anarchic, people who are Confucianists and proletarians at the same time, who cannot be driven backward and are already the image of something new. Impatient as he was ("Ten thousand years are too long—one must seize the day and the hour"), the intervention of Mao makes it henceforth impossible to travel the old road peacefully.

Westerners who believe that at last they are free of the needle that Mao represented are shortsighted and deceived. Choices made on a class basis can no longer be concealed in China or elsewhere. Minds that are neither corrupted nor intimidated will not be misled by attempts to conceal the repression of the many through a pretended struggle against fringe minorities—the "bourgeois elements" (rebellious workers) in China, the "extremist fringes" in Europe. Even as liberty is being proclaimed, liberty is being attacked with every form of violence—economic, physical, moral.

To take refuge behind Beethoven in order to repress the people will be increasingly difficult.

The current "thaw" in China—the concept is borrowed from the repertory of the West, which includes the U.S.S.R.—is the most recent of the conventional images offered the world, those false images of China that Chinese leaders long ago decided to offer us.

This falseness was an integral part of the extraordinary accomplishment of Zhou Enlai. From the "come to see" to the Friendship Stores, from simplicity-order-efficiency-cleanliness to the "do not treat foreigners badly," from the "let us take advantage of traditional culture" to the "let us take advantage of foreign culture" to "we have no illiterates," from the unity of the people to the "women have won parity with men" to the image of the Cultural Revolution as a great pacific fair, a happy folk festival. A country without blood, sweat, and tears, unless they be the purified, antiseptic blood, sweat, and tears of the hero who was conceived a hero in his mother's womb, who exemplarily sacrifices himself for the people. A country without poverty, ignorance, slavish labor, repression by the powerful, a country without howls of protest against an inhuman life. The country of "contradictions within the people," which are mediated by moralizing priestly rulers.

The Four were certainly not offering a "truth" in place of the lie; they lied more than the others in making their impossible claims (the school that was no school, science that was not science, self-government by illiterates?). Still, the Cultural Revolution opened a wound, exposed to the light a lie (on both sides). It was destructive, because it revealed as false the compact between leaders and people, mandarins and illiterates, in which no one no longer believed. It did not

propose alternatives that were practical, since the problems it was treating were
enormous—not only in China—and would require perhaps an entire historical
period to become resolved. But to destroy that which in the consciences of all is
recognized as false also signifies opening the road to truth.

Libraries and Persecutions

The city library, which we have not been permitted to use—the one which
practically from the day I arrived I have been asking permission at least to visit
—has finally been opened to us. My profession in Italy is that of librarian, and
so I was very interested in this tour, and in the hope of getting some answers,
I had prepared four pages of questions on the functioning of this and other
libraries in Shanghai and throughout China. Very soon, however, I understood
that such questions would be ill-advised, since the meeting had another purpose
altogether: to familiarize us with the misdeeds of the Gang of Four through
first-person accounts by their victims.

The representative of the Revolutionary Committee received us in a small
elegant wood-paneled room;with him were a specialist in the history of the book,
a reading-room employee, a cataloger, and the head of the catalog section. After
a lengthy stint of listening, we were taken on a rapid visit of the public rooms
and one stack room.

The Revolutionary Committee cadre was probably not a trained librarian;
in any event, here his function was primarily political. The others were former
victims of the Four and had come to tell us their stories. The representative of
the Revolutionary Committee spoke first. He made a brief statement about the
library's history and its collection. Then he moved on to the principal topic: how
the Gang of Four had persecuted library personnel in order to cover up historical facts. The staff has now discovered in texts from the thirties more than three
hundred instances testifying to the reactionary activities of Zhang Chunqiao and
Jiang Qing. The director actually mentioned only one, which is well known. It
concerns the article Lu Xun wrote against Di Ke (Zhang Chunqiao) in 1935.
According to the speaker, that Di Ke was Zhang's pseudonym is made clear in
a biography of Lu Xun published in 1937, of which very few copies are extant
because most were sequestered by the Kuomintang. One copy is owned by the
library, in its rich collection of writings from the thirties. The man working in
the catalog section came upon this book in the ordinary course of his job, and
he showed it to the Red Guards, to let them know that Zhang Chunqiao and
Di Ke were one and the same person. (This occurred early in 1968, when several
persons unleashed a "bombardment against Zhang Chunqiao.") Zhang was
terrified by the attacks; in June, 1968, through his Shanghai accomplices, he had
the doors to that part of the library sealed; even library personnel were not
allowed to go into the stack room of that section. Nineteen-seventy was the year

of the "white terror,"* and those who knew too much had to be silenced. From then on, some fifty people from among those who worked in the library were singled out; two were imprisoned, ten sentenced to "isolation," and some forty underwent investigation. The employees were tortured psychologically and physically. One died as a result; others suffered nervous disorders.

The next speaker was the persecuted librarian. After some preliminary remarks in which he complained about his persecutors and expressed his gratitude for having been freed, he recounted the entire story of the Lu Xun–Di Ke polemic once more. To ascertain whether traitors and spies might have infiltrated the Party, he, together with the Red Guards, had consulted pre-Liberation newspapers and magazines. Counterrevolutionary articles attacking the Party and Lu Xun had been discovered, particularly in *Huoju*, the supplement of the newspaper *Da Wan Bao*, † among them, the Zhang piece subsequently criticized by Lu Xun. Because the librarian had revealed the truth to the Red Guards, he was persecuted. In February, 1970, he was placed under "isolation," and personal books, letters, and other papers were sequestered. A public interrogation was improvised by an accomplice of Zhang and held in one of the rooms at the library. At all costs, the examiners wanted to learn the names of the people to whom he had given information. They said that the watch tower of the library had been turned into a cannon tower against Zhang. The librarian refused to name names, and a few days later, he was arrested at night and subjected to a new trial; this one was not public. But they could get nothing out of him. They did not have the courage to criticize him at a mass meeting. (This should follow the sentencing.) In point of fact, they were afraid that the pseudonym business would become common knowledge. Therefore they kept him in prison illegally for five years, transferring him from one place to another. He spent a long time in solitary confinement and used to read the papers aloud for fear of losing the faculty of speech. He had to fight to obtain the newspapers. He remained in solitary until April, 1975. His release was brought about thanks to the struggle waged by the library staff and the requests of the masses.

The librarian concluded his account by repeating clichés against the Four,

*"White terror" is the expression commonly used in China when referring, negatively, to someone's repression of another, with this qualification: that "terror" is good if it is revolutionary, i.e. "red," but bad if it is counterrevolutionary, i.e. "white." Since Zhang Chunqiao is by necessity "counterrevolutionary," his being repressed is "red," while his repressing someone else is "white."

†The newspaper *Da Wan Bao (Evening Journal)* and its supplement *Huoju (The Torch),* which the librarians had pointed out as reactionary publications, were papers that gave generous space to the writings of the men of the CCP. That part of the CCP which operated in Shanghai, orthodox and tied to Stalin's Comintern directives, already favored, in 1935, some sort of collaboration with the KMT—unlike Mao, who was in the countryside. Zhang Chunqiao, who was very young, of course followed the Party line in the city in which he lived. Like other men of letters of the time who were close to the Shanghai CCP, he probably had no idea whatsoever of Mao's positions, which were, at the time, heretical. One of those few on the Left who opposed the CCP line in Shanghai was Lu Xun.

in favor of Hua, and about his own dedication in serving the masses. He was a middle-aged, mild-mannered man who wore glasses; his belligerent language seemed at variance with his personality. He evinced not hatred so much as a kind of gratified depression.

The revolutionary committee cadre spoke again. Young people had been persecuted also, he said, and he presented one, who, because he had been familiar with the material at issue, was detained in prison for three years, during which time he suffered from a nervous ailment. He was now better. The young man related how he had been subjected to night interrogations and been man-handled with Fascist methods and beaten about the head. His mother had been forced to hand over his diaries.* When his nerves snapped, he talked, and what he said was recorded.† On the basis of these statements, he was later sentenced.

After further remarks from the director, the fat, elderly man took the floor; this was the specialist in old and rare books. In his official capacity, he had had nothing to do with the famous stack room, but in the early days of the Cultural Revolution he had gone to consult material there. In February, 1970, he was forced to admit that he had taken part in the "bombardment." In June, 1971, for reasons of work he was in the Peking library. During a course of study organized by followers of the Four to criticize certain elements in the ultraleftist "May Sixteenth Group," he was accused of being associated with that group and was charged with eighteen crimes.‡

After concluding statements of hatred and devotion, the old man read a poem against the Gang of Four. In the opinions he expressed, and in his style of speech (full of baronial hauteur), this man belonged to the past; he had never ventured beyond the world of his old books, and all the events of the last thirty or forty years had reached his ears as the sound of some disturbance that was to be neutralized by a surface conformism and opposed whenever an occasion presented itself. He lamented the fact that he had been insultingly called an old bourgeois. "I didn't know what to do," he confessed. Persuaded that he repre-sented the quintessence of what in the West used to be called spiritual values, he protested now against the way in which intellectuals are criticized and undervalued. The Revolutionary Committee cadre wound up the meeting with

---

*It would seem that no Chinese can refrain from keeping a diary, which is used against him by his political adversaries. Even in the charges against the Four, Party Document No. 24 of 1976 made extensive use of their diaries.

†The substance of the charges and of the interrogations remained obscure.

‡The "bombardment" against Zhang Chungqiao in February, 1968, came not only from the Right, but also from the ultra-Left, a fairly strong group in Shanghai which had broken with Zhang the year before because they considered him too moderate. This explains why the librarian—doubtless no ultraleftist himself—could have come to be associated with the May Sixteenth group. The quarrels and hates between various currents of the Left in Shanghai were without doubt exploited by the new leaders during the campaign against the Four, and were some of the reasons that made impossible a coordinated resistance against the Right's coup.

the familiar refrain against the Four, in praise of Hua, about the joy of the masses, etc.

When we asked where the section housing the thirties material was (it is the dream of quite a few Western scholars to be allowed to see it), they answered that it is now in another building. And (obviously) closed. ("What is the difference now, to the public, from when Zhang Chunqiao and his friends were in control?" I asked myself. The answer: none. Access to that section of the library remains prohibited today, as then; the only thing that has changed is the identity of those who hold the keys.)*

In reply to the question whether the accomplices of the Four were a part of the library or not, their leader was said to have been brought in ad hoc. Some members of the staff had been influenced by this man, and they were now "being helped to correct themselves." These librarians we hear seemed to be happy about their personal liberation, yet they shared a peculiar characteristic. I did not find in them one trace of those professional interests that link librarians throughout the world, namely and in first place the preoccupation with spreading the use of books and of finding ways of persuading the public to read. On the contrary, they seemed interested mostly in holding closely to their treasures, to enjoy them by themselves and to conserve their monopoly of them. Perhaps the persecution they had endured had disfigured them, or perhaps they belonged to that type of very conservative librarian of other days which is almost extinct. Because of this, the obligatory words of ritual sounded all the more unreal: "bringing books to the workers, peasants, and soldiers." This was the usual political chit that had to be paid, to safeguard—exactly what, in this case?

As we walked through the public rooms, I was seized by a deep depression. The plain varnished wood tables, the large, modest spaces could evoke a conventlike austerity, an egalitarian, Puritan purpose had the rooms been inhabited, had some form of life circulated through them. But they were dead spots, they seemed created not for reading but to put the public off, even to drive it away. In the whole of the library rooms, there were not more than fifty people. In the course of a day, they might number four hundred at most, surely not three thousand, which was the figure given us. This, in a city the size of Shanghai.

---

*Such a serious conflict cannot be explained, naturally, simply with the little literary polemic between Lu Xun and Zhang Chunqiao as a youth. In the thirties Lu Xun was opposed to the Stalinists who ran the CCP in Shanghai; this opposition was given wide notice during the Cultural Revolution by Lu Xun's widow and his friends, with support from the Red Guards. One of those Stalinists was Zhou Yang, a political leader who was attacked by the same Red Guards. Zhang Chunqiao's enemies wanted to demonstrate that he had shared Zhou Yang's discredited positions —the enemies of the Left, so that he could be denounced as an unrevolutionary bureaucrat, the enemies of the Right, to create cloud of dust and confuse the young leftists' protests against bureaucrats such as Zhou Yang. Confusion won out. The rehabilitation of Zhou Yang came at the same time as the end of any public discussion of these historical matters. The problem is *not* simply one of history, but has direct bearing on the present.

. . . Scattered along different corridors were rows of catalogs. . . . There were no shelves. Walls were bare. When I did not see one encyclopedia or dictionary the public might consult, I inquired and was told that "because of lack of space" all materials must be requested and that they are specially fetched out. This explained why in those dreary, largely deserted rooms, the few readers sat, each leafing through a book as if it were a treasure he had managed to get his hands on. At one end of the room for Marxist studies, neon-lighted glass cases displayed a few classics, Mao's works, and several pamphlets, as if by way of decoration. At the time of our visit vast rooms were set aside for a photographic exhibit on the theme "Learn from Dazhai." Not a single visitor. The only "normal" room was the one in which the old books are kept, and this they did have us visit.

It's possible that the staff permits anyone to enter the library, but it is certain that not just anyone is encouraged by his unit to come here. Or the restrictions on what one may read are such that many people think it is pointless to visit the library. I come from a country that, unhappily, is known to have inefficient libraries, but until yesterday I would have found such a scene as we saw unimaginable. One felt as if one were in a cage where such a foolish wish as to do some research would be frustrated. Maybe behind the scenes a lucky few can take advantage of all that is available here, as if it were a true library.

In Peking it seems things have not come to such a pass, either at Beida or at the central library. (I went regularly to the latter in the winter of '57–'58; it was functioning normally and was crowded.) Is the Gang of Four to be blamed for the situation in Shanghai? Or is the frontal battle between the Four and the librarians at issue? Before taking us back to the elevators yesterday, they led us along a passage, also deserted, and at a midpoint there was a well allowing one to look down, floor after floor, to the ground floor; it brought suicide to mind.

When Chen asked me for my impressions, I turned the conversation around to the pressures a government can put on librarians, and I told her how American librarians had refused to give information to the FBI about what books their readers were consulting, and also how during fascism many librarians in Italy, while pretending to obey, were able to flout the order that forbade reading books by Jewish authors. I tried to make her see that a librarian's function is not to keep the material for himself but to defend the public's freedom to read—something that was far from the minds of the ex-victims we had met.

Cultural Matters
April 17

Classes canceled today, to celebrate the publication of Volume V of *Mao's Selected Works*. On either side of the avenue through the Institute grounds, there were long rows of red flags almost upright on their poles, a short distance above the ground, the way they are when set next to the doorways of private houses. One felt enwrapped in the festiveness of that red. The hoardings where the *dazibao* are posted were covered with red paper bearing joyous inscriptions. Weather was rather rainy, as it almost always is. Our interpreters were waiting for us at the gate, and went with us to line us up in a sort of procession—men apart from women, professors apart from students—and they handed us each a small stick with a small paper flag on which a slogan was written. We were marshaled along either side of the entrance avenue and the rear path that runs from my section to the film auditorium, as if we were waiting for something to pass by in between. And indeed, what was being awaited was the arrival of the books, which the Xin Hua bookshop was to distribute among the various units. We looked like children at a celebration. Finally, the books arrived, and everybody shouted slogans in a chorus and waved flags. Then we moved on into the auditorium. There were girls wearing red ribbons, and girls carrying bunches of paper flowers in both hands. The directors and the cadres sat on the stage. Behind them, to the right and left, two clusters of red flags in a slanting position. Everyone stood to sing *"Dongfang Hong"* ("The East Is Red"). Then, rather like altar boys bearing missals, several people walked single file up onto the stage, each carrying two packets of white books wrapped in transparent paper and tied with a thick red string. They deposited them side by side on a long table, but not before they had turned toward the audience to show them, as in the offertory; then, single file, they stepped down from the platform. The faces of the men and women seated behind the table were as impassive as masks. They looked either very wise or very stupid. Directors, students, workers, professors went in turn to the microphone to recite their pieces, which often ended with the words "to the very end" (to carry on the revolution, to follow the will of Chairman Mao, etc.). The attention and inattention, the involvement and indifference, the speaking style and the substance were those proper to a ritual. Very close to the Catholic rite. What was said was not important; the important thing was the unifying function of the ritual. An effective force.

Slogans were uttered in sequence. A voice—most often a woman's and usually very shrill—would shout in a crescendo: *"Tatatatata!"* And everyone present, raising his fist, would reply in a very rapid, rhythmic litany, *"Tatatatata!"* This would be repeated several times, and then again, after an interval of a few sentences. It was amusing to watch the faces, and the automatic, uninvolved way in which they raised their fists. But no one would have dreamed of not doing so. The rhythm matched the quickness of Chinese speech.

We have visited the Polytechnic, which was founded in 1896 as one of the first "modern" schools for the study of Western techniques. The two- or three-storied red brick buildings stand in a well-maintained park; the architectural style is somewhere between Kensington and South China; the later and even very recent additions are in the same style. In its first fifty-three years, the school produced not many more than five thousand graduates, and after Liberation, it was greatly enlarged and converted into a technical school. Faculty resistance to the Cultural Revolution was sustained and quite solid. There's no doubt that the Polytechnic will be a bastion of strength in the new program.

May 6

On the eve of May 1, a great festive spectacle was held at the enclosed stadium, with government people present—the ranking officials of Shanghai in the first row on a specially constructed platform, perhaps twenty-five people in all, two-thirds of them military. The general of the Nanjing garrison—Shanghai is also within its jurisdiction—was replaced; it seems that the Navy has major responsibility for our city. The public overflowed the available seats. As always, the grandstands were divided into sections and formed vast blocs of color, a spectacle within a spectacle: the white caps and aprons of the women textile workers; the blue of the metalworkers, multicolored paper flowers held by schoolgirls, the khaki of the soldiers. The program included a great variety of entertainment: a Chinese orchestra, a Western orchestra, chorus, soloists, *zaji,* animal acts, gymnastics, ballet, Peking opera.

At the very end, an extraordinary exhibition by the Shanghai Peking opera company. Dressed in track suits, the actors offered the most famous acrobatic excerpts from operas—chosen with great intelligence, in that they seemingly avoided the option between the old-exhumed and the new–now criticized. In close studied powerful movements accompanied by gongs and drums, they simultaneously demonstrated the continuity of their art and affirmed the essentiality of the new, the critical detachment with which bodies stripped of all costume observe that continuity. A *single* bit of scenery onstage toward the end, one chair of dark carved wood, which was felicitously made part of otherwise unadorned dancing. This was no mere allusion; it was a shouted symbol, the pinnacle of their art: "The Investigation of a Chair" is one of the last and the best of the modern Peking operas, which is now banished from public programs.

Storms of applause. . . .

"Is it the landlord's chair?" Roland asked his interpreter maliciously. The man grimaced and turned away.

It was raining in torrents when we left the theater. The city was alight with special illumination provided by the municipal government. We drove by thousands upon thousands of street lamps that outlined buildings and pinpointed slogans, and past multicolored arches supported by bamboo. People crowded the streets despite the hour and the rain—spectators and actors in this nocturnal intermission. As in Hanoi, the celebration consisted in looking at the lights. Here, with less happy resignation and more impatience.

The next morning, notwithstanding my tutors' urging, I didn't go to the ceremonies in the parks, but stayed at the hotel and slept.

In the course of the day, the rain did stop, and was followed by sultry heat. When it was almost dark, people poured out into the streets again, heading for the Bund to watch fireworks; the hum of the crowds reached my window, which was open in that summer heat.

The tourists came in droves, more than three hundred just to this one hotel, and the elevator was sorely overtaxed. The Dasha staff and their families and the foreign guests crowded up onto the terrace atop the hotel. Even our students came to find us on this occasion, or, rather, delegates representing all of them. Maybe it was because of its being evening or the holiday excitement—some of them had drunk wine at home with their parents—but in any case, our meeting was a little more spontaneous and cheerful than usual. My students are restless because they must leave fairly soon for an island off the coast, where they will spend about three weeks in an Army unit. Some look on it as a vacation; others think it's a waste of time and are hoping for rain so that they can stay indoors and study. Tang will go with them.

A political study session based on the fifth volume of *Mao's Selected Works,* with the usual Chinese professors. They started off by asking us, one by one, to say what we thought. Then the professors made their statements. In their speeches the only really interesting bit of information—however confused it was —was that concerning the grave disagreement among members of the commission regarding the publication of the works of Mao. The conflict was so serious that it had blocked publication for years.

Otherwise, the speeches were useful for understanding the orientation of the professors and, of course, of many others with them. Great importance was attached to the struggle among the factions (particularly underlined, as an important event, was the liquidation of Gao Gang and Rao Shushi at the beginning of the fifties). There was a frontal attack upon the forced collectivization in the Soviet Union after 1929 (for the first time in China I heard reported data—widely known in the West—on the economic disaster which then followed). They presented, as a contrast to Stalinist despotism, a supposed analogy between the method adopted in China for agricultural collectivization and the possibilist attitude of the early fifties in dealings with the "national bourgeoisie" in the cities. This last analogy is an arbitrary linking between the reliance upon a revolutionary movement from the bottom up in the countryside and the path of moderation regarding small capitalists, who were to be expropriated only gradually, and only as their entrepreneurial abilities became no longer indispensable. The glorification of this moderate path heralds, at least according to the intentions of one sector of society, the rehabilitation of the "national bourgeoisie" and attribution to it of ruling functions.

Today there is not one single topic of discussion that is new. Each and every issue is one raised by the Cultural Revolution. In turning backward, it is impossible to ignore the movement, so the attempt is to remix and muddle facts, pretending thereby to rebut it.

This is the case also when the thirties are recalled. Problems and dissension continue to be entangled with the knotty conflicts that were interwoven in those years among class components, political groupings, national and international ramifications, European radicalism and Chinese tradition. A Third Internationalist amalgam was fused, with Shanghai as its center, which was made up of militant minor intellectuals (the majority) and urban workers (the minority), who were both Stalinists and internationalists. In Yanan, Chinese autonomy was the dominant option, with the support at the base of soldiers/ex-brigands/and peasants. What bonded the two factions was their shared enemies, foreign (capitalist) imperialists and Chinese proprietors (chiefly landlords).

In the China of the twenties and thirties, the masses were primarily rural and peasant; they knew nothing of bourgeois civilization and lived immersed in a system of profound, sturdy values and hierarchies; in some areas, external aggression had helped to weaken the system, but it had not transformed it. In the course of the gigantic operation Mao carried out, this scale of values and of hierarchies was overturned; the upset was such that "it shook the world," and its repercussion continued long into the later phase in China.

In the wake of victory, the mighty energies released by the revolution formed a new corpus. Zhou Enlai was the major protagonist in this task of organization and stabilization. Within the new structure, new strata and new relationships came into being, as well as new conflicts, while in Europe the Stalinist edifice, which had served as a model in China, was coming apart—noisily so, after the events in Hungary. For a long time, Mao had been seeking ways out of the dilemma that imitating the Soviet model had created in China: on the one hand, Stalinist-bureaucratic centralism, which regimented everything and encased production programs, thought, and culture in a straitjacket of unitarian directives; on the other hand, the educated classes' demands for freedom. It was a dilemma in which the voice of the common workers was not heard.

In agreement with Zhou, Mao first tried to open up society with the Hundred Flowers campaign, in 1956, to encourage moves to explore social contradictions freely. But it was soon evident that the Hundred Flowers opened up no road for the people. Given the mass poverty and the tremendous social and cultural disparities that prevailed, in short order the demand for freedom became synonymous with the educated minorities' resistance to attacks against their privileges from below, and turned into a conservative (rightist) movement.

In order to achieve the freedom they deemed due their class, the educated minorities were, in effect—sometimes without even realizing it—asking for the repression of the people, who were called upon to outdo themselves as producers and to restrain themselves as consumers of cultural benefits, first and foremost, *so as to guarantee intensive scientific growth and autonomy on the higher cultural levels. This program implied a hierarchy of knowledge which helped to create a hierarchy of influence in successive strata of educated ruling elites—the Socialist bureaucracy, with its cultural appendages. Thus, even the minimal preconditions of an effective demand for power on the part of the common workers were eliminated. When the Stalinism-freedom choice is put in these terms, it shows itself to be false.*

In China, both the educated and the bureaucratic classes are the heirs of the scholars and, in addition, have adopted "bourgeois" values—that is, the economic and production-oriented values of capitalism. The old system is welded to the new, which is capitalistic even in the Socialist form of public ownership, and the ruling class is reproduced in the "bourgeois" species. The dominant classes have tended to transform themselves into modern elites.

Their antagonists are no longer the peasants but the basic producers of the contemporary world, the industrial workers. (They began to become relevant long before they constituted the numerical majority of Chinese workers.) In the conditions that obtain when capitalism takes on a despotic form, the workers are the only possible protagonists in the fight for freedom. *The political mediators in this situation will be the "revolutionary rebels." Those who uphold order in the interests of a Socialist development based on the power of educated elites are the despots of today and, all appearances to the contrary, the enemies of freedom.*

The Cultural Revolution was the beginning of the search for freedom by the workers, by the nonbourgeois opponents of an authoritarian system. Historical antecedents made this search dramatically difficult in China. In Europe the bourgeoisie put together elements inherited from a tradition that from its earliest beginnings gravitated toward the question of freedom—from the Greeks, who felt the founding of the city-state a double tragedy in the relationship between nature and freedom and between freedom and institutions, to Christianity, which legitimatized the institution by internalizing the problem and offering salvation to the individual. Even at the height of the Middle Ages, the nonidentity of Church and State made of the Church the supreme paradox, the institution that stood surety for the noninstitutional dimension, that inwardness of conscience in which the poor man is rich and the slave is free.

In China, the scholars ignored the question of freedom both in their thinking and in practice. The Confucianists did not have to betray any principle in order to effectuate nonfreedom; for them, ritual was the sole reality, and the sphere of the individual or of the conscience did not exist as a distinct realm. In Europe, the cultural elements transmitted to the people became tools in their revolt against class power, but in China the ideology the Confucianists transmitted to the people supplied them with no such weapon. For individuals who were not situated on the very highest levels, what resulted was a mixture of adherence and nonadherence to the official creed and a profound impoverishment of the faculty of independent judgment. Ontologically, what comes from the person who at a given moment holds power is what carries authoritative weight. Authority descends only from power.

The need for freedom is a characteristic of the individual in China, as it is everywhere else, and in China the need has found expression in the form of negation—in remotest antiquity, in Taoism, and later, in the various sinicized versions of Buddhism and its philosophical offshoots. These have infiltrated the institutional fabric without rending it, thanks to its great elasticity. (The power of the scholars owed its duration to the capacity to absorb contrary ideas rather than to repressive practices.) But among the people this has led to the permanent existence of a society which is "against" or "other" or subterranean; it knows nothing of the higher society with which nonetheless it has lived symbiotically, and which utilizes the concepts of negation in its own fashion. In periods of political crisis or when material conditions have become intolerable, the subterranean society has asserted itself through periodic explosions of violent revolt, which always have collapsed or have been defeated. (The most recent was the Tai Ping Rebellion, which adopted Christianity as its mode of negative thought; it lasted for almost fifteen years, spread through entire provinces, and left in its wake thirty million dead and a devastated country.)

The victorious revolution that Mao guided was also, in large measure, the continuation of these rebellions. He was able to make his revolt one with that of the people because he shared with them the spirit of negation and destruction. In Western understanding, this spirit is mistakenly taken to be anarchic, and Mao himself, in his youth, somewhat so mistook it. His support of the international labor movement has been construed as his having adopted its utopian aspects. However, one should lend credence not so much to Mao's youthful Westernism as to what he himself said as an old man: "You are Western philosophers, I am a Chinese philosopher." Negation is immanent in history, revolution must be continuous. From Chinese tradition, he drew the elements that led him to transcend both the idea of a completed revolution (which leads to the rise of conservatism) and the definition of communism as the final phase of history. He is reproached for a millenarianism that, in fact, has no part in his vision of an uninterrupted becoming in which new contradictions are ever emerging in the relationships among men. In the last period of his life, he was convinced that inevitably the power of minorities must be continually reestablished, just as, simultaneously and no less inevitably, the struggle of subject masses for their own liberation must continue.

But his unwillingness and his inability to move outside the Chinese universe placed limitations on the great creativeness of his ideas. Within that universe, the revolution of the peasants could grow and be carried through as the negation and overturning of the scholars' power. The truth that bound Mao to the people and made him their greatest interpreter was the fact of his being at one with the peasants and, like them, both inside and against despotism. Since Liberation, the urban proletariat has become the protagonist of the class struggle. The proletarian revolution cannot move forward with Chinese cultural weapons only, for Chinese culture does not transcend the limits of the society that has produced it. This Mao knew; he also was a man of the May Fourth Movement. But he had been driven back into the Chinese universe because he saw that it was essential to lead the peasants to victory without making them into tools serving the power goals of their leaders, of other classes, or of other countries. A withdrawal in the direction of even cultural self-sufficiency occurred after the break with the Soviet Union.

A cultural limitation obscured Mao's description of a Socialist society as one that is divided (and not a monolith that can express itself through a single party) and obstructed the class struggle. New ideas oriented toward communism require new forms. Mao seems not to have looked for these forms. The only system of guaranties to the creation of which he contributed is that of independent and self-sufficient base organizations (the very ones that now, and not by chance, are being dismantled). The hardest struggle lying ahead will turn on this issue, but it will not be readily visible from outside. For the rest, essentially Mao emphasized the transforming power of ideology, which acts dialectically to fracture the organizational rigidity. But when the instruments for maintaining mass democracy are lacking, indoctrination is inevitable no matter what ideas are propagated; the language of freedom will be converted into dogma, which is the tool exclusively of the organization, the instrument of enslavement.

A serpent bites its own tail. Mao came to count less and less on a quick solution, and his reaction was to put ever greater distance between himself and his collaborators, and to distrust intellectuals. During the Cultural Revolution, when the people broke their organic, contradictory bond with the cadres and attacked the Party, he sided with the people.

But once the monolithic institution—the Party—was shattered and mediators were lacking, the only authentic connection that remained was between the leader and the masses. The Chairman represented authority independent of ruling power; he was still a voice from outside, a guiding voice of independent thought. It was no solution, because the connection between people and leader becomes merely symbolic if it endures a long time without mediation. And the connection without mediation also becomes unreal because it presupposes a compact and united people (something that happens in any part of the world only in exceptional circumstances, such as under the serious threat of foreign enemies), and excludes a place where the different ideas and interests of the various social groups can be expressed. The concept of the Chinese people as a unity derives, as we have seen, from the cultural inheritance bequeathed by the scholars and by

*their peasant counterparts. If one does not discriminate between this culture and
the workers' demand for freedom in modern form, it is a sign that one cannot
handle the contradiction between workers and peasants. The new class grows on
this contradiction and uses it for its own ends.*

*Only in a discontinuous and contradictory way did Mao come to see the
power system that he himself had devised not as proletarian dictatorship polluted
by bad leaders—"capitalist roaders"—but as a form of capitalist despotism within
which islands of popular power surfaced and grew. In 1965, when he went to
Shanghai to unleash from that workers' city the Cultural Revolution, he was in
no position to control it, and it was to explode in his hands. From then on, his
remoteness from the majority of the old leaders grew until it changed into hatred.
In his last years, defeated, half the prisoner of those who were waiting for his death
to arrest his wife and the others closest to him, he tried to the end, with means
altogether inadequate, to protect the people from the consequences of the factional
struggle with which the ruling class was suffocating the laborious growth of a
popular opposition.*

Freedom

We "struggled," and we managed to win for ourselves two days of joyous
freedom: a Saturday and Sunday in Suzhou, *alone.* There were no political
obstacles, for Suzhou is a peaceful city, it's been open to tourists for years, and
it's near Shanghai. The objections came from the Institute clan, but were finally
overcome when several people declared that they would not go on the trip if it
were not possible for us to be on our own. We finally obtained a letter from the
Institute for the Lüxingshe office, which got our train tickets, made our hotel
reservations, and arranged for a bus from the station to the hotel. In Suzhou,
we were met at the hotel by a Lüxingshe employee, who made us a little speech
of sensible brevity, and left us to ourselves.

Each of us was able—alone, if he wished—to walk through this, the most
beautiful city in China, to stroll like any ordinary mortal along streets of white
houses with black doors, perfect shapes beneath plane trees that, high above the
rooftops, overhang them in long long rows stretching toward some invisible end.
The luminosity and warmth and freshness of shade and sun. . . . Women and
beautiful children, with immense eyes in oval, full faces. . . . As in Shanghai,
people do their washing in little tubs out on the street; beside every doorway,
there is the refuse bin . . . slow-moving boats on the canals, often loaded with
waste. . . . This is a tranquil, joyful place, where even poverty is beauty—thanks
not only to nature but to enduring work by human hands. To walk about in this
city is to enter and leave garden after garden; some are complex constructions
in which vegetation and open spaces dominate, others have galleried pavilions,
and still others are rock gardens, but water is everywhere. People crowd the little

bridges to watch the big fish below. The long long walls, edged with tiles, are little higher than a man is tall; they are never straight, and their imperceptible curves delight the eye and erase all measure of time. On this trip, for us there was no programmed rushing hither and yon; one could sit lazily on a stone bench in a garden, eating apples and little cakes. . . . We took the bus to Xi Yuan, and then climbed on foot up Tiger Hill, pausing in the pine grove beneath the great pagoda. . . .

In this city of 600,000 inhabitants, people stroll in the evening the way they do in a Sicilian village. *"Hua Qiao,"* they would say to us—"Overseas Chinese" —even to Dagmar, with her mop of blond hair; if they could mistake us for Chinese, it was an indication of how alien racism is to them in high places of their civilization such as Suzhou, and when they do not feel threatened or repressed. We sat on the side of a little bridge, and had long chats with a group of students, and then with some elderly women who joined them. How easy the rapport would be with this intelligent and communicative people if we—we and they—were not hindered and stupefied by the intolerable overwhelming weight of the apparatus. It manages to obscure even the joy of nature.

But these two days belong to me; they are a confirmation that love for China is possible.

Another suicide at Fudan, a few days ago.

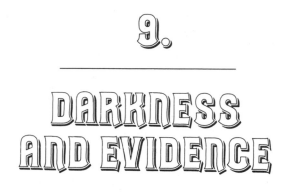

9.

DARKNESS
AND EVIDENCE

More Cultural Questions
May 18, 1977

The students have been authorized to ask me a few questions about Italy. They're full of curiosity, I discover; their indifference had all been put on. My answer to one question dumbfounded them. The wages of an Italian worker are much higher than those of a Chinese worker. Total incomprehension when I refer to the youth movement or to independently owned radio stations. "But who organizes them?" When I say that they organize themselves, they don't believe me. When I refer to the "presalary"—financial aid given, free and clear, to needy university students in Italy—Zhang hastens to add, "A ridiculous amount," and I am obliged to make clear that it comes to more than twice the average wage of a Chinese worker. The students idolize Fiat—the great automobile manufacturing company they wish they had—and for the life of them cannot understand why I should find so much to criticize in what for them is my country's one attraction, why I actually maintain that if the Chinese copy that production method, it will be ruinous for them.

I adopt extreme measures: I tell them about Togliattigrad. That shuts them up, but it doesn't convince them.

I've given a few lectures on the geography and history of Italy. Because the students have trouble following me when I speak Italian, Zhang had asked me to prepare written summaries. Now, at the students' own request, I have to prepare three conversations on current topics. Zhang transmits their requests; he can't not, but he is terrified. "Don't write any summary this time, it's not necessary." Translation: Since the conferences must be held, let them be held, but it's better if they don't understand anything, let's help them not to understand anything.

The present directives opening a window on the outside world are related to a broad policy decision to abandon Chinese economic autonomy. The choice is basic to a full resumption of power by elites that have been frustrated and threatened with disintegration by the economic strategy of poverty and self-sufficiency. But if they are to control the working people, it is essential that they preserve the hierarchy of knowledge and even maximum ignorance among the people today when, to accomplish their plan, they are obliged to subject workers to greatly intensified labor, and to reject their cultural demands. In particular, information about how people actually live in the capitalist West (too well to picture it in the negative, and too badly to imitate it) would risk making the people ungovernable and would contribute toward refueling a revolt that for the moment has been halted by the Left's having been defeated.

The contrast is so glaring that it explains why Chinese professors are concerned when, in order to carry out the directives, they must leave us foreigners at least some leeway in informing our students about the realities of life in our countries. Their concern turns into positive panic when the subject is worker and youth movements. The one loophole is to fall back on the safe terrain of anti-Nazi resistance—as, in the case of China, one falls back on the patriotic war against the Japanese.

Walking stick, parasol, folding scissors, back scratcher, acetylene torch, phonograph, penholder, photo album and corner tabs, blotter and ink pad, toilet chain, fly swatter, ankle boots, derby, top hat, night cap, Panama hat, washtub, rolling the hoop, signet ring, tie pin, tippet, duster, veil, mantilla, muff. . . . This is the Chinese image of the bourgeois West which emerges from the glossary currently in use which I am translating into Italian. Other entries: monocle, étagère, canapé, pince-nez, spats, silk stockings, jabot. . . .

Other word lists conjure up an Italy one has heard of from one's parents. . . . Sicily . . . elderly aunts. The words and the objects, the material civilization one is imbued with. . . . Everything can be told or explained but not this, which must be conveyed in images, the only medium that can give some notion of the changes in our society in the last fifty—and even more in the last twenty—years.

How far do the blindness, the impossibility of approaching the outside world, the being cooped up inside China as if it were a vast cage—how far do they reach into the upper ranks? Is there really some high and secret and unattainable place to which at least information gets through in a normal way? It happens sometimes, but rarely, that a Western traveler tells of some miraculous meeting with one or another Chinese who is informed and up to date. But such meetings do have the semblance of miracles; they happen by chance; we can find no linkage among them. Well, people will say, there's always the Academy of Sciences. Then they read articles prepared by Academy members for Deng Xiaoping, and they throw up their hands. Witke's interviews with Jiang Qing convey a pathetic image of her as being totally a prisoner in China as well as during those terrible visits to the U.S.S.R., hemmed in by walls that prevented her from even formulating clearly her project to revamp the entertainment field, and deprived, as she was, of all tools. And this despite her being the wife of the Chairman. Or was it because of that? One does have the impression, sometimes, of leaders being bound by invisible chains, of a harsh, unremitting blackmail that kept them not only from speaking clearly but also from being able to obtain the means indispensable for creative work. One is all the more persuaded to think this when one considers the things that are imputed to some leaders—as when Jiang Qing is "accused" of having arranged a private screening of *Gone with the Wind* or asking a singer to record an old song.* Their every move, their every word picked up and recorded by spies—including things said by the Chairman in private, as it turns out from the formal charges now being produced.

But the blindness affects the accusers, too. The protective measures, the controls, and the repression have little by little extended everywhere, and become dominant. The leaders have castrated themselves.

In recent days, there have been more trials and executions. Executions by firing squad take place not far from the Institute; some people say they've heard the shots. This morning, I saw a crowd assembling for the confirmation of sentences. (According to current judicial practice, sentences are pronounced by popular assemblies; in practice, the assemblies merely confirm the judgment already reached.) According to the Hong Kong papers, delinquency is on the rise. I don't know how true this may be. I would think, rather, that order is being maintained by means of very rigid control.

Further moves against followers of the Four . . . arrests, convictions. . . . How reliable these rumors are will be known only with time.

Foreigners

Semi-invisible human jetsam floats about this city—the foreign residents who have lived here for many years, either because they are married to Chinese or for some other reason. There are a few at the Institute; I met them at the foreigners' mess. Now that Tang has gone off with the students, I walk over there alone at noon. On the way, I pass students and professors also bound for

---

*Only recently (1981) did Italian scholars of the theater come to know that Jiang Qing had promoted and realized the filmed reproduction of dozens and dozens of traditional Chinese theater pieces for use as documents and study materials. It is likely that Jiang Qing's request to the Shaoxing opera singer (see p. 254) fell into this category of research work.

lunch, enameled bowls in hand. Sheets upon sheets of paper, white, red, pink, are plastered on the walls, one over the other; they are gradually loosened and shredded by the wind.

In the big, dimly lighted room, an elderly, fat Frenchwoman is often seated at the narrow end of the bare table. The weather is not hot yet, but she's already beginning to feel short of breath, and she will have turned on the fan. "It's funny," she says, "but after all these years I've still not got used to this climate." She is the widow of a Chinese whom she married long ago in Paris. Roland lends her *Le Monde* and *Le Nouvel Observateur;* to me she confesses that reading today's French papers makes her feel lost, everything seems so strange to her. She is mildly shocked—for reasons of modesty, not intolerance—by the photos of nudes and the queer ways in which people dress. About what is happening here she knows little more than do we. She lives in a room at the Institute. I asked her whether she has the use of a kitchen; she said no.

There is also a little Russian, with a little mustache, probably in his fifties; he, too, years ago had married a Chinese. He sits opposite me. For a long time we didn't exchange a word, as if that were something one didn't do. Now we smile and say hello. Before he leaves, he always goes into the kitchen and chats a moment with the Chinese cook, the woman who helps him and clears the tables, and whatever young transient may be there. A person who reaches this point with people here has achieved a genuine relationship.

One day, I made up my mind and I spoke to him in Russian. He is, I discovered, quite a sensitive and cultivated man. He's shown me periodicals he continues to receive from the Soviet Union. The Chinese keep him busy doing translations and compiling dictionaries. At the moment, he is translating from German some writings of Lenin that are not included in the Russian edition of the *Collected Works.* "Have you lived here a long time?" I asked him once.

"A long time, yes." He usually exchanges a few cordial words with Kieu, and goes off alone, wheeling his bicycle at his side.

Another guest, recently arrived, is an elderly Austrian, with a big bald head, rather teary eyes, and the air of a whipped dog. They say he comes from Peking. Pascale has managed to exchange a few words with him. He told her that in Peking, after the earthquake, the walls and some gates had been knocked down. This happened many years ago, not after the recent earthquake. Evidently, before coming to Shanghai he had returned to Peking after a long absence, spent who knows where. Every day, before touching his soup, he takes a plastic envelope from his pocket and sprinkles something that looks like black dried leaves over the broth. He finally explained to me one day that it is seaweed; it's good for you, full of iodine.

Other foreigners, who don't come to the mess, I've heard spoken of or seen briefly at city affairs. One is an elderly German woman, who married a local man, too; she's lived here for fourteen years and has never learned Chinese.

If I were to remain here, I would become just like those people. Everything is fairly quiet around me. Who knows where the treatment reserved for me stands on the isolation scale. My impression is that in the last weeks it has intensified, but perhaps it's only that my powers of resistance are lessening. They are allowing me to work a lot now—in my case, as seriously as possible when I am preparing reading materials regarding language, and with this part of my work they do not interfere. Insofar as possible, they meet halfway my tacit request not to be subjected to an excess of political propaganda. In compensation, however, they do their utmost to see to it that I know about and understand as little as possible of what is going on.

An unknowing foreigner experiences the isolation for a while without being aware of it. But the moment comes when he realizes that he is being misled. This has now happened with Mohammed, who has protested because "my interpreter is always lying to me."

There is another type of isolation, which is accompanied by the highest honors. This is the case with old friends of China, guests who have been well treated for years and who travel about surrounded by assistants and wet nurses, like mandarins. These old men know many things, but the ability to communicate with the non-Chinese world has died in them.

The path of knowledge seems blocked for all, but this is not so. There remains a small, authentic, daily human dimension. It is from this that one must take off. For some time the Russians have known this truth.

Like many other people, when writing a letter I've got into the habit of talking mentally with the censor even before I talk with my correspondent. Of all our dependencies, this is the worst because it implies the destruction of any relationship other than the one between you and whatever or whoever controls you.

The only genuine relationships are those among foreigners. For Olga not only do I feel affection, but also I trust her unqualifiedly. She comes for a talk almost every evening. She sits in an armchair, her body slightly heavier from her pregnancy, her face beautiful and serene, and we drink coffee or wine together, while we leaf through magazines from her country or mine. She is a woman of a joyous, free sensuality, and she has transmitted this, as well as intelligence, to her little girl. Aymin loves to be caressed; in play she lets herself go with passion, she rolls about on my bed until she falls asleep. She's jealous of the conversations between her mother and me, and does her utmost to interrupt them and bring attention back to herself. She finds dozens of ways to show off. She will begin by reciting verses she's learned in kindergarten but then elaborates on them and invents her own, mixing words together until she reduces nursery rhymes that are intended to be political to their true nature of nonsense.

Olga has a very precise sense of her own dignity and personal freedom, and she finds the continual interferences and controls more unendurable than do the others. Also, she sees clearly that, all verbal homage notwithstanding, the comrades from the Third World are given the least consideration. After many requests, counterrequests, interviews, and consultations, they have not even allowed her to take part in a course on acupuncture which had been organized for the Belgians, French, and Swiss; several Africans and Lebanese were admitted, too, but they are doctors, whereas Olga is only a nurse. At first, the authorities put her off by claiming that all the doctors speak Chinese. One does wonder at times about such childish lies. Those doctors live at our hotel, they eat in our dining room, we meet them and talk with them every day. How can it be supposed that Olga doesn't know whether or not they speak Chinese?

Olga, Dagmar, and Uta invite me often for lunch or dinner. The Egyptians, too, are kind and affectionate. Since January, Mohammed has had his whole family here—his wife, seven-year-old son Hosam, and daughter Noha. Noha is a bit younger than Aymin, and is looked upon with suspicion by the latter, who fears competition in her previously unchallenged dominion over us all. Hosam has delicate features and dark-blond curly hair. He is a thoughtful, meditative child; he asks his mother questions about the first man, about Satan, about good and evil. He attends the Chinese elementary school, and has grown more dispirited every day; he cannot adapt, and even resists learning the language. Like all the very young children, Noha responds better; over the months, she has grown less aggressive, perhaps through the efforts of the Chinese kindergarten, perhaps because she is dominated by Aymin, who, behind a show of indifference, is aiming to make Noha her personal slave. The relationship between the two is not peaceful; there is an enduring reciprocal jealousy with respect to the adults, and outbursts of rivalry. In the morning, on the bus, they have a contest to conquer these or those knees—first and foremost, Pascale's. Aymin's face bespeaks such anguish when Noha gets there ahead of her that Pascale resigns herself to holding them both, one on each knee. Comes the moment for them to be dropped off at the kindergarten, and Aymin becomes openly rebellious, Noha cast down and disconsolate.

Several days ago, while we were in the midst of our political study session, which seemed as if it would never end, Aymin and Noha suddenly started to shout and race about the room; then they vanished. For the return to the hotel, they were borne separately onto the bus, soaking wet and covered with mud from head to foot; they must have rolled in the mud, and then got under some faucet. Noha buried her head in her mother's bosom, and refused to sit up.

Since the start of the second semester, Mohammed's wife has been teaching at the Institute, too. She comes from an intellectual background, and for a Muslim woman her ways are free, "modern." But in her own apartment at the hotel, when she withdraws to pray or when she receives me in her sitting room and offers me coffee or chocolate, her big, ample body and the very sweet expression of her eyes do put me in mind of something familiar—a woman from the Sicilian lower-middle class of twenty or thirty years ago. Yet this woman has also an unknown dimension, religious and worldly qualities that are strange to me and fascinate me.

"Madame Naga [his wife], Hosam, and Noha wish very much to be in your company, they have such a liking for you, and they would hope that you might dine with us this evening." Thus Mohammed, who came to extend the invitation. I'm the only person, I believe, who is on a footing of equality with the Egyptians; the other "Common Marketers" ignore them or blandly jolly them along, while between them and the Peruvians there is a slight competitiveness. Unhappily, the possibility of our communicating is beset by language difficulties. Naga speaks only Arabic, and Mohammed's English is worse than mine.

By what art I don't know, but Naga managed to prepare the perfect Mediterranean meal—fresh greens, olive oil, rice; food that is seasoned yet easily digestible, like the vegetable dishes one eats in Greece. "We've made nothing special for you, it's our usual dinner." In part that was true, because Naga cooks for Mohammed every evening; but it was also true that tonight's dinner was prepared with me in mind. This was clear from the way the table was laid. It was laden with food, but at my place there was a larger dinner plate, and everything seemed to be oriented toward me. Never have I been the "guest" to such a degree and in so lordly a one—I say "lordly" advisedly, for in homage to my age and out of the respect they wished to show me, they treated me the way Arabs would treat a man.

The food was too plentiful. Standing beside me (her husband and the children were seated, but not she), Naga kept filling my plate. I didn't manage to finish the soup, which was made with meat; then there was an enormous serving of rice wrapped in vine leaves, then more meat and more vegetables. At that point, Naga, smiling wordlessly, took my fork, cut a piece of meat, and held it out to me. And slowly, gently, but firmly, she continued like that to the end. Then, ladling out the rest of the broth, she fed it to me by the spoonful.

This was very strange. My European-conditioned stomach wanted to say no. But a pleasure revived from I don't know what remote sphere persuaded me to accept, and to feel sure that if I surrendered completely it would do me no harm. It struck me then as "natural"—that which is in fact a product of history and culture. Naga's demeanor was gentle and utterly dignified—she who was not a servant served. And I was experimenting with masculine privilege, with what it is for a man to abandon himself to the attentions of the mother-servant that is woman. The depth of my rebellion equaled that of my pleasure.

I am reading poems that Ho Chi Minh wrote in classical Chinese while he was in a Kuomintang prison. They have been well translated into French by a Vietnamese:

> *La rose s'ouvre et la rose*
> *Se fane sans savoir ce que rose*
> *Fait. Il suffit qu'un rose parfum*
> *S'égare dans une maison d'arrêt*
> *Pour que hurlent au coeur de l'enfermé*
> *Toutes les injustices du monde.*

Hangzhou
May 30

The miracle of Suzhou has not been repeated. The trip to Hangzhou was organized by the municipality's cultural section for foreign teachers at the three universities—Fudan, Shida, and the Institute for Foreign Languages. Only thirteen foreigners were in the group, for many people did not go. With us were numerous Chinese: two members from the cultural office, one from our Institute, ten interpreters (one apiece, except for the two Japanese wives and Felicitas). For some of our escorts, an occasion such as this offers one of their few opportunities to take a trip—what's more, in comfortable circumstances—and, understandably, as many as possible try to take advantage of it.

The site that has been celebrated throughout the centuries is the lake to the west of the city, which is called, precisely, the Western Lake. We were put up in a lakeside hotel (the rooms with the panoramic view were assigned to the Japanese), and for the three days of our holiday we walked in the immense complex of parks that surround the lake. This enabled me to correct a mistaken impression I had got from descriptions and photographs, which made them seem some kind of enormous Peking Summer Garden, even if more genuine and with less junk. In a sense, this is the least "Chinese" landscape I have seen in China; here human intervention in nature has not resulted in a garden that is monstrously artificial. Contrived aspects are not lacking, but they are attenuated (and enhanced) by vast, tree-filled spaces, English-style meadows, and paths by the lake or among the groves of trees that mantle the hills. These were "private" parks in the past, but the residence of the scholar was, in actuality, the one great public domain. A rich and joyous nature has been interpreted with extreme intelligence. There is a sense of great ease, or, at least, the dream of great ease in imagining oneself free. Everything very well maintained; the makeshift, dusty appearance so prevalent elsewhere is missing here.

But the delight promised by a Hangzhou sojourn proved to be a dream that did not come true. Our guardians were gripped by an activist fever that, given the place and the circumstances, was gratuitous and incomprehensible. Not for one moment did they abandon us, compensating by their obsessive omnipresence for their inability to give us one iota of serious information. If I hadn't dug it up from other sources, I'd never have known that the island called the Lonely Hill, which we walked over, is the site of a palace built by Qian Long, the great Qing emperor, and of the library of ancient books he founded, which was gravely damaged by the Tai Ping; that today there is a modern library there, a museum, and Buddhist statues. . . . Our escorts had us rushing frantically in a group from one place to the next, without allowing each person a moment to pause, to look, to reflect—in a word, to take in what lay all around him. Chen, whom I had glued to my side, carried zeal to the point of abjuring me, "See that tree, see that stone, see that flower!" . . . Not for an instant did she allow me to forget her presence.

As for the local Lüxingshe escorts, their sole concern was that we should not become aware that certain art works and monuments have vanished, and they were entirely successful in giving us no information whatever. In the vicinity of the Yellow Dragon Spring, we came to a slight elevation dominated by a kind of platform, which you climbed a few steps to reach, only to find it empty. "What used to be here?" No answer. At that moment, the Hangzhou Lüxingshe people were nowhere to be found. I thought it plausible to suppose that some Buddhist building had once stood there. The dragon's grotto was empty, too; once upon a time there had been a Guan Yin and other statues there. These depredations had occurred during the Cultural Revolution. There was nothing shameful about this—especially for people *opposed* to the Cultural Revolution, such as our guides—and no civilization has ever come to an end as a result of statues being broken. But the tactic of lying and concealing wins out over the purported intent of showing the negative aspects of the Cultural Revolution.

As we were passing from one garden to another, over the dike built by Su Dongpo and along Bo Juyi's dike, and I was being cruelly persecuted by tireless chatter, I asked myself why there should be this mania, as it seems to me, to fill up everything with talk or written signs, this *horror vacui,* the ever-present obsession with the analytical, the inability to perceive the sound of silence. Apart from the ironic contrast between this reality and the exotic notions we Westerners entertain about some vague "East," one knows for a fact from the great written works and the paintings that Chinese civilization has been the opposite of this: Chan Buddhism and Taoism. These landscapes that *demand* silence— was it not Chinese who created them?

What upsets me is not the fortuitous cheekiness that is a personality trait of single individuals; the phenomenon is a general one, and it is spreading. Perhaps the only possible answer is that it is a question of two poles: the *no* of Taoism and of Chan Buddhism opposed to *realpolitik* China, which is the second pole. But then you confront another paradox. Chinese thought, both ancient and modern and of whatever tendency, is dialectical. So how can this deep-rooted dialectical propensity accord with such total structural dogmatism, with the total absence of a transition from the "filled-to-the-full imperative" to the absolute *no* of the Great Void? It seems that this dialectic exists only at a very high level, or else among the common people, in their closed and minute analysis of their particular milieu. The two spheres do not communicate. The attempt, which to date has failed, to introduce the materialist dialectic is also the attempt to bring those at the bottom up to the capability of abstract thought —to leave behind their condition as dependent creatures.

I had one high point, during the morning, in a boat out on the lake. Who knows how it happened, but for a short while they had forgotten all about me. The sun was very pale, and the water milky but with bright, luminous reflections. Long, dark rowboats were moving over the lake, carrying people in colorful clothes; the boats were shining and transparent, as if fashioned of light, concrete yet unreal as they swept over that liquid mother-of-pearl. Their bamboo oars were like those you see in Chinese paintings. The light had an improbable, indescribable quality—the point of truth, where the sublime and the lowest are not to be told apart. You could fix no frontiers between the work of nature and that of man.

Among the boats there was one modern canoe, paddled by men in red and blue overalls. It was absorbed into the context. For nine hundred years, they can go on painting their socialist realist oils, with muscular rubicund types gesturing toward the future and thrusting their chests far forward of their buttocks; but they will be nine hundred years of phoniness.

I have had my first closeup view of tea under cultivation. Beautiful, like vineyards, like flower nurseries on the Riviera. . . . In the light of this fluvial southern land, the shrubs evoke a rustic, idyllic Mediterranean, the breath of a vast land but with no salty scorched aridity. The chairman of the plantation brigade's Revolutionary Committee was one of those peasant managers who have nothing of the bureaucrat about them. This man talked only about factual things having to do with his work; he explained to us in detail how tea is cultivated and cured. (He had started out with a few of the routine political clichés. We all know them by heart; anyone of us present could have recited them in his place and saved him the trouble.) Without having to be asked, he told us that the property in his commune operates at two levels—that is, accounting by squad has been done away with—but that the Gang of Four had wanted it to revert to three levels. Any child knows that even in the caricatures the Gang of Four are accused of precisely the opposite. His meaning was clear: "We have to say 'Down with the Gang of Four,' and so we say it, but just don't let them meddle with our Socialist structure." The elastic resistance one formerly found among intellectuals has spread, now with other functions, to base cadres of this type.

We saw the first harvest of the famous Long Jing (Dragon Well) green tea drying, gently turned over by hand in warmed vats, and we drank it brewed in the excellent water of Hangzhou. This is among the most highly prized teas of Asia, and has been grown here for fourteen hundred years. The local brigade is made up of peasants who are better educated and better off than the average.

This trip out into the country provided a sense of serenity and well-being that was matched that evening by a moment of freedom. Dagmar, Uta, Felicitas, and I went out alone after dinner, and walked along one of the lake's many banks, where it lengthens almost like a river between two rows of hills. Vast silence, stars, the lighted windows of small houses mirrored on the water. . . . Along dark avenues among the trees, couples were walking arm in arm, often wheeling bicycles at their sides. Others sat out in the meadows, singing with strong, melodious voices. They were singing from the hill on our side, for the echo replied, very clear, from the other. We were enfolded by sound until we no longer knew which were the voices, which the echoes. "Like stereo," Dagmar said. We sat down on a wooden bench by the lakeside; it was like the kind we have in gardens at home. For someone coming from Shanghai, this was like being in another world. "Paradise," a Chinese proverb calls Hangzhou. A paradise for the poor, as it was for great gentlemen of the past.

Yet these are not tranquil people. For many years, Hangzhou was one of the most tormented areas in the country. It was closed not only to foreigners, except for brief intervals, but also for a long time to the Chinese, too. Serious labor unrest, many strikes. . . . The province, Zhejiang, is one of the richest in China. The official word is that the Gang of Four ruined it. (The same is claimed of Sichuan, another rich and cultivated province.)

For these reasons, it would have been inconceivable even now to obtain permission to come here without escorts, and even with escorts, the city proper was virtually forbidden us. No great loss, I believe, since from the little glimpse I had of it—one main street seen for the few minutes allowed us to shop before we left, and during the bus trip from the hotel to the station—it is rather characterless, similar to the new or relatively modern sections of many Chinese cities, which are bare and enlivened only by trees.

One thing in the city they did show us—the silk factory that had been one of the most famous bases of the Gang of Four. I don't know whether they took us to this particular factory because they thought they could not avoid doing so or whether they were counting on a good propaganda effect.

We talked with a small *ganbu* who described herself as a "member of the office." There was neither hide nor hair to be seen of the factory's Revolutionary Committee; what's more, to judge by the sample we encountered, the people who now staff its "office" know nothing about production and very little about the factory itself. (During our visit, it became quite clear that the *ganbu* had no experience whatever with the work done in the various units.)

In an irritable voice, she delivered first the "brief account" of the factory's history, in the course of which we heard an expression new to the repertory, or recently exhumed: "The factory was one of the buildings *constructed during the First Five-Year Plan under the guidance of Chairman Mao and Premier Zhou Enlai.*" She then moved on to her main theme, which was an attack on the ex–vice-chairman of the Revolutionary Committee, Weng Shenhe, and on this she dwelled for the rest of her talk. Apart from Weng's connection with the Four, his principal misdeeds seem to have been his program to reform the cadres and his criticism of several older leaders. The latter were tortured by having their hair cut off and their hands tied behind their backs. "Weng established a Fascist dictatorship." In 1975, after Ji Dengkui came to establish order in the factory, toward autumn, Weng was arrested. (This was the period of the resurgence of the right, when Deng was preparing his programs, planning for the publication of his magazine, etc.) After April, 1976, he was *not* set free; he remained in prison. Today, the older workers have come to realize that it was the Four who were guilty of everything. A production-incentive campaign is in progress, ditto Socialist emulation, overtime work is "free"; to this end, the workers have been divided up in groups—praise for the groups producing the most.

In this factory, more than in any of the others we have visited, a genuine enslavement of the workers seems to have been put into effect—of women workers, that is, since the majority of the factory hands are women. (However, the other factories visited are all located in Shanghai, where, no matter what, it must not be so easy to use heavy-handed methods; also, in Shanghai we have not visited any of the Gang of Four's "citadels.") The work in silk filatures is very hard, particularly in the initial phases from cocoon to spinning. The women must keep their hands immersed in hot water for long periods; others handle the very thin fibres, keeping them taut, which hurts the fingers. (I've seen some snap the thread between their teeth, to go faster.) In the weaving sections, the noise is unbearable and is amplified by the size of the sheds. I don't know whether in richer countries remedies have been found for these problems; in any event, when one works in such conditions, steps to foster Socialist emulation and unpaid overtime are not only antilabor but inhuman. The workers looked wretched; they kept their heads lowered and did not even glance at us, to emphasize their apartness. We were unable to exchange one word with anyone except the *ganbu*— neither a worker, union member, nor manager, young or old.

Chen, on the trip back: "The situation that had been created in that factory was such that there was a lot of absenteeism, so much that in some cases production was halted." Once upon a time, she added, Hangzhou had been a flourishing market town; one found more numerous products there, and of better quality, than in Shanghai. (Chen's husband comes from Shaoxing, a small city in Zhejiang Province.) When merchandise grew scarce, hoarding and black marketing began. Shanghai no longer receives merchandise from Zhejiang regularly.

Chen was being much more sincere now than when she was telling the little story about how provinces did not want to send supplies to Shanghai because it was the citadel of the Four. And she was now telling the truth; or at least, the rumors among the people in Shanghai agree. And it has happened to me in the Friendship Store that when I have asked for things produced in Hangzhou, the clerks shrug and reply, "We don't know whether they will ever come in. We can only promise for sure what is made in Shanghai." Justifiably or not, the people of Shanghai are all convinced that they are swotting away for the whole of China without getting enough in return.

Chen has also told me that during the Cultural Revolution, when she and her husband were living in Peking, he went by train with a group of other young men, first to Hangzhou and then to Shaoxing. There the group broke up, some going off in one direction, some in another. "I wrote to my husband that that was enough, and he should come home." But two of the men continued on by foot, according to the original plan, as far as Jing Gang Shan, which is farther south in the mountainous region near the Hunan border. (Mao Zedong and Zhu De established the first revolutionary base here between October, 1927, and April, 1928, after their defeats of August and September, 1927.) In those days, millions of young men traveled to the most remote places, even as far as Xinjiang, in the far northwest; not only their train travel but also their food was free, and "they took advantage of the opportunity."

"It's all right for educated young people to get out into the country, but their abilities must be made use of. If they're set to hoeing, they get depressed, and in that way young people no longer have any incentive to study," continued Chen.

In a poor country like China, where the number of those who can go on to more advanced study is extremely small, I believe it will be a long time before disincentives of any kind—even hoeing—will have much effect. The demand for education is widespread and urgent. If the selective criteria which are now being outlined for the recruitment of students are actually put into effect, the distance between those who study and those who remain ignorant will be greatly increased, and the violent conflicts that will result among the youthful elements in society will be the first to explode and throw the new order into a crisis. Conservatives continue to quibble over the allegedly utopian nature of Mao's choices, but they are the only realistic ones for anyone who does not aim at repressing the people—even violently.

Chen referred also to an objective problem—the scarcity of cultivable land —and to the need to build up reserves. Chen is in good faith and full of goodwill, even if her horizon is limited. It is miserable that no one has succeeded in widening the horizons of so many like her.

Theaters and Museums

A little comedy about Red soldiers on Nanjing Street at the time of Liberation: young peasant fellows seduced by city lights—even one so audacious as to forget his wife and chase after a girl. Yet they are the bearers of cleanliness and morality, they conquer temptations, and in the end, with the help of some local people, they get the better of corrupt people who are trying to take them in. . . . In the same play there is a "bourgeois" family in crisis—the mother dressed in a long gown, a living room with drapes, awnings, and piano; however, they are people of goodwill, and they are saved; in the end, the daughter who wanted to become a revolutionary is exhorted by the Army commander to continue with her study of music, for that, too, is useful to society.

Loudspeakers resound in our ears with Hua's address at the conference on Daqing. Around eleven-thirty, I was in the restaurant when one loudspeaker took up the old story again and was joined by others, but they were out of sync so that the voices were jumbled in incomprehensible barks among which fragments of ritual clichés were audible.

In Hong Kou Park, behind the Institute, is the Lu Xun Museum. In a country where museums are open to the public irrespective of nationality, I would have been able to visit it during free hours at the school, and to look at this or that exhibit at my leisure. Instead, I have visited the museum once. In any event, it was interesting, for they were only a few of us, and we were allowed a fair amount of time.

The museum is well arranged; there is some reference to everything, including Lu Xun's polemic with the Creation Society; the more scabrous points are less emphasized, naturally, and especially the 1927–33 period is passed over very quickly.* For the biography, the same rigid and distorted pattern has been followed which is used in schools, but the documentation is good. Several first editions and copies of magazines are on exhibit. However, I don't know where

---

*This was the period of the most bitter polemics between Lu Xun and supporters of the so-called revolutionary literature, among whom are some personalities still eminent today, such as Guo Moruo (though he died in 1978), and Cheng Fangwu, as well as other literary types of the Communist party.

Lu Xun's personal library may be, or his collection of engravings, of which only a few are shown here.

At the end of the visit, Makita and I chatted with the young man who had accompanied us. He was well informed about literary matters and willing to answer questions. His attitude was quite open as long as one did not touch on points too close to specifically political questions; then he lapsed into the usual confusion, mistook one period for another, one tendency for another, and answered with little set phrases.

Peking
June 1

I'm on my way to Peking to celebrate the June 2 holiday (the national day in Italy). In the limbo of the train compartment, I work on my translation of the glossary. I have come to the section that deals with Peking's Summer Palace: the Hall of Regular Clouds.

When you read the transcriptions of names that are assigned to places, buildings, plants, and other material things in a Chinese garden, you could never recognize the real garden from those transcriptions. Examples: the Hill of Thousand Ages, the Jade Fountain, the Long Gallery, the Tower of the Perfume of Buddha, the Sea of Wisdom, the Hall of Goodwill and Longevity, the Imperial Theater, the Jade Waves Palace, the Chamber of the Moon's Invitation, the Pavilion of Contemplation of the Mountains and Lakes, the Walk in a Painting, the Belvedere of Great Happiness, the Tower That Greets the Dawn, the Dragon King Temple, the Bridge of Seventeen Arches. . . .

Almost always, these buildings, gardens, pavilions, chambers, walks, towers, temples, and fountains are so small that you might not even notice them if you were not bade to by aggrandizing words chosen hither and yon to name them, and you would find it hard to recognize any affinity between their actual characteristics and their high-sounding, sublime verbal attributes. The garden as microcosm, as an allusion to something else, is not only a Chinese but a universal phenomenon, at least in some periods—the Italian Renaissance, for one. What is Chinese is faith in the thaumaturgic power of the written word, in its being capable of causing it to exist. If there is the word, there is certainty that the thing is also. This reveals a fundamental uncertainty of self. One defines oneself and defines with words in order to reassure oneself that one exists, that the world exists. One separates thinking and being, interpreting and doing. Every cultural construction, then, is an artifice, an imitation-sublimation of the true and unattainable universe on which one has no hold. And one searches for legitimation in the two directions: the self as existing (the subject), and that existing confronted by the thinking self (that directs, and orders, imperial). The thing without the word does not exist because that would mean it is left to the caprice of possible definitions—an opportunity for heresy. Words come down from on high.

Precisely the opposite of Mao Zedong's "right ideas." His speech about this seems to deal with the obvious, but not if one understands the need for it, not if one places it in this Chinese context. What the Cultural Revolution put in doubt was not so much governmental and production management so much as the consciousness of the subaltern obedient to the word of those on high; it was a leap into contemporary history and the modern world. (Which explains the resentment of many ex–Red Guards toward Mao and his contradictory attitude in this regard.) Every other "modernization" theory implies a return to semicolonial conditions; for this reason, beyond all the conflicts among the contending factions which are the superficial cause of present difficulties, salvation is sought in earlier phases of the revolution. The Chinese have already traveled a similar road with the Kuomintang; they should know that it leads nowhere.

June 4

During the reception given in the embassy garden in honor of the national holiday, I met the elderly Ge Gao, of Beida; twenty years ago, he was employed in the *bangongshe,* but he has made a career for himself and is now a director. We were both moved to meet again, like brothers who see each other after a long, long time and who share a past unknown to others. I shall never stop being grateful to the Chinese for their profound sensitivity in the area of what-is-left-unsaid, of what seems to be entirely excluded from their surface, conversational existence.

Friday evening, on our way back from a dinner party, we drove through a limpidly clear evening—the moon was full—to Tienanmen. The mausoleum was recently completed; it hides the Qianmen Gate entirely, but it's smaller than it looks in photographs, and it's not especially ugly—anonymous, rather.

The eternal game of second-guessing backstage politics goes on here. It strikes me as all the more futile the more completely it absorbs people.

I am on the train again, on my way back to Shanghai; it's late afternoon. Pines and more pines, acacia, poppies, sun-bathed fields, a sunset amid green. . . . While I was in the dining car, the countryside turned dark, the moon rose. We passed by Tianjin. Its industrial outskirts are a world of huts. I couldn't make out whether they are old living quarters or temporary ones put up after the earthquake, but there was frightful squalor and filth and poverty. The shacks are crowded close together, built of odds and ends, scraps of rusted, cruddy iron, half-roofless, riddled with holes. Inside and out, adults and children in evident extreme destitution.

This must be the result of the earthquake. Always, before passing judgment, I must remind myself of this grievously impoverished China.

Morning now, about seven, and a Sunday. The peasants are walking out to work, one behind another, their tools over their shoulders.

A Fudan student from Jiangsu has been telling how the peasants in his village don't even conceive of the possibility of not going barefoot; they criticize the young students for wearing shoes. A very strong man, he says, can manage to earn four *mao* a day, which is about twenty-eight cents. The amount of rice each person may eat per day is controlled. The young man added, "Where there is oppression, there is resistance." If the peasants are oppressed, they will rise up.

China
June 6

I had set out looking for a hidden reality; then, after being shaken by events in a way that seemed destructive, I found myself finally discovering—without realizing it at first, and starting I don't know when—that nothing is hidden, that everything is being made known clearly in words and other ways, in even a superabundance of ways. Only, contrary to what one might expect, one must go looking precisely in those things that are open, that cannot be concealed, that are there for all to see.

I have come to understand that for the person who keeps his eyes open and his mind alert, nothing is unknowable; the limitations that are imposed from outside on both knowledge and expression serve only, then, to refine one's ability to understand and to express, to make reality more lifelike, more real. (In his essay "Voyage with Don Quixote," Thomas Mann asserts that political repression is inoperative in the case of artists, and he adduces the example of Cervantes; the essay is a paradox because it was written while the author was crossing the Atlantic in flight from nazism—but Mann's case was a matter of life or death. We must learn to distinguish between one repression and another repression.)

For some time, the most ordinary facts have become significant, and I couldn't say how this has happened. Contributing to it, perhaps, is a stratification of my knowledge about this "continent," which was latent and has reawakened to make it intelligible to me. The schemata have collapsed, emptied. Between the old and the new China, between this period and that in the new China, there is a prevailing continuity, as there is in the daily life of the individual, for which it is also the thing that supports events and gives them substance.

Joseph R. Levenson seems to me more and more admirable, and I continue a mental dialogue with his work.

June 9

The Suzhou *pingdan* is a traditional kind of theater, which is performed also in Nanjing and Shanghai, in special surroundings called *shuchang*—literally, piazza of books. But it has nothing to do with books. *Shu* is the text, as in the *huaben,* the tales, divided into chapters, which are recited and sung, and lie at the origins of the novel. Its common origin with the earliest beginnings of narrative was confirmed for me by Chen's husband, who is an expert in this area. Through her, I also asked about the number of actors onstage. In some cases analagous to the *pingdan,* there is a single narrator-interpreter; in no case are there more than three. As for the "piazza," that is in fact a particular kind of locale, enclosed but with ample door-windows, and almost round, in imitation of an open pavilion; it is a very agreeable modern solution for a form of traditional theater. Chen tells me that in Shanghai there are several locales of this kind, and that so far she has avoided going to them for fear of becoming like those people who are so attached to the *pingdan* that they can't do without it, for whom *pingdan* has become an addiction, almost a vice. There are other versions of the genre in various cities and provinces, but Suzhou's is considered the finest. They don't all have the same name. *Pingdan* means "squabble" and "ballade."

To what extent the genre has been changed and modernized I don't know. Now only one evening performance is given, but once upon a time the *pingdan* used to last without interruption all day long. (Naturally, they're saying that the Gang of Four sabotaged this form of theater. However, when I inquired, I gathered that it's never been discontinued, indeed it is one of the things that has enjoyed a peaceful continuity, apart from adapting itself somewhat to the prevailing political current. It was even included in the Peking festival last summer.)

The plot comes from some preexisting work—a novel, opera, film. . . . The action is divided into *hui* (chapters or "turns," as in *huaben* and novels). In the course of one evening, several *hui* are performed, but not necessarily the whole story, especially if it is long. I've attended the performance of the first part (four *hui*) of a story taken from a 1962 film that actually has to do with the Great Leap Forward and the first People's Communes. Wife and husband are both peasants; she is "advanced" and aggressive, a spokesman for the public interest; he is "behind the times," an easygoing fellow who's for taking things as they come. The performance lasted from seven until almost ten, with a ten-minute intermission.

There was no set. Just a long, narrow table stage center, the narrow side facing the audience; to stage left and right, two velvet-covered chairs were placed on high wooden platforms. The table serves to hold the musical instruments—the lutelike *pipa* for the women, the two-stringed violin, *erhu,* for the men. *Pipa* and *erhu* are also leaned against the two chairs with, I believe, symbolic significance. Two or three actors are present onstage. With each *hui,* they change. Most often, they are a man and a woman; sometimes two men and a woman, or two women and one man. When they are in three, there is a third seat upstage, and the table is placed so that the wide side faces the public.

The actors enter, and take their places on the raised seats. They rest their feet on the narrow platforms, and look as if they were standing on tiny podiums or sitting on a kind of shooting stick. If there is a third person, he sits behind the table. They all look out at the audience. They are not in costume. The men wear the habitual Sun Yat-sen jacket and trousers, the women wear a blouse with trousers. Their cheeks are slightly roughed and their eyes are made up, which is customary when appearing on a stage. One person begins to tell the story, and at a certain point, with no interruption, he begins to act one of the characters. Even during the narration, he has somehow already been that character. He is not a detached narrator but someone who first tells about, and then acts out, that character. Mostly, the speeches are long, varied, and recited in various ways depending on the actor's taste—Punchinello-like or statically, with a little or a lot of mime, but always delivered with a very pronounced rhythm, which turns the monologue into a song or, in any case, speech in verse even if literally it is prose. The meter is approximately iambic, with run-on lines. While one person is reciting and acting out his character, the other sits motionless, his eyes fixed on the middle distance. Throughout a single *hui,* a character is always interpreted by the same actor; the actor, however, does not necessarily play only one role—on the contrary, usually more than one; his shift from one to the other is not very rapid and is always accompanied by connective narration. Generally, one major character is assigned to each of the two actors. The third person is a sort of extra, at least this was so in the one performance I attended, and he supplies something on the order of stage directions provided in a scenario. The sex of the two leading characters matches that of the respective actors, but this does not necessarily hold for other roles. For example, I saw the role of an old woman consistently played by men throughout the several *hui.* So, the same performer recites the lines of and acts out more than one character; and from one *hui* to another, the same character may be interpreted by several actors. The acting styles are determined by the individual actors, and can change from one *hui* to another. For example, in the third *hui,* the peasant husband was played by a rather elderly and, so I was told, quite famous actor. He had a Neapolitan face and style, and disregarded the standard of remaining motionless (which the women faithfully observed, being on a level too far below that of the men to dare take any initiative on their own). This man also acted all the time, even when the other was speaking, miming in a way that might suggest a curtain raiser but was actually calculated and stylized.

The play we saw seemed to be only a work of folk-realism; it was a comedy, and the purpose was to make us laugh. Now and then, the spoken narration changed into song. With precise gestures, the two actors picked up their instruments, and each, in turn, sang his piece, the rhythm always strongly marked. As at the opera, the words being sung were projected on two panels on either side of the stage. The women playing the *pipa* had round, closed faces; apart from the sounds of their instruments, they acted a *silence,* in which juxtaposed allusions were without number. The infinite as limitless repetition.

Full of goodwill, Roland tried to interpret this art form with paternalistic-folkloristic sympathy. It was one of those instances in which the foreigner plays the role of barbarian (or of idiot).

Criticism Meetings

"When we go to a foreign country, we know that we must obey its laws. But in China the foreigner can't even find out what the laws are, what is allowed and what isn't allowed, what are one's rights and what one's responsibilities. If we knew the regulations, no one would make any fuss, and it would be easier for you, too."

I had no sooner finished saying this to Chen and Zhang, when Xing—*el calvito*—walked into the office. He sat down in Chen's chair, and launched into his communiqué: "This afternoon, there will be a mass criticism session of the Gang of Four, specifically of the sabotaging activities their accomplices within our Institute carried out during the movement of criticism of Lin Biao and Confucius. . . . Several foreign instructors have asked to attend the assembly. The school has considered the matter in depth and has concluded that you"—addressing me directly—"cannot attend since you are working here on the basis of a cultural agreement with Italy." The reason adduced was nonsense, but apart from that, I didn't understand why they went so far as to justify their decision since I was not one of the people who submitted the request.

The business began some days ago, when Pascale learned of the forthcoming meeting (although officially it had been carefully concealed from us). She had declared that since it was a mass meeting (not Party or *neibu*), she intended to go to it, on the basis of Zhou Enlai's directives and in her capacity as a teacher at the Institute. She had been told that this was not possible, that the meeting would be *neibu.* She very calmly repeated that she knew it was not to be *neibu,* that she would go, and that she would not enter the hall only if they physically prevented her from doing so; in this eventuality, she said, she would no longer appear at the Institute and would do her work at the hotel—preparing material, obviously, but no longer conducting classroom lessons. This threw directors and staff into the greatest consternation, and even her own interpreter would not look at her. The matter was referred on up to the municipal level; there the decision taken was against admitting foreigners, although the reasons were not made clear. That's where things stood as of last evening.

What surprised me today was not the refusal to admit me, but their taking the trouble to inform me. However, I replied that I had, in point of fact, not asked to take part in the meeting. I was not greatly interested in attending it, I added, since I already deduced from *dazibao* what it was to be about.

And indeed, for some days I've been reading in *dazibao* uncut versions of an old article published in *Wenhui Daily* more than three years ago (March 10, 1974), in which several Institute professors were criticized for their Confucian spirit, for having opposed worker squads' admission to the Institute, and for having sabotaged the studies of the worker-teachers—for example, contemptuously giving them material in foreign languages which they knew was incomprehensible to them. Now the professors are striking back. Who passed on the details to Wang Xiuzhen? Who then had them published in the paper?

Someone reported to Chen having seen me reading the *dazibao* with the *Wenhui Daily* article, and naturally she delivered a little sermon, saying that *Wenhui Daily* was lying, that the professors had been unfairly accused by the propaganda squad, which was an offshoot of the Gang of Four and was determined to ruin the school by making people go to classes for the sake of going to classes but doing nothing, etc., etc.

Interest in today's meeting lies in the fact that Wang Xiuzhen, who is currently in prison, is to be produced in person as the Number One culprit to testify against several worker-teachers at the Institute.

At lunch at the hotel, I learned from Uta that, at the last moment, the municipality changed its mind during the morning: foreigners may be admitted to the meeting. (That an order came down from Peking is not to be excluded.) Pascale said that as late as nine this morning the Chinese professors and her interpreter knew that the veto had not been lifted, and were not behaving normally toward her. Uta was stunned that I should have been barred, and at the excuse given. I was much less so, for I know the ways of this bureaucracy.

When Olga got back from the meeting this evening, she came to see me, much upset, and told me how the ceremony had gone. Other people gave me more details later. In the unanimous opinion of the foreigners present, the meeting was so much theater. It was not a place for seriously raising or discussing charges of wrongdoing, even in the sense in which "discussion" is construed in China. Nor was there any attempt at a defense. The one permissible way to defend oneself is to recognize one's guilt and promise to change. "To persist in denying one's own guilt" is in itself, as we know, criminal behavior.

On the stage, the leaders of the Institute sat in the center, in an area reserved for them. To one side, on a small raised platform was a place for the Number One culprit, Wang Xiuzhen—who was also serving as a witness. On the other side, and somewhat lower, a place for minor offenders, the two worker-teachers from the Institute. Culprit Number One, because she was under arrest, was fetched and taken away by car.

Each person had been assigned his role. Six people spoke, four accusers and the two worker-teachers from the Institute. (Whether they were the only Institute people facing criticism, or were token representatives, I don't know.) The accusers were professors. No student spoke. The performance was, in effect, a settling of accounts. The professors belonged to different sections. It seems that numerous others had prepared charges, which were all checked, screened, and recombined. In a word, everything was predetermined prior to the performance. The charge was as known, but many analytical details were offered which, if anyone intended to challenge them, would lend themselves to endless hairsplitting; they were precisely calculated to transform the whole thing into a futile game and to frustrate anyone so foolish as to aspire to contest them. An abundance of detail acts to so muddy matters that one no longer understands what is being talked about. The professors adopted an aggressive tone.

Then the worker-teachers spoke; they corroborated the charges and admitted their guilt. With respect to them and other worker-teachers of the Institute not present at this criticism meeting, a decision, it seems, "has not yet been reached."

The reactions of the public were the usual ones at a big meeting: lack of interest, no concern for the issues involved, a compliant submissiveness. Some people read, some dozed. Everyone raised his arm when there was a slogan calling for a response, and the slogans were stock anti–Gang of Four and their accomplices.

Throughout, Wang Xiuzhen sat with her head bowed. While she was being interrogated, she was addressed directly: "Is it true that you did this and this? Why did you do it?" Her replies were always couched so as to admit guilt, but in general terms; she kept reiterating current set phrases, such as "they wanted to usurp power in the Party and in the State." Her accuser would press her to make her replies "more concrete." To no avail. In the end, he answered his own questions, and then asked: "Is that the way it is?" She confined herself to answering "yes."

Olga was upset that the woman had been humiliated and that her conviction was baseless; yet it was given that she had lost, and that she would not be permitted to defend herself.

Susan is more cynical, and remarked to me, "Wang Xiuzhen answered questions in an insolent way." I believe Susan, who is competent to interpret the underlying sense of people's behavior. Very likely, Wang was not permitted to deny her guilt, she had no loophole, but she kept strictly to the ritual and avoided making any admission of substance prejudicial to herself and to the others against whom she would be expected to appear as a witness. In this fashion, she not only avoided supplying a list of real charges, but also made it quite plain that she was being forced to say things she does not think at all.

The municipality is very busy putting on these shows. The ex-leaders of the city are being taken around to dozens upon dozens of public meetings, at which they are assigned simultaneous roles as defendants and as witnesses for the prosecution. It was because of Wang Xiuzhen's presence that the foreigners' attendance at the meeting was to have been forbidden. Pascale put them on the spot, especially now when the propaganda campaign about the Gang of Four violating civil rights is in full course.

When the actress friend of Zhou Enlai was subjected to treatment similar to what is now being meted out to followers of the Four, she spoke of "Fascist dictatorship." There's nothing for it. The little word "fascism," which once upon a time no one would have dreamed of uttering, has been put into circulation and is gaining currency, buzzing about like a pestiferous insect, and no one knows anymore whom it will end up biting.

Certain methods have been overused, especially given the public polemical exposure about the use of them by the Gang of Four and their accomplices. To adopt them now against the Four is proving ineffectual. The ritual is losing credibility, it is ceasing to be a ritual. Cynicism is encouraged. But once the Chinese people are more mature or more organized, they will begin to demand that bureaucrats give an accounting of why they have leveled charges against the Four for doing what they themselves have done in the past and continue to do today. The political defeat of the Four has been achieved; inevitably the forms of protest will be supplied with new fodder, including issues the conservatives, relying overmuch on the passivity of the people, will clumsily raise.

This evening in the restaurant, Uta called me over to say that Mohammed had been invited to the meeting, although he, too, was sent here on the basis of an agreement between the Chinese government and his own; ergo the directors of the Institute are caught out in a flagrant lie in relation to me. I knew from the outset that they had lied to me and had seized on any excuse to prevent my being admitted to the meeting. For reasons of "face" and because, after all, here I represent not only myself but also my country, I am writing the directors a short letter of criticism.

June 25

There was a mass meeting at Fudan today, similar to the one held at our Institute, against someone associated with local friends of the Gang of Four. The meeting was held in the open on an athletic field near the university. People got up at five in order to leave for the meeting at six, and they were still arriving at seven-thirty.

A few of the French students, mostly girls, went along with the Chinese. The others couldn't have cared less. At the gate, the foreigners were refused admittance. They stayed until the meeting was over, half of them climbing up on the wall around the field, the others hanging onto the gates, and talking with whomever passed by.

The young foreigners were very much excited as they told us about all this, and quite convinced that they had been waging an important battle not only for themselves but also for democracy in China.

However, freedom does not gain ground behind a structure of lies. The essential problem is not that foreigners should win the status of third- or fourth-class sub-Chinese. Indeed, the question is not one that foreigners can even help to resolve, for they are slotted into false categories—a false "friendship" or an even more false "proletarian internationalism." The Chinese people themselves must break down the Pan-Sinitic structure, and this they will not be able to do as long as they are suffocated by the lies of the old bureaucrats who govern them.

Among those who are fighting for greater integration are two young women —one French and the other Australian—who so far have been unable to obtain permission to marry two Chinese. The Australian's case has attracted great attention and has reached the upper echelons of government without a solution's being found. Obviously, the young women are right to fight their personal battle, and no doubt the moment is favorable. Their marriages will be a fine propaganda card.*

Possible conflict with the authorities in the matter of matrimony is a privilege available to people with white or yellow skins. It would never cross the mind of a Chinese to want to marry a black man or woman, because, they say, society would not accept a black person.

As for human and civil rights, the only one among us who has shown that he has a clear notion of what they are about is John, who refused to be present at the vile comedy surrounding Wang Xiuzhen that took place in the Institute salon.

In my glossary, I found the following quotation of Mao:

"To remain quiet, tranquil, unhurried; to allow the organism little by little to generate resistance and fight through to final victory—this is the method for treating a chronic illness.

"Even in the case of an acute illness it is good to allow the remedy to be generated out of the illness; haste serves no purpose, haste is harmful. One must have a stubborn will to fight against the illness, not haste. This is my position with respect to illness."

In the antiquarian bookshops on Fuzhou Road stocks of dusty old volumes have appeared, exhumed from who knows where. Lots of Russian books: Mayakovsky's poetry, dictionaries, technical books, Lenin. Also some rubbish. A sprinkling of old Chinese books. Everybody, it seems, is taking advantage of

*They were, in time, to get permission to marry through the personal intervention of Hua Guofeng and Deng Xiaoping.

the moment to drag out everything he has, provided that it is old and antedates
the Cultural Revolution.

> *The colonialist spirit is not extinct. These days it is flowering anew among
> sinologists of assorted extractions, camouflaged in all the colors of democracy,
> from liberal to Communist.*
>
> *Colonialist-minded sinologists love the concept of the "national," or even of
> the "national-popular." They fret over the damage to production that the "follies"
> of the Four provoked in China, and they rejoice over "the Hundred Flowers."
> They band together with petty bureaucrats who are gratified to be taken for
> persecuted intellectuals, and with poor elderly writers and artists who were indeed
> persecuted and are now exploited in shameful fashion. They rejoice that politics
> is being banished from the schools, and smile benevolently on the performances
> of national minorities that, in group and in costume, dance, wave flowers, sing,
> smile, and demean themselves.*
>
> *"How sweet and attractive and likable these savages are [twice savage be-
> cause not modern and not pluralistic]," the colonialist thinks, "and good, really,
> now that they've stopped destroying temples."*

Summer
June 29

Another mass meeting at the Institute, with the widow of an ex–Red Guard
from the entourage of Zhou EnLai; the woman had been persecuted by the Gang
of Four (with the complicity of someone associated with the Institute). Tearjerk-
ing anecdotes, I was told later. The other foreign professors were invited to
attend, but not I.

Some days ago, *el calvito* turned up in my office and delivered himself of
a few introductory remarks in which he praised my industry and inquired
whether I had any comments to make, and then went on to explain the treatment meted out only to me in relation to these gatherings. Mohammed could
be admitted to them because his status was a little different from mine. With
Italy, there was a genuine two-way exchange of instructors, whereas Egypt sent
instructors to China but China sent none to Egypt. When I had recovered from
my surprise, I said to him that I thanked him and that I interpreted what he
had said as a statement to the effect that they did not wish to give me a reply
to the letter of protest I had sent. He started again, and yet again, to repeat the
same idiocy until finally I asked Chen to make him stop because I felt sorry for
him.

Suffocating heat has arrived. Everyone is tired, and the children are at the
end of their tether. Hosam begs his father to go back to Egypt. They tease him
all the time—the adults, not the children—and say insulting things about his

country. Hosam is a gentle, introverted child, and his reply is *"Zhongguo bu hao"*—"China is mean," "China's no good." Aymin still recites her little Chinese poems and songs, making the small gestures that are always the same and have no relation to the text. The moment she speaks or sings in Spanish, she is another person. And she changes yet again when she talks with the waiters in a very vulgar Shanghai dialect.

Aymin isn't well; she has intermittent fever and suffers from nosebleeds; the doctors don't understand what is wrong. The conditions in which we live make for a feeling of insecurity about not only our own health but the health of people we care for. I am painfully worried about Aymin.

Again many *dazibao* in the units, in a fresh attack on "accomplices of the Gang of Four" at the base, and an effort to have them purged. People have even been seen (but not in Shanghai yet, as far as I know) being transported about with pillory posters hung around their necks.

At the Institute, the polemics against several members of the Party Committee drag on and on. Every once in a while, someone launches a fresh attack; this has been going on for months now, has become part of the routine.

Our most recent visits have been to a middle and an elementary school. Both were model or experimental schools, although nominally; since the Cultural Revolution, such schools no longer exist. They seemed to be well integrated with their neighborhoods, and if not entirely, then very close to being full time. In any case, student life is organized around them. In the afternoon, there are numerous and varied recreational activities: drawing (even from life), calligraphy, singing, collage. There was even a small orchestra of Chinese instruments and violins. One child, so tiny she could hardly hold her *pipa,* played a solo for us. Already her large, dreamy eyes were fixed on that middle distance, focused on those images of another world toward which the faces of Chinese adolescents seem ever more turned. The child pressed her face against the instrument she struggled to embrace; she was composed, entirely absorbed.

In the courtyard, the students were playing Ping-Pong and badminton. Model makers were flying their planes. No model makers among the little girls, who were busy with needlework.

There were small workshops set up after the Cultural Revolution. Those in the middle school were making simple medications and attaching snap fasteners to cardboard. In the elementary school, they were making sock pieces (to be sewn together later) and battery components. Display cases along the hallways, which remind one of the good old schools of times past: straw animals, ship models, a toy telephone, and other odds and ends.

In the lower as in the middle school, our visit ended with dancing. Here again, as with the tiny *pipa* player, we were fascinated by one or two figures that

moved in some timeless world, intent on the unseen, as if they knew all myster-
ies, or were totally possessed.

July 14

The unbearable heat has produced widespread bronchitis among Dasha dwellers. The one possible way to fall asleep is to stretch out naked on a mat directly
in line with a fan. My window is kept closed because they are making repairs
with a welding machine on the iron bridge below; the motor runs all night and
is so noisy that it drowns out the boat engines and sirens. There are residences
in the vicinity of the hotel, and a hospital nearby, but nobody protests this
assault on one's rest. Traffic could be diverted to another bridge and the work
done during the day, but people seem to have no idea of their right to protest;
they let themselves be beaten down.

When I look out my window, it isn't so much a fog I see as streets and
houses shrouded by millions upon millions of droplets of hot moisture. People
live six to a room here, sleeping in bunk beds; on nights like these, they invade
the streets, bearing stools and small chairs; if they have bigger chairs of bamboo,
they stretch out on them; the men may strip to the waist and pull up their
trousers. Some read under the faint glow of the streetlights; many play cards.
But most simply sit, limp, amid the dust and smells.

Kieu has learned that at the end of the semester I will be going home, and
he came to the office to say good-bye to me. Zhang was there, but we chatted
in French and paid no attention to him. Kieu brought me a gift, a poem he wrote
in classical Chinese and has copied in small-seal characters; it has to do with
homesickness for his country on the day of the lunar New Year (when I was
in Vietnam). He told me that if one is to get to know China, one must speak
daily and at length with the plain people; he described how, when he goes to
the country during his vacation, he talks with the peasants about the everyday
things of their lives. "Of course, it is easier for me," he added, "because they
almost take me for a Chinese."

What we have in common which makes us close is the feeling of international fraternity, which was once widely shared among all Communists and
which history has destroyed.

The students have given performances in the languages they have been
studying—in my section, too: Spanish, Russian, Italian, and Albanian. Twenty-
five-year-old young women in pleated skirts and socks; babyish-looking young
men. The program comprised sketches, selections of things they had translated
from Chinese (my students offered Italian translations of dialogue in the film
Hai Xia), and old songs. The students of Russian, in addition to singing "The

Internationale" (badly) and "Varshavyanka" (even worse), put on an excerpt from *How the Steel Was Tempered*. The students of Spanish (middle school) performed, according to Olga, excerpts from a Spanish comedy (but if it was, who could guess which?). It had to do with a school where they gave high marks to the children of the rich and flunked the children of the poor, although they were the best, the villain-schoolmaster roaming the corridors meanwhile, walking stick in hand; the student body was represented by two girls who, to look like Occidentals, wore plaid shirts and white cotton baby bonnets with little visors.

As I was watching all this, especially "How the Steel Was Tempered," I was thinking to myself, This is how they cheated the Russians for thirty years, and now how they're cheating you, you poor Chinese. If you knew what works of art are being made in Eastern Europe today—the films of Andrzej Wajda, for example. And you, who don't even know anything about *Zhivago*. They show you this unreal Soviet Union—for that matter, you call the Russia of 1905 the Soviet Union (it's not only my students who do so; one sees it in print), which doesn't exist today, which never has existed. The entire world that you are shown is unreal, a ridiculous model of a false good and a false bad. What they would like is for you to be made unreal, too, strangers to yourselves, clothed in infantilism and stupid obedience and fear.

The one true and beautiful thing that took place—by mistake—was the mimed work about the struggle of Peruvian peasants which Marcial had prepared. For a whole month, he had worked his head off rehearsing his students. He was annoyed and frustrated by their prejudiced resistance to non-Chinese forms, symbology, the mime makeup, the peasants' ragged clothes (because onstage one must be beautifully costumed, if possible in silks). And none of them wanted to play the "negative" characters.

For all that, given the problems, Marcial's efforts produced an extraordinary result. He was able to convey to them a sense of movements and rhythms and gestures, and to teach them how to perform them; in a word, he taught them how to set aside their Chinese imprint and made them participants in something heretofore unknown to them.

The audience understood nothing, laughed in the wrong places, and made fun. Chen, who was sitting beside me, thought Marcial's involvement was a joke, and he some kind of silly monkey. But actually, she, like the other less ingenuous spectators, was diffident because of what the miming was about: the peasant revolution, the betrayal of agrarian reform and of cooperatives formed by a semi-Fascist government. These are painful subjects, like all serious discussion which has to do with the true substance of ownership policy in the West. Behind it is an awareness of those who are everywhere becoming the allies of the representatives of the bosses *(and not only in international relations)*. The suspicion and finally the hostility are directed against those people in the world who want freedom for the common people—which is to say, another form of communism.

"At least, anybody who goes to the Soviet Union does eventually make contact with the dissidents," Susan says ironically. "But here you don't have even that diversion." Nontheless, since all of us have been asked to communicate orally or in writing our opinions about the teaching, Susan has delivered to her section a twenty-page paper of well-reasoned, concise criticism. It should have been circulated among the other teachers, but a little trick was devised whereby only a few pages were given to each. Susan patiently made the proper number of complete copies and personally distributed them.

Lao Bai and his acolytes find Susan hard to stomach because she is so outspoken, but especially because she knows too much. They offered inconsistent excuses in rejecting her request to continue to teach at the Institute for one more year (after reading her correspondence with her mother, from which they learned that for the moment she has no work in England). When the French instructors intervened in her behalf, they replied with the usual mixture of cavils and lies.

Now they are making life difficult for her with a host of petty spiteful things having to do with arrangements and payment for her return trip, and the shipment of her luggage.

John had a chilly scene with the people in his section, calling them reactionaries. He said that he had come to work in a Socialist country and found himself in a nest of Fascists. They undo or ruin everything that he tries to do, and make it impossible for him to work. His interpreter told him to talk with Lao Ji and Lao Bai face to face, and his reply to that was, "Which face do you want me to talk to?"

John is as fine as ever. But the interesting thing is that now he is much more of a Socialist than when he came.

July 23

A cycle has closed in these last days. Yesterday, at eight in the evening, announcements were made on the radio and TV of the convening of the III Central Committee of the Chinese Communist Party. The institute alerted us by phone about the broadcast, even calling several times people they had not reached on the first call. One saw Hua Guofeng, Deng Xiaoping on his right, Ye Jianqing on his left. Hua was smiling genially; he was wearing his hair shaved in front in an attempt to look like Mao. Deng looked thinner and older.

The event had been expected, and foreign radio services had been speculating for a long time about the new leadership. Deng had been repeatedly—and erroneously—put forward as the probable Premier—a sign that there had indeed been such an attempt. Now we know that that "news" came from a Chinese source, not officially but from one or the other competing groups.

The school year is coming to an end, and the students are breathlessly preparing for exams. Examinations were given in the middle school as well; if they fail in just one basic course, they will have to repeat the year. (In the middle school attached to the Institute the basic subject is a foreign language.) Texts were written on long strips of paper, which the students drew by lots. They were terrified. The Chinese professors tried to insist with Olga that she grade the papers, which she refused to do, so instead they will have her listen to tapes without telling her who the speaker is, and she will have to evaluate them. They did not ask me. Zhang's indifference to principles aims at merely smoothing away obstacles. The selections that the students in our class should read and report on will also be drawn by lots, but in actuality each person knows which will fall to him and is preparing himself accordingly.

Despite the exams, a kind of demobilization is in the air which always comes with the approach of vacations. The foreign teachers are making preparations to travel, either in China or to return home. I won't go on the trip the Institute has organized; it will be to the northwest, and I already know some of the cities there, and a visit to Dazhai, as it will be conducted now, doesn't interest me. Also, it's too hot, I am very tired, and I would not put up with two weeks of obsessive protection-control. I would rather really rest at some vacation spot, and will go to Beidaihe, where I've been invited by the ambassador, and then on to Kyoto for a week. At the Institute, they are very pleasant to me and do everything to accommodate me in these travel requests. Their attitude is one of formal friendliness. Why? Unlike the English, I have avoided a frontal encounter.

Final meetings. . . . I did not go to the one for foreign professors, at which the innovations for the coming year were announced. Admission will be on the basis of examinations (in English, for our Institute); people under twenty-three will be eligible to take them—which is to say, almost exclusively students from the middle schools, and no longer from the base units after a year or two of work following the diploma (which peasants rarely attain before the age of twenty-one or twenty-two). Thus is closed the experiment in permanent and independent education—independent of age—initiated after the Cultural Revolution. The criteria determining whether graduates should either go to, or return to, the countryside have been declared a mistake. Graduates should enter government service—i.e., follow a civil-service career. (Some time ago, I saw middle-school graduates leaving for work in the countryside; who knows if they will continue to go from the middle schools—those, that is, who are not admitted to the university.) At first, it was explained, the students did not understand, but now they have understood, and now they are happy to take the examinations. "Before," the school had a few shortcomings but in all essentials it was functioning; "then" it no longer functioned. Someone asked what "before" and "then" meant; reluctantly, they answered that the terms referred to the Cultural Revolution.

The directors have come to bid me farewell, and then there was a further farewell meeting with the people in the section, at which I presented orally my observations. I was afraid I would be too aggressive, but then, as always happens, what I had to say more or less fell apart. The problem is that I was confronting a soft, compact wall which can be attacked only with violence, and if by a solitary foreigner acting alone, it can only boomerang. They complimented me on the work I had done, and they added that "someone" had failed to understand the matter of the Gang of Four. It is the European's unavoidable misery here that "to persist" in being European and not to be sinicized is to be aggressive.

When judging Chinese behavior, one must be mindful that the "yes" said to something coming from on high embraces numberless potential "no's." This is impossible for us; we perceive it as the disintegration of personality. My need to return to Europe comes from my knowing that were I to remain here long, I would in the end be destroyed.

The sultry weather is sometimes broken by very violent thunderstorms, which turn the streets into rivers. We take refuge in big doorways, happy as children for the rain—even people on their way home from work, who still have a long way to go. Despite the heat, I am making my last bicycle excursions; I take advantage of the exceptionally serene gray-and-red sky that follows a storm. I've gone back to the ex–French Concession area to see once again the beautiful twentieth-century buildings, which have a strength that resists dirt and discoloration and even the washing hung out to dry (much like the eighteenth-century buildings in Naples, which are now dilapidated and no less covered with laundry).

In a perfectly orderly, disciplined way, people are putting up strips of pink paper in which they rejoice over the "happy event" of the Central Committee Congress.

Departure
July 30

Everyone else has left, and I am alone in the hotel. Even most of the students have gone home, after the examinations, for which they appeared shaking with apprehension. They knew that their future hung in the balance. We had a farewell meeting, which was planned but affectionate, and at the end a group photo was taken out of doors.

I leave the door to my room open, as I always do when it's hot. And I see Aymin pass by. While her mother and father are traveling, she has stayed behind with an *ayi,* for children are not permitted to go on strenuous tours. Her fever has gone, and she's happy to be with the *ayi.* Olga had the woman on a trial basis for two weeks before leaving. And Aymin, who has grown no fonder of the nursery school, was happy finally to have a slave at her beck and call.

She is peaceful now, but is behaving strangely. She passes by my door but does not come in, and doesn't even call me *"italiana,"* as she always used to. Aymin is exceptionally intelligent and sensitive, she demands love and freedom and a ruler's role, and she knows with certainty where she can find and enjoy them. And with prodigious acumen she also recognizes nonapparent repression. The *ayi* are very indulgent with the foreign children in their care; they want no trouble and give in to them utterly. The Aymin of today, however, is not the Aymin one knew before. She used never to want to eat, and one had to stand over her with great patience to get her to swallow something. Now, what the *ayi* prepares for her she immediately eats. At night, she would never go to bed until, in spite of herself, she fell asleep, and she never napped during the day. Now she not only goes to bed early but sleeps half of the afternoon. She used to burst into everybody's room, and now she doesn't dare come to see me. If I call her, she will come in, but with a furtive, guilty air. "Recite something for me," I'll say to her. She will recite a poem, but without showing off in her usual way—she recites modestly, as if she were giving a demonstration of virtue for the benefit of the *ayi* who is not even present. But she does it with a kind of hypocrisy, and of complicity with me.

The recitation and everything else she does in my presence have two clear meanings: one real, unstated, repressed; the other visible and virtuous. The *ayi* walks by my door, perhaps looking for her, but she doesn't glance in. Almost as if Aymin were committing a heinous transgression, the child puts her finger to her lips and looks at me, bidding me be quiet, not to give us away.

But she behaves with an even ostentatious pride toward the Chinese (a pride she does not show in relation to any of us non-Chinese; with us, she is aggressive). I see sometimes that, when she thinks of her parents, she's on the verge of tears, but she holds them back with all her might. She is disciplining herself.

So tremendously vital a creature is transformed into the brave little orphan. She's changed even in her clothing—no more bare legs; now she's bundled into a pair of wide pants. Luckily, it's only a matter of two weeks and then her parents will be back; they are people capable of great love, which marks out the way for the happiness of a life. But these two weeks will leave their mark. Of "naughtiness" and, I hope, of rebellion.

August 6

Today, I left for Peking. It was not the directors but a group of friends who accompanied me on the bus to the airport: Chen with her young daughter, the thin woman who works at the *bangongshe,* the head maid on our floor at the hotel, Aymin, and the *ayi.* I was happy to be leaving, and happy and touched to have this kind of accompanying group, which exactly met my unspoken wish.

Aymin was a little groggy—it was early afternoon, and the *ayi* said she was sleepy; that is one way to drug emotion. We passed along the long, tree-lined streets as far as the well-groomed area around the airport—neat, planted with evergreens—which is the same in all cities. We were early, and I sat beside Chen in the waiting lounge. The two little girls let go, then, and played at taking running slides over the floor. Chen called her little girl back; she is nine, very pretty, and well cared for. Chen told me that lately the girl's not been concentrating on her studies as her father would like.

The kind of near-friendship which binds us to the people we work with could have grown between Chen and me, had an obstacle external to both of us not intervened. For this reason, when our conversations touched on the private sphere or on ourselves, we involuntarily lapsed into a tone of resignation. I remember that once, when we were together at yet some other departure, we talked almost sincerely of how hard it is for the teacher to find the right position vis-à-vis the students, embattled as the instructor is between the need not to repress yet at the same time to discipline, not to classify yet at the same time to help the children of the poor emerge from their cage of cultural inferiority. But Chen has been, first and foremost, my control, and she knows that I know it, and for this reason it has been impossible that there not be some diffidence between us, and a hostility born of our uneasiness in the roles imposed on us.

When they called me for departure, I said good-bye to everyone in some confusion and kissed Aymin. To leave Shanghai was both pain and liberation.

10.

BEIDAIHE

Beidaihe
August 13, 1977

We arrived here in a downpour, after more than five hours on the train from Peking, although Beidaihe seems only two steps away. (The staff and employees of the foreign embassies think nothing of making the trip to spend weekends with their families who are vacationing here.) Waiting for us at the station, with car and umbrellas, was a tubby little man who bustled about rather like an American tour guide; he runs the International Club in Peking during the winter, and moves out here in the summers to manage the foreigners' vacations. He drove us (the ambassador and his wife, two other Italian families, and me) through empty pine-bordered avenues—in the distance, lovely countryside under cultivation—to the bungalow, with a terrace looking out over the sea, where we will be staying.

We are in a submonsoon area here, and the summer is always a bit rainy, but except for the day we arrived we've had only occasional showers. The air is fresh and pleasant, and when the sun shines, the light is splendid. From our roofed terrace a small lawn, with trees, extends to a low wall bordering the sea. In the middle of the wall is the round opening that in China is essential for framing all images, which otherwise are considered invisible. (Groups of Chinese come to have themselves photographed in front of this little window.) To reach the beach, we walk down steps bordered by rocks and plants. We have other bungalows on either side (these are the most desirable residences) and one small building with long terraces, which is a hotel. A few steps farther on in the direction of town there is a large one-story building, which is a restaurant. Opposite the restaurant, the office of the government unit responsible for this area, which is reserved for diplomatic personnel and therefore is under the Ministry of Foreign Affairs.

353

As I lean against the low sea wall, the silence is enormous. Not only are there no loudspeakers but not even a portable radio may be played loudly. The sea below moves gently; and as always the figures of Chinese, fully dressed, are standing on the rocks in groups or single file. After midday, the fishermen arrive by boat out beyond the rocks; even when the fishing is poor, crabs always abound. The men maneuver almost to the shore, lower their sails, and, helped by others, push the boats up onto the beach; their movements are rhythmical and slow, and they laugh as if it were all a game. The Chinese have a capacity to identify with objects, and this, together with their diffused eroticism, predisposes them to be happy when they are in the midst of plenty. In extreme poverty, they become governable, maneuverable, pliable, but with a capacity to resist that is not easily assessed.

This seaside spot was invented by the colonialists around the turn of the century. It is one of those discreetly luxurious places created in seemingly deserted locations, with large, comfortable, unpretentious villas—in taste like the controlled wilderness of the English garden. There is even a Viennese restaurant serving both hot and iced coffee.

Solitude, silence, repose, pure air. . . .

The Chinese keep things up, in slightly run-down fashion, and they add. But they impose restrictions on space. You are allowed an hour-long walk by the sea, to the left; a half hour to the right. Walking inland, you are not permitted to go as far as the railway station. You swim within the bounds assigned. If you pretend to forget that the barrier exists, everything is fine. Excellent shops, the most luxurious I have seen in China, are located among modest modern buildings. Many items of straw are displayed, and you can buy American-style T-shirts with the name "Beidaihe" surprinted. A little cooperative was organized to make these stencils, since foreigners like the shirts—one point where the taste of our young people coincides with the Chinese mania for covering everything with ideographs.

If you follow the inland avenue to the left, you come to a Chinese hamlet that was somewhat damaged by the earthquake, as everything except modern buildings was from Tianjin on. What was already dilapidated is now mixed in with shanties. Roofs are secured with the usual stones and bricks. The same small muddy streets which you find everywhere in this watery land, where the only alternative is drought and dry dust. . . . The water is canalized, regulated —managed but never dominated. The unceasing activity to systematize everything down to the smallest detail and even to the point of artificiality is governed by a universal uncertainty that is both existential and ecological. There is no benign Providence watching over, but generation after generation of professional regulators of the waters and land.

The beach world here is what the Chinese imagine it must be in the capitalist West—the beach as it was when a vacation by the sea was a luxury for the few. Old wicker armchairs are set out under light, crumbling trellises. Space, the sound of the sea, a few people in the distance, who wrap themselves in great towels after their swim. . . .

Walking along the shore to the right, you come to a barracks for soldiers on furlough, built in the style halfway between Yanan and Dutch-Germanic that prevails here, with cloudy-white glazed bricks and green trim. Big arched windows, flags, the red star. . . . At noontime, the soldiers go swimming in a group; they march into the water in rows with identical movements—perhaps they are being taught to swim. Also, in addition to the villas, which now are reserved, surely, for high-ranking cadres, there are groups of buildings that belong to factories and to unions, which send workers here who need detoxification— miners, for example. There are small coves, one after another, between the rocks and the shore, and each unit has its own reserved space. They bathe, and then dry themselves; they seem not to like to lie in the sun, especially not the women, who cluster together, fully dressed, in the shade of the trellises. In China, a suntan is considered ugly.

Still farther on there is a public garden with densely planted flower beds on the sand, paths, and enclosures painted red and green, like toys. Beside them, canals with flowing sweet or salt water. . . .

On the inland walk, to the right of and beyond the Chinese hamlet, a rather narrow but well-kept street slopes gently upward, following the curves of the hill. To the left are cultivated fields and an occasional villa; to the right, a very long, low stone wall interrupted at intervals by gates; between this wall and the parallel shore line is a zone that is occupied entirely by villas and a few rest houses of more recent vintage. Nature here is fresh and joyous; the buildings, set behind the wall and among shrubbery are a discreet, unforced blend of Chinese and North European elements; the light is southern but without the Mediterranean violence we associate with light in the latitudes of Naples or Barcelona. These spaces, which were laid out by foreigners in China and are now owned by the Chinese, are for me on the shores of this ocean a nostalgic reminder of the Tuscan countryside.

At the end of the area allotted to us, you turn to the right and reach the sea near an elevation called "the pigeons' nest."

Today, the sky was gray. I climbed up to the pavilion on the little hill. Rocks rise above the surface of the sea, but inland there are swampy fields and grass. The gray brought out the yellows and reds and the dark green, as in Van Gogh or some Cézannes. Pines and large villas. . . . Inside the courtyard of the largest villa a soldier was standing guard by his sentry box. The section where we are staying is guarded by soldiers, too. Once upon a time, one of these villas belonged to the parents of some unpleasant English people who take their meals in our restaurant.

I have felt well here and have got back my health and balance. Also, I have rediscovered even a mental pleasure in a marine world which I believed belonged to the sensibility of youth and was therefore forever lost to me.

In the evening, out on the little terrace, a young Spanish couple sing Spanish and Latin-American songs, accompanying themselves on the guitar. Radical background. . . . She is small, dark-complexioned, very intelligent and sensitive; now and then she explains to us who wrote the words or what protest incident the song is related to. "We used to sing this song when we were students and were demonstrating against the police." How many ambiguities there have been in the last twenty years in our Italian democracy and their Spanish fascism. Their society is ours, in effect; the differences, especially in the educated class, are marginal.

A trip to Shanhaiguan, the first pass in the Great Wall. (The point where the Wall enters the sea is a military zone and off bounds.) The town's ancient walls have been preserved, and you enter through an arched gateway to find yourself in what seems a Chinese Far West: streets of low houses in orderly rows, enlivened by shops, all of brick, and hanging objects. Peasants are dressed in black, and wear pointed, slightly curved straw hats—the kind that in old illustrations were called "typically" Chinese, which was a mistake because each region has its distinctive style of hat that is unlike any other. Girls here have thick, very long hair, and they wear straight skirts that completely cover the calf —a traditional style, surely, and far more elegant than the pleated model.

The gate in the Wall is a noble Ming structure, which has been restored. It bears an inscription: *Tianxia diyi guan,* "The First Pass [or Gate] in the World."

China offers a continuous lesson in sociology in which contradictions that in other countries are concealed by a surplus of abundance, including the cultural, are open and openly stated. The lying, the governmental abuse, the class divisions, the repression, the obedience are direct and shameless. Here you learn to recognize the substance of things.

Socialism exists in many countries, M—— F—— says: the Soviet Union, Italy, China. . . . That is certainly true. Socialism is nonanarchic production, the prevailing of order and of good mandarins who follow the way of the kings, the equitable division of tasks and of manual and intellectual labor, the governance of all by all, construction that is as rational as are regulations.

When the mandarins do not serve the people, the division of tasks and of labor becomes inequitable, the standard of living and of culture diverges too much from class to class; when private interests rise and the public interest falls, there is speculation and corruption. These are signs of internal crisis, of disorder that grows within order; at that point, the class struggle will have to be resumed, not against the bourgeoisie but against dominating forces of socialism that are no longer "rational."

After the defeat of the Cultural Revolution, Mao spoke of himself as a monk "without Law and without Heaven," but he knew that the defeat was not final and that cultural revolution was a necessity. There will be "building" in China today, but it will be construction that is weakened from the outset and that will fool no one except those at home and abroad whose interest is served by their allowing themselves to be fooled. It is undermined by the "mole" of communism. Standing against the possibility of reopening a path of liberation —beyond the illusions and errors of the past—is the great reaction, the possible evolution of the mandarin system into nationalistic fascism. This is a possibility because the people are partly prepared to submit to it. Yet many factors, even within the composite alliance now in power in China, may prevent such a development. The dialectic is not closed. For this country, "there is hope."

August 15

I am going back to Peking, tomorrow will leave for Japan, and then, after half a day in Shanghai to pick up my luggage, will fly to Italy.

I could not remain in this country, but it is lacerating to leave it. The country rejects me because it wants to conquer me totally, to be the universal theater of human events, and to expand within me until it excludes everything else. To avoid that, I have to practice violence against myself.

Why is it that to be in China is to think and to talk continually about the Chinese, and not *with* the Chinese? Again now, as it was so many years ago, at the moment of leaving there will be the pain of something that has remained suspended, that should have been communicated but has not been or not entirely or not in the right way—an interrupted message, an unfulfilled relationship.

INDEX

Academy of Sciences, 34, 166, 321–322
Africans, in China, 91, 325
agriculture, 5, 8, 16, 23, 203–206, 313
  accounting systems in, 206–207
  reform in (1930s), 12.
  See also communes; peasants; rural areas
"Ah Q" (Lu Xun), 229
"Analysis of Chinese Rural Classes, An"
  (Mao Zedong), 10
"Analysis of Classes in Chinese Societies,
  An" (Mao Zedong), 10
anarchism, 17–18, 301–302, 316
ANSA (Italian news agency), 139
Aquinas, Thomas, 128
art forms, "traditional," 234–238
Association of Chinese Women, 37
athletics, 53
Aymin (Olga's and Marcial's daughter), 71,
  117, 233, 274, 324–325, 345, 351, 352

back door *(hou men)*, 177
banners:
  mourning, 88, 97
  political, 185, 219
banquets, role of, 55–56, 149
BBC news, 138, 139, 140, 141, 153
Beethoven, Ludwig van, 302–303
Beidaihe, 353–356
Belden, Jack, 13*n*
bicycles, 116–117
Bob (French instructor), 89, 115, 149, 160,
  232
Bo Juyi, 328
bookshops, 64, 76–77, 156, 183–184, 343

bourgeoisie (urban middle class):
  in alliance with international capitalism, 7
  as "capitalist roaders," 17, 84, 106, 243,
    298
  as caste, 84
  CCP vs., 15, 17, 21, 298–299
  ethic of, 14, 290, 314–315
  Kuomintang and, 5
  Mao's use of term, 10
  "national." *See* national bourgeoisie
  as new mandarins, 14
  political bureaucracy and, 15
"bourgeois revisionist line," 166
Breakdown, The (Juelie), 82, 134–135, 142,
  288
Buddhism, 130, 316, 328
buildings, public, 53, 57
bureaucracy, bureaucratization, 31, 177*n*,
  349
  as class enemy, 94
  May Fourth Movement and, 4
  as new mandarins *(guan)*, 32
  political, cadres as, 15
  power of, 32–33, 34
  Socialist-Confucian, 172.
  See also cadres; *danwei*
buses, 53

cadres *(ganbu)*:
  control of ideological discourse by, 300
  in cultural movement, 5
  danwei system and, 54
  defined, 31*n*
  educated middle class vs., 15